DON'T DIE WONDERING

A TALE OF BETRAYAL

MICHAEL NEWMAN

PRAISE FOR MICHAEL NEWMAN FROM REVIEWERS:

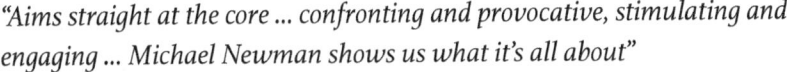

"Aims straight at the core ... confronting and provocative, stimulating and engaging ... Michael Newman shows us what it's all about"
  – Neil Stagoll

"An absolutely compelling read for anyone ..."
  – Jim Aitchison

"A rich soup of insight and inspiration"
  – Jack Vaughan

"This is certainly an easy and readable book – a must ... "
  – Florence Oh

"In all this is a wonderful book, enjoyable, revealing and ultimately educational ..."
  – Mark Gabbott

"His interesting and well written book will go a long way ..."
  – Al Ries

©2018 Michael Newman

ISBN 978-0-6482494-4-3

info@dontdiewondering.info

Dedicated to Les, to Maureen
and, with thanks for all her patience, to Jennifer Wendy

DON'T DIE WONDERING

"He who trusts the world, the world betrays him."
Hazrat Ali Ibn Abu-Talib A.S

"I have, he went on, betrayed myself with belief, deluded myself with love, tricked myself with sex. The bottle is damned faithful, he said, the bottle will not lie."
Charles Bukowski

PROLOGUE

Gorma, Afghanistan – 2011

CARRICK WOKE COVERED IN MOONDUST.

In his mouth and eyes, up his nose, pouring like gritty grey flour from his battle rattle as he tried to sit up.

Except he couldn't sit up. There was a foot on his chest.

That made him focus.

The foot was attached to a blood-splattered muj who was raising an old Kalashnikov in the air. In the half moment before Carrick's jawbone was shattered it all came back to him.

He'd spotted them more than a mile away and prayed they were another of the passing militia on the pitted track out of Gorma. Two earlier convoys had already jolted along the MSR (hardly a Maine Supply Road, more a goat herders trail), roughly in the direction the second half of Carrick's four man patrol was positioned. Ten clicks south, in an area the U.S. satellite boffins suspected might have insurgent tunnels.

But this lot hadn't passed by, they'd wheeled into the ruins of the bombed out qala where Carrick had made his close observation hide. He waited long as possible before engaging, silently willing them to carry on, but they were drawn to his flame like moths.

Of course, he shouldn't have been alone, shouldn't have been setting up the observation post on his own. SNAFU from the start.

The op was preparation for a strike on some Taliban HVT called Mullah Noorullah, a suspected insurgent commander who'd been fingered for organising a series of roadside attacks on allied troops. That won the man High Value Target status.

Carrick's team from the 22nd had been dragged out of Kandahar at short notice to join the U.S. paras. Gaffney, Peters, Dewey and himself. That wasn't unusual, tier-one forces from different nations routinely worked together.

At the briefing, the latest Int reported Noorullah holed up fifteen miles from the designated drop zone. But the show was delayed three days because of a northwesterly shamal. The parachute drop was sloppy in the unpredictable winds of the dying dust storm, Dewey came down hard, smashing bones as well as the TACBE pack.

Carrick pushed them to carry on and not abandon the job. There was an exfil route and emergency pick up point that Dewey could get himself to by daylight; he had his full-sized Minimi and Browning 9mm as back up.

Gaffney and Peters took themselves off into the gloom while Carrick helped strap a 66mm Law rocket onto Dewey's back. Carrick loaded the remaining gear into his own Bergen and legged it all night to the qala carrying his M16/M203 and 120lbs of sandbags, observation post equipment, extra ammo bandoliers, PE4 play doh, detonators, Claymores, Elsies, four days rations and intravenous drips for emergency.

He'd made the lying up position just twenty minutes before he sighted the first of the approaching militia. No time to lay toe poppers.

As firefights go it had been pretty one-sided.

Carrick took out everyone in the convoy's first vehicle with the M230 grenade launcher as they rounded the corner of the compound, couldn't fail at such close range. Three or four more in the second truck cost a handful of rounds.

But the heavy lorry veered crazily when he shot the driver and somehow kept accelerating, flipping on its side and crashing at speed *through the far wall of the ancient compound, setting off a series of collapses along the whole length of the mud brick structure that literally brought Carrick's world down on top of him.*

How long had he been unconscious?

Seconds?

Minutes at most.

But too long. Far too long.

Now he was on his back and fighting angry. It was half a moment too late as Carrick swivelled to break the bloody knee that belonged to the heavy foot on his chest.

The wooden stock of the AK hit him like an IED, little bursting points of moonlight eclipsed in a great big darkness was the last thing he knew before the nightmare began.

CHAPTER 1.

Two years later ...

Provençe, France – 2013

Jonas Shackleton's body was found five paces inside the tiled entrance of the hotel suite. Air Jordan sneakers, Italian designer jeans, alligator-skin belt, baby-blue silk twill shirt with an open collar.

And a wide-open neck.

His throat slashed from ear to diamond-studded ear.

On the floor beside him, a German-made straight razor with an ironwood handle.

The corpse was encircled by a vivid starburst of blood on the pale stone tiles, a giant asterisk like a *Red-Spot Special!* in a newspaper ad. The man had flowed, rich life had poured from him.

For Inspecteur de Détective Gerrard Lacont, who had considered many crime scenes, thickening pools of blood always smelt like apples that had fallen to the ground and rotted.

Une pomme pourrie.

It was an observation that caused the already wan faced hotel manager to reach for his handkerchief and rush from the room.

At the edge of a fashionable hill town, St-Paul-de-Vence, La Colombe d'Or was a local icon. Being a few pay grades below such pleasures, Lacont had never before set foot in the place, a large rehabilitated farmhouse, but he knew it well enough by reputation. Picasso had left several works in lieu of paying his bills. Hemingway too dined and drank in the bar.

'Mostly drank, they say', the manager had commented when he guided Lacont through the rambling building like any other guest, reciting its history along the way, pointing out minor artworks by Matisse, Braque, Giacometti, Bonnard, Modigliani, and Chagall adorning the soft-mauve walls. Paintings that Lacont didn't understand, but he kept an open mind.

The victim had been a special guest at the Mayors' Lunch for the VIPs judging the annual Cannes Lions awards. The hotel manager described him as an imposing Englishman with a broad moustache and a completely shaven head.

There had never been the violent murder of a VIP during festival season before, as far as Inspecteur Lacont could recall. It was a most unwelcome novelty.

Every summer three great festivals invade the Riviera in quick succession. First into the spotlight, the famous Cannes Film Festival. Hot on its stiletto heels comes the annual Cannes Porn Festival. Last up the red carpet, the Cannes Lions Advertising Festival.

The locals call it *Le grande déclin moral.*

Each is a cutthroat affair, a meat market dusted with glitter.

Naturally, crime figures spike during festival season, more pockets picked in the crush of the steep narrow lanes, more hotel suites burgled, a rise in assaults and rapes. People died too: heart attacks, weaving drunks run down on the Boulevard de la Croisette, stoned delegates plopping overboard into the Baie de Cannes during all night yacht parties.

But never a murdered VIP.

Yet now, just one day before the official start to the 2013 Cannes

Chapter 1.

Lions Festival, an advertising guru's throat had quite literally been cut.

Inspecteur Lacont understood the seriousness of the situation, a murdered adman was bad *publicité* for the Lions, for Cannes, for his own department; a catastrophe that had to be solved quickly and quietly.

The three great Festivals are the locomotive of our local economy, the Mayor invariably told any audience he addressed. Where that locomotive was headed Lacont couldn't say, already you could walk the length of the boulevard and not hear a single French voice.

The Mayoral lunch had apparently been drawing to a cheerful close when an upstairs chambermaid shrieked, turned on her heel and clattered down the oak stairs with a sound like automatic gunfire to alert the manager that a guest, the bald one she said, *le crâne d'oeuf*, lay in his suite in a sea of blood.

Why had he gone upstairs to his room?

Witnesses said he'd risen from the long table on the terrace during the cheese course, apparently to fetch something from his suite, leaving his smartphone, a three-pack of Montecristo No. 2 cigars and an unfinished bottle of rosé at his place. Clearly he expected to return.

Why had no one at the lunch looked for him, even after some time elapsed and he'd failed to reappear?

It was common knowledge, answered an Englishman with red-framed spectacles, to the stifled amusement of his fellow diners, that Jonas Shackleton was travelling with a young and exquisitely beautiful Thai girl.

"One could understand that, having gone back to his room, he might have been, um, waylaid."

The couple's suite overlooked the vine-hung terrace where the lunch was held, and beyond it the perched medieval village. From the window, the girl could have watched him leave the VIP table to make his way upstairs.

Inspecteur Adjoint Rolande, Lacont's diligent but dour deputy, a gaunt man with a permanent 5 o'clock shadow, trudged up the dimly lit staircase and confirmed what his boss already half-suspected, namely that the dead man's exotic companion had not been seen by anyone since the murder.

Lacont took in the room. A stone pitcher and finely cut glasses on a marble-topped desk, splay-foot furniture in dark mahogany, an elegant vase on an occasional table, good taste and Provençal antiques wherever the eye was drawn. Everything in its place. It didn't look like a robbery, the couple's belongings seemed undisturbed. The victim's money and credit cards still in his wallet on the four poster's bedside table. Their clothes neat in the Louis XIII armoires. A woman's hooded-jacket with pink fur-edging folded neatly over the back of a chair.

The victim's passport, tucked into a frayed Louis Vuitton travel pouch with two return air tickets, was in a desk drawer.

Name: Ronald Jonas Shackleton, 57, born Northampton, UK.

His business cards showed his title as Worldwide Creative Director and gave office addresses in New York, Bangkok and London. No wonder the travel wallet was well worn.

Neither the girl's handbag nor her papers could be found in the suite, but a photocopy of her passport taken by the hotel at check-in confirmed she was a Thai national.

Name: Pornthip Ausanat Sinn, 19, born Bangkok.

She was beautiful even in her passport photo.

Lacont shook his head at the age difference. Almost forty years. "Sex and advertising," he muttered.

A chartered helicopter thrummed down into the quiet airport on the outskirts of the Provençal town of Apt, one hundred and forty miles west of the crime scene. Its only passenger, Tony Maine OBE, Chairman and Chief Executive of Maine Hyland & Blix.

It was three hours since news of the murder had been posted on social media. No time to lose. Shackleton's violent death rang all sorts of alarm bells. If what Tony Maine thought *might* have happened had *actually* happened, he would have to act very fast indeed. If his worst fears were true then the inevitable chain of events would be unthinkable, the cost incalculable.

But Tony Maine's mercurial career was built on well-timed decisions, first mover advantage. As he transferred to the black Mercedes Pullman ready to chauffeur him through the grey villages and vivid lavender fields of the Luberon, Maine clicked open his cell phone, made the first move, created options.

The limousine pushed into the gathering twilight passed the walled farms into the valley, xenon gas headlights probing the quiet rural world like thin, pale fingers delving through the night's secrets.

By the time the Pullman crackled along the driveway towards the brightly lit villa awaiting him, Tony Maine had just one more call to make.

Andy Carrick wasn't exactly sure what time his phone started ringing.

Lying on a lumpy couch in a rented cottage near Bonnieux, shirtless, sweating in the early summer heat. Staring at the century old ceiling, studying its heavy timber beams, contemplating their checks and cracks. Pondering their weight. The burden they bore. It seemed to him a maudlin metaphor, his cracks also ran deep. He carried a weight.

He sucked at the rim of the drink balanced on his chest but it was empty. Again. How many times had that happened this evening?

He let the phone ring, the sound bouncing round the old stone cottage with its small draughty rooms and heavy hand-hewn beams like a trapped dryad.

Whole weeks in the Luberon passed without him having to speak to anyone else, well, anyone who spoke English. He'd rented the place from friends, Didier and Emma Luc, who owned a handful of gîtes in the area. He'd taken the unrenovated one but insisted on paying full whack.

Chapter 1.

"No mates rates," he told Didier, "I don't want favours, I want quiet."

There was something about the mute stone, the sharp morning air and hanging wood smoke, the small square of whispering forest, Mont Ventoux standing watch in the distance. The crushing world was held back. The four-week sabbatical from his London security business had turned to five, then seven.

'Jacko' Jackson, a former squaddie mate looking after the shop meantime, told Carrick he was AWOL, grizzled each time he extended his stay.

"You're probably doing no worse a job running the joint than me," Carrick said.

He'd just cut Jacko into a share of the company so his conscience was clear on that at least.

Thoughts bubbled up about selling everything he owned in London, the Hammersmith flat, the company, everything he'd ever been or wanted to be. It would bring enough cash to survive in stasis for some time. Maybe he'd buy an ancient *petite maison á la campagne* like this. Do it up. Keep life simple.

But by morning he'd be sober and change his mind.

About the only thing that had got his heart racing was yesterday afternoon's episode with the snake in the kitchen, he felt it was an omen of some kind. He was not a fan of snakes. The only other encounter he'd had with them was a McMahon's Viper in the desert, a small buff-coloured thing that becomes very irritable if you get close. A lifetime ago, during his final tour in the sandbox. And that *had* been a bad omen. It seemed a different man's life to him now.

It was more than two years since his discharge from the regiment with a gilt medal and pieces of wire holding his face and fingers in place. One year and eleven months since the Major made him a partner in the security company. Which made it almost a year since the Major died under a car, leaving the whole company to Carrick.

It was a kind of betrayal letting the Major's business slowly go sour, but Carrick was no businessman and tonight he was drinking his shame in full draughts. As usual, he told himself if his marriage

Chapter 1.

hadn't fallen apart it might have been different, there would've been something to fight for. But he was never persuaded by that argument for more than a couple of glasses.

The business still ticked over but it wasn't the precision clockwork it had been with the Major at the helm. He'd been a genius with people. Carrick always thought of him as 'the rock', though in real life no one called him anything but The Major. Without him, Carrick didn't have the substance to even cast a shadow.

The phone was still ringing from across the far side of the room, like a signal from another dimension. Apparently the world wasn't going to let go without a fight.

Putting down the empty glass he shuffled across the room and in his best French said, "Allo?"

"Andy Carrick? It's Tony Maine calling. How are you this brilliant evening?"

He was stunned for a moment, electricity ran up his back straightening his spine, it was like being rung by a Brigadier. *Fuck me, Tony Maine.* Carrick tried to jostle his thoughts into line.

"Tony!" his voice thick with disuse and pastis, "How are you?"

"Did I wake you?"

"No, no, not at all. Just a local frog in my throat."

"Apologies if I did. Thing is, I'm just down the road from your place — at the humble villa of your charming landlords'. Say hello, Emma."

Just down the road? Didier and Emma's villa was in Oppéde, three villages away. Carrick had successfully avoided them since he arrived, along with the rest of the world. His regime of savage self-reproach had descended into a lifestyle unsuited to company and he'd lowered the curtain on friends and foes alike.

In the background he heard Emma calling across the room, "Come on and get over here, you antisocial *étranger*."

"I thought you might enjoy joining us for a drink? Not too late for you hermit types is it? It would be great to catch up with what you're doing?"

Chapter 1.

A drink? With Tony Maine? Not a catch up, there'd be a catch. He was a heavy hitter.

"Sure, I guess," Carrick rubbed his head hard, dragging himself back to the surface, "Yes, yes, of course I... "

"Brilliant," you could hear the smile in Maine's voice, almost feel the warmth, "Can't wait to see you, old man." Then the tone modulated to a note of fatherly concern, "Look, I can send my car over for you if you don't want to drive?"

"No that's fine. Just don't drink everything in the house till I get there, I know what Didier's like."

"Just the two of us here at the moment, unfortunately, Didier's away on a job doing whatever structural engineers do. I got here fifteen minutes ago and we've only just opened the bottle, the first one anyway. Thought we'd get you over and make it a threesome."

Emma laughing in the background, "Mind your language, Tony. You'll start rumours that way."

Carrick hung up and sat down again. Pushed stiff fingers through snarled, unwashed hair. You'd think a man like Tony Maine would have better things to do Friday night in the South of France than ring me for a drink? The last time he'd seen him was in a newspaper photograph, his arm around the British Prime Minister's shoulder, it made the PM look like one of Tony's account execs being congratulated for some good work on an ad campaign.

Britain's Maine Man, the tabloids dubbed him.

Maine's agency had been a client of the Major's for some years and so Carrick had met him a few times, had even handled a job for him personally looking after a production crew filming in the Czech Republic. He remembered now that Maine was an old friend of Emma's. She'd worked as an art director or some such at his agency for a time before she married Carrick's drinking mate, Didier Luc.

He pulled on boots, went to the sink to splash cold water from the shuddering tap over a stubbled face and round the back of his neck, wet his hair in an attempt to impose order.

Emma and Didier must have told him I was here. *Just down the road.*

Chapter 1.

He had a funny feeling. Maybe he was chuffed that Tony Maine had called. Over the next few days he began to see it as a siren call back to the real world.

Maybe he'd stewed in his own juices long enough.

Twenty minutes later Carrick was squeezing his battered Land Rover Defender through the country lanes toward Oppéde, between the fields and small farms, exploding panicked French hens into the night air and waking sleeping dogs in the passing blur of the narrow *hameaux*.

He drove too fast, a habit he blamed on the locals, almost missing the *rue blanc*, the white dirt road lined with oaks that curved like a serif towards Emma and Didier's L-shaped *mas*.

Their squat farmhouse was blind to the madness-sparking mistrals on its northern side, no windows at all, but along the southern wall every casement blazed with light. Outside, a black Mercedes crouched like a large shadow in front of the building. He could see Tony Maine and Emma in silhouette, sitting inside the brightly lit kitchen at a big oak table Didier had made as a wedding gift, copper pots and pans hanging above, a bottle of wine in front of them.

Didier Luc was a handsome, energetic Frenchman who'd grown up in London. He'd been a drinking buddy whenever Carrick came down from Hereford on leave. Ironically, when Didier's career took him back to France a couple of years ago he met an English girl, Emma Browning, who'd just left advertising and opened an art supplies shop in St-Rémy-de-Provence.

Soon after they were married in a fourteenth century chapel in Gordes. It was all very fairytale as Carrick saw it.

The wedding was the first time Carrick had met Emma and he approved; she was an English rose, tall, wispy, beautiful skin, southern counties accent. He liked the way she watched Didier all the time, her big eyes following him around the room as if he were an exotic animal.

At the time Carrick had just taken the job with the Major and was still with his wife, Robyn. After the nuptials the two of them toured around the area for a week, Fontaine de Vaucluse, St Rémy, Cannes, Nice, the usual tourist track, trying to reignite the flame of their own relationship. Somewhat pointlessly as it turned out.

"You've been hiding out here for weeks, I'm told," said Tony after the greetings were completed, cheeks kissed, hands shaken, backs patted, "Not thinking of doing a Peter Mayle are you, buying some renovator's delight in this windy hole?"

"Not when I'm sober."

Maine poured a generous Bandol, "You look like you could do with one of these."

Emma smiled winningly at him. She hitched the recalcitrant strap of her sundress back onto a tan shoulder and slapped barefoot across the stone floor to the Aga, she'd baked *gougères* and the hot pastry smell filled the room with a cheery homeyness Carrick hadn't felt since his divorce. The evening was flooding him with memories, unfiltered things that swirled around his head for the next few days.

Tony sipped his wine, loosened his tie and pulled a face. Recently turned fifty, slightly built, with tightly coiled hair that had started life ginger and was worn slightly too long, Tony Maine was a pleasant if unremarkable looking man, even wearing H. Huntsman & Son suits and quarter of a million pounds worth of Tourbillon Relatif wrist-watch. Unremarkable, that is, until he started talking, then he was captivating, hypnotic some said. He possessed that most valuable of all advertising industry qualities, likeability, combined with the most valuable of business assets, ruthlessness.

"God, I remember when Ridley renovated the tower at his little pile, they took him for a fortune. Apparently the real killer in France is paying the workers' social security. Speaking of Ridley, I must introduce you while you're down here, you might pick up some work from his production company."

Carrick couldn't decide if he wanted to be introduced to Tony

Maine's rich friends just now. The Major had handled such networking effortlessly but Carrick winced internally when he was treated like a CEO, he felt like an imposter.

He changed the subject and began to tell them about yesterday's slapstick episode with the snake in the kitchen.

But before the punchline Tony's phone rang. He looked at the incoming number and frowned at the interruption.

"Bugger, bugger, bugger. Sorry, Andy, *Jokus Interruptus.* I've got to take this, tell me the rest when I come back," he walked outside, handset to his ear.

The voltage in the room seemed to drop to normal.

"What kind of snake?" Emma gasped.

"Hang on, I'll save it for when the other half of my audience returns. It's very funny. Anyway, how's Didi?"

"Great. He's down in Portofino with a client. Can't tell you who but he's an American rock star. They're building an amazing cantilevered house hanging out over the cliff. Didi's staying on the guy's yacht, working out a few things and schmoozing. I told him you might be coming around, he said to say 'Hi'."

Maine's voice reached them indistinctly through the door, he was sounding displeased with someone at the other end of the phone.

Carrick indicated in that direction, "The wheels of industry still turning at this time on a Friday night? No wonder he's rich as Croesus."

"Tony's making a speech with Sir Richard Branson down at Cannes in a couple of days, I believe," she reached across the table, topping up his glass, "Still, 'whatever-it-takes'," she said it in a funny voice, wobbling her head.

"What's that mean?" Carrick wobbled his head in imitation.

"Oh, that's his agency's cultural mantra. W.I.T. — Whatever It Takes."

"Mantra? What is it, an ad agency or religious sect?"

Emma laughed. "I know what you mean, but agencies are very big on company culture. Got to keep the loonies on the true path. You know the kind of stuff, *One-team-one-dream ... Shoot for the stars...* Years ago when Tony started his agency he originally wanted the maxim to be *Disruption!* but that was already taken by a French agency. So he went for *Whatever It Takes.*"

"Thought it was just Americans who bought into that raa-raa corporate stuff?"

"Oh no, advertising agencies want a consistent brand culture all over the world. Makes it easier when a big client shops around. The client can choose a McDonald's style of agency — big, safe and friendly. Or there's the Virgin style of agency — more attitude and entrepreneurial. There's even your Harley Davidson style of agency culture — maverick and sexy. Well, maybe not too maverick, it's only advertising. Want another biscuit? I did a t-shirt when I worked for him that read: *Just do W.I.T.*"

Carrick took another *gougère*, he had almost forgotten real home cooking.

"How would you categorize Tony's agency," he said as the hot smoky cheese cut through the wine coating the inside of his mouth, "Maverick or big, safe and friendly?"

"Oh, Maine Hyland & Blix used to be very sexy; they've done some super creative work," said Emma, "As an agency brand they're somewhere between a Virgin and a Harley, I suppose..."

"Between a virgin and a Harley? The mind boggles."

"... But he sold his company to one of the big networks a few years ago for an obscene amount of dosh, InterGroup-Publicity they're called, they're not nearly so sexy unfortunately. They put a lot of pressure on Tony for big returns, his staff call them the 'Evil Empire' behind his back."

"How shocking, a parent company that's only in it for the money. Poor old Tony, how does he sleep at night?"

"How does Tony Maine sleep?" she laughed in an appealing way he'd never noticed before, "In a penthouse on the finest silk sheets, with the nubile twin daughters of his biggest client, I imagine."

Chapter 1.

They were both giggling into their glasses as Tony returned to the kitchen and put his cell phone down on the table, "Sorry, boys and girls. Did daddy miss much drinking?"

"You've got a little catching up to do," Carrick filled his glass. Emma fetched another bottle.

"Andy," Maine looked at him searchingly, "Have you got much going at the moment? I mean anything that you couldn't drop to do a little job of work for me?"

Business was rearing its ugly head. "What's up?"

"I've got a problem and you might be just the man to help solve it."

"What kind of problem?"

"There was a creative director murdered today near Cannes. Jonas Shackleton," he indicated his phone, "I heard the story on my way here."

"Murdered? I'm sorry," said Carrick, "Was he a friend of yours?"

"A prick of the first order." Maine said it without the malice the words might suggest, a statement of fact.

"What happened?"

"Killed at a restaurant this afternoon."

"Which one?" asked Emma.

"Up at La Colombe d'Or."

"How awful."

"So how's it your problem?"

"Shackleton worked for the international network my agency is affiliated with," he began.

The Evil Empire, thought Carrick, but managed to stop himself saying.

"Jonas was usually based in Bangkok for InterGroup; they put him there out of harm's way, I suspect. But recently they shifted him to New York because they needed to appoint a worldwide creative director. The thing is, we're doing a few projects in tandem now — I mean the network company and mine — we're tapping new markets, China, India, maybe Indonesia soon. At the moment we're combining to make a joint pitch for the biggest advertising account in China."

"Who is it, can you say?" asked Emma.

"It's a Chinese government energy project, called the Qi Project. Qi Energy. Three hundred and seventy million Euros total billings."

"Wow," Emma opened her eyes wide, "Big bikkies."

Tony pulled off his Jermyn Street tie as if it were a hangman's noose. He looked several years older since taking the phone call.

"The Qi Energy Project. Ironically, it means life force in Chinese," he leaned forward, serious again, "I think the murder might have something to do with the pitch. However, the police at the moment seem to think the girl did it. I'm not so sure."

"Girl?"

"Jonas always takes some floozy or other around with him, fresh flesh for the old ritual; usually some Asian girl. They think she did it."

"I see. How was he killed?"

Tony swallowed uncomfortably, "Throat cut, I think."

"How horrible," Emma was genuinely shocked, looked down at the floor, "How could she?"

"At a restaurant?" Carrick said.

"In his room. Apparently he went upstairs during the lunch and … somehow got his throat cut."

"Doesn't sound much like women's work."

"No. That's why I'm going to hire you to find out who really killed Jonas Shackleton."

"Why would you want to do that? What about the police investigation?"

"Let me put it this way, in revenue terms this Chinese business is worth almost twenty million euros to whichever agency group reels it in, after costs … that's year one. It will be a four-year contract."

Maine let the figures hang in the air for a moment.

"But Tony, I don't …"

He raised a practised palm stopping the interruption, "I don't want to try and explain the subtleties of a highly political international advertising pitch to some local Inspector Clouseau who's half-convinced he's chasing a Thai hooker with a sharp nail file. Let them get on with their theories, we'll follow our intuition. What do you say?"

Next morning in Cannes it looked like the carnival had come to town.

Saturday was the Festival's registration day and thousands of newly arrived zombie-faced delegates wandered in jet-lagged stupor along the beachside boulevard, mingling with them a sideshow of rowdy buskers, shouting souvenir hawkers, fire breathers, mimes, face painters, jugglers, henna-tattoo artists, ice cream sellers, sunglasses pedlars, over-tanned bark-faced local women with ludicrously small dogs, a pair of garish whores wrapped in leopard-skin and some of Europe's most experienced pickpockets.

The night before, Tony Maine described the Lions as the "Olympics of Advertising, ninety countries competing tooth and claw."

To Carrick it looked more like a 3-ring circus.

Worse, he felt like the elephant man. His hangover was ugly.

Emma and Tony put him down in a spare bedroom sometime in the early hours of the morning after his long and liquid 'briefing' was complete. He woke at dawn and saw Tony's Mercedes had gone.

He'd left a note for Emma, driven back to the cottage, shaved for the first time in a week, showered and packed a small bag. In the hard light of day, he couldn't escape the notion that he'd been press-ganged in the nicest possible way by the nicest possible people.

But that was probably being a little ungrateful. After all, fifteen thousand was plenty to be grateful about.

It was close to midday as Carrick crossed La Croisette to join the steady pilgrimage shuffling towards the festival mecca — the Palais de Festivals et Congrès — sitting like a monumental bollard east of the port at the edge of Cannes' old town. A great, white blockhouse of a building at the end of the beach, eighteen auditoriums, 25,000 square metres of exhibition space all boxed up in charmless white concrete modernism.

Chapter 1.

The first day's award judging had begun in the screening rooms at 8.45am. Secrecy is strict Emma had explained, but rules are for other people, "Nothing keeps Tony Maine out."

Tony arranged a five-minute interview for Carrick during the lunch break with the creative director of his own agency, Ray Doyle, one of the judges representing the UK. *Dear old Ray*, he called him.

"A bit of a worry wart, dear old Ray, but he'll get you in to meet all the judges."

Carrick was about to press the intercom button at the Palais' heavy stage door when it opened suddenly. A large security guard was ejecting a straw-haired man with sunglasses perched on his head, he was hunched over protecting something.

"Go easy, mate, watch the camera," he was yowling, "We've all got a job to do."

Carrick recognised Benny Sewell, the advertising journo who'd once interviewed him when word of his adventure in the Czech provinces had got out. After some consideration, the Major had encouraged Carrick to do it for the publicity, provided he didn't admit to any violence.

Diplomatically ignoring the kerfuffle, Carrick gave his name to the door attendant, explained his appointment and was admitted inside.

The bowels of the blockhouse were full of movement. Tech people running around talking into headsets, efficient looking girls in uniformly tight little black dresses sashaying down hospital-bland corridors clutching tablet computers to their bosoms. They looked half-automaton, half-model agency, foot soldiers for the great organ churning out glamour on an industrial scale.

One of them introduced herself as Melodie and Carrick was shown to a plastic chair next to the Pepsi machine.

"You are 'ere to see Mr. Doyle? Ee'll come through zis door in five minutes," she said, "You cannot go in, I'm afraid, it is ze judging room. And please, don't keep 'im long, *s'il vous plait*, we are most busy."

Carrick waited obediently. His hangover keeping him company.

In the dim, air-conditioned cool a constant background hum was interrupted now and then by bursts of music or electronic voices from behind closed doors.

He let the ordered energy of the place flow around him while his mind replayed snatches of last night's conversation, trying to explain to himself exactly why this had seemed a good idea.

When Maine made the offer Carrick shook his head, "I'm no sleuth. Maybe you should give the police a chance to get somewhere. I mean, the guy was only killed this afternoon, you say?"

"Nothing happens unless you make it happen."

Nothing happens unless you make it happen. A saying of the Major's. Carrick wondered if Maine knew that and was trying to coax him by using it.

Tony held his eye with a look that seemed to stress that what he was about to say was really consequential, "Listen, I want you to do it personally, none of your lackeys. Keep it to yourself. If you start tomorrow you've got a week to talk to as many agency people as you need while they're all here in one place at the festival. Let's see where that leads," he smiled and put out his hand to shake, "Fifteen thousand pounds, plus expenses."

"Fifteen thousand pounds?" Carrick was suddenly several glasses soberer, "For a week? You must be joking?"

"Plus expenses. Of course, it'll take more than a week. But these next seven days are key, while everyone's here."

"For that kind of dosh you could hire a professional. You could hire an army of professionals, not just some amateur out of the army. I'm just a security guy, Tony."

Despite what he was saying, Carrick felt a quickening of some kind. Or maybe it was the Bandol on top of the pastis he'd been drinking at the cottage.

Maine patted his shoulder, "Trust me, it's brilliant," an air of having already considered every option, "You might have to ruffle a few feathers, but I know you're not afraid to do that."

Tony winked. Carrick recognised this as a reference to the Czech adventure.

"Depending what you find we'll decide who to get involved next, maybe Interpol. I've got some contacts in Marseille."

Interpol? This was getting way out of proportion.

"You'd be throwing your money away on me, Tony."

"Don't believe it. You special forces guys know covert surveillance, intelligence gathering and the like, a murder investigation is hardly a stretch." Carrick was shaking his head, eyes averted. "You're already here on the spot. Plus you've seen a bit of the ad industry from the inside. It's perfect!"

"Go on," advised Emma, "Take his money. He won't leave you alone till you do what he wants, believe me."

Carrick had heard the stories. Maine's presentations to clients were legend. Other agencies prepared Powerpoints and chart attacks in stuffy meeting rooms, Maine famously presented his agency's campaign ideas wherever he could corner the client to his advantage; in First Class during trans-Atlantic flights using the back of drinks coasters, in a Japanese bath house near Nagoya, on the squash court at the club in St. James, and once, most notoriously of all, with one foot on the outside window ledge of a high-rise office building while threatening to jump if the client didn't approve it.

In some industries he'd be called a control freak, but as this was advertising he was called dynamic.

"Fifteen thousand is a hell of a lot, Tony," Carrick was trying to be grown up, swimming against the tide of Tony's enthusiasm.

"Don't worry about that, my friend."

Maine reached across to a yellow hand-painted vase in the centre of Emma's table and pulled out a couple of long-stemmed flowers, "Firstly, fifteen thousand is not a lot of money considering the circumstances. The network has key executive insurance covering its top people, two million pounds in the case of sudden death. I can afford to give you fifteen thou plus expenses every week for a year and not feel a thing."

He handed him the first flower and smiled.

"Secondly, most of the people you need to speak to are in Cannes right now. It's too good an opportunity to miss. Ask a few questions, stir things up, report back. Just remember, look for the profit motive. This murder is nothing to do with Shackleton's women, trust me; think money, let that be your guiding principle."

He handed Carrick the second flower.

"Fifteen thousand, plus expenses."

Carrick knew ridiculous sums were spent when ad agencies wanted something done fast and it concentrated his attention wonderfully. The routine with the flowers was a nice touch too.

"Well, OK, if you think I'm the right man," he heard himself say to the two smiling faces on either side of him, Emma's cheeks glowing with the effects of the red wine; Tony, eyes shining, looking like he believed in him.

Carrick felt like a kid with a new bicycle. He felt wanted, part of a team.

He felt less alone.

Emma stood up to get some olives while Tony poured more wine, and just like that Andy Carrick slipped down through the cracks into a battlefield as deadly and asymmetrical as anywhere he'd been in the Middle East — the dark unchartered continent of Adland.

CHAPTER 2.

Eighteen months earlier ...

Česky Krumlov, Czech Republic - 2012

As Carrick approached, the heavy set man in the long black coat spoke
quickly into a cell phone before sliding it back into his trouser pocket.

Flowing around them, a troupe of costumed Baroque musicians led a
throng of medieval towns folk, shopkeepers, miners, artisans of every
description, a donkey pulling an ornate cart, a company of colourfully
dressed soldiers with swords in hand and three peasants wrangling a
squealing pig. Carrick was walking against the crowd so his progress was
slow and the big man standing in the middle of the cobbled street near the
Old Inn came in and out of view as the strange procession of people made
their way in the direction of the catering trucks near the river.

It was an impressive number of extras and the detailing of the costumes
and props were a surreal sight. Carrick was still getting used to the film
world in those days and there was something dreamlike about it. That
didn't suit his mood.

Instead of confronting him directly Carrick walked passed the behe-

moth in the coat, gesturing for him to follow into the adjacent laneway out of sight of the passing crowd and the production crew.

"You in charge? You the boss man?"

The man raised his chin and stared down at him. One word rumbled from deep in his chest, "Cash."

"No. You're just a little fish, aren't you?" Carrick said. He knew the words 'fish' and 'small' from the menus on the banks of the Vitava back in Prague, "Malé ryby, eh?"

The man looked hewn from a block of granite. And just as smart.

"Cash," he growled.

"No more cash."

The big man shrugged and adjusted his gaze to something indeterminate over Carrick's head, some parallel world Carrick had no place in.

"Just for my conscience, I'll say please," Carrick made an exaggeratedly polite motion ushering him in the direction of the public car park and away from the area of town where the scene was to be filmed, "Please? Prosím."

The big man's chin jutted a fraction more, "Píčo. Cash."

"No cash," shaking his head, "Ne."

"Zkurvysynu," the man spat on the ground between Carrick's feet.

Carrick hit him in the throat, fingertips extended, and the big man halved in size. Retching violently, he fumbled for something under his coat as Carrick's knee came up hard and flattened his nose. The big man went down, a dark slag heap in the gutter.

"I don't know what you said to me, but if it was anything to do with my mother you're probably right."

He frisked him and found a Russian Makarov 9x18 in a shoulder holster and the cell phone in his trousers. He checked the magazine and the safety and tucked the semi-automatic under his belt at the small of his back, then stood a couple of paces away to take a photo of the prone man with the phone's camera. Five seconds later he sent it as a text attachment to the last number listed on Recent Calls and waited.

Carrick saw little choice in the time available but to play offense.

The film company had run out of cash and the constant delays were eating into profits. The whole thing was a standard shake down, local heavies offering the company protection from their own interference. It wouldn't happen in Prague, but Krumlov was out in the regions.

Carrick had organised three locals to marshal the crowds and close off the streets, but apparently none were keen to cross the town's mafia boys. Russians by the sound of it.

The Major's security company worked on film sets regularly, usually 'security' for commercials meant little more than keeping the public safely clear. Money for jam mostly and they simply hired ex-police for a day or two. If it involved close protection of VIPs or celebrity actors Carrick or Jacko would be assigned. The Major looked after the corporate stuff, risk assessment and analysis. Only occasionally was it more challenging work, like this time in the closed off streets of Krumlov.

Silent figures in sunglasses and big coats had been appearing in the background of every shot in the picture-perfect bohemian location since Day One of the shoot, standing rigidly behind the actors and positioning themselves directly in line with the camera angles, refusing to move, ruining set-ups that the Director and Cinematographer had taken hours to get right.

Just standing there. Not speaking.

Not moving.

It spooked the actors and the crew, the hard faces, the big coats.

The Director abandoned shot after shot, moving to different angles. The silent figures then moved to new positions, ruining each new shot, and so the dance went on.

They'd considered trying to fix it all in post-production but that would cost thousands and the budget was already stretched.

Meanwhile, Carrick had been in Prague for four days, baby-sitting the expensive BAFTA-winning star who was to appear as the handsome Nobleman in the climactic crowd scenes on the last two days of filming. Quite what the meticulous recreation of medieval times had to do with advertising a Financial Services brand he didn't know, he hadn't read the script. His job was simply to keep the lead actor sober and away from rent boys and the paparazzi.

He'd been wondering about the reason for the delay at the location.

"It started soon as we were ready to turn over on the first day," explained the Producer when Carrick got there.

He was a pasty-faced man with a public school accent and a perpetually worried manner. The four of them were squeezed into the Wardrobe Unit's caravan — Carrick, the Producer, the Director and the Cinematographer — a place they hoped the agency's creative team wouldn't find them.

"The set build went fine," continued the Producer, "We did camera rehearsals to get the crane and the moves right. Brought in the extras for a run through. But once we were ready to actually shoot something suddenly there he was. Just walked straight into frame and stood there. Wouldn't say a bloody word. Ignored the crowd marshals. Wouldn't move. I remonstrated, threatened to call the cops, told him I'd send a couple of the gaffers over to sort him. He just stared back at me. Hard."

"When I went over with a couple of the Grips with me he kind of leered at us, patted his shoulder like he was wearing a holster under his coat. Then just stared into the middle-distance like we weren't there," said the Director, opening and closing a small nervous fist.

Carrick nodded. "Then?"

"A phone call," said the Producer, "Don't know how in blazes they got my cell number. Voice says, 'My friend accepts cash'. I said, 'Who is this?' He answers, '€5,000 and my friend will find somewhere else to go.'"

"You didn't pay?"

"No," said the Director, "Not right away. I set up a different shot. Tried to work around it. We sent the extras back to the hotel for the afternoon. Instead, we turned the camera around to shoot the road scene with the cart trundling over the bridge and the castle in the background. Didn't get even one take. Soon as everything was in position a different fucking guy appears on the bridge and lights a cigarette. Just stares at us. Expressionless bastard. I mean, Jesus, it's supposed to be the twelfth century."

"Cell phone rings again," said the Producer, "Voice says, 'Price gone up. £10,000 for being smartarse'."

"And?"

"We paid. Took it out of the per diems and cash expenses kitty. Better than holding up everything."

"And they went away," said the Director.

"And our medieval setting was medieval again."

"Until ..." said the Director through grinding smoke-yellow teeth.

"Next day, the first guy was back. Stood in the same place just before we were ready to roll. I marched up to him, said 'We paid!'

"He just shrugged, 'New fee today'."

"This time we called the cops."

"While fifty-five fuckin' extras sat around," said the Director and threw his head back to emphasise his disgust.

"While the agency guys got twitchy. They'd already been on the phone to London and their Chairman gave us the hurry up. Anyway, the cops were useless. I told them we'd already paid the council the full location fees and they said, 'The streets are public streets. You have to let the residents come and go when they need to.'

"I told 'em these bastards come but they don't go. Just stand there and demand money. Straight extortion. They said they can't make the locals stay indoors if they don't want to. It's all down to good will."

"So?"

"I gave them twenty thousand to stay away the rest of the week."

"Twenty thousand?"

"Look, I've got an expensive crew sitting around and the agency's got a media deadline. Either way, we're haemorrhaging money. I can't believe it. For god sakes. What happened to the Velvet Revolution? This is worse than the Czechoslovak Communist days."

"Seems they've embraced capitalism," said Carrick.

"We're way behind our shooting schedule, we've got the biggest scene to do, the key dialogue sequences with our expensive BAFTA-winning nancy boy lead talent, and now they're bloody back for more. I've got to get this scene in the can today or we're totally screwed," the Director grimaced as if he'd had a bad oyster, "It's like they've got their own copy of our shooting schedule. They turn up at precisely the wrong time, like they know when they'll be the biggest nuisance."

"Who gets the shooting schedule? The extras?"

"No, no. Only the crew."

"No outsiders? No locals?"

Chapter 2.

"The Construction Unit has a copy," said the Cinematographer coming alive for the first time like a roused puppet.

"Construction?" prompted Carrick.

"They're local. Contracted from Krumlov. Built the market stalls and the medieval wagons."

"The agency is getting seriously shitty back in London," the Producer was gnawing at his nails.

All eyes turned to Carrick.

He knew what they wanted.

He asked himself what he wanted. To let nature take its course? Anything else was beyond his remit. No. He wanted to be loyal, unhesitatingly. The unwritten law melded into his soul. The only one. But whenever it spoke to him another voice, thin and bitter and unsettling, asked *Was life ever so faithful to you? The army? Married life? Where is this precious loyalty obvious anywhere in your miserable existence?* The Major was the answer. And these pathetic three were an extension of him, weren't they? They were paying the bills and he was there to solve their problems. Yes, he had to help this overgrown public schoolboy who was out of his depth and his short-arsed Director with the little fists like half-baked scones. Right or wrong. So he'd have to play offense.

"Call all the extras and crew for an early lunch. I'll go have a word with your friends."

Just a few minutes after texting the photo of the big man lying in the gutter, Carrick heard running footsteps coming towards him. There was another laneway off to the right where a sign pointed to a gun dealer, two men appeared suddenly at its mouth.

They found Carrick sitting on the body of the unconscious heavy with what he imagined was an nonchalant smile. They exchanged looks and immediately advanced on him. The taller of the two pulled knuckledusters from the pocket of his brown leather jacket. When their shadows reached him Carrick took the Makarov pistol from his belt and they stopped dead in their tracks.

Carrick stood up slowly and turned the gun around in his hand, holding it by the barrel, and offered it.

"Shall we strike a bargain?"

Chapter 2.

Then he coshed the tall one across the forehead with the gun handle and swung around stomping down with all his weight onto the side of the second man's kneecap with his heel. Both fell at his feet.

Carrick frisked them and found two more pistols. Another robust old Makarov and a new Walther PPX 9mm.

He called a taxi and told the driver to take his passengers to a medical centre in Sobêslav. There is one closer said the driver. I want it at least an hour away, said Carrick. He put the fare on expenses.

When the Major heard the details back in London three days later, he wasn't pleased with his protégé's negotiation technique and told him so in clipped, deliberate language. Carrick accepted the rebuke but knew he'd done the right thing.

The agency behind the shoot, however, was delighted. It was called Maine Hyland & Blix.

Their Chairman, Tony Maine, rang in person to thank Carrick for his work and sent the Major a case of vintage Krug.

~

Cannes, France – 2013

"Are you Andy Carrick? I'm Ray Doyle."

For ten minutes Carrick had watched the choreography of tightly dressed sashaying girls until the door of the judges room opened and a man emerged with a soft round face, bright red-rimmed glasses and a receding chin.

"Hello Mr. Doyle," Carrick shook a doughy hand. *Dear old Ray.* Early forties but dressed like a Hampstead yuppie's toddler. Over-sized baseball shirt, wide cotton trousers and sneakers with little Mickey Mouse images above the plimsoll line.

"You're from the insurance company, right?"

"Yes; Mr. Maine explained everything I hope?"

The insurance company identity was Tony's idea. Part of what he called the larger strategy, a plausible cover so Carrick could interview the advertising people without having to admit who he was really working for.

"You're certainly quick off the mark, but I guess that's Tony's doing."

"There are certain protocols when making claims on key executive insurance, especially in unusual cases like this." Carrick hoped it was sufficiently cryptic.

They moved into a quiet corner and stood awkwardly close, two strangers trying to be genial.

"Tony didn't actually tell me much, he's not always particularly forthcoming, but I gather you chaps do an investigation in these types of, er, circumstances?"

"I'd like to get some sort of overview if that's OK. You were at the lunch yesterday when it happened I understand?"

"We all were, all the international judges on the main jury. First I knew anything was when the maid screamed and next thing the police arrive. None of us actually saw a thing."

"Was anyone away from the table, apart from Shackleton, when the murder happened?"

"No."

"Did you speak to Mr. Shackleton during the lunch?"

"We didn't get much beyond 'Hello again' I'm afraid. The first I noticed him he was with Eugene Choi, he's another one of the judges. I heard the shriek."

"Shriek?"

"Jonas snuck down the *Hotel Guests* stairs and goosed Eugene with a fire poker. Juvenile stuff."

"Goosed?"

"Jonas was a joker. Everyone in advertising is in touch with his inner child, I suppose. Some more so than others."

"Did you know Mr. Shackleton well?

"I've known him a few years, professionally, not well. We run into one another on the annual award show circuit."

"In Cannes?"

"And some of the others. D&AD, the Campaign Big Awards,

London International Awards, the Effies, the IPA Effectiveness Awards, though Jonas didn't bother with that too often."

"And have you..."

"That's in London. Then there's the American ones, New York One Show, the Clios, the ADDYs; we go to the Asia Pacific Awards most years and the Irish awards in Kinsale..."

Carrick shook his head, "When do you get time to actually write any advertisements?"

"How do you mean?"

"Nothing. Did you see Shackleton here in Cannes apart from at the lunch yesterday?"

"Yes, I did actually, briefly. I ran into him in the Carlton Hotel bar Thursday night. I'd just checked in, but he'd been here a day or two already apparently. I went over to his table for a few minutes. Didn't stay long."

"Why was that?"

"Had his girl with him. That's who the police suspect did it, if you don't already know."

"The Thai girl? What's she like?"

"A beauty pageant contestant he'd seen in the Bangkok fashion pages. Believe it or not, he only wanted to meet her because of her name, Pornthip Sinn. Can you imagine? He told me that right in front of her. No shame. Said he always loved getting into Porn," Doyle sniggered, the back of his hand to his mouth, "Amusing in a Shackleton kind of way."

"Did they seem to you like they were getting on well?"

"Splendidly. She was rubbing his leg with little painted toes the entire time. Said she was very excited to be here, her first time in France. First time anywhere, I'd say. She's rather young."

"Did he say anything unusual, anything that caught your attention, anything that suggested he was worried?"

"No, just the usual banter."

"About?"

"Nothing really. I remember he said, 'Wasn't the recession great? Stuff's been so cheap.'"

"Tell me more about the lunch? Did you pick up any tensions among the judges?"

"Not really. We all get on pretty well, until the judging starts anyway, that's when the politics come out to play."

"Politics?"

"Professional rivalry, shall we say, between the regions."

"Do you think there could be some business motivation behind the murder?"

Carrick didn't want to mention the Qi Project by name, wondering if Ray Doyle would suggest it himself.

"Business? Advertising business? I doubt it," he said flatly, "Perhaps it was just his past caught up with him." Doyle looked at his watch and suddenly looked worried, "Sorry, I've really got to get back inside, but I've got an idea if you want to speak to the other judges. Why don't you come over to the Carlton this evening? Our jury's having dinner together and a little wine tasting in one of the function rooms — they like to keep us out of the public eye while the judging is on. I can introduce you to the rest of the jury if you like? Anyway, that's what Tony suggested I do."

Tony Maine, always a step ahead.

"Great, thank you. I want to explore potential business angles to this."

"Really? Well, whatever you think. I should warn you, everyone will be pretty shot after the first day's judging, it's going to be a long one and we've got two more days to get through after this."

Carrick gave him his number and they shook hands again. "Before you go, Mr. Doyle..."

"Call me Ray."

"Ray, you said something before about Shackleton's past catching up with him?"

"There was a seedier side to Jonas," he hesitated, "I don't want to speak out of school but — well, when you asked about business it just occurred to me that Jonas owns a club in Patpong. In Bangkok. A girlie bar thing, you know? Called, *Inn the Pink*. Inn spelt with a double n."

"I see. What about it?"

"It's probably nothing, but I heard a rumour a while back that he was wanting to create a franchise chain on mainland China. There are some tough characters in that industry. Who knows, maybe Jonas stepped on someone's corns? He was just an advertising guy for all his bluff, he knew nothing about real business."

Doyle shrugged and made for the judges' door just as a tablet-holding-sashay-girl came out looking for him.

He wheeled around before disappearing, "Call it creative instinct, but I don't think this has anything to do with us, you know, the advertising business. He might have been a bit of a scammer, but mostly we're a pretty harmless lot."

Scammer?

~

Emma had been busy refilling the glasses with the velvety Bandol last night, explaining to Carrick, "Shackleton was down here for the judging. The Cannes Lion awards are on, and he's won a few of them over the years."

"Some," Tony corrected, "Not for big clients. In reality, he was Prince of the Scammers."

"Scammers?"

"A scam ad is an ad done without proper client approvals, so it's usually more creative," Emma smiled mischievously, "Sometimes it's not even for a real client or for a client you actually have."

"What's the point? Why do an ad for a client you don't have?" asked Carrick.

"To win award competitions. It's much easier to write a clever ad when you don't have to deal with a client. Often you don't even need to run them."

"Fake ads?" Carrick laughed hard at the notion, "They allow this?"

"No. It's against the rules, of course. But award shows make their money from the number of entries they get, the Cannes awards get maybe forty, fifty thousand entries. They can't check the bona fides of everything."

"You'd be surprised how often it happens. But Shackleton made an art form of it," said Maine.

An industry as fake as advertising spending their time making fake ads, Carrick wondered if it was the wine that made it sound so surreal.

"You're not saying this guy might have been killed because he made scam ads?"

Tony laughed, rocking back in his chair with delight, "I wish. But no."

When Tony smiled it was like the sun had come out.

After Doyle, Carrick thought he'd try to see the Chairman of the Lions Festival, Rémy Barré. The sashaying girl frowned fetchingly and expressed reservations about his chances, but directed him to the elevator.

She was right, he got no further than an anteroom on the Executive Level before a pencil-thin woman in her late thirties appeared and put him straight.

"Monsieur Rémy is not available without a prior appointment."

"Would it be possible to make an appointment?"

"Of course. Please apply in writing and it will be considered after the judging and presentation of the awards are completed."

"Next week?"

"I would be surprised. Perhaps next month. Thank you for your interest, we'll await your correspondence. *Au revoir*, monsieur."

Outside the Festival building bright shards of sunlight ricocheted off the concrete surrounds and spiked Carrick in the eyes as soon as he came out the stage door. Squinting, even in sunglasses, he made for a street vendor's mobile wagon selling beer to the lucky few on the *Plage Publique,* the Cannes' Public Beach, fifty yards from the blockhouse; a tiny stretch that is the only patch of sand on the glossy bay not designated for the exclusive use of hotel beach clubs.

Sitting on the sea wall Carrick thought he could make out the figure of the journo he'd seen being ejected from the stage door.

Stiff straw-yellow hair, the same colour as healthy urine someone once quipped, short-sleeve shirt, short pants, kicking his legs like a truant schoolboy, staring out to the yachts in the bay. It was Benny Sewell. Couldn't mistake him. He had a plastic beer cup to his lips and a Bluetooth in his ear. BS, as he was known, was from the notorious UK-based webzine, *InCreative*, a publication the advertising industry on both sides of the Atlantic fondly referred to as 'the gutter press'.

BS was always *there*, wherever *there* was this week. If little else, he was admired for his Energizer Bunny energy.

"Persistence is genius," Benny would say, running a nail-bitten hand through the flaxen hair and grinning like a kid. It was his slogan.

BS published the industry news without fear, favour or, at times, fact. So he was reviled by the corporate types, the client executives and ad agency suits in equal measure to the welcome he got from advertising's freewheeling creative fraternity. His blogs painted the top copywriters, designers and commercial directors as cavalier geniuses with the quick brilliance of young gods (no-one believes their own publicity quite like an advertising man). In return, Benny successfully wheedled the creatives for campaign information and insider tip offs.

Carrick had met him twice before, the first time for an interview about the danger to international film crews posed by local mafia standover tactics in the Czech provinces. The second time was the production company's Christmas party on a boat cruising down the Thames. It rained cats and dogs so the two of them held up the bar for the duration of the trip, grey London sliding by on both sides in a watery blur.

BS was good company even if his range of subjects was somewhat limited, his tales growing taller the lower the level of his pint. His information might be opinionated, plain wrong or wishful thinking but at least there was lots of it.

It occurred to Carrick that BS would know the gossip, Shackleton's Bangkok girlie bar for example. A thread Tony Maine hadn't mentioned last night. Maybe he wasn't even aware of it?

"You're a bit old to be playing Humpty Dumpty," Carrick called.

They abuse body and brain cells in pursuit of their profession, but nothing seems to damage journalists' memories. BS plucked the name from his internal file within a couple of seconds, "Andrew Carrick! Mr. Security. How are you, my old son?" They shook hands. "What are you doing hobnobbing in Cannes?" A thought occurred to him, "Doing security for someone important?"

"We've only just met up and already you're grilling me?"

"Avoiding the question, eh? So you *are* here with someone famous! Knew it. Who? At least give me a clue, English or American? Neither?"

"Whoa, steady. You haven't changed, same old BS. I'm just down for a day at the seaside. I've been renting a cottage up in the country."

"Really? Cool. Where?"

"Bonnieux."

"Never heard of it. If it's close, I could bring some of the dudes over for a drink."

"Thanks for the opportunity," Carrick said, "but it's not five-star. Found a snake in the bloody kitchen the other day. Funny story. Anyway, it's two and a half hours away."

"Gawd, the sticks. I only know Nice, Cannes, St-Paul-de-Vence, oh and Paris. That's France enough for me, what more do you need?"

"So what's up at the Lions this year?"

"Haven't you heard about Jonas Shackleton?"

"Never met him."

"Guru, one of the judges this year, murdered at lunch yesterday. I was there. I broke the story. More or less. Picked up by the Murdoch media overnight with a by-line, thank you very much."

"You were there? Let me buy you another beer and you can tell me all the gruesome details."

"Can't right now, Andy. Got to go and do an interview with Sir Richard Branson at two this afternoon, he's staying over at Eden Roc. Take me a while to get there in this bloody traffic. Why couldn't he stay in Cannes like the rest of us plebs?"

"Interviewing Branson? You've come up in the world."

"Yeah, well, it's a press conference, really. There'll be a few of us there, but I'll ask him some questions."

"Forget Branson, tell me more about this guy Shackleton, I didn't know they had murders in Adland. My buy?"

"Alright, just to be sociable. I suppose I've got a couple of minutes yet."

Carrick bought two large plastic cups of 1664 from the street vendor and BS was still sitting in the same precarious spot on the ledge, digital camera clutched to him like a comfort bear. It was a boyish face under the straw-broom hair but at the same time the old man was forcing his way through the crazing at the edges of his eyes and the deep lines running down both cheeks. There'd be no middle-age for Benny, he would grow old quick as falling off a cliff.

"Cheers."

"Cheers."

The beer eased Carrick's head. They sat in the warm silence a moment letting the sun iron their faces, light filling the crevices. Persil-white yachts drifted across the sea in front of the green Lérins Isles hovering on the horizon of the blue day. Fifteen minutes and centuries away from the glamourfest of Cannes — the islands of Sainte Marguerite and Saint Honorat — silent forests and ruined monasteries where couples took long walks and families took picnics. Carrick had been there with Robyn once upon a time in a different life. Andy and Robyn. Robyn and Andy.

"Reminds me," said BS, "I was at the local award show in Croatia a while back. I discovered their word for 'Cheers!' is dangerously similar to a word they use when inviting a person to engage in a kinky sexual encounter..."

That broke the mood.

Carrick sighed and went back to work, "What's the scoop on the Shackleton thing then?"

BS took another swig, "I was right there when it happened."

"Right there?"

"Outside the Colombe d'Or ..."

"Right there, but outside?"

"Initially. Then I went in. Point is, I was the first member of the press on the scene."

"What did you see?"

Benny didn't tell Carrick that he'd been sitting in the sandy pétanque park opposite La Colombe d'Or for an hour and twenty minutes, the post-luncheon doorstop interview being one of his most successful news-hunting techniques. It had been a long lunch but advertising lunches usually are. Whoever thinks there's no such thing as a free lunch doesn't know how to fill in expenses, Benny always said.

What he did tell Carrick was that he got a text message from someone inside La Colombe d'Or.

Jonas Shackleton killed!

Benny admitted with a laugh that he initially wondered who Shackleton had 'killed'? Had he put on a performance that 'killed'? Shackleton could do witheringly cruel impressions of his peers when he had a captive audience. Who would Shackleton have turned on in such an elite gathering?

Or did it mean something more sinister?

'Killed' as in Shackleton's career killed?

"You see, Shackleton would get drunk and aggressive pretty much whenever and wherever he felt like it, I wondered could he have blown his new job already?"

"Who was the text from?"

"Whitey. Malcolm White, one of the UK judges, Creative Director of HypKno. Über creative London agency. I know him pretty well, so I thought maybe it was a wind up?"

"New job?" asked Carrick, though Tony Maine had already briefed him last night about Shackleton's new role at InterGroup

40

"Jonas gave me an exclusive Skype interview a month ago from New York when it was announced he was being made Worldwide Creative Director there."

Titular, Shackleton called it, putting a punning leer into the word like he always did. "Everyone loves a tit-ular job," he boomed and laughed like a pirate across the Atlantic.

The photo Benny used on the interview's webpage showed a big-boned man with a polished skull and a big moustache of the kind only a big guy can wear. Larger than life, staring down the camera; big hands, big rings, a fat cigar stuck between his fingers. With his leather jacket and looming presence Shackleton looked like the drummer from some ageing heavy-metal band.

Benny began the article with the famous story of the time a younger Shackleton had ridden his Harley Davidson up the elevator to the top floor of his then agency and along the hall to the chair-man's office where he burst in to announce that, following the success of his most recent campaign, he had decided to go to Barbados on holidays, starting immediately. And, by the way, he was taking the chairman's pretty new secretary with him. A year later he wrote an award-winning chocolate bar ad based on the same scenario.

"You gotta laugh," Shackleton said when Benny reminded him of it.

Shackleton wrote funny ads, made funny speeches and told excruciatingly dirty but very funny stories. Then, Benny got another text message and that's when he realised this was no joke.

Jonas Murdead!

This came from Eugene Choi, Chief Creative Officer at the O&W agency in Beijing. Choi isn't a funny guy, said Benny, couldn't afford to be, not with those huge Chinese Government accounts his agency handles. This was the real thing. Authentic. He knew Eugene Choi couldn't spell.

Benny leapt from his park bench and ran across the street, he'd never had a scoop bigger than insider industry news, the defection of a creative director from one agency to another or the sudden move of a blue-chip account from one hot-shop to its fiercest rival. A real life murder was a gift on a different level. Benny's steps grew longer as he jumped the gutter and vaulted towards the restaurant gate, his ambition keeping pace.

The way Benny told the story, he burst through the heavy timber door at the entrance as though they were the gates of a dream, writing headlines as he went. *Death in Cannes! Ad Guru's Last Supper!* He was hoping to spot Whitey, who sent him the first text message.

Instead he ran, quite literally, into the tallest man in the vicinity, Jay Carlsson, just as the Swedish advertising judge was leaving the Gents and walking along the terrace back to the bar. Carlsson saw the official press pass hanging from the blue lanyard, registered the mop of straw hair and realised Benny's small digital camera was already rolling.

"Oh, BS. What are you doing here?"

"I heard about Jonas. What do you know?"

"Already?" Carlsson looked around and saw a row of bow-backed tweeters sitting on the low terrace wall messaging, and understood, "Um, don't know what I can say really, I just heard the scream."

"He screamed? Wow. Hang on ... I'll do an intro for that and ask it again. OK?" BS put on his 'announcer's voice', "The hugely talented Mr. Jay Carlsson, the man behind last year's breakthrough Volvo campaign and one of Europe's new wave of creative directors, was a witness today. Did you hear what it was the victim screamed at the time of his murder?"

Carlsson took a step backwards, "No, *she* screamed. The woman. Sorry, BS, I can't really talk now."

"Woman?" said BS still filming, "Which woman?"

"A chambermaid, I think. I just want to say I'm shocked and saddened. See you later, BS."

Benny's was pondering the notion of Shackleton and chambermaids when he saw Eugene Choi standing alone on the far side of the garden, the judge from Beijing, a fat man in tailored black, 'Buddha in Armani' they called him behind his back. BS bolted around the trellises towards him.

"Benny? You here?" said Eugene Choi.

"You sent me a text, of course I'm here."

"But so quick?" said Choi, wide eyed.

Benny didn't want to explain he'd been outside the restaurant waiting for trivial gossip, now he was planning the syndication of a big story.

"Um," he said, trying to get a sense of urgency into the conversation, "What happened, Mr. Choi?"

"Oh, Benny, it is awful," Choi stared downwards, adding nothing more.

BS raised his camera, "Great, go on."

Choi said slowly, "I am talking to Jonas, you know? We are finished lunch but still sitting at the table, well, he was talking really. I don't know. Telling something he is doing ... or wanted to do. You know, a project or something. I'm not so sure, you know my English? He was very excited. Talking quite fast. Talking, talking. A little drunk, maybe... "

Choi stared out across the garden to the egg-shaped hill opposite, the orderly French countryside sloping down towards Cannes and the distant sea, clearly affected by the situation, his smooth round face sad and golden in the afternoon sunlight. But Benny couldn't wait for a Zen moment of reflection, other journos would be getting their texts by now, and they'd be getting them from judges with a better command of the language.

He asked urgently, "Was he poisoned or something? Oh, and where's the body?"

Once more Choi's answer was painfully slow, "He got up ... to show me something. Something I would like, he said ... or something else ... not quite sure," he was frowning in the effort, "then he went upstairs ... I don't know ... and that's where the maid found him. Mur-dead."

Choi looked up at BS, suddenly saw the camera and put his hand up in front of his face, "Maybe I shouldn't have call you," he added almost to himself, "I just thought 'news', Benny would like to know. I didn't think you could come here, I didn't think I ... I didn't want to talk."

Out of the corner of his eye, BS saw the first gendarmes arrive and knew instinctively they would shut him down soon. He lowered the camera and said in a conspiratorial tone from the corner of his mouth, barely above a whisper, "Who killed him?"

There was silence for a long moment.

BS tried to catch Choi's eye but his expression was unreadable. BS raised an inquiring eyebrow, the hush getting awkward now.

"Pardon?" said Choi.

The ad man's attention was on something behind Benny and just as he looked over his shoulder someone called, "*Sortez. Allons! Allons-y!* Hey. You shouldn't be here. How long have you been here?"

It was Rémy Barré, a man who could normally smell a journalist two towns away and happily crawl across broken champagne glasses to speak with him. Not today.

"This is a private function with no press passes valid. You must leave now," Barré said, his busy hands wringing.

"Is it still a private function after a murder, Monsieur Barré?" countered BS, holding his digital camera behind his back now, still rolling, trying to do a slow pan across the terrace, "I'm a member of the world press covering a crime scene. This is not advertising, this is real life. I don't need a press pass for that."

BS hoped he wasn't overdoing it, he didn't want to get his press pass revoked for the rest of the festival. Then came another voice followed by the sharp pain of his camera being taken away and his arm being bent up to his shoulder-blade. A gendarme had spotted him filming.

"*Cesser. Arretez.* No journalists. *Sortir. Media interdit.* Leave immediately."

BS was bum-rushed from the La Colombe d'Or as the *ambulanciers* rushed in.

"It was over," he said to Carrick, "No pics of the body. No interviews to speak of. It was only when I was back on the bench across the road in the pétanque park that I realised I should have asked Rémy Barré who was going to replace Shackleton on the judging panel. That would have been a great exclusive."

Carrick laughed, "Yeah, it's hard keeping things in perspective after a murder."

"Well it's not much of a mystery is it? Open and shut. I found out later that his girlfriend's gone missing. She's a Thai tart. Get this: her name is Pornthip Sinn. Can't be a real name, can it? *Pornthip? Sinn?* She's got to be a dancer at Shackleton's club, right, with a name like that?"

"Shackleton's club?"

"He owned a club in Bangkok."

"Really? Tell me about it."

"Called *Show Me The Pink* or something. It's just a side business — Jonas bought it to stick it up the network straights probably. It's the usual Patpong thing, girls everywhere, pole dancing, lots of hostesses walking around wearing nothing but a smile. Only been there once myself, from what I can remember."

"When?"

"The Pan Asian Awards two years ago, the year Shackleton was Chairman of Judges down there. He hosted a huge night with special shows, you know, ping-pong, the lot, everyone got an eyeful."

"What makes you think this girl, Pornthip, worked at his club?"

He snorted, "Had to, surely? I saw her when they arrived at Nice airport. Gorgeous. Tall. All cheekbones and legs right up to heaven. She'd have been a star in a club like that..." he chuckled again, wiping his mouth with his sleeve, "God, it was so funny last night."

"What?"

"And sad, too, of course," he added, his face squirming like he'd just swallowed an eel, reluctant to continue but couldn't stop himself, "I was just remembering last night, the boys around the pool at the Martinez, once word got around, you know, about Jonas."

"Funny?"

"No disrespect. But a lot of slit jokes, about her *and* him. You know, her being a slit-eye and him having his throat slit."

"Classy."

"You can imagine what the creatives came up with, all bad taste, nothing I could publish, but sometimes you've got to laugh, right?

Jonas would've, I'm sure," Benny pulled hard at his beer, "He would love to have gone out this way I reckon."

"His throat cut?"

"Maybe not that bit. But killed by a tart, you know."

"Were the other judges there?"

"God no. They're locked away, even I can't get to them. It was just the lads trying to guess what his last words might have been. Taking it in turns, y'know, a kind of drinking game. Sounds silly now. Just a lot of pissed delegates from all over, copywriters and art directors, a couple of agency producers. The Aussies had a Cannes Opening party at the Martinez, lots of cans of Foster's. Get it? 'Cannes/Cans'. Those Aussies love a pun. Started with cold beer and ended with warm champagne. It was huge. There was a lot of booze spilt to toast ol' Jonas last night, I can tell you that. Anyway, 'nuff said.

"Sounds a riot. So tell me, what did these creative geniuses come up with as his last words?"

"Whatever he said, he was talking out of his neck."

Carrick shook his head. He didn't mind gallows humour from squaddies, men who knew how easily a person is torn apart, who've seen the obscenity of human meat, purply-blue guts spilling like reels of unspooled tape from the bellies of children, they deserved the release; but lily-white civilians mocking savage death was somehow unearned.

"Anyone have a clever theory about why it happened?"

"I figure the new girlfriend thought she was special, he'd brought her over to Cannes, you know, but then she got mad 'cos Jonas was playing around on the side. Sometimes girls don't get it."

"He was playing around?"

"Why else would he have installed her at La Colombe d'Or? You see, the judges are put up for free at the Carlton here in Cannes. Always have been. Shackleton, sly old dog, had her tucked away from prying eyes up in Vence, so he could still use his judge's suite at the Carlton for dalliances with any young creative talent who might benefit from his, um, experience. He was a devil."

"You don't think his death might have been connected to business? Rival agency networks maybe? Someone trying to nobble a new business pitch, or something?"

Benny looked at him suspiciously.

"Gee, it's not like you film crew-type people to take an interest in the movement of clients in new business pitches?"

"I'm just tying to think laterally, trying to think beyond the-girl-did-it cliché. Is that too creative for Cannes?"

"Mmm," BS looked chary.

"Tell me more about what happened at La Colombe d'Or. The conversation with Choi."

"Nothing to tell, his English is about as good as my Mandarin. Apparently he went upstairs for something and Choi thought he'd be right back."

"Upstairs for what?"

"'Something interesting' is all Choi said. My bet is probably naughty photos of Pornthip, knowing Shackleton."

Carrick tried Ray Doyle's theory, "Maybe Jonas wanted to start some more girlie clubs in China? Maybe Choi was going to help?"

Benny laughed, "Nah. Can't see that, Choi's an ascetic, more like a Zen monk than a typical creative guy. I think the last time Eugene Choi was inside a woman he was in the maternity ward waiting to be born. Jonas always called him the Not Very Mad Monk."

Benny's phone beeped and he stood up stiffly, threw the dregs of his beer at an unsuspecting seagull.

"That's my appointment alert. Better go see Branson do his spiel. Listen, Andy, we're having a wake for Jonas on Monday afternoon at a big empty villa up on the hill. Come if you want. Free drinks. Great view. Should be fun."

And he was gone, dashing onto the flag-festooned boulevard like he was late for the school bus. Carrick looked out at the Lérins again and finished his beer.

A wake.

Free drinks. Great view. Should be fun.

An advert for a wake.

CHAPTER 3.

Carrick's coffin closed.

A neat, decisive sound.

"You've made you're bed, now you're lying in it," the journalist smirked.

The young woman in the tight black dress frowned, whispered, "Toi, toi, toi" and thought how strangely changed Carrick's face looked.

Gone the hesitant smile, the steady eyes that held her at the rooftop bar just a few nights ago. Un air canaille, she'd decided. Rakish. A weary face, not old, but somehow vulnerable.

Almost unrecognisable now.

Now the face of a murdered man.

The hard-edged shadow of the coffin lid wiped across the freshly shaved skull and filled the casket with darkness.

The lift lines tautened.

The coffin descended slowly into the murmuring, unnatural glow below.

Then the music started. Nihilistic rumbling from deep in an orchestra, a martial kettledrum punctuating the air with thirteen ominous blows, boom-boom-boom-boom-boom-boom-boom-boom-boom-boom-boom-boom-boom, amplified everywhere, like the boots of an approaching army. Mighty trum-

pets sounded three long, clear notes and crescendoed to a pair of clashing chords that hung like infinite possibilities in some huge space.

"Pretentious or what?" the journalist groaned, "Fat Elvis used this track to start his Vegas shows. Thus Spake Zarathustra."

But no one was there anymore, the French girl in the black dress was gone.

Inside the casket, darkness deeper than midnight. The music muffled, compressed, eerily distant. Carrick's feet pressed stiffly against the base of the casket, the white skin of his head touching the top, knuckles tight at his side scraping the raw pine-smelling timber, clenched into strengthless fists.

His eyes stared straight ahead, widening in the dark.

Rising panic filled his chest.

Wild thoughts rushed like schoolchildren fleeing a burning hall, tripping over themselves, screaming unintelligibly. Thoughts of Afghanistan, a bombed out qala two years ago. The mujahideen tried to smother him in heat and darkness, buried him inside the rusted turret of a dismembered tank after breaking his face and most of his fingers.

But he'd pulled through. Robyn saved him. Pale-eyed, beautiful as marble, pure as a dream. Their bright future a beacon in the deep, burning black.

No.

No, no, that was all wrong. A survival program obsolete now. A desert mirage.

She was gone.

There was nothing but a coffin lowering into chaos below. Him inside.

How?

How had it come to this?

He fish-gasped for breath.

∼

Inspecteur Lacont scratched his head.

Footage from the CCTV camera at the hotel entrance showed a tall girl La Colombe d'Or staff had identified as Pornthip Sinn, dressed in a pink hoodie, leaving the hotel at 8.17am Friday morning.

Chapter 3.

Some six hours later, at 2.35pm, the camera sees the figure returning. The pink hoodie identical to the one found in Shackleton's room.

Roughly an hour before the murder.

Another camera is at the bottom of the Guests' Only stairway vectored along the hall towards the dining room, but ill-positioned, trying to catch both areas and only half succeeding. It only managed to cover the right-hand half of the stairway, so anyone using the left side of the staircase, by chance or stealth, is effectively invisible.

Pornthip Sinn was not seen again by any of the staff and not picked up by any other camera in the hotel. She somehow disappeared.

Lacont rewound through all the earlier CCTV footage of the couple again, back to when Shackleton and Sinn first checked-in Wednesday afternoon.

But it is their activities late Thursday night that causes the head scratching, through bemusement rather than prudishness.

The stairway camera shows them coming down from the first floor, time code reading 1.43am. A third camera inside the dining area picks them up a moment later, the restaurant is closed and deserted, the tables cleared. The couple are apparently there to look at the art collection on the walls, hands clasped behind their backs in the universal art gallery position.

The manager had explained, "It's one of the benefits of staying at La Colombe d'Or that you can browse the collection in your own time."

After a minute or so, Shackleton fixes on one painting in particular, he comes close but doesn't seem to be looking at the painting as such, instead he fingers its frame, the shell-shaped picture light flaring over his hand as he gently tilts it off the wall as if examining how it's hung.

He replaces it, curiosity evidently satisfied, and steps away.

After a cursory look around he moves to the other side of the room behind Pornthip who is gazing at a different work. The soundless grey-blue footage sees him suddenly grab her, roughly pinning her wrists up her back before plunging his free hand down her neckline to squeeze her breast.

He bends her over one of the tables, her arms still pinned, his other hand now under her dress between her legs.

Then he looks up, directly into the eye of the camera above them, releases his grip and says something to her. She giggles, steps out of her panties, turns into his arms and they kiss. Then he squats down and she swings a long leg over his head and jumps onto his shoulders, sitting astride his ears. While she holds onto the polished dome of his skull, he stands up, grinning like a sailor, walks across the room towards the high-mounted camera. She reaches out towards it, poking her tongue out lewdly, her hand growing grotesquely large as it comes close to the lens.

She tilts the camera up to the blankness of the ceiling.

What happens next is left to the viewer to imagine.

These creative directors were a strange breed, Lacont mused, switching off the machine. Arrogance he was used to after working eight years on the Riviera, but these people exuded something else.

"An adolescent triumphalism of sorts," he described it to his deputy, Rolande. Lacont had spoken to each of the award judges after viewing the body; though they came from half a dozen different nationalities most shared the same air of naughty boys who'd won the lottery.

Rémy Barré, the President of the Cannes Lions International Festival of Creativity, a short, dapper and fidgety man in an impeccably cut grey suit, had hosted the VIP lunch. In the commotion that followed the discovery of the murder, Barré had the presence of mind to gather them all in the La Colombe d'Or's small vaulted bar and beg them to remain on the premises until the police arrived.

Better to get the inevitable official questioning out of the way immediately, he said, he didn't want them interrupted during the upcoming awards judging.

In festivals past, Barré explained to Lacont, he'd coped with drunk, high and hallucinating judges, prima donna judges, gone-missing judges, overworked and jet-lagged judges who wanted nothing but to sleep, judges who'd sent someone else in their place without notifying him, judges who wanted to change the rules of the judging and judges who wanted to be awarded all the awards themselves. He could cope with a dead judge.

The award show must go on.

Most of these renowned creative gurus would have stayed anyway, Lacont decided, they were exactly where they liked to be, at the hub of the interesting universe. Few saw any threat to themselves despite a murder being committed at such close quarters.

No one was gauche enough to say it in as many words, but they seemed unsurprised someone wanting to kill Jonas Shackleton.

"He was popular but not well liked," is how one of them summed it up.

When Lacont first arrived on the scene those judges not gossiping quietly in the bar were sitting in the overflowing garden on the terrace messaging with busy thumbs or talking guardedly on cell phones. No doubt that's how the press arrived so quickly.

Lacont had the press removed just as quickly.

Barré explained that the VIP lunch had been dignified by the attendance of mayors from both St-Paul-de-Vence and the City of Cannes, Lacont was relieved to hear that both mayors were swept from the restaurant (one by his driver back to Cannes, the other back to his residence on the far side of Vence) even before the Gendarmerie and Ambulance were called. Lacont didn't want the press talking to them or, for that matter, them talking to the press.

This was even more important now that there was a salacious CCTV tape to keep under wraps.

Even Tony Maine hadn't been able to get Carrick a hotel room in Cannes with all the advertising illuminati in town, instead he found himself booked into an inconspicuous 3-star in Juan-les-Pins, 25 minutes further down the coast.

"This isn't a complicated ploy," Carrick asked Emma the previous night, "to get me out of my cottage so you can install a couple of tourists from Arkansas over summer?"

"Didi would never allow it, he thinks of you as a brother," she laughed, "He wouldn't even charge you rent if it wasn't for me doing the books."

There was a small package waiting for Carrick at reception.

250 fake business cards for his cover as an insurance man, organised by Tony and printed locally that morning. They identified Andrew Carrick as an agent of Lloyd's of London, based in the Nice office.

A famous brand is trustworthy, Tony said, as a Lloyd's man you'll have permission to ask questions in an official-sounding capacity.

Carrick changed into a suit to look even more trustworthy and put a bunch of the cards into the breast pocket. Next he rescued his dusty Defender from the hotel's open-air car park across the Rue de l'Oratoire and made his way easily to the D36 from the motorway in the direction of St-Paul-de-Vence, only to snail up to the hilltop village behind three tourist buses.

La Colombe d'Or was open for business as usual when Carrick walked in through the big doors under the famous golden dove logo, he figured the crime scene must be restricted to Shackleton's room. The old walls glowed like fiery honeycomb in the afternoon light as he picked his way through the green shade towards the bar, under the gnarled vines and white umbrellas, passed an unsettling marble sculpture of a giant painter's thumb. The terrace was quietly buzzing with cicadas and the sound of a dozen tables enjoying the good life — mostly civilised grey heads and their coiffured wives.

He gave the barman a freshly minted business card and asked discreetly if he'd been working yesterday when the guest was killed?

The man shook his head.

Carrick asked if the chambermaid who found the body was working today?

"*Non*, monsieur."

Carrick asked if any of today's staff had been on duty yesterday?

Chapter 3.

The barman shrugged in the patented way the French have of annoying the English. Carrick asked if he could see the manager.

Long minutes passed.

Carrick studied a peeling, faded fresco behind the bar, a hunted deer leaping through a tangle of forest. There were black & white photos on the wall of celebrity drinkers who'd perched on the stools before him — David Niven, François Truffaut, Yves Montand, Earnest Hemingway, Roger Moore, Tony Curtis. All the time wishing he'd ordered something to drink, but supposing that would be out of character for an insurance investigator.

Eventually a thin, long-faced man wearing a pencil moustache, an old-fashioned dark suit and an even darker scowl came out from the back office. He was holding the Lloyd's business card between bony fingers.

"You are Monsieur Andrew Carrick?"

He pronounced it Carrique. Careek.

"*Oui*, monsieur. *Bonjour.*"

Carrick's smile wasn't returned, his outstretched hand was left mid-air, unshaken.

"I am Inspecteur de Détective Gerrard Lacont, from the Unité des Crimes Graves. Come with me, please."

It's a truism of military strategy that no plan survives first contact with the enemy.

Now Carrick was in a stupid dilemma, he hadn't reckoned on giving a fake business card to a police detective on his first day on the job. Tony Maine had got this bit wrong, it was too soon to go to the crime scene.

He followed Lacont down a narrow corridor that skirted the dining rooms, passed the guest staircase to the first floor, and through a door with a small nameplate reading, *Bureau du Directeur*. The manager's office was large, decorated in the rustic-chic style evident throughout the inn, art on the walls, heavy antique furniture; without the modern technology sitting on every surface — a couple of computers, CCTV monitors, all-in-one scanner, printer and fax, multi-line telephone — the elegant room may not have changed for fifty or sixty years. There was no sign of the hotel manager.

"Why are you here, Monsieur Carrique?"

Small, penetrating eyes assessed him, they didn't seem to like what they saw.

"Shall we sit?" suggested Carrick.

Lacont turned the business card over in his fingers a couple of times, then brought it up to his nose and smelt it. Freshly minted, ink newly dried, just baked plastic coating. Carrick went cold.

"Do you have photo ID please?"

Carrick handed over his British driver's license, Lacont glanced at it before giving it to a younger detective in a brown suit who had materialized at the door; he proceeded to photocopy it.

Finally Lacont moved behind the manager's desk and sat down, motioning Carrick into the visitor's chair.

"I ask again. Why are you here?"

"I'm investigating the sudden death of Jonas Shackleton on behalf of his employers for insurance purposes," Carrick began, "Mr. Shackleton, when travelling, was covered by one of Lloyds' Key Executive Policies to the value of two million euros."

Lacont tilted his long face as if taking aim down his nose, "May I observe how diligent your company is, Monsieur Carrique, and how prompt? His death was only yesterday."

"Thank you. Our client, InterGroup-Publicity, contacted me at home through their Vice Chairman, Mr. Tony Maine, who is currently in Cannes. He was most keen for me to come up from Nice immediately and find out as much as I could. He is a very important client."

Lacont wrote down the name, Tony Maine. Asked for the spelling of InterGroup.

Carrick noticed a diary on the desk in front of Lacont, it had pink edging and Hello Kitty on the cover. It didn't look like it belonged to the hotel manager. Or the policeman.

He indicated with a tilt of his head, "Anything helpful in Miss Sinn's diary?"

Lacont picked up a manila folder and placed it over the book, "Why didn't you ring the Sûreté before coming here, Monsieur Carrique?"

The inspecteur didn't have a particularly large frame for a police-man, but there was something about him not to be taken lightly. A serious man from the Serious Crimes Unit.

Carrick decided that the best defence was attack.

"Look, Inspecteur, I don't want to waste your valuable time. I came because I was hoping to ask just a couple of questions and be on my way."

Lacont considered for a long moment, the hangdog face raised itself to target along its nose again, the mouth turned downwards and he sighed, "Monsieur, I can tell you the basics."

"I'd appreciate any cooperation you can offer us."

"Inspecteur-Détective Adjoint Rolande, my deputy," he indicated the policeman in the brown suit, "will supply your office with the time and place of death and copies of necessary morgue certificates. The autopsy report can be sent also, once it is complete. For the moment I can tell you that the victim's throat was cut and he likely died of asphyxiation and blood loss at the scene, Suite 12 on the first floor, as a result of those injuries."

He opened the manila folder in front of him and pushed it across the desk, police photos of the body in situ. He watched closely as Carrick examined the glossies.

"What caused the wound? The razor on the floor?"

Lacont nodded, "It is likely."

The only wound appeared to be the sliced throat, Shackleton's clothes weren't disarranged, no sign of struggle or fight, his rings was still on his fingers, a fat watch on his wrist.

"Suicide a possibility? Have to ask. It affects the policy, you see."

"We are treating it as murder, monsieur."

"Fingerprints on the razor?"

"We are checking."

"What of the young woman, Miss Sinn, you believe she was involved?"

Lacont's black looks darkened a shade, "That is surely not relevant to your insurance policy?"

"It's just that I understand Miss Sinn has gone missing?"

"Does your policy cover her also?"

"She might qualify as next of kin, Inspecteur."

"Monsieur Carrique, our investigation proceeds, I don't think I can help you further at this stage."

"Come now, it's already in the newspapers and all over the internet that she's done a runner. Just put me in the picture and give me the chance to do my job."

Lacont drummed the desk irritatedly.

Carrick prompted, "Can you tell me anything about her?"

"I can tell you she is a Thai citizen visiting France on a holiday visa. She's a student of languages at Bangkok National University, the only daughter of..." he opened a small notebook, "... Dr. Niran Sinn and Mrs. Sukhon Sinn. He's a dentist. She's a housewife. I can only say that Miss Sinn is a person of interest in this case and we hope she can help us with our enquiries."

"When you find her..."

"As you say."

"How long do you estimate it was between the murder and the discovery of the body?"

"A matter of minutes. Fifteen perhaps."

"Long enough for her to leave the hotel?"

"Apparently."

"Did she leave with anybody?"

"When we have concluded you'll be given a summary of our report, Monsieur Carrique."

"How do you know she was in the hotel at the time of the murder?"

"May I observe that you are acting more like her lawyer than an insurance man?"

"It's a two million payout. We must be thorough."

Again the drumming of the fingers, "We believe she returned to the hotel an hour before the murder. She must have slipped away during the confusion when the body was discovered."

"Is there CCTV footage?"

The monitor on the sideboard was flicking between four scenes, the front gate outside the high perimeter wall, the dining room, a partial view of the guests' internal stairs and the bar.

"Nothing helpful. France is not watched over by cameras like your English places."

"Is it possible for me to see where the murder happened?"

"No, it is not."

"Any chance she was abducted?"

"Why would you ask that? There is no evidence indicating such a thing."

"What I'm getting at, is there a chance it wasn't her, that the murderer was a person unknown?"

"It does not appear to be a robbery. It does not appear to be an abduction."

"Maybe it was an assassination? Maybe business related?"

"Why do you say so?"

"I'm looking for a motive. I understand the Lions festival brings many powerful business competitors together. The rivalries must be fierce?"

"There is no evidence indicating such a thing," he said again. He closed the folder and stood up, "I think I can say I have cooperated in all necessary respects, Monsieur Carrique. Now, if there's nothing else…?" he gestured toward the door, making an unsuccessful effort to contort the long face into a thin smile.

"Let's go back to my first question," said Carrick, remaining seated, "Anything helpful in Miss Sinn's diary? Had the couple been fighting for example?"

Lacont picked up the pink book from under the file, turned it round and pushed it across the desk.

"You tell me."

Carrick opened a few pages.

This time the policeman did manage a smile.

Chapter 3.

Each page of the diary was neatly handwritten in Thai script.

Carrick sighed with relief behind the wheel, motoring slowly out of Vence down the bends towards the A8 and back to Cannes. Questions winding around his brain in tightening circles.

If the girl *wasn't* the killer, why did she disappear?

If she *was* the killer but it wasn't a crime of passion, as Tony insisted, how was she connected to a business plot?

Doyle said it was Shackleton who instigated their relationship because of her double entendre name. Though just because Shackleton said so didn't make it true — advertising men and the truth weren't always close buddies. But if she *was* involved in a business plot, why wait until they were in France to kill him? And why do it in such a risky way, with only minutes to escape?

It was disconcerting too that neither Ray Doyle nor Benny Sewell gave much credence to the idea of a business motive behind Shackleton's murder. Both of them were naïve, he decided. And what of the girlie bar in Bangkok? A possible link between such a place and Pornthip Sinn couldn't be totally ignored.

The scale of difficulty was the only thing becoming clear.

He should have asked to see the guests' register for a full list of who was staying at the hotel; though he doubted Lacont would have allowed it. He sighed again, this time with frustration.

"God, what am I doing?" he said out loud, not sure if the question was rhetorical.

The truth was, talking to Maine on Friday night Carrick had been surprised to feel something in him stirring. Like he was rediscovering an edge of excitement, a quickening, the feeling of being close to something real again. Something at the centre of things.

The Major had an expression, *the pull of action*. Perhaps that was it.

The pull of action. Something he was missing but couldn't quite admit.

But duelling with the policeman unnerved him, his head was spinning. He needed to absorb a few things. He needed a drink. Only a veneer of confidence had saved the day, a confidence he didn't feel.

The Major would have handled it so much better, Carrick never once saw him off balance; he'd envied his poise, the effortless mastery of self and circumstances, but he hadn't found a way to emulate it. Didn't someone once say that you admire in others the qualities that you lack in yourself? Carrick didn't have the Major's analytical ability, just his client list.

When he reached the freeway near Cagnes-sur-Mer a truckies' bar came into view and he pulled onto the ramp, parked the Defender beside a monster 18-wheeler Fiat and went inside for a cognac.

Inspecteur Lacont summoned the hotel manager back into his own office. "Did you recognize that man, calling himself Andrew Carrique?"

"No, monsieur."

"Do you know the name Tony Maine, from the company Inter-Group-Publicity?"

"I don't believe so, monsieur."

"Check your records and tell me if either have been a guest here."

"Of course, Inspecteur."

Lacont beckoned to Rolande, "Talk to Lloyd's in Nice first thing Monday morning and see if this Carrique checks out. Meanwhile, find out if this Tony Maine and InterGroup-Publicity exist and, if so, what kind of animal they are."

Rolande hovered, waiting for more, "Do you trust an insurance man who works weekends?"

Lacont scratched his head.

9pm and the town was ablaze.

Smoke and sulphur clouded the night air like the devil himself had materialized in Cannes. Huge balls of light bloomed high over the Carlton Hotel, great bangs boomed off the façade and bounced across La Croisette echoing out to sea like a wartime bombardment. Every few seconds more pyrotechnics sprayed lurid colours over the upturned faces in the crowded street below.

"The fireworks for us?" murmured one of the judges as he glanced through the second floor window sipping a glass of wine and helping himself to a piece of ripe brie.

The Lions jury had been mini-bussed from the Festival's block-house to the Carlton's underground car park and ushered straight upstairs to their private dinner and sponsored wine tasting, the slick operation coinciding with the opening fireworks display launched from the beach club across the boulevard.

Ray Doyle's phone call had directed Carrick to a plush confer-ence room called 'Elba'. Time to meet the little generals, he thought.

It was a large, timber-panelled room configured with a buffet sideboard and a selection of hot dishes along one wall, enough food for twice as many people. Under the chandelier, a carved mahogany banquet table had twelve places set with heavy ornate silverware and an array of varying sized wine glasses. Three uniformed hotel staff were serving from a selection of six reds and six whites and providing tasting notes for each. The rich smells reminded Carrick he'd eaten nothing all day.

Outside, the light-show climaxed in a last thunderclap as Doyle introduced each of the international gurus, explaining that unfortu-nately three of their number had already gone to their rooms, too tired to participate.

Carrick noted the judges were using the vacant chairs to create several distinct groups around the table.

At the head sat a handsome grey-headed man in a high-backed chair, Francesco Ferreira from Sao Paulo, sleek and watchful, mid-forties. Next to him, Alberto Lopez from Argentina, younger, squatter, with large sad Latin eyes, and on the other side, Rocco Jiminez from Barcelona, angular nose at the front, grey ponytail at the back.

They offered polite handshakes but stayed aloof, imperious; they weren't pretending disinterest, thought Carrick, they were genuinely indifferent.

Sharing the centre of the table were two American judges, New Yorker Eddie Schwarz, square head, buzz cut and bright blue eyes. The other was the only woman present, Taylor Simmons, LA thin, well-cut clothes, mid-thirties.

At the far end sat a tall, softly spoken Swede called Jay Carlsson who, Doyle explained, was working in Amsterdam. Next to him a blond Englishman with long, expensively chopped hair and a languid manner, Malcolm White.

Carrick gave each a business card.

Gone to their rooms already, Doyle said, were Vince Delahunty, the judge from South Africa, another woman, Bec Woods from Australia, and Eugene Choi from Beijing.

Just as the introductions was complete and Carrick was ready to say a few prepared words the door opened and one of the tightly packed little-black-dress girls he'd seen at the Palais shimmied in.

"*Bonsoir* monsieur, I am Melodie, from the Lions Committee's Judging Co-ordination Team. We met this morning I believe?"

"*Bonsoir*, Melodie."

He gave her a card too.

"Monsieur, I have only to ask you, please, do not keep my judges too long. Zay 'ave 'ad a long day and zere will be just as mush to do tomorrow," Melodie's sex-kitten accent made her consonants sensuous, they were laid out softly across her tongue in a way Carrick thought delicious, specially so after the truck-stop cognacs.

" ... but of course, we understand you 'ave to do your duty in ze, er, *enquête*, um, investigation, but take not a minute longer than needed, I beg you," she smiled and tilted her head, "I'll come back and check how zings are going in a short while. *Merci* for your cooperation, Monsieur Carrick."

Everyone watched her cross the room as she left, even Taylor

Simmons, the American judge. Her eye caught Carrick's and she smiled amiably.

As Melodie closed the door he said to Doyle, "I'd like to say a few words to everyone if that's all right?"

Doyle shrugged as if to indicate he had no authority in the room either way.

Rattle their gilded cages, Tony had instructed, *these are some of the most coddled people in the business, it's the only way to get their attention.* It seemed to Carrick the judges' demeanour was a caricature of self-importance, they had the assurance that success and wealth confer but an arrogance that spoiled it.

"Gentlemen ... Ms Simmons ... it's an intrusion that I'm here tonight, I know I'm interrupting you and I apologise, but one of your fellow judges was murdered horribly yesterday and I'm here to investigate it. I'm not a policeman, but I am a licensed insurance investigator here in France," he paused to give the lie more weight, "So your cooperation is not only appreciated but also required by law." He looked around the table slowly, "I have the authority to apply to a Magistrate to stop you leaving France if I feel there is evident cause to believe you could help the investigation further."

Carrick wasn't sure if 'evident cause' was a real legal term, but it didn't matter, he'd got the tone of voice right, he could see it in their faces. Tony Maine said there'd be nothing the judges would fear more than being stranded by some long investigation. They'd have tight schedules and important meetings planned since months ago, deadlines looming and clients calling.

"Of course," he continued in a friendlier tone, "I can't see anything like that eventuating in these circumstances. I'm sure I can rely on each of you for complete cooperation to expedite this."

Expedite? Carrick was better at sounding officious than he'd imagined.

"You saying you're gonna try to stop us leaving the goddamn country till the investigation is over?" bristled Schwarz, the New Yorker.

Several judges glanced at their cell phones instinctively.

"No. All I'm trying to say is ... as an investigator I have teeth as well as a smile."

Malcolm White flicked his long blond hair, pushed his plate away, leaned back in the chair, put brown cowboy boots on the table then made his fingers into a pyramid and tipped his head to one side. It looked a well-practiced piece of body language.

"So what do you want, mister investigator? Let's get shot of this so we can all get on. I'm sorry about Jonas and all that, but what can we do? We've already told the police what we know, which totals sweet F.A. far as I can see."

Carrick stepped forward and rested his knuckles on the table in an attempt at informality.

"At the moment, the police are working on the premise that Mr. Shackleton was murdered by his travelling companion. I'm exploring other avenues and that's where you guys might be able to help. For example, I'm looking at the possibility he was killed for business reasons?"

Carrick looked up and down the table.

Nothing.

"Such as...?" prompted Taylor Simmons.

Ray Doyle said, "You mean the girlie bar?"

"Girlie bar?" said Jiminez, the Spanish judge with the pony-tail, wondering if he'd heard right, interested for the first time.

"Jonas owned a bar in Bangkok," Francesco, the smooth-looking Brazilian explained, "I have even been there. Excuse me," he motioned to one of the staff, "I'd like to try the Puligny-Montrachet now."

"*Les Folatiéres*, monsieur? Broad and buttery, excellent," cooed the waiter.

Carrick would have preferred to get rid of the staff but figured he would have to rise above it; they were servants in a stately world, hearing nothing, reacting to their betters only when called for.

"I mean the advertising business," Carrick continued, "You're the top guys on the planet, I'm told, nothing much goes on in big business without you knowing, right?"

Several of them chuckled disconcertingly.

It was Jay Carlsson, the tall judge from Amsterdam, who spoke first, "You have an exaggerated view of us, Mr. Carrick. We creative directors are usually locked in our own bubble, head down and arse up, we don't see much of the real world."

"Which of his competitors would benefit from Jonas Shackleton being out of the way? Which agency? Maybe even one of yours...?"

They continued looking at Carrick quizzically.

Jiminez raised his hand, "Yes, I'll have a little Montrachet too."

Carrick wondered if he was being mocked.

"I thought you were going to ask if anyone in the business had a grudge against Jonas," said Schwarz.

"Grudge against Jonas?" laughed Malcolm White, "Any number of pregnant secretaries."

Some of the judges chortled.

"And plenty of junior creatives..." said Taylor Simmins seriously.

"Top me up with that St. Emilion, will you? Quite like one more gargle before we go. I like 'em meaty," Malcolm White held out his glass.

"*Chateau Angélus*, much intensity and concentration of flavour, monsieur," burbled a waiter.

"Junior creatives? How do you mean?"

"Ideas are the currency of our business, Andy," Ray Doyle responded patiently, "If someone steals your idea he's taking money out of your pocket, he's stealing food off your dinner table."

"Sure...?"

"I hope I'm not speaking out of turn or ill of the dead. Let's just say it's suggested on some occasions that Jonas, God love him, did sometimes overlook the names of junior creatives when preparing the credits for an award-winning ad."

"Overlook? Spit it out Ray, he was worse than that," exploded Taylor Simmons from the middle of the table, "He told Rita Tyson — you remember her, young Californian went to work for Jonas in Bangkok? — he told her he was taking her credit right to her face.

Rita wrote that wonderful Lynx spot, you know, with the naked girl and the anaconda?"

Several judges nodded.

"Nice spot," said Malcolm White.

"Nice spot," echoed Jiminez.

Must be no higher praise, thought Carrick.

"She showed him the basic idea on her layout pad and Shackleton said 'That's great. That's really great, let's do it,' and took it from her. He stopped at the door, Rita told me this herself: he stopped before leaving her office and actually said, 'You know, Rita, you don't get many big chances in advertising ...' and, like, she was expecting him to say, 'Well done!' or something, you know — 'You're gonna be a star'. Instead, he said, 'Rita, you don't get many big chances in advertising ... and I've just taken yours.' And the bastard did!

"She thought he was joking. But he sold the ad to the client next day, got it made, entered it in awards, and when it won her name wasn't on the credits. It destroyed her; she hates the business now."

Francesco Ferreira, the urbane Brazilian spoke from the other the end of the table, "There are always stories like that, I've heard them too, but it's hard to know about credits for an idea, is it not?" He ran manicured fingers through grey close-cropped hair, "Just because you were in the room when an idea comes up, should you get a credit for simply being there?"

"Rita *wrote* the damn thing," Taylor put her wine glass down decisively.

"I'm not disputing that case of your friend, she sounds very talented," Francesco threw Taylor a knowing smile, "Regardless, no-one murders someone for award credits. We don't want to confuse Mr. Carrick."

"If stealing credits was motive for murder, there'd be ten thousand suspects in town," murmured the New Yorker, Schwarz, to general amusement.

"Great title for a murder mystery," White chuckled, "*Ten Thousand Suspects.*"

Carrick persisted, "I'm curious about the big stuff. Big business.

Let's talk about agency rivals who would be advantaged with Jonas out of the way," he played his trump card, "For example, the competition for the Qi Energy Project in China? That's a pretty big deal, isn't it? A lot of money at stake?"

No immediate comment from anyone.

Carrick surveyed the room. Jiminez was looking at his watch. Others were reading the wine tasting notes. Their insouciance aggravated him.

"I'd like to try a different red," said the Argentinian, Lopez, addressing a waiter, "I'm used to wines with body."

"Qi?" said White dismissively, "Qi's China. That's a real lottery. Chinese clients aren't swayed by one *gweilo*, whoever he is. They don't care who's on the creative team, you could wheel in Jesus Christ and they'd ask what has He done lately? The Chinese will want to see an army of resources at their disposal, a red army," he laughed at his own humour, "It'll be down to numbers at the end of the day, whichever agency cuts the best deal on service fees etcetera, while providing the most bodies on the ground, that's what will win the pitch. One thing it won't be about is great ideas, you'll never see an ad for Qi winning at Cannes. It's just about money."

"Anyone here personally involved in the pitch?"

"All the Big Four networks are in the pitch," explained Ray Doyle like a patient host, "So we're all involved, in one sense, even if none of us personally do any work on it. The Big Four own most of this room between them, as parent companies they control most of the ad business globally."

This didn't go down well at the top of the table and once again the discussion veered off course.

"They don't control us, we at A.G.A.S. Brazil are a totally independent company. We barely see them," Francesco said curtly.

Doyle put his palms up in retreat, "Same with us at Maine Hyland & Blix — InterGroup rarely interfere. My point was about who *owns* us; just trying to explain it simply to Andy here. I meant financial control, not creative control."

"We are not owned by any of them," said Jay Carlsson, the tall waif from Amsterdam, a strong whiff of moral superiority in his voice, "My agency values its independence."

"That's why you only have domestic business," scoffed Taylor Simmins, "You'll stay a local boutique handling rats and mice accounts unless you get a network behind you."

Carlsson tremored slightly and looked away.

"Any of these big bad networks evil enough to kill to win the biggest advertising account in China? Twenty million Euros in profit every year I'm told."

"It wouldn't be anything like that," muttered Schwarz.

Carrick wasn't to be deterred, "Evil empires must be run by some pretty evil suits? What about the Account Service guys?"

"Most suits are evil in the sneaky, venal, obsequious, selling-out-your-idea-to-never-ending-client-changes kind of way. Not the killing people kind of way, Mr. Carrick," said Jiminez smiling, "Account Service guys only kill creativity."

"And the atmosphere at lunch," White drained the last of his wine.

They all laughed and some started standing up, preparing to leave.

"Sorry, Mr. Carrick, you might be barking up the wrong tree, I think," Francesco Ferreira gave him a glassy smile and a magisterial wave from the top of the table.

They'd lost interest and Carrick was losing control of the meeting. They saw him as just another suit.

"I don't think there's much we can help you with," said Doyle, half-apologetically.

He had to do something.

Carrick hardened his voice and thumped the table with his fist before anyone could take another step, the nearest wine glass jumped in the air, "I'd be thinking carefully about this if I were one of you. Because if there is someone with a lot to gain by having Jonas Shackleton killed — and doing it cleverly enough to make it look like the girl did it — then maybe there are other creative directors here in this room who are in imminent danger too."

He stared at each of them hard, one by one.

"You're all sitting ducks. It's very convenient to have the world's elite advertising people all in one place if you're going to kill a few of them."

"Why would anyone want to hurt us?" Taylor Simmons challenged, though her voice betrayed a nervousness.

He prowled around the room, "Rivalry? Extortion? Influencing a new business pitch? Maybe just payback for reducing the world to such a shallow and trivial place? Believe me, it wouldn't be hard to cull the odd lion, I could imagine it being the latest blood sport for some mad man. I don't know. I came here tonight to warn you. You need to help me if I'm to help you. We used to have a slogan in the army, *Be careful — the life you save may be your own.*"

That put the wind up the haughty bastards, one and all.

CHAPTER 4.

"I'm getting some funny looks this morning."

Ray Doyle's voice over the phone just before 8am.

Could be the Mickey Mouse plimsolls you wear, thought Carrick. Instead he said, "How so Ray?"

"From the other judges. Over breakfast. You came on a bit strong last night in the Elba room, you know."

"D'you think? It is a murder we're talking about here."

"Yes. Anyway, look, when you asked who'd benefit, you know, who'd benefit from Jonas being, well, out of the way? I'm worried. I'm sure some of the other judges think that I'll benefit."

"Will you?"

"I won't because I won't take the job. But they don't know that."

"What job?"

"With Jonas, er, no longer in the frame, another creative director will have to run the pitch for the Qi Project in China and no-one else in the InterGroup-Publicity group is up to it frankly. The network's full of hacks. I'm the most senior creative director at Maine Hyland & Blix and we're their best agency, the network board will want to conscript me. Plus, I'm used to working with Tony Maine, as far as one can be. *Ergo*, me."

Carrick wondered if the network rated Ray as highly as he rated himself?

Poor old Ray, Tony called him.

"You don't want the job?"

"Of course not, who wants to work in bloody Asia? They'll throw money at me, of course, Tony will turn on the charm, but ads for Qi will never be any good, you heard Malcolm White tell you that last night. Maybe I'm being paranoid but if any of the judges say anything, even wonder out loud, the gutter press will pick it up, guaranteed. I've got my image to protect."

"Why not tell the gutter press you're not interested?"

"Can't deny it. Everyone will definitely think it's true then."

"So you're not worried that they might think you're behind a brutal murder, you're worried they think you'll take a job in China?"

"No, no, both, of course, I mean ..."

"If you got that job, or whoever gets it, would it mean a significant cut of the profits? I don't mean just a raise?"

"God no. You're just another employee. It's the network that rakes in the serious dosh. The shareholders get the benefit ultimately."

"Who are they?"

"Big institutional investors, super funds, merchant banks, the usual corporate nightmare. Anyway, maybe you could put the word around that you're not looking at me," he paused, "I mean, you're not, are you?"

"I'm looking at everyone, but you're not high on the list of suspects."

"Well, that's something I suppose."

"I appreciate you telling me your situation. Best to hear it from you."

"Look, Andy, I'm not trying to tell you how to do your job, but I do think the Bangkok connection feels a more fertile area, know what I mean? The girl is from Bangkok, after all."

In Carrick's experience any sentence that starts, *I'm not trying to tell you how to do your job* usually ends up contradicting itself.

"I can't jet off to Bangkok, Ray, not without anything to go on but your feeling."

"People have spent far more than that on my gut feelings, you know, it's what I do. It's called creative instinct. Anyway, you don't have to go anywhere, you can talk to people here in Cannes who know more about Jonas's seedy club.

"Look, I've got to hurry to the judging now but I'll give you two names. Nick Bailey and Liang Weh — a couple of young guns, a freelance creative team who work around Asia a lot. They knew Jonas better than most of us on the jury. They're delegates here right now, I'll get contact numbers texted to you, I'll get Melodie on the job. Will you speak to them?"

Doyle's suggestion of dark dealings to do with the Bangkok girlie bar was a possible scenario, no doubt there were some seriously bad people involved in that business, but the question was, why kill Shackleton here in France? It felt more like an opportunistic crime.

Truth was that Carrick had hoped his speech to the judges the previous night would have a bigger effect than just Ray Doyle worrying about his image. He'd left the Elba room feeling his performance hit home, the judges were tired and suggestible and he'd appealed to their self-interest. Like a good advertisement.

Afterwards he'd been mulling things over in the Carlton's downstairs bar, decompressing since immersing himself in Cannes' craziness, hooking up with Benny, encountering the police inspector, bullying the award jury. The place was pumping with party-focused young delegates looking cool and aloof — the slouching merchants of popular culture — when out of the corner of his eye he'd noticed Melodie, the judges' sashay-girl, picking her way through the crush from the direction of the elevators. No tablet or cell phone in hand. Off-duty.

"How was the first day's judging?" he called, getting to his feet, dropping some cash on the table and slipping into step beside her as she cut a swathe through the lobby.

"Oh, Mr. Ca*rr*ick," he loved the way she rolled her 'r's, "You're still 'ere? *Oui, ze* first day was good, *merci.* But also quite long."

Chapter 4.

She smiled apologetically, kept walking.

"Call me Andy. Look, Melodie, if you're finished for tonight, maybe I can buy you a quick drink? To thank you for letting me speak with the judges?"

"Mr. Doyle was very insistent I allow it. We could not refuse in ze circumstances, Mr. Shackleton being a judge and so forth. *Merci* for not taking too much time, zay're tired puppies."

Puppies? More like rottweilers.

"Don't worry, I wished them sweet dreams when I finished. A drink?"

"*Non*, I'm sorry, I've got to get my car..."

"I wanted to ask you about Jonas Shackleton in a less formal way than an official interview. But I can book a time during work hours tomorrow, if you prefer?"

"During work?" She looked at her watch. Bit her lip. "I really aven't mush time." She suddenly made up her mind, "Not here, too many delegates. My car is parked in ze Palais car park. We can go to the roof bar at White Palms, it is quieter, and I can walk to my car from zere."

It was a short cab ride along the beachfront, they didn't speak, watching the festival people promenading through the warm night was a full-time job, even Melodie was transfixed with the parade of oddity.

At the Hotel White Palms the lift doors opened and the nighttime view from the sixth storey rooftop was intoxicating; the dancing reflections of the party lights from the anchored fleet of super yachts on the bay, an otherworldly yellow glow from the winding cobbled lanes of the old town, Le Suquet. The stars in Cannes, they say, are not in the heavens but here on earth.

Melodie ordered a glass of champagne, Carrick had another brandy. Up close she was quite lovely. Lit by a single candle on the table, he watched her sip, soft light moulding the curve of cheekbone down to a pointed chin and long neck, he felt like the only person in the theatre watching a beautiful movie. A strange and forlorn feeling.

"Do you live in Cannes?"

"Is zat an official question or an after-hours question?"

"It's an ice breaker."

"I live in Cagnes-sur-Mer. I study in Nice, normally, when I'm not working with ze festivals I mean."

"What do you study?"

"Languages. Japanese and Chinese."

Carrick smiled, wondered if her accent overwhelmed her Mandarin as much as it did her English. She could make Mao Tse Tung sound sexy.

"Pornthip studies Languages too," he said.

"Who?"

"Jonas Shackleton's companion."

"Oh, Thip? Yes, Languages. I know, we talked about it. What did you call her?"

"Pornthip. Her full name. When did you meet her?"

"I picked zem up at ze airport when Mr. Shackleton arrived last week. 'E was the first of ze judges to arrive." She traced a finger along the champagne flute, "Pornthip is a funny name, no?"

"Not in Thailand. They'd probably think Melodie was a funny name, though personally, I think it's lovely."

She pouted.

"It's a stupid. Mel-o-die. My parents meant it to sound cool but it sounds like *mal*, you know, that means bad or evil in French. My brother called me *Mal-Aimer*," she laughed, "and *mal aéré...*"

"Evil? I don't believe it. What's *mal aéré*?"

"Erm, 'stuffy'."

"A little brother I bet? You bullied him and he taunted you?"

"It's true. Am I such a cliché?"

She laughed, wonderfully. Soft freckles were just visible on her cheek and the top of her nose. The down on her arms shone pale in the candlelight.

"No, you're the realest thing I've seen in Cannes."

"You don't like it here?"

"Not this week. They're all liars for hire, aren't they?"

She thought for a moment.

"To know Cannes is to see its ironies. During zis year's film festival I worked at a conference in ze Grand Hotel du Cap, you know it?"

"The grandest in the Riviera."

"*Oui.* During the Cannes Film Festival it is ze favourite of ze very richest Jews in ze film industry — ze most successful from all Hollywood. One of zem told me why it is zeir favourite hotel."

"Why?"

"Not because it is so grand and beautiful, *non*, but because it is where ze Nazis 'ad zeir headquarters for southern France during ze occupation. Strange and ironic, *non*?"

"What do you think of the advertising people?"

"I zink they are creative. Insecure. Egotistical."

"Do you think they tell the truth?"

She wrinkled her nose, "Erm, advertising people I zink, maybe zay believe what zay say when zay say it?"

"Really?"

"Everyone lies to zemselves a little bit, *non*?"

Yes, he thought, I certainly have.

"It's the big lies that make the money though, isn't it, lying *en masse*."

"You know what my boss says?"

"What?"

"Advertising is a useful industry, it keeps a lot of unemployable misfits off ze street."

"Except the streets of Cannes."

They smiled together, sipped their drinks in sync.

"What else did you and Thip talk about when you picked Shackleton up at the airport?"

"Mostly Mr. Shackleton talked. Thip and I chatted only when 'e got a persistent journalist badgering 'im. She was very excited; first time in France, a big adventure, she said. *Charmant*. It is hard to believe such a tragedy, what do you zink 'appened?"

"What do you think?"

"People say she killed him. I cannot believe it."

Chapter 4.

"Were you there, at the judges' lunch, on the day?"

"Me? *Non! Dieu merci.* We were at the Palais, all ze 'elpers, ze 'ole team, setting up final arrangements for judging. It's very big to coordinate, you know, over six zousand TV commercials alone zis year. All judged in five days. Ouf! I don't know 'ow our judges maintain concentration so long. Zay are *grandissime*, quite marvellous."

"They certainly seem to think so."

"Oh, zay are very busy, working very hard for sure. Zay 'ave to fast-forward through so many or we'd never finish."

"Fast forward?"

"Ze ones zay don't like I mean."

"Really? What does it cost for people to enter their work in the awards?"

"Between 500 and 1,400 euros per entry, depending on ze category. Why?"

"And the judges fast-forward through them? How do they know they don't like them before they've seen them?"

"Oh, zay make up zeir minds very quickly."

"How much money do the Cannes Lions make?"

"Last year about 40 million euro."

Carrick made up his mind to start an awards festival one day, especially if you don't have to actually watch the entries.

"You'll never go broke providing awards to advertising people, vodka to Russians or guns to Americans, zats another saying by my boss," laughed Melodie, enjoying the effect the figures were having on Carrick.

He drained his drink and ordered another round. Expenses are a marvellous invention.

"Had you met Jonas before, other times he'd been to Cannes?"

"*Non*, I recognised 'im from 'is picture. 'Av you seen 'im? Easy to remember."

"What was he like as a person?"

"Oh, you know 'ow zay say, Talent does what it can, genius does what it pleases."

"Jonas was a genius?"

"Zay are very clever people ze judges."

She was probably trained to think that way by the Cannes committee, he thought. All part of the orientation. How to sashay across the floor in a tight black dress and don't forget that advertising creative directors are geniuses.

"So you drove Jonas and Thip to La Colombe d'Or?"

"*Non*, ze Carlton. Zat is the official hotel for judges every year. 'E must 'ave booked La Colombe d'Or privately, *a mon insu*, I did not even know about it until, er, ze incident. No one knew. 'Is parcels and messages from 'is agency were all waiting at ze Carlton."

"Parcels?

"Yes, *colis en souffrance*, parcels waiting? I saw Reception give zem to 'im at check-in. I zink 'e was going to stay at ze Carlton during all judging days zis week, ze sessions often go quite late."

"What was in the parcels that were waiting for him?"

"I don't know. *Dieu seul le sait.* 'E 'ad zem sent to his room."

"I hear there's a lot of politics involved in the judging?"

"Zay argue a lot. Is zat the same as politics? It's really up to ze Chairman to keep control, we don't interfere. Not zat I could, I 'ave no status. But even Rémy can't interfere. Judging is sacrosanct."

"Rémy?"

"Rémy Barré, my boss.

"Of course. How's he taking the fact that one of his judges is dead?"

She lowered her eyes, "Everyone is so shocked. 'E is very worried about bad *publicité*. Who'd expect such a 'orrid zing here? *Méchant.* 'Orrid, that's right, isn't it?"

"Yes, horrid is right."

"Do you really zink she did it?"

"I don't know. But perhaps advertising might be a more competitive business than people believe."

"What do you mean?"

"I think there's the possibility someone made it look like she did it."

"*Vraiment*? But she ran away, *n'est-ce pas*?"

"Maybe."

Melodie looked out across the old port, her profile sharp against the diffused lights. A warm salty breeze wafted across the rooftop. Carrick took some more brandy.

"A Cannes award means a lot, doesn't it? Brings a lot of kudos? So whichever of the networks wins the most Gold Lions must get more than just bragging rights?"

"What is 'bragging rights'?"

"Boasting in the corporate schoolyard. What I'm wondering about is the financial benefits that flow from doing well in Cannes? It can be significant, I imagine? For both individuals and companies?"

"I suppose so, but I don't really know if ze clients zemselves care about awards."

She was right, advertisers would care for results in the market-place more than on the award stage.

Carrick kept digging for a financial motive, "Who would gain from Shackleton's death? Anyone on the jury?"

Her hand rushed to her mouth, "Ze jury? *Non!* You zink one of ze jury is a murderer?"

"I'm just trying to understand the dynamics at play, that's why I asked about politics in the judging, I noticed at dinner tonight the Latin countries all sat together, for example? The British were at the far end of the table. Jay from Amsterdam in the middle. The Americans and the British split up. Tell me, do they tend to vote in blocks? Asia versus Anglos? Or Latins versus Poms? You know, collusion?"

She looked offended at the word, "Zay wouldn't do zat. Besides, judging is secret, with a button, no talking: red is 'out', green is 'in'. Ze Chairman of Judges should be on guard for your 'collusion'."

"Who's the Chairman of Judges this year?"

"Francesco Ferreira."

Made sense. Ferreira seemed the most poised of the jury members. Carrick thought back to his calm when things became heated with Taylor Simmons and her story of Shackleton stealing a young woman's credits.

"Why didn't Rémy Barré replace Shackleton? There're ten thousand delegates here, someone must be able to step in?"

"It was felt to be disrespectful to Mr. Shackleton, just shoving in someone else to replace 'im."

"The graveyard is full of irreplaceable men," Carrick said. The Major on his mind.

"Pardon?"

"Doesn't matter, just a saying we used to have. Go on."

"Nothing like zis ever 'appened before at ze festival, no-one knew ze correct protocol."

Carrick was silent a while, thinking hard.

"Can you remember anything about the parcels that were waiting when you dropped him and Thip at the Carlton? Where they were from? Or who sent them? Anything?"

"No, 'e didn't open zem in Reception, like I told you, 'ardly even looked. I remember one was a folio. The kind used for carrying around print ads artwork and illustrations. Ze desk sent everyzing to 'is room, 'e just wanted check-in formalities done so 'e could have a cigar, 'e said."

"What then?"

"'E sent me away. I went back to Nice to pick up another judge from ze next flight. I went back and forwards many times over."

"Who was the next judge to arrive?"

"Francesco."

She looked so serious behind her young girl's face. Maybe she was simply tired. Carrick shifted gear, put work aside, no golden clue was going to manifest itself tonight.

"Ever tempted to leave the judges to look after themselves and get on a plane yourself?"

She laughed, "You are a psychic. Yes. I zink about zat all ze time, on every trip to Nice airport."

"Where would you go if you could? If you ran away from it all?"

She smiled again and looked up to the sky, "Oh, I've always wanted to see Afrique. Or ze Amazon. Somewhere deep and dark and wild. Indonésie." Her eyes widened at the thought. "'Av you travelled a great deal? Where would you go if you dropped out of your world?"

"I've already dropped out of my world."

"Oh no. Surely your fantasy is a better place than this?"

"Not when I'm opposite such a beautiful girl."

She laughed, "*Flirteur.*"

"What could be better? On the Mediterranean, rooftop view, glass of something nice in my hand, vision of loveliness sitting close."

"Hardly," she demurred, "Now you are being smooth."

"Well, here is a definitely a fantasy where I come from, let me tell you."

"Where's that?"

Where did he come from? An alcoholic mother? A poxy orphanage? The dead end of the world? When they first met, Robyn commented that he never talked about his past. *I spent my first fifteen years wishing I'd never been born*, he said, *I've killed the past and I'm dancing on its grave.*

"The military," he answered.

Her features became troubled, "A soldier? Did you go to Iraq? Afghanistan?"

"Both." And Croatia and Northern Ireland. But he wasn't giving her a CV.

"What was it like?"

"Heat. Cordite. Moondust." Ragged zombies in the streets, hollow-eyed children made deaf by the bomb blasts, veiled widows picking amongst the rubble.

Laughter peeled up from the streets and ebbed away again. Melodie's eyes were downcast, "I can't imagine it, I can't understand killing, it seems barbaric."

"It is."

"Oh, pardon! *Je suis vraiment désolé,* I am so rude, I did not mean it zat way about you, in the army," she was flushing, "... it's because we've been talking about Jonas, ze army is different I suppose, oh, I don't know what to say," her hand darted across the table to his, "I'm sorry."

"No offence taken, you're right. I agree with you. Killing is animal behaviour."

She looked at him for a drawn-out moment.

"Did you have to kill anybody in your army job?"

"I'm afraid so."

The candle flame twisted in the breeze, "But you are not a killer like who killed Jonas, you 'ad a duty ... for your country... a cause ..." she trailed off.

The court's out on that one, he thought, but said nothing.

"I have put my foot in my mouth and can't get it out."

Even woebegone she was beautiful.

"Your mouth looks fine to me. Let's talk about you instead and see if your foot reappears."

She smiled.

They talked about her favourite music, her part time modelling which she hated but it helped pay for her studies, her interest in the brocante markets in Aix.

Carrick told her about Camden Passage and Spitalfields.

"You like bric-á-brac?" she asked suddenly.

"Why not?"

"It doesn't seem manly enough for you. Why do you like?"

"Why? I don't know. A bit of people's lives stick to old things, I suppose. How they thought or felt. There's a subliminal language of things, isn't there? Everyday items handled by someone years ago, it still holds their love or laughter or sadness. Maybe it's a way to touch people you can never know but can glimpse through this ... this husk, this piece of junk."

He was embarrassed trying to explain a notion he'd never consciously thought about, "I guess it's a type of small connection."

"You are sensitive," she made it sound endearing, "It is nice in a man."

He thought it made him sound dismal.

Another twenty minutes passed quickly before she could no longer stifle a yawn, "Oh, I am sorry. *Excusez-moi!* I didn't mean to, champagne makes me sleepy. It is late."

She rubbed her bare arms and blinked a couple of times.

"I don't want to keep you out of bed."

"I should go before I say anyzing silly again. *Merci* for my drink, Andy. If you're still 'ere when this fuss is all over," she waved her hand to indicate everything below, the crowded harbour, the bright town, the stretching coast of tiny lights, the Lion awards, "maybe you will buy me another?"

She smiled shyly and they locked eyes momentarily, "*Bon nuit.*"

She leant across to kiss him on both cheeks, he moved his head and kissed her lightly on the lips. She didn't pull back.

"Are you trying new tactics to interrogate me?" she said, breathing close to his mouth.

"Whatever it takes."

"You don't seem mush like an insurance man," she stroked the pale scar on the side of his face with the edge of one finger.

"I'm not a very good one."

"I zink you are kind, but also raffish, you 'ave ... *un air canaille* is 'ow we say it," she leant back in the chair, considering him, "Zere's a mischief about you, somezing dangerous. In school you would have been doing some naughty zing when you were meant to be doing work. It would have led to the science lab being blown up."

He laughed, "You're closer than you think."

The fire in the school hall.

"Right now, I zink you should walk me to my car and no more mischief. I 'ave mush to do tomorrow."

On the way back to his hotel in Juan-les-Pins Carrick dared to think that perhaps he might enjoy being back in the land of the living. Tony Maine had opened a new chapter for him.

Maybe the story would even have a little romance.

After Ray Doyle's phone call first thing Sunday, Carrick sweated out the previous day's alcohol on the pavements; there'd been better endurance runners than him in the regiment but not many.

His exercise regime had been shamefully disregarded in recent times so it felt good pushing around the Juan-les-Pins beachfront in the morning air in a trance-like state. Through the pines and plane trees. The scent of mimosa and the sea, hot croissants in waterside cafés. Sprinting passed posters for the jazz festival, the antiques fair, the mariners' festival, conferences, summits, synods. More conventions than NATO around here.

Back at the hotel an hour later there was a text from Melodie. No personal message, just two phone numbers as Ray Doyle had promised, for Nick Bailey and Liang Weh, the creative hotshots from Bangkok who were friends of Shackleton.

He showered, breakfasted on his balcony and tried Bailey's number.

The phone clicked through to voicemail, a working-class London accent, off-hand and sarky: "You've rung Nick who is in Cannes getting pissed. If you're a suit, hang up. If you're a girl I met last night, leave your name, number and a brief description so I can remember. If you're my boss, I'm working on that thing right now."

Carrick tried the second number, Liang Weh. It answered almost immediately, a softly spoken Singaporean accent with a touch of American school. Carrick told Weh he was investigating Shackleton's death for Lloyd's and wanted to ask a few questions.

"You think you can find Thip?" he asked.

"You know her?" Carrick hadn't expected that, "When can we meet?"

"Dunno. Today we're going to lunch, then to the Palais for the *Legends Debate*."

Carrick remembered that Tony's speech with Branson was Sunday's major show, slotted sometime early afternoon.

"Who's we?"

"Me and my copywriter, Nick Bailey."

"Great. How about I meet you at lunch? Where are you going?"

"Hadn't really thought, somewhere near the Palais."

"I know somewhere."

Make a place your own, the Major used to say.

He meant make a base where you can operate with the comfort and security of one's London club. For the Major it was the Imperial Hotel in Prague, Brasserie de l'Isle St Louis in Paris, the New York Athletics Club, Hotel Maria Theresia near St Stephen's in Vienna, the Sala degli Uomini Illustri in Venice ... he had somewhere everywhere. Carrick had watched their eyes come alive when the Major arrived, they'd do anything for him, run special errands, dig up inside information, keep his confidences and movements private. They indulged him at all hours with endless pots of tea and a small jug of water with his favourite malt whisky. His personal authority had nothing to do with his old military rank, the Major knew the first names of regular staff everywhere he went, knew about their families and pastimes, their passions and prejudices, their politics and peccadilloes, he made them trusted friends and allies.

Carrick didn't have a London club or the people skills, but he understood the principle.

"What about the rooftop bar at the Hotel White Palms? My buy."

"A rooftop bar? Awesome," said Liang.

"You'll like it."

"You said you're paying, right?"

"Yep."

"We'll like it."

Carrick hoped the young creatives would find it impressive, but what seemed a smart idea at the time was less so when he got out of the capsule-shaped elevator at the White Palms; he should've thought ahead to book, the place was packed.

It didn't help that half the dining area was being used for a photographic shoot being set up poolside. Arc lights, a big square-format camera on its tripod, a smaller digital one beside it, a clutch of assistants moving reflectors around the edge of the pool. It looked quite a production and it didn't look like it was going anywhere in a hurry.

Carrick thought he recognised a tall woman dressed like she was going on a cross-country hike, sturdy boots, khaki pants and checked shirt, she prowled the area like a big cat, getting things moved a few inches this way or that. Surely it was Annie Leibovitz? No wonder the assistants were running around so intensely.

She turned suddenly and brushed past him, picked up a large duffle bag sitting on top of the nearest table and took it to the edge of the pool.

"Excuse me," he called after her, "You still need this table?"

"All yours, honey," she drawled over her shoulder.

He liked this place. It had good karma, made him feel lucky.

In fact, since Tony Maine called on Friday night his life seemed to have acquired a new battery pack. The fifteen thousand winging its way to his bank account was giving positive energy too, it didn't even seem such an embarrassing amount now that he had a table and a ringside view of a famous celebrity photographer at work.

The waiter brought him a drink soon after.

A couple of guys stepped out of the elevator and into the sunshine, one a tall Asian wearing John Lennon glasses. That was how Liang Weh described himself so Carrick waved.

"Andy?"

"Liang? Hi. Appreciate you coming."

"This is my copywriter, Nick Bailey."

"How did you swing a table like this?"

Bailey was attitude on legs; sunglasses, unwashed hair, three-day growth, bad posture, baggy adolescent clothes on a man of thirty. He shook hands sloppily, no attempt at a grip, sat down with a proprietary air and spread himself out.

But he was observant, "Li, look there, Annie Leibovitz."

"Cool. Awesome camera."

"Li said you were an investigator? I gotta get a drink. Want something, Li?" Bailey looked around for the waiter, clicked his fingers, "*Garçon*. You a private eye or a proper copper? If there is such a thing. Hate coppers, but you look OK. Nice tatts. Where'd you get them?"

There was no pause, Carrick wondered if it was ADHD or coke.

"I'm an insurance investigator," he gave them each a business card and rolled down his sleeves a little.

"Bit late to sell Jonas insurance," Bailey laughed at his own joke.

The waiter took their drinks order.

"I'm investigating various possibilities about who might have killed him. I'm told you might know about a bar he owned in Bangkok."

"*Inn the Pink*? Brilliant place. Saucy wenches for all my friends ..." Bailey boomed the last sentence and gestured theatrically to an imagined audience. The table behind turned to look, Liang giggled, obviously accustomed to Bailey performing large.

"Remember the first time he took us there, Li?"

"Yeah. It was cool."

"It was fantastic, that's what it was. You won't believe this, Andy, we were sitting on these high bar stools at one of those tall, round tables, you know the sort. It was me, Li, Jonas and... who else was there?"

"Francesco Ferreira," said Liang.

"'Course. Francesco, yeah, that's right," Nick sniffed unselfconsciously and continued apace, "I was so out of it that day," he nudged Carrick's elbow conspiratorially, "Listen to this, we're just drinking away, the four of us like, you know, having a laugh. Then this totally fit Asian bird in a tight satin dress comes to the table, doesn't say a word, kneels on the floor and unzips Jonas's pants. Jonas continues chatting away as if nothing has happened, right? Chat, chat, while she's going gobble, gobble.

"We all look at each other. We're all thinking, what the...? Well, guess he's the boss of the joint, you know. When he's in town he gets good service, right?"

Liang giggled, "It was funny. We thought that. No-one says anything at the time, we are all too cool."

"Then another girl comes over, gets under the table and unzips Francesco's fly and begins to go to work on him. Then a girl comes for me and another one for Li. And they're doing us all at the same time. Four of them."

"Wow," said Liang, "It was so awesome."

The table behind turned around and glared again.

"All the while Jonas is just chatting and Francesco's like, sipping his drink, 'cos that's the game, you see? You're not allowed to show any feeling, any enjoyment, any reaction at all, you just gotta carry on as normal. The deal is, first to come buys the table a bottle of Krug, second one to come buys a cognac, third one to come only has to buy the snacks, last to come pays for nothing. Better than winning a Gold Lion, I tell ya, ha-ha-ha."

"It was cool," said Liang.

"Same lunch, remember Li, when Jonas had the idea of doing an illustrated pop-up book of sex games?"

"Would have been amazing. It was Jamie Tan going to do the illustrations."

"Yeah. Jonas was getting LaChapelle to shoot it, that's right. Wonder what happened?"

"Too expensive probably," said Liang.

"Too late now," said Bailey, "Unless Jonas makes a big comeback."

"Did you ever hear talk he was going to open some bars in China?" Carrick tried out Ray Doyle's theory.

"In China? Never gonna happen. Place like that wouldn't be the same in the PRC, would it? No fun."

"He liked fun. A fun guy," lamented Liang.

"Was Jonas sole owner, any silent partners? Other stakeholders?"

"Dunno. His name was above the door as Proprietor, he was proud of that, but he had local management. Some people have a set of golf clubs wherever they work, Jonas had a nudie bar."

"Jonas told me it was a birthday present he gave himself."

Bailey chipped in, "The gift that keeps giving, ha-ha-ha."

"Probably costs a lot of money to run a girlie bar," mused Liang, "Fees, security, light-show..."

"And Jamie Tan," interrupted Bailey, "He wouldn't be cheap."

"Who's he?" said Carrick for want of a better line of questioning. Let these two flow.

"Jamie Tanyapongpruch, everyone just calls him Jamie Tan. He was the hottest wrist in Bangkok for a while," said Bailey.

"Wrist?" Carrick's mind boggled after the last story.

"Yeah, illustrator."

"Could draw anything, so many styles," Liang was changing his Lennon glasses for identical Lennon sunglasses, "He was an art director for Jonas, always by Jonas' side." He turned to Bailey, "Remember that Hewlett campaign Jamie did? Shame he's gone."

"Gone?"

"Gone from advertising. Jamie went to work for Jonas at Four Floors," Bailey turned his head and belched towards the ocean view.

"Where?"

"*Four Floors of Whores*," explained Liang. "That's our nickname for *Inn the Pink*, it's a joke," he sipped his lemon squash. Bailey's bourbon and coke was long gone.

"Jamie went to work there more than a year ago now."

"What does an illustrator do at a girlie bar? Interior decoration or something?"

"Wouldn't that be great? Ha-ha. Nah, Jamie only does exterior decoration," said Bailey, still laughing, "'Interior decoration', I love it." He stood up and made for the bar, "I'll get us another round."

"Jamie illustrates the girls," explained Liang. "Very beautiful. He paints their entire bodies."

"Like Goldfinger?"

"Yeah. But not one colour. Pictures, intricate paintings. Real art, every style. Impressionist, Cubist, Expressionist, Classicist. Every girl he does different. And different every night too. They look amazing. People come back to see what he does next. *Four Floors* has dancing on the first floor. Usual stuff, you know, for the tourists mainly, topless girls dancing on stages, hanging onto the poles. Second floor, more expensive, strips and naked girl shows, that's where they come out painted. People pay a lot to see the show, very erotic."

"Always start with a well-prepared surface ..." said Carrick.

"Ha-ha. That's funny too," said Liang. "Jamie's a lucky guy. Not as much money as in advertising, of course. I'd do it for free. He says everyone tells him it's the best job in the world."

"More intellectual stimulation than creating ads, I suppose."

From the corner of his eye Carrick watched Bailey veer away from the bar and slip into the gents instead, one hand reaching into his pocket for a little plastic packet.

"Not really. Ads are much harder than you think," said Liang, taking him seriously, "He could have been great, Jamie. Cannes Gold even, one day. But it's too much for him, maybe. He spent most nights partying then couldn't work so well next morning. Too much chasing the dragon."

"You call it *Four Floors*. What's on the third and fourth floors?"

"Third floor for lots of fun, private booths. Fourth is offices, you know, business, admin," he dismissed it with a downturned mouth, "The office girls all wear clothes."

"Is this guy Jamie, this friend of Shackleton's, is he in Cannes?"

"No way. Bangkok. Don't think he leaves his room unless he's at *Four Floors*. He's always painting."

Bailey came back and sat down extravagantly. Carrick liked Liang, an easygoing fellow, but Bailey was a slob, a soccer lout with an advertising-sized ego.

"You mentioned on the phone that you knew Thip?" Carrick said to Liang.

"Only met her the once. With Jonas about two weeks ago at an art gallery opening in Hong Kong."

"That was Gallery 88 Republic wasn't it?" Bailey trying to pries himself back into the conversation, "I got an invite but couldn't be bovvered. Was it alright? Did you see that dozy creative director from YS&J there?"

Liang opened his mouth to answer.

"I'll ask the questions," Carrick growled, now that they were on a useful path he wanted to stay on it, "The last time I looked I was the one with 'investigator' on his business card."

"OK, OK," Bailey held up both palms and grinned, "Long as you're paying the bills I'm your whore."

The waiter arrived with another round of drinks, handed the menus around like a croupier.

"Did Thip work at Shackleton's bar?"

Liang shook his head, "No way, not that kind of girl I think. She's nice. We liked a lot of the same music. Jonas was being very serious talking to the gallery owner about a painting or something. Left her on her own most of the evening. So we talked."

"On the phone this morning you asked whether I thought I could find her, where do you think she is, what do you think happened?"

"Don't know. I thought she must have run away," said Liang, "Scared when Jonas was killed."

Carrick's soul searching had led him to the same worry.

If she wasn't a killer she might be a witness. A potential victim? It wasn't just Tony Maine's Qi pitch at stake, he was becoming anxious about a middle-class girl mixed up with a man three times her age who seemed to treat the world and its women as personal entertainment.

"You don't think she killed him?"

"She not like that sort of girl," Liang spoke feelingly, "Just nice."

"Where would she run to here? Did she know anyone else in Cannes?"

Liang shrugged

"Hey, Li, look," said Bailey suddenly, "It's the Rockett Man."

He was pointing at a short man in mirror sunglasses wearing a costume better suited to a magician; Carrick had seen him arrive a few minutes earlier but pegged him as another Cannes whacko. He was talking to Annie Leibovitz on the other side of the pool. She towered over him comically despite his knee high boots.

"Who?"

"Stevie J. Rockett. Only my favourite commercials director in the world," said Bailey like a smitten girl.

"Irish guy. Friend of Bono. Does great work. Great reel," said Liang.

"Won the Grand Prix here last year with a commercial he directed for Heineken," Bailey couldn't take his eyes off him, "And Gold at the New York One Show."

"Yeah. Nice spot," said Liang.

"He's making a movie next year apparently, big Hollywood budget with Johnny Depp. Still doing loads of commercials, though, Jonas wanted him for his Hong Kong Bank spot, remember Li? His quote was quarter of a million over everybody else, ha-ha."

"Anyway, back to business, have either..."

"Wonder if we can meet him?" Bailey ignored Carrick, still staring at the short magician.

"Is he always like this?" Carrick said to Liang.

"No. Usually he's pissed."

"There's a dirty girl," bellowed Nick Bailey across the hotel rooftop to the dismay of nearby tables, "Sammi!" he jumped up, "Come and sit on me, I mean sit with me."

They were halfway through lunch, but with the distractions of the Leibovitz shoot, Bailey's coked-out concentration span and the street life of Cannes at their feet, Carrick hadn't put together much that was meaningful. He'd just asked what they knew about the pitch for the Chinese Qi Project, both shrugged and simply quoted what they'd read in the trade press.

Now yet another diversion, Bailey had spotted a woman he knew emerging into the rooftop's lunchtime glare looking for a table. Late twenties, tall, burgundy hair down to her shoulders, bright lipstick (the mark of advertising girls everywhere, Carrick thought), black sleeveless leather vest and tight leather pants suggesting she'd left her motorcycle running outside for a quick getaway.

As Bailey brought her over she scanned the rooftop for an alternate table or perhaps someone else she knew, but there was no one to rescue her.

"Andy Carrick, this is Sammi Walton. You know Liang."

She stretched over the table and kissed Liang, "Hi gorgeous, how are ya? Hey, Andy, nice to meet you," a peculiar mixture of American and British accents.

The waiter came with yet another bourbon for Bailey. Sammi ordered a vodka and soda. He didn't really want one, but Carrick got another beer because this was the place he was making his own.

Bailey explained, "Sammi works in New York for, who is it again? Empire Productions...?" a tease in his voice.

"You know damn well I left those mental midgets months ago," she turned to Carrick, "I work for Backroom Boys Productions out of New York. Don't mind his little games, he's jealous 'cos he's never got the budgets to work with a decent production company."

"Now, now, Sammi, be nice. What did I tell you last time about sucking up to creative people? Pucker up, that's your job," Bailey pulled a cute face.

"Suck on this," Sammi gave him the finger. She turned to Liang Weh, "How are you, darling? How are you liking Cannes this time? Does it feel a little flat this year?"

"Maybe. Because of Jonas. Andy is investigating who did it."

She flicked hair from her eyes and looked at him appraisingly, "You a cop?"

She had an intelligent face, not a classic beauty but plenty of moxie.

"Insurance investigator," he gave her a business card, her eyes glazed slightly.

"Oh right, I think someone told me about you."

Carrick was pleased. Tony Maine told him to make some noise so it probably wasn't a bad thing becoming gossip in this small town.

"Getting anywhere?"

"Early days. Did you know Jonas?"

"Did she know Jonas?" Bailey guffawed.

"I worked as a producer in the same agency as him for a while in Bangkok, before I moved to New York."

"Did you see him here in Cannes?"

"I only got here this morning. We, er," she hesitated fractionally, "we're having a client party on a yacht we've hired for a couple of days. Picked it up in Nice and sailed it round this morning. I've been running all over town organising last-minute things."

"Party on a yacht? Which one?" Bailey asked, looking across the bay at the anchored flotilla.

"Aphrodite," she said as if she didn't really want him to know.

"Is it big? Can we come? When is it?"

"Uh-uh, no way, Nick. It's for VIPs, the chosen ones." Then after a beat, "Unless you can grow a man-size budget."

Bailey snapped his head sideways as if she'd slapped his face. Liang laughed.

At poolside, the photographic shoot was over, lackeys were packing up. Annie Leibovitz was kissing the strangely dressed little man goodbye.

"Is that Stevie J. Rockett? What on earth is he wearing? And Annie Leibovitz! Cool," Sammi was just as excited as Liang and Bailey had been.

"He's doing the big speech on Friday's award night," Liang said.

"He's such a fabulous director," she made a low noise in her throat, "... He stirs me."

"Fancy the Rockett Man, do ya?" said Bailey.

Rockett looked a scrawny bantam to Carrick. But if Annie Leibovitz was taking his portrait he must have stature somewhere, she'd photographed practically every cultural icon of the last forty years.

Sammi was almost drooling, "He's got such a bent mind, I'd love to get my hands on that."

"Hey, look at the time. We gotta go, Li," Bailey was getting up, skolling his drink and belching again, "You going to this *Legends* seminar-debate-thing, Sammi? Lee Clow, Richard Branson and big daddy, Tony Maine?"

"Pass."

"Let's catch up for a drink somewhere later in the week. Thanks for the lunch, Andy," said Liang, "Hope we helped."

Bailey was already gone.

"Just you and me then," Sammi said.

"Cheers."

"Cheers."

"Well, I don't think I can be much help to your investigation, Andy. Were they?"

"Hard to say. We were talking about Bangkok, they mentioned

someone called Jamie Tan who seems to have a lot to do with Shack-leton. Do you know him?"

"I don't think poor Jamie could have done it, he's not even here." She sipped the last of her vodka soda, shifted in her chair, "I thought everyone was convinced his dopey girlfriend did it?"

"Maybe. Was Jamie Tan at the agency same time as you and Shackleton?"

She looked surprised at the question, "Yeah, we crossed over. Everyone moves around a lot in this industry, nothing's a job for life, it's not like an insurance company."

"Hey, save the attitude for young Bailey."

"It's hard to make a dent in him, skin of a rhino. And the manners. Anyway, I wasn't having a go at you, I was just saying that advertising people are restless."

"You have an interesting accent."

"Stopping all stations, my father calls it. It's all over the shop, I know. I was born in England and lived in the States after my parents split, worked in Barcelona soon as I left college, bummed around the world, lived in Ibiza for two years before running away to the Far East in search of a career. Now I live in New York, I have a Green Card and a UK passport. The end. I'm difficult to put in a box."

"Never a dull moment."

"I like it that way."

"The guys were saying Jamie Tan still works for Shackleton, though not in advertising?

"Just how is Jamie connected?" she sounded irritated.

"He's probably not. They said he was close to Shackleton, that's all. I'm just trying to build a picture, find out who's connected. How much do you know about this Bangkok bar, *Inn the Pink*?"

"What kind of girl do you think I am, Mr. Carrick?"

"Adventurous, by the sound of it."

She laughed, "No, not my kind of place. What can I tell you? Jamie works there and wastes his life. I've moved on from Asia, I don't look back. Never have."

Carrick tried the business angle.

"Do you know anything about the big business pitch for the Qi Project in China?"

"Never heard of it. Like I said, everything about Asia is behind me now."

The Qi Project angle was drawing a blank every time.

She opened her handbag, "Anyway, I'm on the run, I only came for a quick look. I see the boys stuck you with the bill for lunch, let me pay for my vodka."

"No need, I'll put it on expenses," he pointed at the hotel beneath their feet, "You staying here?"

"Oh, no," she said quickly, "I've got a cabin on the yacht. It's just that this is one of my favourite bars in Cannes, whenever I come to the Lions I come up at least once."

"Maybe we can have another drink here later in the week, when I've had a bit more time to dig around?"

"I don't think so."

"I'd appreciate being able to ask a few questions of someone who's worked with Jonas. It was hard getting much sense out of those two guys."

"I'm sure. But I'm afraid I can't. Normally I'd love to, but I've got a lot to think about at the moment."

"I'd really appreciate it."

She crinkled her mouth, changed gear, "You don't give up do you?"

"I'm the dogged type."

"And you're on a scent?"

"I'm sniffing around."

"I can see that. Listen, here's an idea, I think you should come along to the party on the yacht? That would be fun. We can talk then."

"I thought it was for clients only?"

"That was a way of saying to Bailey: no peasants."

"You won't be tied up with bigwigs all the time?"

"I won't be tied up. I'll make sure I've got enough time for you Andy Carrick."

"In that case I'll be glad to come."

"Meet me at the port 9am Tuesday. You don't need to bring anything, everything a bloodhound needs is on the boat. Just don't tell anyone else about it."

Alone, the table crowded with empty glasses, Carrick wondered if he was getting anywhere. He called the waiter again, surveyed the beach and the gleaming yachts, comforting himself with the thought that at least he was getting there in style.

CHAPTER 5.

"What is it you are looking for, Monsieur Carrick?"

The hotel suite was high-ceilinged and classic, the parquetry entrance opening to a wide lounge, rococo sofa with two matching chairs, a sturdy coffee table between them; under the smallish window a work-desk and an elegant straight-backed chair. Between heavy curtains, a doll's house balcony overlooked La Croisette and the rich man's playground bay.

Shackleton had not spent much time in Suite 613 at the Carlton, the room that he was officially booked into according the Lions' committee.

Carrick checked the bedroom first, opened the wardrobes — just coat hangers. In the dresser there was nothing but lavender-scented drawer liners. The bathroom cupboard had no personal affects other than those the hotel supplied. One hand soap unwrapped but hardly used.

The duty manager was hovering, a nervy stick insect called Bernard Perott. Carrick looked at the man's reflection over his shoulder in the bathroom mirror, and replied, "Answers."

Perott had expressed concern for 'procedural correctness'. The police had ordered no one touch anything or service the suite.

Monsieur Perott was, however, willing to 'acquiesce in these special circumstances' to a private inspection by Lloyd's of London.

It's amazing what can be achieved with an important-looking business card and the special circumstances of a crisp, yellow €200 note.

Carrick went back to the lounge. On the desk a monogrammed message-pad had an abbreviated quick-dial number handwritten in pencil. A hotel extension? He picked up the phone using a handkerchief and rang the three digit number.

"What are you doing?" protested Perott.

"Avis, *bonjour*," answered a clerk at the car-rental desk.

Carrick asked if a car had been rented and charged to this room number? A handful of taps on a keyboard.

"But yes, of course, Mr. Shackleton, three days ago."

Clearly news of Shackleton's demise had not reached the hotel rental desk.

"I'm calling on Mr. Shackleton's behalf. Can you give me the make, colour and license plate please, for our business records? Expenses, you see? I can't bother Mr. Shackleton with it right now."

Avis was happy to oblige.

Carrick asked, "Just checking, is Ms. Pornthip Sinn noted as a second driver?'

"Yes, sir. Is everything in order?"

"Indeed. Thank you."

Where was the vehicle now, might it lead to Pornthip? Or was it parked at La Colombe d'Or? Presumably Lacont would know? Maybe, maybe not. Carrick needed to build bridges with him, any tidbits of information he could trade might help.

"You were not to touch anything, monsieur," the duty manager chided.

Carrick crossed the room to examine the coffee table, about the only area of the suite that showed someone had been in residence at all.

A *Cannes Lions Welcome Pack* lay open with its goodies, gifts and guff spread around; folders, schedules, blurbs about festival events, invitation cards to parties, screenings, cocktails, speeches. God these people kept a punishing schedule.

Amongst it all an A4 pad, the lower half of the first leaf torn away.

He picked it up and looked for the indentation of the pen on the page beneath. Perott started, looking concerned. Angling the paper against the light Carrick made out an imprint.

9am Fri.

The handwriting was large, the full stop after the word *Friday* was made as a small o. The dot on the lowercase i also a small circle. A feminine hand. Pornthip's?

9am Friday.

Shackleton was killed Friday afternoon.

What did he do in the morning? Had he gone to a meeting? Or was it Pornthip's appointment? Or neither? Might be just an arrangement for breakfast or a phone call?

Then he saw something really interesting, the black edge of a large folio bag propped between the back of the couch and the wall. Melodie mentioned Shackleton had been sent something the size of a folio and had it delivered to his room when he checked in. The police obviously didn't regard it as material to the murder otherwise they would have taken it away by now.

He reached over to pick it up but stopped himself and turned around, "Monsieur Perott," he smiled, "You should know that there is a great deal of money at issue in this investigation. Mr. Shackleton had substantial insurance cover in the event of his death while travelling on business. Two million euros worth."

The duty manager looked at him enquiringly.

"You can understand I have a grave responsibility to be thorough?"

"Of course, monsieur."

"Now, I'd like to be able to say in my report that you have been totally cooperative, helpful at every turn... a credit to the hotel. I'd be grateful if you could take a seat over there and busy yourself for a moment."

Perhaps this appeal to responsibility and reputation spoke his language, or perhaps it was the second fresh €200 note Carrick handed him.

"*C'est un plaisir*, monsieur."

"I appreciate your constructive attitude."

Perott sat down in the straight-backed chair at the desk, pulled out his Blackberry and started punching the keys.

Carrick lifted out the big folio from the back of the settee, unzipped it and flicked through the artwork inside. Illustrated images for ads, cover designs for fashion and music magazines, mostly Asian titles but a couple of English-language mastheads. Some ink drawings too. And paintings. The artwork was startlingly good, even to Carrick's eye. A diverse range of styles. Three of the paintings were on canvas, which struck him as notable only because the rest of the pieces in the folio were prints, coated in plastic.

Paintings?

Impressionist, Cubist, Expressionist, Classicist, Liang had said, Jamie Tan could paint every style.

Could this be Jamie Tan's work? But hadn't he left advertising? Why would his portfolio be in Cannes?

Digging further into the folio's pockets Carrick searched for a covering note or something identifying the owner. Nothing. He glanced over to see how Perott was occupying himself when, from the corner of his eye, he saw under the couch the discarded packaging that the folio was wrapped in when delivered.

Perott looked up when he heard him fumbling with the express shipping docket,

"*Qu'est-ce que c'est*? Found your answers?"

The docket, addressed to Shackleton at the Carlton, showed the package had been air expressed to Cannes from Bangkok. As well as who paid the freight. It was a TV production company.

The Backroom Boys.

Sammi Walton's company.

"No," Carrick said, "Just more questions."

~

Chapter 5.

At the Palais, Tony Maine's big grin was everywhere, larger than life posters advertising *The Legends Debate* with an equally beaming Sir Richard Branson and, by contrast, a reserved looking bearded man called Lee Clow.

Carrick paid at the entrance, waving away the girl's protestation that the show was almost over, bounded up the stairs to the main auditorium and slipped inside. With a schedule like Tony's, God only knew when they'd have the chance to speak in person again.

It was an elaborate stage set for a bunch of businessman debating each other.

Nothing as pedestrian as a podium or rostra of any kind, instead some sort of chat-by-campfire theme. Spotlights above the darkened stage were directed downwards in a series of pale pillars creating a forest-at-night look, artificial stars twinkled in a purple 'sky' behind the three legends who were sitting on low benches dressed to look like felled logs. Leaves and small rocks were scattered artfully around the stage.

Between them a roaring campfire somehow burned, Carrick wondered about health and safety regulations.

In such a theatrical setting, the three men looked incongruous in normal day clothes. Tony, the most out of place in his smart navy business suit. Branson, in open-necked shirt, jeans and cowboy boots looked more at home. Lee Clow, all in black with long grey hair and beard of biblical proportions, looked like a Californian philosopher.

Tony was holding forth, enthusiastically chasing down some point, eyes shining like they had the other night when he'd outlined the scenario for Carrick's role as an insurance investigator.

"... to that extent, I agree with Sir Richard absolutely. But 'cool' is just one word. It doesn't help every brand. Not all brands in a given category can be, or should try to be 'cool'. Every brand needs to worship a different key word, carve out a differently flavoured brand equity.

"Some should be traditional, some should be cheap and cheerful. Why? Otherwise, they'd all be the same. At its most fundamental, advertising is simply about differentiation..."

Carrick found a spare plush seat at the end of a row next to a young woman with spiky gelled hair who glared at him suspiciously as he sidled in.

"... What's interesting is that the actual differentiation doesn't have to be big or significant. It just has to be, well, interesting. The small things matter. It's the same with people, or political parties. In most western countries the major political parties are more or less interchangeable, jostling for the same centre ground. Often the smaller the actual differences, the fiercer the battle."

In the darkness, the spot singled Tony out as he stepped forward, highlighting him like an evangelist. But his enthusiasm was catchy rather than preachy.

"... Today, big brands are becoming commoditised, in both performance and service levels, so as products become more and more a parity choice the fight for differentiation will cause a lot of heat.

"Now, Lee Clow, sitting right here, he knows this. As you all remember, Lee wrote the classic *Think Different* advertising campaign for Apple that won so many awards on this very stage some years ago..." the crowd spontaneously applauded the mention of the old campaign, "... brilliantly tapping into our psychographic need to differentiate ourselves, preferably by buying an Apple computer.

"Freud wrote about this too. Differentiation, I mean, not Apple computers. Freud called it the *narcissism of the small difference* ..."

Lee Clow chipped in with a good-natured drawl, "Wow, you Limeys have read everything."

The audience laughed.

Maine waited until they'd subsided, "We have this wonderful thing in England, Lee, called 'Education'".

A bigger laugh. Tony Maine with a microphone was deadly as a sniper with an AI.

"Freud pointed out that it's the minor differences between people who are otherwise alike that is, ironically, the basis of many of the feelings of hostility between them. Visit Punjab and see if you can detect the smallest real difference between those who are Indian and

those who are Pakistani — appearance, language, ethnicity, literature
... indistinguishable. Yet they hate each other.

"Can you tell the difference between a Catholic and a Protestant
in a street in Belfast? Sounds like the beginning of an Irish joke,
doesn't it?" Maine's boyish grin made you want to smile back, share
the same wavelength. "Or a Turk from a Greek in Cyprus? Of course
not. It's artificial differentiators — things like nationality and religion
— that have succeeded in keeping all of them fighting for years. The
Jews and the Arabs have been proven to be genetically the same race,
for God's sake! Hutus and Tutus believe they have slightly different
hairlines from each other and that was enough for genocide.

"My point is this: differentiation, even if it's an artificial kind of
differentiation through advertising or packaging, the very belief in
differentiation itself, is a powerful motivator — a need at the most
basic human level, deep in our psychology. We are hard wired to look
for novelty, distraction and disruption.

"If there is no difference, we humans will make one up. It doesn't
matter if it's real or make believe.

"The lesson here is that marketers in charge of the big brands
must stop copying other marketers, stop being lazy, stop asking their
ad agencies to produce 'something like' such-and-such a brand or
such-and-such a campaign. They must start demanding 'something
unlike'... something different ... something original ... something no
one else has dared. Then your brand can *own* that difference. Own
the experience and you can own the category.

"Now Sir Richard, I'm sure you'd agree, that would be cool."

The audience of creatives applauded wildly, they loved him.

A call for originality in advertising couldn't be that original,
thought Carrick, but it was all in the delivery, Tony Maine's brand of
attractive certainty carried the crowd with him. A sunny positivity
that persuaded because of its own breezy confidence.

It was like the Major's *sprezzatura*, seemingly effortless, concealing
the thorough preparation behind it.

Carrick clapped as hard as the rest. While the MC closed
proceedings he left the auditorium and walked around the outside of

the Palais to the stage door, imagining Tony, Sir Richard and Lee Clow toasting the success of their session backstage with champagne and caviar, swapping insider-trading tips or whatever the super rich do together when they're relaxing.

After waiting a couple of minutes he rang Tony's cell phone, half-expecting it to be turned off, planning to leave a message to say that he was outside if Tony had time before his flight back to London.

To Carrick's surprise, he answered.

"Andy Carrick?" and with mock gruffness, "Where the hell are you?"

"At the east-side stage door."

"Here at the Palais? Are you following me?" delivered in the same tone.

"Yes. I thought I'd give you an update before you head back to London."

"I can't talk here. I've got a helicopter waiting for me. I'll meet you at the helipad in five minutes. Know where that is?"

"Yep. Great speech."

"Ah, how can I believe you, Carrick," he proclaimed, "You're just after my money."

"See you soon."

Suddenly Carrick sensed movement close behind.

He braced instinctively and swivelled.

"You still here?" grinned Benny Sewell, camera in hand, slapping him on the back, "This is where I left you yesterday."

"Benny, I could hear you sneaking up behind me from ten yards away. You shouldn't do that. Were you trying to listen in on a private phone conversation?"

"I've sussed you, haven't I, old son? You *are* doing security for someone. It's Branson, isn't it?"

"Wrong. But if I was, Benny, I'd certainly want you to be the first to know."

"What are you doing hanging around here then? I know for sure that you're up to something."

"As you saw, I was making a phone call."

"Why at the stage door entrance? You can walk with those things, you know. The French call them *portable*. Means mobile."

"Very droll, Benny."

BS was scoping left and right in case there was anything he hadn't noticed. Enthusiasm draining a little he squinted at Carrick in an attempt to look hard, "Don't bullshit a bullshitter, Andy, if you don't want to tell me what you're doing it's no skin off my nose."

"Don't get all out of shape, Benny, I'm not doing anything more interesting than meeting an old friend."

"Guess I'll let you off with a warning this time. Speaking of which, just remembered: I've been warned off talking to you."

"What? Who by?"

"I tried to interview the police detective investigating the Shackleton case this morning. Dour bloke, called Lacont. He knows you. Doesn't seem to like you much. Said you'd been asking questions." Benny saw his advantage, "Didn't know that, did you? See, I tell you stuff, even though you don't reciprocate. Haven't you heard of the scratch my back system...?"

"What did he say?"

"He asked me what I saw at the Shackleton murder scene," he smiled, "Must've read one of my articles."

"Oh, I'm sure he subscribes to *InCreative*."

"It was syndicated. Remember? I told you."

"What did he say about me?"

"Asked if I'd come across you, were you a reporter of some kind?"

"What did you say?"

"Told him that you weren't a reporter. He asked if you worked for Lloyd's of London? I said of course not, that you worked for yourself."

A heaviness settled in Carrick's bowels.

"And?"

"Told him I didn't know what you were doing in Cannes. And as you're still not telling me I ... hang on a minute ... gotta go, catch you later."

Then BS was gone.

The door to the blockhouse had opened and Lee Clow was

coming out chaperoned by one of the Cannes committee's sashaying girls in a tight black dress. She tried in vain to get between them but BS was all over Clow in an instant, camera running.

"Mr. Clow... Sir? Hi, sorry. Benny Sewell from *InCreative*..." He started shooting questions and footage at the same time.

Clow walked briskly, answering politely as possible while the girl continued her protestations. The three figures disappeared down the side of the building in the direction of a white limousine parked in the forecourt. Carrick turned the other way and headed for the helipad on the far side of the Palais.

He was late. Tony said five minutes and Carrick had to get round the entire monolithic building, he picked up the pace and broke into a fast trot, distancing himself from what BS had said as much as hurrying to meet Tony.

That the head of the police investigation was telling people not to talk to him was bad enough, but the reason was potentially worse.

Carrick's cover was blown.

Building bridges with the Inspecteur might be a problem now.

He'd have to tell Tony things weren't going quite to plan.

"What's the penalty for impersonating an insurance man?" Carrick greeted Tony Maine with the question.

Maine didn't answer. He'd been kept waiting and looked tense, the helicopter was already warming up to take him to Nice airport.

Ushering Carrick into the rear seat of the tinted cockpit he yelled over the noise of the rotors, "The money's in your account now. It should be enough to pay for a cab back."

The pilot threw a disapproving look at Carrick, nodded to Maine as he slammed the door closed.

Seconds later they were lifted into the sky above the Iles de Sainte-Marguerite ferry, its wake a comet's tail in the blue sea. Carrick could no longer ride in a helicopter without being transported immediately back to the desert, that jump with Dewey,

Chapter 5.

Gaffney and Peters. The blowy shamal. The firefight with the convoy. The Kalishnakov in the face and all that followed.

He shut down those thoughts, closed his mind's eye and concentrated on the view.

They reached a thousand feet over the Palm Beach Casino at La Pointe, the smiling expanse of Golfe Juan opened up below as they tracked alongside the Boulevard du Littoral. Tony looked preoccupied. They didn't speak, the chopper pilot sharing the headphones' wavelength, so Carrick gawked at Cap d'Antibes' real estate.

The glossy ultramarine bay changed colour to a deeper blue as they tacked northeast passed Biot and Cagnes-sur-Mer. "Klein Blue", Robyn had called it the first time they'd come here. She'd been doing art classes at night back home and hauled Carrick to every bloody gallery and museum in the area.

Ten minutes later the helicopter sat outside Nice airport's private jet terminal and Carrick was giving Maine his report.

"I spoke to most of the judges last night while they had a wine tasting."

"Any good?"

"They didn't offer me any. They weren't overly helpful as you predicted. By the end I tried to ramp up the tension."

"Good stuff."

Tony's mood was more avuncular now they were alone.

"I also went to La Colombe d'Or."

"Great."

"Not altogether. I ran into the police investigators."

"A-ha. And?"

"They wouldn't let me see the room where it happened. The police seem convinced it was the girl-fiend. But I've got to say, the few people who've met her don't seem to think she's capable of it, his throat was cut ear-to-ear you know. I've seen the pictures. Not very ladylike."

Maine grunted.

"The fact that she's disappeared made the police suspicious, but if anything I'm worried about her well being."

"Mmm."

"Ray Doyle has a theory."

"Does he now? What does dear old Ray think?"

"Ray thinks it might be something to do with Bangkok, maybe to do with some girlie bar Shackleton owns in Patpong. He said that was his intuition, anyway."

"Bangkok. How?"

"He's vague on that. But the way I see it, if it were something to do with a Bangkok bar, why would they kill him here in France? Does it mean the girl was a plant? From what I've heard of the triads that's a little complicated, they prefer the direct approach. Do you know anything about Shackleton's bar?"

"I'd heard he bought one, now that you mention it. Must admit I didn't think it connected with this, it's a possibility I suppose..." Tony looked thoughtful but his expression managed doubtful too.

"I met a couple of creative blokes, Bailey and Weh, freelancers who knew Shackleton and his Bangkok bar pretty well, but they didn't help much."

The more Carrick spoke, the more it sounded to him like he'd achieved bugger all of substance.

"I also met a TV commercials producer who worked with Shackleton in Bangkok, Sammi Walton. I'm hoping she can tell me more about him when I see her again in a couple of days."

"Really? Such as?"

"I'm fishing. I did, however, manage to look around Shackleton's suite in the Carlton."

"How did you manage that?"

"Had to part with a few crisp notes. The duty manager obliged."

"Bribery? You beauty," smiled Tony, "Find anything?"

"Some rather good paintings and illustrations sent to Shackleton from Bangkok, though I don't know if there's any connection between that and his death. I think they might be the work of a Jamie Tan. Name familiar?"

"No. Anyway, creative directors are always being sent material to feed off. Think money, money, money, Andy. You've made a good start, meet as many people as you can, needle, push, probe, make a nuisance of yourself and ring me at the end of the week. I'm flying to China tomorrow for a series of meetings so I'll be hard to reach for a while."

He didn't seem to expect to hear any more but Carrick had saved the worst till last.

"I spoke to Benny Sewell, the journo from *InCreative*."

Tony rolled his eyes, "The gutter press. What's he have to offer?"

"He said the policeman in charge of the case, Inspecteur Lacont from the Serious Crimes Unit, told him not to speak to me. I think Lacont has rumbled my cover thanks to Benny and doesn't like me asking questions."

Something crossed Tony's face but Carrick couldn't read it.

"Has this Lacont talked to you personally?"

"Yes, we met. I told him I was working for Lloyd's, gave him the business card. Said you were my client, etcetera. He may ring you."

Tony didn't seem troubled, mildly amused if anything, "I thought you'd be talking to the police at some stage, but not this soon. Anyway, you're right, if he doesn't believe you he'll ring me to check."

"That's why I asked you earlier: what's the penalty in France for impersonating an insurance man?"

"Keep stirring things up, you'll be able to afford the fine, don't worry." He checked his watch, picked up his briefcase and stood.

At the *Private Jet Passengers Only* door he stopped and called brusquely across the lounge, "I'll talk to the police and tell them about you."

A flight attendant appeared, she looked from Maine to Carrick and back, puzzled, smiled uncertainly.

Minutes later, Tony Maine took off. His charter jet shrinking to a dot with a series of slow reverberant booms as the sky swelled with bruised clouds in the early evening. Carrick watched it disappear, experiencing the emptiness felt by all those left behind at an airport. Going nowhere. He would have liked to explore things a little more with Tony, used that famous brain.

He was flat, the meeting had been a mistake, he was trying too hard, pathetically seeking approval from the boss as a substitute for actual achievement. What was it about Tony Maine that made him want to impress?

Carrick's next move was another mistake.

"Hotel Négresco," he told the cabbie at the airport rank.

CHAPTER 6.

"Hotel Négresco."

As soon as he said the words, it set off a different train of thought a world away from the investigation. Andy and Robyn, Robyn and Andy, Andy and Robyn, Robyn and Andy. The rhythm of a train wreck.

The young lovers were dazzled by the glamour of the Négresco, a romantic fantasy built on the grandest of scales by a one-time gypsy violinist. It was the year before they were married and the boy soldier Carrick was equally dazzled by the young Robyn Cooper.

He had a ten day furlough so they took Ryanair flights to Marseille and spent a week camping in the mountains, sleeping bags zipped together, waking in the forest to frosts and heart-starting nips of cognac, hiking, climbing, making love on smooth warm boulders in the afternoon sunshine above virgin valleys.

The last few days they headed for the coast to thaw. The rented campervan corkscrewed down the corniche, the outside temperature rose with each descending mile as the sun flashed through the windscreen and the blue sea ("Klein Blue") stepped up to meet them. Every few minutes Robyn stripped off another layer of mountainwear beside him in the passenger seat. By the time they slipped into the Monaco traffic she was down to bra and pants, they stopped beside the park near the casino and never got around to breaking the bank at Monte Carlo.

She showed him Le Carré's sporting club with its underground pigeon tunnels full of unlucky birds trapped on the casino roof to be used as post-lunch target practice by wealthy shotgun wielding members. Seems symbolic of something, he'd said. Capitalism? she suggested. Everything, he answered.

Not for the last time Carrick marvelled at Robyn's wide-ranging grab bag of bits and tangents beyond any knowledge that his world showed him.

Later they pushed onto Nice and got drunk in the bar of the Hotel Négresco. "High-class drunk is the best kind," Robyn said.

A few months later they were engaged and after a civil ceremony on a rainy September day in Richmond she became an army wife.

Andy worked hard in the ranks, Robyn studied during the day and jobbed in a Hereford jody bar three nights a week. They were a normal, uncomplicated couple, the kind you see holding hands outside shop windows fantasising about things they can't afford.

Time passed in seamless years. Two, three, five...

Inevitably, without either noticing, the first flush of intensity gave way to a kind of parallel comfort, they stopped living inside what Robyn called the *shared moment*. Robyn's parents helped raise the deposit and they moved out of the married quarters and into a small flat of their own. They were happy. Happy enough, he supposed.

Life was orderly. Something Carrick's life had never been before. They were settled, yes, but he was surprised to find it strangely unsettling. He confessed his restlessness to the Major one night who suggested applying for Special Forces selection.

"You think I should?"

"Don't die wondering," the Major answered, as he did to all such questions.

Carrick jumped at it.

"Four months of hell on earth," promised the Major.

And hell it was. Hell in mountain mud and tropical lowland

swamp. Hell in heaving seas, in barbed-wire cold, under the pressing weight of tunnels and buried pipes, hauling, crawling, clawing, climbing, carrying, half-drowning, hardly sleeping, marching, marching, marching, evading, resisting, extracting. Surviving. Elbowing through stress and duress and misery and bastardisation and finding a little more in himself each time. He could do it because none of it was bad as what he was running from, nowhere was bad as the nothingness behind him, his childhood, his bitterness, his lowliness. Not even the high, hard, broken country of Brecon Beacons.

When he was badged, Robyn was jubilant, intensely proud, he'd really grown into something, he was becoming a hero in front of their eyes. Other people looked at him differently too, instead of a journeyman they saw a man of the right calibre, a special breed.

It changed him. He'd spent his entire life on the outside looking in and now he was inside and looking out. He could slough off the petty things, the normal drudge of suburban people, all that could be put aside. Ordinary life was small and mealy when a man could think and act on a martial scale, walk down the street in a way others can't. Calls to a hot spot anytime of the day or night, real action. Real highs after an operation.

Like a high-flying executive he lived for the job, loved the swagger, believed in the bubble; an elite soldier knows he's superior, at the top of his game, ready to prove it anytime.

Robyn took on the supporting role to the hero's performance, like all good SAS wives she was sympathetic, never asked questions, always careful not to tread on the overbearing testosterone that accompanied a mission. She never let on about the sleepless nights after he left for an op, when she saw him dead or horribly hurt and bloodied, the isolation and utter loneliness of the endless 3am.

But imperceptibly, a distance grew, though neither admitted it.

As the missions got more diverting they delayed having kids. He said he didn't want the distraction. She laughed, said he was the centre of the universe and didn't want the competition.

Then came his last Afghanistan tour and everything changed.

Carrick had been killing time in CHUville, the containerised housing units in Kandahar. His two closest mates in the regiment, Dave 'bloody' Fergusen and Brett 'Jacko' Jackson, had been rotated back to Hereford so he had no one to play with.

Dave 'bloody' Fergusen was good value in the desert because you never knew what weird piece of kit he'd buy from the Americans. He was a geardo, whenever he walked in wearing that sly, lopsided smile you knew he'd wasted some hard earned on new paraphernalia, a fancy custom rucksack, GPS watch or some weapon accessory. The same smile was a tell when he was bluffing in poker.

Four Brits were assigned to join the Paras for a special op, at that time tier-one forces from different nations routinely worked together. Carrick, Dewey, Gaffney and Peters were sent to southern Oruzgan, in the Deh Rafshan district west of the Bamiyan-Kandahar Highway.

The HVT was a Taliban high up, Mullah Noorullah, a senior insurgent commander apparently involved in the successful use of IEDs and rocket attacks against the coalition. That made him a High Value Target.

But target elimination wasn't their job this time, it was purely an information gathering role. If they found what they were looking for the Australian SOTG had a combat outpost Forward Operation Base nearby and would take over. It was a variation of the old CIA Phoenix Program. Ruthless stuff. The allies' emphasis had recently shifted from 'clear, hold and build' to 'land, kill and leave'.

US satellite pictures suggested there were Taliban tunnels situated near a village. Carrick's team was charged with surveillance, they were dropped northwest of Sorhk Morghab, fifteen miles in a straight line from Gorma where the latest Int said Noorullah was hiding out. They'd trek cross-country under cover of darkness and take up two different OPs (Observation Posts).

What changed everything wasn't that Robyn was unfaithful during that exact time.

Chapter 6.

What changed everything wasn't that her choice of bedfellow was Dave 'bloody' Fergusen.

What changed everything was that Carrick only managed to stay alive during those three days by focusing his whole being on a vision of Robyn as his holy saviour, his destiny, his belief in her complete and utter golden perfection.

He was captured at the start of the operation.

Delayed three days because of heavy weather, a northwesterly shamal, the parachute drop was sloppy in the unpredictable conditions of the dying dust-storm and they were blown off course. Dewey came down hard, breaking bones as well as their TACBE communications pack.

Carrick immediately pushed to carry on and they decided not to abandon the job, there was a designated exfiltration route and an emergency pick up point Dewey should get to by daylight. A sortie would be flown over their last known position if he didn't make it.

They left Dewey with his Minimi machine gun and a Browning Hi-Power pistol as back up. Gaffney and Peters went their way while Carrick helped strap their 66mm Law rocket onto Dewey's back and then he took off alone.

He loaded the extra gear into his own Bergen and legged it to his LUP in just over three hours carrying his M16/M203 and 120lbs of sandbags, observation post equipment, extra ammo bandoliers, PE4 play doh, detonators, Claymores, Elsies, five days rations and intravenous drips for emergency.

His lying up position was a bombed out qala, the place had been abandoned for years, probably since the Russian invasion, there was even wreckage from an old T-62M battle tank blasted to pieces but still recognisable in its rusty bones. Carrick set up a hide in a ditch sheltered from the nearby road by the old walls.

He arrived just before dawn and broke open the first of his MREs. Meals Ready to Eat, known as the Three Lies. Not meals, not ready, not edible.

Within twenty minutes he sighted the first militia jolting down the pitted track coming out of Gorma. Then another, both travelling roughly in the direction Gaffney and Peters were positioned. Before he could lay the Claymores and Elsies a third convoy of mujahideen appeared. This lot didn't pass by.

He waited as long as possible before engaging, silently willing them to carry on, but they were drawn to his flame like moths.

As firefights go it had been pretty one-sided. He'd taken out everyone in the first vehicle with the grenade launcher as they came around the corner of the compound, couldn't fail at such close range, and two or three in the second truck went down with a handful of rounds.

But the Toyota lorry veered crazily when he shot the driver and somehow kept going, flipping and crashing at speed through the far wall of the compound, setting off a domino effect of collapses along the whole length of the mud brick structure that literally brought Carrick's world down on top of him. The enclosure he was using as cover caved in, his kevlar saved him from serious damage but he was knocked over and out. In the smoke and confusion Carrick considered the manoeuvre an accident, he was simply unlucky.

It was weeks later that he found out the mujahideen had known exactly where to look for the surveillance team, but hadn't expected them to be in place so soon.

There'd been an incident at the allies' base while the team's chopper was in the air, an 'insider attack' as the media call it. *Green on Blue.* There was a strong feeling among many Afghans that NATO missions were obsessed with taking out names on a list, regardless what the ops did to ordinary civilians. The assailant was an Afghan working as a Terp, he machine-gunned a roomful of US special forces, killing three, escaping through a check point.

Turned out the bastard had blown the gaff on the whole operation and Noorullah slipped into the night.

Gaffney and Peters shot their way out and made it back to the pick up point. So did Dewey. Carrick didn't.

The jihadists who survived the firefight didn't know what to do with him. Carrick supposed they kept him alive with the idea of using him as a bargaining chip. At any moment he was expecting the heated spoon treatment or the teeth extraction routine, but instead they exhausted themselves giving him a protracted beating and then broke eight of his fingers with a rock to nobble him.

When he regained consciousness he was in utter darkness. Shackled inside a heavy metal container that he eventually realised was the detached turret of the ancient dismembered Russian tank he'd seen on arrival. It was high 40s Celsius in July and inside it was twenty points hotter. Carrick baked in the iron oven in the desert sun for three days without food, water or light, his tongue swollen in his mouth like an old leather cricket ball.

Periodically they opened the hatch to check if he was still alive or to torment him. Once dousing him with petrol. Once dropping in a small buff coloured snake, a McMahon's Viper.

The US flew two sorties over the area but could see nothing except wrecked vehicles from the firefight, heat sensors couldn't pick him up inside the tank.

Training kept him calm. He knew help would come. Focussing on Robyn kept him positive.

Everything about her became sanctified, holy images scorched into his brain — the exact shape of her eyes, cream-white skin wet with bath suds, her sudden smiles, her instinctive goodness, her shining bliss when she spoke about the "purity of moments" — he knew absolutely he would survive, for her, for them. Start a family, build a house. A boisterous family full of life, sons and daughters who'd grow fast and have their own families and spread into the lively, laughing future.

That was something worthy of a man, he realised, maybe the only thing. He finally knew his place in the world.

Inside the darkness he saw her and she was spring water. An angel delivered unto him who'd given his dreams wings; his life, up to and including now, was his earthly purgatory. These visions kept his mind intact even as his body fell apart inside the tar-black, sun-blasted furnace.

In the end, Command scrambled a Predator to check his last known location one more time and they decided to go in, the Black

Chapter 6.

Hawk boys lit up the handful of ragged mujahideen before landing and eventually finding him. When they opened the old Russian tin can they said he smelt like hot bacon. All senses virtually shut down, he was a piece of meat wrapped around a hopelessly idealised Robyn — lovely, diaphanous, flawless Robyn — Robyn and Andy and their crystalline future.

Base hospital wired his jaw and worked on saving his fingers before shipping him to the infirmary back in England.

The allies got Noorullah a month later. The Aussies did the job, but only after first blowing up a civilian family with grenades in their home in the wrong village.

∾

By then everything was changed.

Everything changed the moment he learned that all through this time his ephemeral darling had been getting physical with Dave 'bloody' Fergusen, *writhing in the hot and salty juice of fevered infidelity*, as the poet wrote.

The first time she came to see him at the infirmary he still couldn't speak, otherwise he would have announced his plan to start a family, a real life, straight away. She brought biscuits he could not eat and books whose pages his broken fingers could not turn.

On the third visit she said there was something to tell him and it couldn't wait and it might be better that he couldn't talk yet; so it was that in a tumble of words and tears she sat by the bed and revealed her brief affair with Fergusen, all the details. She sobbed, buried her face in the hospital blankets, squeezed his arm, and cried some more.

A sick fury that he couldn't vent took hold, not so much with her, or even Dave 'bloody' Fergusen; worse, and mostly, with himself.

He lost faith. Not in some sublime ideal of a woman he'd invented, that had served its purpose. He lost faith in himself. All his assumptions were wrong, conceited delusions. Nothing was shared, he was isolated as before. A dribbling orphan from a dead-end street whose mother had given him away and whose woman had thrown him over.

His fight to have the world just so was lost, he no longer trusted the self-serving ideas devised from inside his own hopes and dreams. It was his own ego that betrayed him. The ironman inside that metal prison in Afghanistan had been reduced, unmanned by hubris, just when he thought he was a man ready for family it all misfired.

Left Robyn alone too long, hadn't he? Left her open to the tender mercy of a calculating swordsman with a crooked smile who delighted in friends' wives.

It wasn't the sex, the flesh on familiar flesh, the where of the adulterous hands or the how of wet tongues, or even the why or the bloody who that broke everything.

It was the when.

Just when he thought he could beat life at its own game.

Robyn had let go the ladder that held him out of reach of his worst fears and he tumbled down to a place inside the dark where there was no swagger, no strut. The idea blistered in his brain, a betrayal needs someone weak enough to be betrayed. All his life had been self-inflicted harm, an undermining voice said, his own neediness had mastered him.

Their marriage lasted another few months and when they finally divorced it was just another numbing endurance test.

Since then he'd rolled his ball of pain around his mind countless times and his precious certainty abandoned him.

However, the Major didn't.

After Carrick's physical recovery, the medal and his honourable discharge, the Major reached out and gave him a place in the small but thriving security company. A partnership and a place. Like a father to a son.

Then a year later the rock was split under a car, the Major was gone in an instant and the world was worse than before. The tumbling started anew and a dull void yawned for Carrick.

The couple of years since of playing the businessman hadn't been as satisfying as people thought.

Chapter 6.

Neither was the bottle in front of him now, he realised, just another dead man, another empty vessel. Slowly, Négresco's busy rococo came into focus again and Carrick looked around to find the disapproving waiter and ordered more.

But the next bottle didn't answer the call either.

Nothing changed. Nothing ever did.

He knocked it off the table just to see it smash on the mosaic floor.

He paid and left, cursing Tony Maine for summoning him back to a world full of ghosts, stumbling into the street swearing not to visit Nice again for another lifetime.

CHAPTER 7.

"What did you do? *Mon dieu*, what zings did you say?"

"Melodie?"

10.09 am, Carrick was lying on top of his hotel bed in last night's clothes, head hurting and tongue thick, Melodie's voice on the cell phone shattering the night's bitter crust.

"What's going on? What did you say to 'im?"

"Who?"

"Eugene Choi!"

"What about him?"

"He's gone."

Carrick sat straight upright. "Dead?"

"Of course not dead. You are always talking death. *Merde*! 'E's left Cannes, e's flown home. In the middle of ze judging 'e's gone back in China ... zere is still many awards to decide. I was short one judge and now it is two. Because of you!"

"Why would Choi leave because of me?"

"It is you scared 'im off. I 'eard ze judges talking. You said bad zings to zem. Choi went to 'is room after zay told 'im about it and ze 'otel says to me just now 'e checked out last night to catch a midnight flight! Before my judging is finished!"

Chapter 7.

"I haven't spoken to him, haven't seen him. Last night I … had my own problems."

"What am I going to do? It's unprecedented to lose one judge and zen another."

"It's not good news for me either, let me tell you."

"Men! You zink first of yourselves. You make me mad and you are no help. *Au revoir*."

She hung up.

Not a good start to a Monday. It got worse when Carrick remembered he'd left his Defender parked near the Palais when he took the helicopter to Nice with Tony Maine the afternoon before. Accruing expenses. He couldn't remember anything about coming back from the Négresco.

After showering and shaving he went to the further expense of a taxi to Cannes.

Choi doing a runner was plain annoying. It hadn't done much for Melodie's opinion of him either. And if word reached Inspecteur de Détective Lacont that Carrick had put the frighteners on the judges then the notion of bridge building with him was dead and buried too. He didn't want to be run out of town by the sheriff, and it was beginning to feel like a very small town.

Tired of the traffic and needing fresh air, he jumped out of the cab at the Palm Beach Casino and walked beside the beach to clear his head.

But Robyn was still there. Last night's thoughts were clinging to him like a conscience and everywhere he looked dragged him back to the past.

Young Andy and Robyn had visited Cannes on their way to catch the charter flight home from Marseille. They walked the length of the beach before clmbing the steep Le Suquet laneways to a restaurant at the top of the hill for a last splurge before going home. The chef's wolfhound took a liking to Carrick and lay under their table passing wind throughout the lunch. They drank too much for the second day in a row, sitting with the chef and his wife till the sun was aslant and they were tilting.

Later they staggered into an art gallery and played with an exhibition of painted mirrors; they didn't break any, so that wasn't the cause of their bad luck together.

It was years since Carrick had thought about those moments and now wasn't a good time to start. He mentally gathered himself and instead of walking along the sea, which seemed far too cheerful for his mood, he veered a few streets inland until he reached Rue Meynardier, one of the gourmand streets of the Côte. At its western end it meets Forville, the covered market.

Food took Carrick's mind off most things and by the time he reached the *marché* his stomach insisted he eat something instead of just looking at it, he hadn't had anything but red wine and old bile the night before in Nice.

Crossing to a laneway he was drawn to a dated Bar Tabac next to a florist, he ordered from the chalkboard and asked for a large pastis so the locals would stop looking hard at him. Unlike tourists, drinkers are accepted everywhere in France. His reflection stared back from the corner of a freckled mirror behind the zinc bar, it asked if the reason he rented the cottage was really in subliminal homage to Robyn's passion for all things French? Why hadn't he gone AWOL to Spain? Turkey? Cornwall?

Robyn and Andy, Andy and Robyn.

A young wife at home, a girl really, left in a cheap flat waiting to start adult life while her inattentive husband was gripped by a different world altogether, something that had to be played out with other men, something that propelled his ego more than her plain and simple love. A betrayal of her in its own way.

You're getting into deep waters here, son, he said to himself and wished he knew as much about Freud as Tony Maine did.

Tony's name in his thoughts brought Carrick back to the now. He had to get on with the job, had to find a thread to follow or madness would take him. He threw down one more pastis before sauntering into the laneway to collect the old Defender, head buzzing slightly.

His cell phone beeped twice, a text from Benny Sewell giving the address of the wake for Shackleton. Maybe that would turn up something? He was tapping in a reply when he became aware of a high-pitched engine noise approaching fast from behind him. He glanced over his shoulder, the car a red blur, tyres screaming, fender rearing as it accelerated. He made a couple of long strides to get off the road but it swerved to follow him and surged.

Blocked by a sidewalk fruit-stall he pinned himself flat against it, but the car was going to hit him anyway and he jumped at the final moment to protect his legs from the leading edge and rolled into a ball, bouncing up over the bonnet and onto the roof before spinning off in a somersault and falling backwards into the gutter.

Black.

~

Back.

Water at his lips. Voices. Cognac at his lips now. He coughed. He opened his eyes. Vision blurred, pain in the head.

Arms were lifting him straight, a purple shawl was wrapped around his shoulders.

Then, "Andy?"

He recognised that name.

"Andy? Are you OK? Andy?"

Funny Anglo-American accent. The leather girl, Sammi, she talked like that.

He was back in the Bar Tabac, he realised.

How?

A red car, that's right. He remembered now, he had been hit, that's why he hurt. It all made sense. And Sammi is here.

Therefore, he must be the Andy who's being called.

"Andy, say something."

~

He could stand.

"Are you sure you're up to this?" Sammi said.

"I've got to avoid pastis. It slows you down."

His right hip was pivoting more slowly in its socket than the left, without Sammi to lean on he might have had to walk in a circle. They doddered around the bar like an elderly couple.

She laughed, "Are you drunk? That's why you didn't hurt yourself more."

Two strong coffees later he began to feel more like a human being, a bruised human being with a road-shaped bang on the back of his head.

"The café people scraped you off the road and brought you inside," she explained, "I saw the kerfuffle and recognized you, thought I'd better check you out."

"I'm grateful you were passing by."

"No problem. Just tell me when you're going to meet with an accident and I'll make sure I'm there." She smiled, "Any idea what happened?"

"Didn't see much, I was busy trying to get out of the way. Small red car, Renault maybe, headlights on, I didn't get the plates. The rest was spinning through the air."

"French drivers," she scoffed.

"I'm not sure it was an accident actually."

"What do you mean?"

"He seemed to be doing his damnedest to hit me."

"Who'd want to run down an insurance guy? Have you knocked back someone's claim lately?"

"I'm wondering if it's to do with the Shackleton case?"

Sammi considered this. "Did you see him? The driver?"

"Nothing."

"What are you going to do?"

"Keep asking questions. Maybe you can help?"

"I don't see how."

"Come with me this afternoon, tell me who's who. Who I should speak to, who I should trust."

"In Cannes? You can't trust anyone here."

"It's Shackleton's wake."

"No-siree, I hate those kinds of things. Besides, I've got plans."

"Like what?"

"Like a party on a yacht tomorrow or have you forgotten after that blow to the head?"

"If you haven't got the catering sorted out by now you're not going to make it anyway."

"So that's what you think I do? Organise the catering? You sexist schmuck." She seemed about to launch into him then hesitated, she pinched his arm instead, "I'm a TV producer, I schmooze. I solve. I need to make sure certain people are looked after. Like you, Mr. Lloyd's of London."

"I'm sure there'll be lots important people at the wake. Come along and mingle — network, I mean — in between I can pick your brain. How about it?"

"Don't give me that pathetic puppy look. I hate puppies."

"I'm still feeling a bit wobbly, I need a guardian angel."

"Trying to play on my maternal instincts now? Haven't got any, buddy, sorry."

"What did I divert you from?" he tried a different tack, "When you were passing by and I was having a near-death experience?"

"I was just, well, checking things out, window shopping. I've got to go to a dive shop, get some equipment for tomorrow."

"There's plenty of time. Afterwards I'll drive you to the dive shop and help carry your parcels. Look, my car's parked not far from here. Has been for about a day actually, collecting *amendes pour stationement genant.*"

"What's that?"

"Parking fines. I've got to rescue it. Come on, free drinks, great view?"

The address BS had texted was a villa halfway up Le Cannet on a hilltop overlooking the bay. A ritzy area. Every estate had its wonders hidden behind stone walls or impressively high hedging, only treetops and the occasional roofline were visible from street level.

It was just fifteen minutes stuck in the Defender's driving seat, but long enough for Carrick's leg to stiffen painfully. They entered

through unmanned security gates at the bottom of the property —
two CCTV cameras, old models, probably analogue surmised Carrick
— then walked slowly uphill along a white stone avenue lined with
plane trees.

At the top, a gleaming pink-and-white vision emerged, a miniature chateau that looked like a half-scale model of something
designed in Bohemia's golden age, all pointed turrets and fairytale
twee, too small to be anything but a folly, too big to be called a mere
villa. Double storey and framed by two corner towers, the building
had a large paved terrace on the south side overlooking the pool, the
eye was then pulled across sweeping manicured lawns to the gardens,
the view of Cannes and the Mediterranean beyond. A huge eucalypt
completed the postcard vista. Not the obvious place for a wake,
unless it was Walt Disney's.

Hundreds were there already.

"I didn't realise Shackleton was so popular," said Carrick as they
squeezed through to a vantage point.

"Not with everyone," Sammi said quietly.

Fair enough, he had been murdered.

There was a large banner hanging from the chateau's portico, a
pixelated black and white PR photo of Shackleton's face blown up to
almost ten foot across, his derring-do moustache and striking bald
head made him look like a South American dictator ready to address
his grateful nation. In front of it, a microphone and p.a. system with a
row of chairs, presumably for the eulogists.

A platoon of black-tie waiters were distributing drinks and
canapés, there was an animated buzz among the mourners. Two
merry fountains splashed away any remaining solemnity.

"The advertising industry can't take anything seriously," said
Carrick.

"Except itself."

Sammi's always 'on', Carrick wondered if she ever relaxed; like
Tony Maine she was perfectly adapted to an industry where energy
itself is a talent.

"Who you gonna talk to?"

"Anybody involved in the pitch for the Qi business in China?"

"I told you that's not my bag, I produce the commercials once the agency's won the business. We don't care which agency wins as long they've got the budget. I told you this wasn't going to work, me coming here."

"The Big Four networks are all involved," Carrick looked around for any of the judges, "The big holding companies. Do you know who they are?"

"Everyone's owned by someone else in this business, it's hard to keep up, they're always changing names, merging, buying each other out. OK, see over there, that woman with the Cleopatra haircut and earrings? The guy she's talking to is boss of Unicom in the States. They're one of the giants."

"What's his name?"

"Tad Jacobson. He's their CEO. Out of New York."

"Not a creative guy?"

"Money guy."

Jacobson looked like a lawyer, compared to the aura of the Cannes judges his demeanour was quiet confidence rather than preening. The dark-haired woman next to him was more flamboyant: bright clothes, big earrings, severe fringe.

"Who's Cleopatra?"

"Just some art director angling for a job."

"How can you tell from here?"

"Everyone who comes to Cannes is. The whole Festival is all about mutual exploitation. I think of it as a kind of orgy, the same urgency, the same stony-faced enjoyment."

As they edged through the crowd towards Tad Jacobsen, Carrick said, "I had a look around Shackleton's suite at the Carlton hotel yesterday, found a folio sent to him from Bangkok."

"So?"

"So I was wondering..."

Suddenly there was a camera pointing at them with Benny Sewell behind it.

"Hold it ... OK, rolling..." Then in his announcer's voice, "A real mixture of Cannes delegates brought together at Jonas Shackleton's wake. Next we meet Backroom Boys producer from New York, Sammi Walton, with security expert, Andrew Carrick. Would you guys say something about what Jonas's death meant to…?"

"Get out of my face," screeched Sammi as she slapped Benny's camera away.

It burst out of his hands, flew several feet in the air, bounced and rolled across the grass. The people around reeled back and stared. Benny puled.

There was laughter from the crowd nearest — "See that? She bitch-slapped his camera right out of his hands. Whoa."

Carrick took Sammi's elbow, keen to get her away while BS picked up his technology, swearing and looking daggers. Carrick didn't know why Sammi reacted like a paparazzi-hating prima donna, but didn't care. When Benny had said "security expert" instead of "insurance investigator" he thought his cover was in danger again. Out of three hundred or so people in the chateau grounds, Benny alone knew who he really was. BS needed to be muzzled.

He delivered Sammi to the group near the pool, comprising the Cleopatra woman and Tad Jacobson, who seemed oblivious to the kerfuffle, engrossed with a tray of caviar and toast fingers a waiter was handing around. It seemed a safe place to install her for a few minutes.

"I believe you good people know each other," Carrick smiled like a toothpaste ad.

Sammi gave him a withering look as he turned back into the crowd to find BS still squatting down checking his tech, sour as a spoiled five-year-old.

He crouched beside him, "You right there, matey?"

"She's a bitch."

"I'll let her know you're not pleased."

"What's her story? What was that all about?"

"Don't know, Benny. She didn't want to come here in the first place. It's been a difficult day all round."

"A 'difficult day'? Someone try to steal your parking space?" he said bitterly.

"Someone tried to run me down. Sammi was in the street nearby and helped. We're both a bit stressed, that's all."

"I'm a bit stressed right now myself."

He looked ruefully at his camera, though it looked indestructible.

"It's fine, Benny. Look, can I talk to you about something?"

"What?"

"Come over here," Carrick moved to a space away from the crowd, "I need to come clean."

That brought BS trotting over, smelling something, tongue lolling out like a star graduate from obedience school.

"Listen. I've been hired to investigate Shackleton's death, Benny," Carrick said quietly, "That's why Lacont warned you off me. I'm not here to do security; I'm not on holiday," he waved a waiter away, "though at times it might be hard to tell."

"Private investigator, eh. For who?"

"Benny, if I told you that, it wouldn't be private for long. Someone who thinks there's more to Shackleton's death than meets the eye. Thing is, I'm telling people I'm working on a life insurance claim. It's my cover so I can talk to the top brass at the ad agencies without raising too much suspicion. Look, here's my card."

"Wow, you're well prepared. That's why the local cop was asking about you and Lloyd's," he said tapping the business card, "I get it. That's why you were on about that new business pitch?"

"Right."

"Hey, did you know Eugene Choi's gone home already to Beijing?"

"I heard. What do you make of that?"

"Question is, what do you make of that? You're the investigator. Why should I help you? Have you helped me? Hasn't your girlfriend just smashed my Sony?"

"It's all right, isn't it?"

"Might have internal damage."

"Jeez, Benny. Look, here's two hundred euros. Buy another one."

"That wouldn't cover it," he said, pocketing the notes. He grinned,

"You've got a good budget, 'aven't you? You wouldn't give me two hundred out of your own pocket. And you bought me a beer the other day when we met. Must be a serious client."

"Take the money and run away, Benny, before I change my mind. And keep quiet about me, OK?"

"Off the record, Andy."

Carrick looked around for Sammi in time to see her striding back down the avenue of plane trees towards the street. She was leaving. She threw a look across the crowd that could kill, tossed her chestnut head like a wilful thoroughbred, gave Carrick the finger like a wilful New Yorker. He shrugged in reply.

Benny saw the whole thing and smirked. "Told you she was a bitch."

~

"A few words now, *s'il vous plaît*. Quiet please. *Silencieux*."

The dapper little man tapping the microphone was the same Carrick had seen on stage hosting yesterday's *Legends* event at the Palais. The same man who wouldn't meet him without an appointment. Now he was standing in front of the giant Shackleton poster in an commanding pose, ready to introduce the generals to the rally.

"Ladies and gentlemen, *mesdames et messieurs*, I am, as most of you know, Rémy Barré, Chairman of the Cannes Lions International Festival of Creativity Committee. It is my sad duty to be here to mourn the passing of one of our advertising giants, Mr. Jonas Shackleton, gone too soon…"

A loud stage whisper from someone behind Carrick, "The only deadline Jonas was ever early for."

Barré was saying, "… I sincerely hope matters associated with his sudden death can be cleared up soon. I won't dwell on that. Instead, let me indulge a little and tell you something indicative of Jonas' love of life.

"I vividly remember inviting him to speak at the Cannes Awards ceremony two years ago, probably many of you were here and recall his talk and its little bit of theatre with the, um, blow-up doll. Anyway, after the show …"

Standing was making Carrick's leg ache again.

A waiter drifted past, he took two drinks from the tray, drained the first in gulps then started on the other when a voice at his shoulder said, "You must have heard Rémy speak before."

Eddie Schwarz, the buzz-cut judge from New York was winking.

"Mr. Schwarz! You guys having a break from the judging?"

"Call me Eddie. Yeah, a short parole. Just don't ask me about any results."

"Eddie, you're looking at the only person in Cannes who couldn't care less about who wins a bloody Lion award. All the other judges here?"

"Yup. Francesco's saying a few words after Barré. We got limo'd up in convoy straight from the Palais, except for Eugene Choi. He's left already."

"I heard. Wish I'd had a chance to speak with him first."

The crowd was tittering at something Barré said about Jonas and his dedication to uncovering new talent.

Schwarz leaned in close, "The whole scenario frightened the bejeezus out of him, I think. The things you said at the wine tasting about us all being in danger didn't help. I told him you were only trying to make yourself important, am I right?"

Carrick shrugged, wondering whether to say someone had tried to kill him less than two hours ago.

Schwarz said, "Advertising guys are gullible, they always want to believe. I guess Choi got spooked."

"Do you think he might know something?"

"Who knows? Jonas talked to him quite a bit over lunch."

"What about?"

"The usual most likely. Jonas always talked a lot about himself, you know? Talking up his own ads, bad-mouthing other people's, complaining about clients, all between telling how life is one big adventure. Same as most of us to be honest."

"What about Eugene Choi?"

"He's the exception. Choi's not much of a talker. He's like a sponge, soaks up conversation, lets people prattle on so they generally do. Don't know how much he actually takes in, but he's a fine art director."

"Who else was sitting close by?"

"Well, it was one long table, Jonas in the middle, let's see, he had Francesco on one side of him and Vince Delahunty on the other."

"Delahunty's the South African judge? I haven't met him yet."

"Great guy. Then there was me, Choi sat across from Jonas. He had Jay Carlsson next to him, another quiet one."

"Jay's the skinny guy from Amsterdam?"

"Yes, from Hershell's Mirror, good little agency. And then Malcolm White was on his other side. That Malcolm can be a funny dude — you Brits love the wind up, don't you?"

"How d'you mean?"

Schwarz indicated in Rémy Barré's direction at the microphone, "Malcolm helped old Barré with his speech today. Made up all kinds of crap for a laugh. One of the Brit journos bet Malcolm that he couldn't get Barré to say three random words in his speech, I think one was 'slapper', I'm pretty sure 'bonza' was another. Yeah, and 'Shakespeare'. He-he, everything Barré just said about Shackleton being an ex-drummer and moving to Australia... the bit about Shackleton writing all his TV scripts in iambic pentameter in honour of the Bard, it's all a wind up."

Liars for hire, thought Carrick, what could be believed around guys who told porkies just for practice?

"Why do you think Jonas went upstairs to his room before the lunch was over, Eddie?"

"It was late, maybe he just wanted a take a piss in his own bathroom. Last I saw of him he was leaning right across the table showing Eugene Choi some chain around his neck, half-standing half-sitting. He seemed to think Choi would find it interesting. Next time I looked around he'd gone."

Desultory applause rippled through the audience as Barré finished his speech. Next at the microphone was Tad Jacobson, the straight-looking guy he'd deposited Sammi with before she'd stalked off.

Jacobson's voice was a mid-Western American twang made thin through the speakers, "To tell you all the truth, I can't say I knew Jonas Shackleton that well, we watched from a safe distance over at Unicom, ha-ha. I just flew in yesterday from our shareholders' meeting in Delaware and I told…"

Something suddenly clicked in Carrick's mind.

Chain around his neck?

He turned to Eddie Schwarz, "What chain around his neck?"

"Say what?"

"You said Shackleton showed Choi a chain?"

"Some amulet on a gold chain around his neck. He was into jewellery. Wore big rings, big watches and so on."

"What sort of amulet?"

"Like a pendant. Coin shaped. Roundish."

Carrick was remembering the photos Lacont had shown him of Shackleton's dead body on the hotel room floor at La Colombe d'Or. He could picture other jewellery, yes to rings, yes to a chunky bracelet, yes to a gold Rolex, yes to an ear stud.

He could picture the slashing wound across the neck, but no gold chain around it, no amulet.

"How big?"

Schwarz made a circle with his forefinger and thumb.

Shackleton had gone upstairs wearing an amulet and gold chain around his neck and a few minutes later his body was discovered without it. Had it been stolen? Was it a motive for the murder? Or maybe he'd simply taken off the chain in the hotel room and put it in a drawer before being killed? Did Pornthip take it when she disappeared? If so, why? Where was it now? Where was *she* now? Questions for Lacont.

Lacont — Carrick's headache came back at the thought of the dour Inspecteur.

Jacobson finished his short speech and the Brazilian Chairman of Judges, Francesco Ferreira ambled to the mic like he'd just stepped from the pages of a magazine shoot. Light blue suit, tieless, whiter-than-white shirt, sunglasses. Loose limbed, composed, casual. He smoothed his perfect hair, the gesture came across somewhere between thoughtful and vainglorious.

"Jonas was my sometime friend, sometime rival ... here at Cannes," Ferreira said quietly in his careful English. Short even phrases. His voice soothing as a breeze after Jacobson's harshness, the amplifiers carried it down from the chateau across the lawn over the crowd and out to sea. The whole gathering seemed to pause from their drinks and turn like a herd of antelope sensing something in the wind.

"Jonas was an adventurer, never afraid to try things."

He spoke simply, but as if each word was loaded. Carrick saw a girl mute her phone after taking Francesco's photo with it.

"I think that's what the advertising industry needs more of today. That's what the world needs. More adventurers, not fewer. There is too much formula today," he said in sad pronouncement.

Carrick marvelled how these people sounded like they were pitching all the time, even when supposedly paying tribute to others.

"Jonas was not interested in the ordinary, everyday people and everyday things, but he understood them. He understood what was behind their daily impulses. And he appealed to that ... to that ... primal part of us in his ideas. That unfettered emotional part of our ancient lizard brains."

Ferreira lowered his head, drenched every gesture with meaning. His particular brand of charisma. He mentioned a few of Jonas's campaigns, the crowd nodding in acknowledgement, though Carrick couldn't recall any of them. For all his satin cool, Ferreira's speech rambled without real direction, it was his studied seriousness more than the actual content that made people listen.

"I've been wondering what Jonas might have achieved if he hadn't been in the advertising industry? I'm sure he would have left his mark. He would have made an excellent criminal mastermind," the mourners laughed, "Perhaps we should be grateful Jonas did not enter politics?"

Chapter 7.

Francesco Ferreira seemed a silky fake to Carrick, but he had them in his thrall.

"I'd like to propose a toast ... if you could raise your glasses to Jonas' memory and to the spirit of adventure."

Meanwhile, Eddie Schwarz had been discovered by a band of young acolytes eager for hints about the award winners. Carrick mimed a farewell to him and limped off through the shady cover of the big eucalypt, around the flank of the main group to the western side of the mini-chateau. He found the door to the kitchen where caterers were preparing to serve the next wave of canapés.

He decimated a tray of savouries and helped himself to another drink, swallowing another painkiller in the same mouthful.

The speeches were pleasantly muffled inside the house as he wandered down the central hall passed the formal dining room through to a huge, two-level L-shaped lounge area. Apart from a life-sized suit of medieval armour standing like a sentinel against the far wall, there was barely any furniture. Three small stairs led down into a square sunken pool of crimson shag-pile carpet edged with super-sized yellow cushions, a stone fireplace at the far end. It suggested an adult playpen.

Propped into one of the levered windows overlooking the terrace and garden was Benny Sewell's digital camera recording the speeches from behind the speakers. A cunning point of view, Carrick realised, the audience was facing the camera so the delegates would be able to look for themselves in the crowd when the footage was uploaded to Benny's *InCreative* website.

Slumped inelegantly on a big yellow cushion in the sunken playpen was Benny himself, talking to a broad-faced man with a South African accent.

"Andy. You didn't bring that wild woman back here, did you?"

"She's at a safe distance by now, Benny. Hello, I'm Andy Carrick," gingerly he made his way down the steps and gave a business card to the man, figuring if Benny was spending time alone with him he must be someone important.

"Vince Delahunty," firm handshake, congenial smile.

Chapter 7.

"Glad to meet you. You're the judge from South Africa?"

"Guilty."

"I'm investigating Jonas Shackleton's death, Mr. Delahunty. I've spoken to your fellow judges briefly; I wonder if I could ask you a few questions too?"

"I know who you are, the others told me about you. You threatened to stop us leaving the country if we didn't cooperate with your investigation. Then you said one of us could be next on the list to be killed."

"Is that true?" said BS, sounding thrilled.

Carrick didn't want to risk becoming the subject of the next *InCreative* blog, "Benny, you might like to excuse us? Everything from the moment I walked in here is confidential. Understand? Off-limits. This is an official investigation." Then to the South African, "I don't think there's actually much chance of either of those things happening, Mr. Delahunty, I was only trying to get everybody's attention."

"I've got as much right to be here as you. I'm investigating too," Benny stood his ground.

"You're trying to find out who won the damn awards and I'm trying to find a killer on the loose. Now, please, before your camera has another trip through the air and out that window."

"Don't worry about Benny, I wouldn't let him probe me about who won the awards," said Delahunty, neutralising the bickering, "In fact we were just talking about your suspicions regarding the Qi project."

"Really? What do you think?"

"Well, I guess it's an interesting theory."

BS nodded, "If you're right about the murder being done to influence the pitch it'll be a big story, if you can prove it."

"Ah, self-interest to the rescue."

"Could even be a book in it," BS grinned.

"Not a word about this conversation, Benny." Carrick pointed a crooked forefinger at him. Turning to Delahunty, "Do you think there could be something to the theory about the Qi pitch?"

"Well, frankly, I can't see it. There's big money at stake, sure, but murder? I suppose a scandal at an agency could influence the client. But the demise of a creative guy? Anyway, you're in the right place, quite a few of the top people involved in the pitch are here..."

"Like Tad Jacobson?"

"He's one. Boss of the biggest agency communications group in the world, Unicom. Not that I'd suspect him of anything but crimes against good advertising, don't misunderstand me." A throaty chuckle, the usual creative guy's jibe against suits.

"Who else is here from the top of the big networks?"

"Tony Maine's was here but he left on Sunday."

"Who does Francesco Ferreira work for?"

"Francesco? The controlling share of his agency is owned, ultimately, by the Cloud Group network. Gregory Cook is Cloud's worldwide CEO. He's here, I saw him earlier."

"Is Francesco involved in the Qi pitch as part of the Cloud network? "

"Doubt that. Francesco's too important to Brazil to get him involved in Asia, I'm sure."

Outside the chateau, the amplified voices had been replaced by the sound of a New Orleans-style funeral band marching around the pool.

"The speeches are over. Come outside and I'll introduce you to a few people if you like. I'll have to get back to the judging soon."

They stood up awkwardly from the yellow cushions, Carrick stiffly, "I'd just like to ask you something about the lunch," he said to Delahunty as they climbed the three stairs out of the crimson play pit, "Did you notice a gold chain and amulet Shackleton was wearing around his neck?"

"Amulet? Can't say I did. Why?"

"Yeah, why?" said BS, instincts twitching.

"Anyone take photos at the lunch?"

"It was a no-press event."

Carrick looked at BS, "You were outside, weren't you, I don't suppose you have a photo of Shackleton from the day of the murder?"

"There's a giant banner just outside on the terrace if you look closely."

"I want one from the day he was killed, I want to have a look at what he was wearing around his neck."

"Why?"

"Because he was wearing it at the lunch but not later when the police examined the body."

BS scratched at his straw head, "I interviewed him at Nice airport the morning he arrived, is that footage recent enough?"

"You could be useful after all, Benny."

"Hey, you guys looking at porn?" Nick Bailey wandered in from the garden, he still hadn't shaved despite being at a wake, still hadn't tucked in his shirt. His pants and coat matched, both had stains.

Delahunty, BS and Carrick were peering at the small playback screen on BS's digital camera. BS had searched back into the memory to find his interview with Shackleton at the airport and there it was in the first frames: an amulet around the man's big neck. They were in the process of trying to enlarge the freeze frame for a closer look.

"Just looking for the barf-room," Bailey sniffed, "Whatcha doing?"

Carrick was in no mood for his louche version of charm, "Go powder your nose, Nick, leave us be."

"Hey, that Jonas?" he pushed BS to one side to get a view of the screen, "Oh, Nice airport, innit? Why are we looking at this?"

Then he noticed Vince Delahunty, you could see dollar signs spinning in his eyes like a cartoon character, "Hey, Vince Delahunty. Glad to meet you, I'm Nick Bailey," he reached across to shake his hand, "I've done some work for your office in Hong Kong — Ossie-Cossie swimwear. I'm a freelance team, me and Liang Weh."

Carrick cut in, "Nick, please. Schmooze elsewhere or I'll put a crimp in that snorter of yours."

He ignored this and said to Delahunty, "Hey, was the judging a blast this year? Did you vote for Ossie-Cossie?"

Carrick straightened up and looked at him hard.

"Nick, he means it, mate," said BS, "He used to be special bloody forces. Leave us alone. We're doing some investigative work here."

"Really? Cool, cool, whatever, keep your shirt on," he winked, "Special forces, eh — explains the tatts."

Bailey sloped off a little way, walking around the lounge like he was inspecting real estate. He noticed the lurid sunken area and fireplace, "Hey, BS, great place to bring chicks."

BS zoomed into the image of the amulet on the camera's little screen. Delahunty squinted, angled his head, "Looks kind of like a..."

"Hey, this thing's a fake," said Bailey interrupting from the safety of the other side of the room, examining the life-size set of armour against the wall.

"Yeah," said BS, "everything here is fake, the whole place is about as solid as a film set, all cladding and plaster. It's only about ten years old, it's just made to look stately and aged. The marble portico is plaster of Paris. The gargoyles are polystyrene. It's really just a party house for his stable of *artistes*."

"Whose artists?" Bailey asked.

"He calls them *artistes*. Bobby Best. The Bristol music producer, you know, Hot Machine Music?" said BS, "This is like his holiday house where he puts the bands up when they're writing or resting or whatever. It's seen a few parties, I bet. If these paper thin walls could talk..."

Bailey banged his knuckles into a wall, "See what you mean. Bobby Best, eh? Cool."

"It was the only villa that we could get on short notice for the wake. Everything else is rented out by the agencies and production companies for accommodation."

Bailey started down the steps of the sunken lounge to look at the fireplace, "Is Bobby Best here today? Love to meet him. Hate his music though, white soul shite."

"T'aint what you do, it's the way that you do it," chanted BS, tunelessly; one of Bobby Best's sexed-up retro hits.

"Hey, Andy, bad news about Jamie Tan, eh?" said Bailey.

Until that moment Carrick had been trying to remember where he'd seen the design on the Shackelton's amulet before, it seemed somehow familiar. The freeze frame was so pixelated it was hard to be sure. He looked up, "What about Jamie Tan?"

"Apparently he's been in a coma for two weeks."

"Coma?"

"Overdose."

"Jamie Tan," said BS, "I know that name, don't I?"

"Jamie Tanyapongpruch," said Bailey, "Used to be an art director in Bangkok, worked for Jonas. Did that Martini campaign, you know, the magazine ads that picked up a Bronze Lion a few years ago? Remember? He repainted glasses into the hands of the figures in those famous pantings, Rembrandts, Picassos, all the old masters."

"Picasso's not an old master," said Delahunty, "He was a Cubist."

"Yeah, right, Cubist," said Bailey, "Like Che Guevara."

BS snorted.

"Tell me more about Jamie Tan?" Carrick asked, trying to keep the conversation on track.

"Dunno any more, I'm sure Sammi Walton knows all about it. Where is she? I saw you with her earlier..."

"She left in a hurry."

"Spoiled brat," muttered Benny, still sore, "Her father should have spanked her more often."

Carrick turned to BS, "Can you email this freeze frame image to me? Or should I just take the memory card?"

"No, no. I'll do it now. Where do I send it?"

He gave him an email address while Bailey moved furtively down the hall looking for a bathroom.

As Delahunty led Carrick outside to introduce some of the network bigwigs, he warned, "They won't say too much in front of me. Best you make a time to meet each of them separately, away from here."

In his peripheral vision, Carrick saw BS quietly join Bailey in the bathroom.

Outside, the wake had crossed the line and turned into a party,

143

the crowd had broken into small boisterous groups with the volume of chat and laughter competing with the band. Without Delahunty's god-like status as a Cannes judge getting through the tight rings of disciples surrounding the head honchos would have been impossible.

Mostly, the executives were politely baffled by questions about Shackleton and the Qi business.

Gregory Cook from Francesco's Cloud Network, holding court beside the laughing fountain, was outright derisive, "I heard about you from one of my creative guys," he chuckled, "I said you must've seen a re-run of *Who's Killing the Great Chefs of Europe?* and got the industries confused. I didn't think you were for real?"

Carrick kept it short, made times to meet later in the week.

After an hour and a half of shaking hands and being polite, the bang to the back of his head and the ache in his hip were winning the battle with the painkillers and the free alcohol. The waiters had started to avoid him.

Eventually he limped down the tree-lined drive to the chateau's gatehouse wondering about Shackleton's amulet and humming a song BS had intoned earlier, *T'aint what you do, it's the way that you do it ...*

He had a clue now, maybe he was going to get somewhere after all?

Back on the street he checked both directions for a red Renault or similar. The coast was clear. The thought occurred that if someone *was* trying to kill him, perhaps he might be closer than he realised?

CHAPTER 8.

Tuesday morning, 9am. Early for his appointment with Sammi Walton. A military habit.

Carrick strolled the Quai Saint-Pierre and appraised the yachts at their extravagantly priced moorings, beautiful things, like a row of thoroughbreds.

She had the same air. Lean muscled and athletic. Skittish. He wasn't totally sure if he was still invited to spend the day on her company's yacht, she hadn't called to cancel but who could tell with these people? They lie for a living, they lied for amusement in eulogy speeches.

The general incredulity he'd encountered everywhere regarding a connection between Shackleton's murder and the Qi business pitch might be another instinctive lie, but the uniform response from the executives yesterday had made Carrick worry. Yet Tony Maine was certain enough to put money on it.

Work the angles, the Major used to say.

Well, Sammi Walton might be the tangential approach he needed.

First he wanted to ask her about Jamie Tan. A man in a coma according to Bailey (but who could believe him?). Tan was clearly a close associate of Shackleton's, following him from advertising into the girlie club. Or was he just another creative person being used and used up by Shackleton? Was Tan the creator of the incredible artwork in the folio in the Carlton hotel suite? If so, what significance did that have?

Then of course there was the missing amulet. Why was Shackleton showing it off to Choi? There was something quite familiar about it to Carrick, teasing at the edge of his memory, like it was a famous antique glimpsed once upon a time in a magazine. Maybe Shackleton wore it when he worked with Sammi in Bangkok? She might know if it was valuable?

Carrick smiled to himself. At least if he accidentally managed to light her short fuse today Sammi wouldn't stalk off. Not without a lifeboat.

No sign of her yet so he bought a small bunch of flowers and a copy of the *Riviera Times* from the news kiosk, the local English-language paper, and turned to the back pages for the football results.

Half the people on the street were wearing Lions lanyards. Not far away a pretty girl was handing out leaflets to delegates for discounted speedboat joyrides. A one-man band marched past playing a tin whistle, ukulele, cymbals and a bass drum. Two gendarmes watched the crowd, probably to deter pickpockets.

Carrick wondered if any of the milling crowd were also guests on Sammi's yacht. None looked self-important enough. He watched as the two gendarmes spoke to the driver of a police car parked on the double lines behind a street vendor's portable stall. The three of them were consulting a piece of paper and talking rapidly.

He checked his watch. He'd wait until ten past then ring her.

When he looked up again the two gendarmes were advancing briskly on him, the taller one called out, "Monsieur Andrew Carrick?"

"*C'est moi.* Can I help?"

The second gendarme grasped him by the arms without breaking stride. The first one consulted the picture on the piece of paper and Carrick saw it was a grainy blow up of his own driver's license photo.

The policeman said again, "You are Andrew Carrick?"

"Yes."

"*Dépeche-toi.* Come with us, please, monsieur. *Immédiatement.*"

The tall gendarme was older, he'd lifted people off the street before, his movements were sure and economical. The younger one thrust his chin forwards, a little tense, expecting trouble, readying himself.

"What's this? *C'est a propos de quoi*?"

They steered Carrick roughly to the unmarked car and bundled him inside. His newspaper and bunch of flowers fell into the gutter. The driver nosed out into the traffic and then put the siren on.

"If this is about the parking fines," Carrick said, "Inspecteur Lacont promised he'd look after it for me."

The mention of Lacont's name drew nothing but Gallic indifference. "Where are we going? Policeman's picnic?" he turned to the younger one next to him, "You've been at the garlic snails already haven't you?"

Silence.

"Look, if I'm being arrested I'd like to know what for? If I'm being kidnapped I want to know the ransom? Answer me, *réponds- moi.*"

The tall one finally spoke, "We are going to the Commissariat, monsieur."

"Why? *Pourquoi? J'ai besoin de savoir pourquoi?*"

The answer was more indifference.

Inside the station's interview room the air was oily with old sweat and the smell of strangers' fear, the walls bilious green, no windows, space only for a small table and one chair either side. A CCTV camera stared down from the ceiling.

Nothing happened for thirty-five minutes. Standard procedure, worry and anticipation have overcome as many people as coercion.

Carrick wasn't worried about an interrogation, but ever since Afghanistan he hated small rooms.

When Detective Inspecteur Lacont finally opened the door his air wasn't good either, his demeanour even colder than the day at La Colombe d'Or. His 2IC, Rolande, came in after him and stood by the entrance. The room was full now.

"*Bonjour*, Inspecteur, I'm glad you could drop by, I've been missing civilised company."

"Monsieur Carrique," Lacont sat down and opened his file, "We must start all over as you lied to me last time we spoke. Something I do not appreciate."

"Look, I'm happy to clear up ..."

"Where were you last Friday afternoon, monsieur?"

Carrick was surprised. Last Friday? The day Shackleton was killed, surely Lacont wasn't implicating him in that?

"At my cottage in Bonnieux."

Seemed a thousand years ago already.

"You don't work for Lloyd's," Lacont said plainly, not a question.

"Why am I here, Inspecteur? I've committed no crime."

"Monsieur, you are not what you say you are..."

"That applies to half the population of the Côte d'Azur."

"I am looking for a murderer, Mr. Carrique, it is possible you may even be who I am looking for."

"That's ridiculous."

"Is it? You appear in Cannes directly after the murder of Jonas Shackleton, going straight to the scene of the crime, returning to it perhaps? Posing as an insurance investigator, lying to the police. You've intimidated witnesses. A key witness flees the country because of your threats. You ignore the police barrier at Shackleton's other hotel room at the Carlton where the duty manager informs me that you interfered with evidence."

Lacont didn't mention bribing the duty manager, the treacherous bastard must have kept quiet about the four hundred euros Carrick gave him.

"Perrot informed on me?"

"I've more than enough to charge you for hampering a police investigation."

"Not guilty, Inspecteur. *Non coupable.* The truth is I am investigating Shackleton's murder, OK, it's not for Lloyd's, I admit. That wasn't true. I'm working for a private party. But I've broken no law," Carrick looked around the dismal room, "Other than Murphy's."

Lacont interlaced his fingers and placed them on the table, a man with time and patience.

"Your whereabouts last Friday, monsieur?"

Three times over Carrick explained the phone call from Tony Maine on Friday night and the long briefing at Emma's, Maine's suspicions that the murder was an attempt at sabotaging the multi-million-euro Qi business pitch in China, the plan of posing as an insurance investigator for a quick *entré* into the elite judges' circle, the fake business cards to help facilitate the meetings. He told Lacont about the security firm in London and his background in the military.

Carrick admitted that he might have gone too far in terms of alarming the judges but said his intention to use mild shock tactics to get their attention was a harmless advertising technique, nothing more. He repeated Tony's words to explain the strategy, *Shake their tree and see which of the blasé bastards wobble.*

"And have you found evidence of a link between Monsieur Shackleton's death and this Chinese business project?" asked Lacont.

The answer had to be no, "Not so far."

But Maine predicted no one would be forthcoming without pressure. Sincerity is the first thing they fake, he'd said, otherwise they wouldn't be where they are. Carrick trusted Maine's unblinking certainty. It was what made Maine successful, what made him compulsive, Carrick had seen its powerful effect on the audience at the Palais debate on Sunday.

But how to convey this to Lacont in a stinking little interview room? Carrick needed a little of Maine's charisma himself.

The policeman was not well pleased, but Carrick's answers were direct and consistent.

After three quarters of an hour he tried going on the offense,

"Inspecteur, can I ask you some questions now that we've established this atmosphere of mutual trust?"

"Ask *me*? What kind of questions?" Lacont looked just shy of scandalised.

"Getting anywhere finding Pornthip Sinn?"

Lacont paused a full five seconds.

"She is missing still," he replied cautiously.

"What about fingerprints on the murder weapon?"

"What do you think about fingerprints on the murder weapon?"

"I'm guessing wiped clean."

Lacont said nothing.

"Has it occurred to you that Pornthip might be another victim, not a perpetrator?"

"You have a theory Monsieur?"

"She doesn't strike me as the murdering type, that's all."

"You know her?"

"No."

"You know the murdering type?"

"She sounds like an ordinary, nice girl."

"In affairs of the heart, ordinary people sometimes do extraordinary things."

Carrick asked something else that had been on his mind, "By the way, how did you know where to find me this morning?"

"We have been watching the airport, trains, ferries, looking for you since Eugene Choi left town."

"Sammi Walton didn't tip you off?"

Carrick disapproved of naming names, but his need was greater than hers at the moment. He knew that Lacont had interviewed Benny Sewell about him, and clearly some of the judges as well as Perott the Carlton's Duty Manager, it was possible the police had interviewed Sammi too, and equally possible she'd disclosed where he'd be.

"Sammi Walton...?" Lacont wrote down the name on his pad, "Who is that?"

So Lacont hadn't heard of her.

"She's just one of the Lions' delegate, from New York, she helped when I was hit by a car yesterday morning."

Carrick decided to keep quiet about her connection to Shackleton.

"What do you mean?"

"What's the word? *Écraser*? Hit and run."

"Hit and run? An accident?"

"Deliberate."

Lacont sat back in his chair trying to appraise him.

"I didn't get its licence. Red car, small Renault perhaps."

"You are saying someone tried to kill you? This Sammi Walton is a witness? Where will I find her?"

"On a yacht called Aphrodite, anchored in the bay. But it won't do much good speaking to her, no one actually saw anything. That kind of driving doesn't raise an eyebrow with the locals. Besides, Sammi didn't arrive until they were carrying me into the bar. She simply stopped to see if I was OK."

"Did you report this incident to the Sûreté?"

"No, I had other appointments. I spent yesterday afternoon at Shackleton's wake."

"Wake? You went to a wake for Jonas Shackleton? Here in Cannes?"

"Most of Cannes attended. You should've been there, Inspecteur. Lovely canapés, fascinating eulogies."

Carrick decided to give Lacont some metaphorical flowers, as Tony Maine had done for him.

"Have you found Shackleton's car?"

"Car?"

"The white Mercedes convertible Shackleton rented from Avis at the Carlton."

"How do you know he rented a car?"

"How do you not know, Inspecteur?" he couldn't resist the taunt.

Carrick dictated the license plate and model while Lacont stared at him like he was hypnotising a cobra, then he flicked a spiky look at Rolande at the door.

"I shall make some enquiries about these cars, both the Mercedes and the red one you say hit you. Meanwhile we will transfer you to the Commissariat Centrale in Grasse," Lacont was matter of fact, "They have more holding cells there."

"Am I under arrest?"

"We are simply questioning you, Mr. Carrique. But who knows, you may be under arrest by the time the questioning is done."

"We're finished," Carrick challenged, "You know I'm not a suspect."

"I don't know what I know about you except I don't trust you. I am ready to make more enquiries before resuming the questioning, Mr. Carrique. The law in France allows me to hold a suspect an initial seventy-two hours to do this. Would you like to make a phone call? Your Consular?"

Lacont stood up to leave.

"*De mal en pis,*" Carrick hissed, "Wait, I have more."

"Meaning...?"

A second metaphorical long-stemmed flower that, he hoped, might justify putting him back on the streets.

"When Shackleton was at lunch at La Colombe d'Or he was wearing a gold chain with an amulet around his neck. A kind of pendant about so big."

Lacont blinked for the first time. Carrick could see the inspecteur examining the body's details in his memory as he himself had done and knew his mental rewind would come up with the same answer, nothing around Shackleton's neck but a god-almighty slash. Lacont sat down.

"How do you know this?" he opened his file again.

"I've spoken to witnesses who noted it at the lunch. He was showing it to Eugene Choi. I've also seen a photo of Shackleton wearing it when he arrived in Cannes."

"A photo? Where is it?"

"Ah, that's my point exactly, Inspecteur, I don't have it."

This wasn't quite true of course, BS emailed him the jpeg and it was on his smart phone which had been taken away from him before the interview started. But Carrick did not want to be detained in a small cell for any money, even what Tony was paying him.

"I can't do my job sitting here. But I can help you do your job if you'll let me go about my business ..."

"You think this amulet has to do with the killing?"

"You said there was no evidence of anything being taken from the Shackleton's room, well, there's some evidence for you. Leading one to assume that the murderer took it with him."

"Or with her. Get me this photo."

"Deal. Let me go. Let me close a couple of loops then I'll give you the picture of Shackleton wearing the amulet and everything else I've got so far, OK?"

"What else have you got?"

"I've got ... some ideas."

"I'll give you two hours."

"Give me twenty-four."

Lacont gave him the death-stare again.

"Be here at twelve midday tomorrow," he said eventually, "But be very careful, Mr. Carrique, keep away from the frontier and the airports. Be punctual or be prepared for a problem."

"Let's keep things civilized, Inspecteur, meet me at the Carlton instead, in the lobby bar. I hate small rooms. And no uniforms, you won't need the muscle. I need to feel safe if I'm going to share."

Detective Inspecteur Lacont had already used up his best stares, so he had to repeat one of them.

"I must warn you, Carrique, you are former soldier by your own admission, you are skilled, a trained killer. While you are in France I am legally entitled to treat your person as a deadly weapon, even if you are unarmed. I will instruct my men to shoot you if you resist any lawful instructions."

Five minutes later, outside the Commissariat, even the blue diesel fumes smudged along the narrow street by a passing lorry smelled sweet.

Carrick took a deep breath of freedom.

~

You've missed the boat, loser.

A text from Sammi sent at 9.32. So she had turned up and, no doubt, thought she'd been stood up. Terse, but fair. Before ringing to apologise, Carrick decided to make some rather more urgent calls.

First he wanted to call the cavalry, Tony Maine.

No answer. Just a perky-sounding assistant with a Sloane accent on a recorded message. He left a message of his own saying that he needed a contact number for a lawyer in case things went badly with Lacont tomorrow.

If Maine was in a client presentation or on a plane to China it could take all day to get in contact, so Carrick went to Plan B — Didier Luc, he would know where to find a local *défenseur*.

Didier's phone rang forever, then finally, "*Salut!*"

Carrick could hardly hear over the white noise in the background.

"Didier?"

"*Allo? Qui parle?*"

"Didi, it's Andy."

"Andy! How are you, *mon ami*? *Tres longtemps.*"

Carrick stepped into a doorway recess and took shelter from the din of the traffic. "Where are you, it's a terrible line?"

"I'm away on a job. On the client's yacht at the moment having a look at the building site from the sea. It's fantastic. Hang on I'll jump in the cabin. Can you hear me now?"

"A little better."

Carrick noticed a man who had been pacing him on the opposite side of the street suddenly stop and take an interest in the window of a dog grooming business.

"How are you, shipmate?"

"I'm having an adventure here in Cannes. Trying to stay out of gaol."

"Nothing's changed."

"I mean literally. The police threatened to hold me for

seventy-two hours."

"What?"

"I'm OK at the moment, but I might need a local lawyer to support me until Tony sends in a heavyweight."

"Andy," Didier was suddenly serious, "What did you do?"

"I've been asking too many questions about Shackleton's murder. The local police wants to think that I'm involved in it."

"*Doucement*, Andy, slow down! Murder?"

"Yes, Shackleton's murder, last week."

"Who's Shackleton?"

"He's the guy Tony wanted me to investigate."

"Tony?"

"Surely Emma told you about it? We planned it all at your place last Friday?"

"My place? Tony who?"

"Tony Maine. He dropped in on his way to the Cannes awards festival and the three of us planned it all, my investigation, that is. Now I've stuck my nose in the local police aren't taking kindly to my presence."

"Is Tony Maine in France?"

"He was. In China now, I think. Doesn't matter. I'm doing this job for Tony but I've ended up being picked up by the constabulary."

"*Mince alors!*"

"Emma didn't mention anything about all this?"

"No, I'm afraid not. It sounds bizarre, Andy."

"It is. That's why I might need a lawyer."

"Look, don't worry, I'll do whatever I can to help."

"You must have noticed the dent we made in your supplies of Bandol?"

"No, I've been staying in Portofino, close to the site. Haven't been home since last Thursday."

"I'm afraid your cellar sustained severe damage."

"You're always welcome, you know that. Anyway, let me get a number and talk to someone for you. Don't worry, Andy."

Carrick gave him the details of his hotel in Juan-les-Pins with one part of his brain, while wondering with a more suspicious part of his cortex why Emma hadn't mentioned anything to her husband about last Friday, Tony or the investigation into what happened to Shackleton?

After ringing off, the walk from the police station in Avenue de Grasse back to the car park near the port took less than half an hour, but since the first five minutes Carrick was certain he was being tailed.

So Lacont didn't trust him; no news there. But he wouldn't stand for being followed, it was against his training and his self esteem. If he was going to get something better than vague hunches by tomorrow he needed time and elbowroom.

He wheeled the Defender east out of the car park and a dark blue Citroen immediately appeared behind him, a *voiture banalisée*, an unmarked police car. Just four vehicles back in the right hand lane. In the rear vision Carrick thought he recognized the silhouette of Deputy Rolande.

The traffic moved with a reptilian slowness. By the time he'd reached La Croisette it was laughable, so congested along the boulevard that they could have tailed him on foot and saved the fuel.

At Rue de Canada Carrick checked the mirror again.

Judging the traffic lights as they changed he made his move, banged his foot down on the accelerator, running the red light from the far lane and turning sharp left across the edge of the palm tree lined median strip into the traffic on the other side, the old Defender screaming on full lock. He hooked right again immediately into the short crescent driveway of the Carlton Hotel in a cacophony of rubber and abuse from the scattering pedestrians.

Ugly, noisy, but effective. Lacont's tail saw it all, but boxed in the traffic they were going to take a couple of minutes to catch up. Even just four car lengths back it was worth half a mile in ordinary traffic. The world's shortest car chase.

He braked hard under the small white portico and gave the valet twenty euros.

"Suite 613."

He used Shackleton's room number, and bolted through the revolving door into the lobby, steering quickly around the forest of marbled columns to the luxury retail area at the back of the ground floor, exiting into the side street under a yellow-striped eyelid awning across from Rue Rouaze.

Half a block of jogging later he was in Rue Pasteur at the desk of Triple A Car Rental spending more of Tony's expenses, signing for their standby express deal. A shiny BMW Série 4. Such a vehicle might be conspicuous in a lot of places, but not Cannes.

He hustled the convertible through the roundabout at the beginning of Avenue Maréchal Juin and this time saw no tail in the rear vision.

Cannes was claustrophobic, a party with too many people, Carrick desperately needed space to think. He took the A8, then the A7 to Cavaillon and left to the D99, not the most scenic route but the quickest.

At first, the relief was substantial; sharp Provençal sunshine, the rush of air, the Beamer's smooth progress.

Carrick knew the way, but his thoughts wouldn't go where he wanted. Instead the three-hour drive to St-Rémy went down a dangerous and familiar road, the well trodden tour of his self obsession and savage self reproach.

The vivid few days of activity and strange people in Cannes, the mind games, the straining against Lacont, it was all so suddenly different from the mute weeks that had slipped into months in the Bonnieux cottage; talking to no-one, drinking enough to fill an early grave, trying to tidy his life but instead thinking in circles, staring at a face above the bathroom sink that he hardly recognized.

Carrick had come to France to shake off the past, his personal history was too messy, a life of loose ends with a nostalgia for an ill-defined future.

He'd taken the cottage in the hope a quiet place might lead to a quiet mind, a new version of himself. But the quiet let in all the noise that London held back. The sunny Provençal skies pressed down on him, made him a round-shouldered downward staring figure that the locals avoided, a man grappling with some unspoken pain, some self-imposed problem shadowing him.

Constantly at odds with himself, Carrick's internal dialogue was usually angry. Which of the voices in his head should he listen to? The reasonable? The agonized? The mocking? Was there a reasonable one or just a tone that imitated reason, that faked calm?

I should have bought a dog, he'd said to Jacko during one of his infrequent phone calls to the office.

The murder had been a lifeline.

He was grateful to Tony Maine, or should it be to Jonas Shackleton?

Without knowing it they'd given Carrick something he was greatly missing: a sense of being part of something larger than himself.

He'd lost meaning when he quit the regiment, he knew that. Problem was it hadn't been replaced with anything that meant anything. A cog in a wheel has momentum, a reason to be, a cog without impulse is a hollow thing. He needed the whirring and the adrenaline and the momentum. Freedom was a burden, not being part of something big or real was heavy work.

Tony's mission was something, it was real, a murder was real. He didn't care much for Shackleton, but Pornthip's fate was real. Something big was afoot and Carrick was looking for answers that mattered.

The Major's security business had been something once, when the Major was at the helm. A man to admire, a fully formed man, real as the whole world. He was worth serving in himself. Carrick would have died for him. But after the fatal hit and run the heart had dropped out of the thing. The Major's wife had died a decade earlier from cancer, his only son had been killed in North Africa, so the Major gave the business to Carrick in his will and he'd had to become the businessman.

Chapter 8.

But he didn't know what to do with a secretary, he despised dealing with the accountants, was bored by meetings, didn't enjoy making connections and manoeuvring through relationships. Carrick functioned well as a deputy sheriff but he was no Matt Dillon.

The clients soon made it clear they missed the Major too, his parade ground perfectionism, his poised shrewdness, his steady hand.

The powerful private defence contractors who shared their ever increasing volumes of government work with the Major's company began to drift away apologetically. The specialized services and big security advisory projects, the risk assessment and tactical training assignments began to be replaced by mundane operations, physical security jobs, protective assistance.

The puffy-eyed stranger in the Major's seat in the boardroom was no leader. He was a blunt instrument, a component, a wind-up lion, an automata with gears and springs that could be cranked up to serve a purpose, to amaze or frighten, but he wasn't a first mover.

When he looked back he saw a life riddled with bad responses, poor decisions, compromised pleasures. The wings had fallen from his shoulders and he remained a slug. During long hateful nights he remembered little but failures, misjudgements, mistakes, half-measures, withdrawals. In the midst of it all stood an undignified man, unwise, inadequate in the face of a quest as yet undiscovered. None of the Major's composure. A confused child half-grown into a false adult.

Which brought him back as always to Andy and Robyn, Robyn and Andy.

That could have been a larger thing worth being part of, something to serve, something to fill the hollow centre.

Could have been a family.

But family had always been an abstract concept to Carrick; a drunken mother, unknown father and an orphanage hadn't given him much experience.

He used to wonder if he looked like his father? Whose characteristics had he inherited, whose eyes, whose chin, who was to blame for his moodiness? Maybe he had some endearing mannerism the very mirror of an uncle or the same stubborn stamina as a stoic grand-mother? He'd never know. There were no photo albums, no postcards from family holidays, no birthday card messages, no hand-me-downs or yellowing letters.

Foster homes and reform schools followed the boys' home for the young Carrick, teenage years spent in truant backstreets, railway yards, his youth a coliseum. But gangs weren't family.

The regiment used the term sometimes, but he knew intuitively that it too was just another tribe. The joy of the special serviceman was a simple, brutal brotherhood, perhaps even a thing of beauty when all was done just right. Shared maleness builds a bond, tight-knit units proud of their discipline and teamwork. But it wasn't a family. Testosterone doesn't feed the soul it feeds the ego.

And it was ego that betrayed him.

He'd always known exactly what Dave 'bloody' Fergusen was and he'd been cocky enough to pity him. It was his own conceited delu-sion, an invisible unspoken thing, the cosmic conjoining of Andy and Robyn, Robyn and Andy, that was fucked. Carrick stopped believing in Andy and Robyn. He stopped believing in Andy.

Deceived in love, impotent in hate, the betrayed have trust stolen from them.

He didn't even blame Dave 'bloody' Fergusen, though he loathed him as only a traitorous ex-friend could be loathed. Sure, at first he wanted to kill him in a thousand ways, but everyone knows it's in the nature of a scorpion to sting.

No. It was Carrick himself most at fault, who overreached, no wonder the stranger in the mirror couldn't look him in the eye. He embarrassed himself.

He squeezed the steering wheel of the rental car with both hands until his knuckles bleached, as if he could strangle his circuitous thoughts into black oblivion.

∾

Chapter 8.

Self-pity requires full attention. The tedious need for a parking place momentarily brought Carrick back from his fugue.

He scanned the old streets of St-Rémy — tourist bars, boutiques, perfumeries, wine shops. And the Hotel de Sade. When he'd told Lacont at the Commissariat that he had 'some ideas' he really had nothing more than the vague shape of a memory. He knew he had seen Shackleton's pendant somewhere before.

Now he was searching for that blurred recollection at the Hotel de Sade, the birthplace of the Marquis of the same name — ironically, a character who might have had much in common with Jonas Shackleton.

The ancestral home of the de Sade family throws up a forbidding tower and high walls in the heart of St-Rémy, but these days the heavy Gothic buildings house the Musée Archéologique, a showcase for the 2nd century BC sculptures and artefacts excavated nearby. The objects are the remains of an ancient city, called Glanum, that pre-dated the Roman occupation of the area, its ruins lying south of the modern day town.

Carrick knew the basics from two previous visits, the first made by the young Andy and Robyn during their camping trip before they were married. They'd strolled hand in hand under the broken remnants of the triumphal arch along the grassy promenade, the stony ruins a contrast to the warm skinned girl, her shoulders turning golden in the sunlight. They dallied in some temple to a Celto-Ligurian goddess set around a healing spring, drinking Luberon wine from the bottle and sharing a breadstick, laughing at the strangeness of forgotten worlds, intoxicated with some unexpressed future of their own.

An older and sadder Andy and Robyn visited again just a few years later, after attending Didi and Emma's wedding, perhaps looking for that state of innocence but finding only broken remains, buried streets of white rubble cut through by dark afternoon shadows.

"Looks like the Americans bombed it," Carrick said, still with wire in his jaw and pins in his fingers, thinking of Afghanistan, sabotaging any hope of comforting memories.

Every conversation was prickly, there was no way out of this with words, their magnetism had reversed its polarity and they looked for reasons to push away from each other. Their marriage was failing in every room, the cold bedroom, the kitchen where he sat stubbornly sullen through meals, the lounge where the tv sat between them and talked to itself. He had tantrums, showed a contempt that was new to him then wished he could call back some last remark, but everything was full of trapdoors and an awkwardness that made him dislike himself more and more. She withstood his taunts, kept her head high, but at the time he couldn't see the good in her. She lost her playfulness, he lost his candour.

Hopeless love had become hopeless and they became unjoined; it was as if they were under instructions not to love each other anymore, not to concede the slightest moment. He only relaxed in the locker room atmosphere with squaddies or strangers after a drink or two, filling with self-disgust. He'd invested too much in emotion for the first time in his life, he told himself, and the repayments were gouging.

By the time they were in France for Didi and Emma's wedding ordinary conversation was impossible, tangents flared because of the most banal things and they became the glum married couple you see in suburban restaurants, bowed over their meals in dull silence. They'd thrown the key into the sea.

Now, here he was again. Back in St-Rémy.

Maine and Shackleton hadn't rescued him after all, it was just a new route into the abyss.

But he had no choice. Somewhere here, Carrick was sure, back when he was Andy and she was Robyn, Andy and Robyn, Robyn and Andy, somewhere here he'd seen the design on Shackleton's pendant.

He couldn't imagine how else he recognized it?

So he had to come, had to remember all this and endure the torture once more.

He was studying the permanent exhibits and the glass cabinets like a visiting schoolboy cramming for an exam, jaw grinding, rigid with determination, when he was approached by a smiling old man wearing a name tag: *Artifacts, Gabriel.*

Gabriel had worked with the exhibits for thirty-two years he said, "What you're looking at now was excavated in the 1920s, that's when the biggest finds of pottery, coins and jewellery were discovered."

"What relics is Glanum most famous for?" Carrick asked, searching for inspiration.

"The magnificent triumphal arch, still standing on the site," Gabriel said proudly, "the oldest in all France, a powerful ...."

Carrick shook his head, "No, I'm looking for something smaller, a kind of symbol," and told him that he had visited the site before and remembered a spring with some sort of holy water?

"Oh, yes, Glanum had a sacred spring. It fed into a renowned healing pool. When the Romans came Agrippa built a temple to the goddess of health. Valetudo was her name. It was health in the sense of vitality, you understand, a sort of fountain of youth, energy and renewal with the usual overtones of sexuality. Before the Romans, the spring was the centre of the cult of the Hammer God. Pilgrims would come to wash and purify themselves."

Gabriel chuckled nostalgically, as if he'd been there at the time to enjoy it, "Yes, he was a big celebrity in his day. There were over a hundred small shrines advertising the Hammer God around the healing-spring, some exquisitely carved, usually with the same distinctive motif."

"Motif? Can you show me?"

"They'd call it a logo these days," Gabriel leading the way to a different room, "There aren't many surviving, but in the ones we have you can see that he was portrayed with striking homogeneity," he tapped a glass cabinet of relics.

Carrick looked and recognized it immediately.

"See?" said Gabriel, "He was always depicted as a god of mature age, which is unusual. And always with a big moustache and a serene expression."

There it was.

A big-moustachioed pre-roman god.

The Hammer God.

"That's him," Carrick said in some wonder.

"Impressive fellow, isn't he? The most famous example of the logo is on a pendant around the neck of a statue of a young Roman in a toga, it was found in a narrow space between two geminated temples."

Gabriel pointed to a plinth. The statue was headless and armless, about two and a half feet high, the Hammer God's image clear on the pendant protruding from the marble folds of the toga.

"We think it was probably worn as a protective amulet to ward off evil spirits and the like. Wearing it around the neck meant that no one could attack him without incurring heavy judicial sanctions."

"Yet he lost his head," said Carrick, remembering also Shackleton's sliced neck. "How would I get an amulet like this?"

"Today? These come from the 2nd Century AD, my friend, they are priceless antiquities, you can't buy one. Our student archeologists are still occasionally excavating new finds, but mostly fragments, broken pottery and the like. Another might turn up, you never know, but I'm certain it won't be for sale."

"And none of the amulets have been stolen over the years?"

Gabriel eyed him warily, "No monsieur, not yet."

Carrick pulled out his cell phone and asked if he could photograph the item, Gabriel indicated the sign prohibiting such things and then pointed at the wall clock, "Excuse me, but closing time is approaching, monsieur."

Carrick bought a €7 catalogue in the gift shop and left.

Outside the Musée Archéologique he tempered his elation, wondered what he'd achieved? Didn't want to get ahead of himself. He'd answered one question but it begged others. How did Shackleton get hold of the big-moustachioed god? How did this help the investigation? What would Lacont make of it?

Not enough, Carrick suspected.

He looked again at his phone. No call back from Didier about a local lawyer. No call back from Tony Maine either. Not great backup.

"Friends like these," he muttered.

Even Sammi hadn't rung to abuse him for not meeting her at the old port this morning, but then again maybe she wasn't speaking to him.

His next thought was Emma.

Her art-supply shop in Boulevard Marceau was at the end of a block of cafés and galleries, a few minutes walk away. With luck she'd still be there and he could take her for a drink and a bite, he'd eaten nothing since half a croissant and an oversized cup of French coffee at breakfast.

Eaten nothing all day, that is, except his own liver in Lacont's small interview room.

Something felt not right with what Didier said on the phone. Why had Emma mentioned nothing of the Shackleton caper to him, Tony's visit or the long and liquid briefing they'd delivered over Didi's dining table?

When Carrick turned the corner from Rue Carnot he realised he should have phoned ahead.

Emma's shop was busy. A police car outside and two uniforms inside.

He backtracked down the laneway to the rented BMW.

It was after 9pm by the time he was back in Cannes, a fierce strip of lurid colour in the sky behind the city of yachts anchored in the bay. On the street the night was young and the festival delegates' favourite boulevard was boisterous, smelling of suntan lotion and hot food from the beach clubs and sticky ganja in the shadows.

Cannes was in full party mode.

He tried Sammi Walton's cell number. To his mild surprise she answered immediately.

"Hello, sailor," Carrick said.

"Ah, my man overboard."

"I'm afraid I was unavoidably detained this morning. Sorry I couldn't make it. Where are you, still on the yacht?"

"No, I'm on dry land."

"How was the party?"

"Oh, not as interesting as if you'd turned up..."

"I wasn't sure if the invitation stood after you deserted me at the wake."

"Deserted you? You fawn over that sewer rat so-called journalist, treat me like a little girl, depositing me with some adults... and now you have the..."

"Whoa there, if you're going to chew my head off at least let's have a drink to wash it down with? Give me a chance to apologise?"

"I'll want more than an apology, mister."

"Would champagne help?"

"Keep talking."

"Let's meet at the White Palms rooftop bar, you said it was your favourite?"

"Did I?"

"Let me make it up to you?" he said as warmly as he could, after what he'd seen in St-Rémy he more than ever wanted to talk to her about Jamie Tan, the master copyist.

"Oh you'll make it up to me don't worry about that, I always get my revenge."

"How about tonight? I think I'm getting somewhere with the investigation."

She paused long enough to be considering, "Alright, I can be there in one hour."

"Great, 10pm, it's a date."

"You better turn up this time or I'll bloody kill you." She hung up.

There was something anxious in her voice, he could feel it even through her rolling aggression. But before he could think about it his cell rang in his hand.

Benny Sewell.

"Andy, you in Cannes?"

"Yeah."

"Anywhere near the Martinez?" There were loud bar noises in the background, BS sounded lit up, a little ebullient as the Major used to call it. "Look, I'm having a chat here with someone who's got an interesting story about China."

"China? The Qi pitch, you mean?" Carrick said, trying to make the creative leap.

"You got it. Like to meet her?"

"The Martinez? I'm practically outside."

"You're about the only one, the whole of Cannes is inside. We're by the pool."

Five minutes later Carrick walked through the hotel's circular porch on the corner of Rue Latour Maubourg and a wall of white noise straight from Babel assaulted his ears, every language on earth being shouted over every other. The decorous timber-panelled bar was standing room only with a crowd showing all the restraint of cup final fans.

He shouldered a path through a plantation of advertising folk and colourful Cannes flotsam towards the folding doors that led to the pool area. A sequinned female impersonator squeezed passed holding a trombone case above her head, an albino giant in a tuxedo retrieved helium balloons from the ceiling for a group of giggling women who immediately let them go again. Even the leopard-skin mother/daughter whores were there. Carrick doggedly pressed on, one arm across his breast to hold onto his wallet.

At the far end of the pool area BS was standing unsteadily on a banana lounge, waving at him like a drowning man in a heaving swell, "Andy Carrick," he called hoarsely above the heads, "Come and meet an Australian."

"G'day, I'm Bec," she reached up from a deckchair and shook his hand, "Been an amazing day all round, and now I meet a private detective."

"Carrick — meet Bec Woods, one of the judges. From Australia," said BS needlessly.

Bec Woods was younger than most of the other judges, late twenties he figured, skinny as an empty sack. Her cheeks blotched with a ruddy glow that suggested a few rounds of drinks might have helped make her day amazing. Carrick mumbled that he wasn't a private investigator but an insurance investigator and gave her a business card.

Benny slipped into the crowd in the direction of the bar, his bobbing yellow head a cork in the sea of drinkers.

"BS is very excited about your investigation," said Bec Woods as Carrick perched on the edge of the banana lounge beside her.

"BS is excitable, full stop."

"Hang on, I'm gonna hiccup," she said, holding up a small palm, "No," she lowered her hand, "it changed its mind. Anyway, how's the investigation going? Do you always get your man?"

"It's coming along. Tell me, did you see much of Shackleton here in Cannes before he died?"

"No, the official lunch was the first time I've ever met him. First time I'd met most of the judges actually. See, I'm the token antipodean. They usually hook in one of us each year, an Aussie or a Kiwi. It's mostly a club for the big boys."

"What did you make of him?"

"Bit of an old perv, gotta watch his hands when he's behind you. But he had an aura, y'know? What can you say about a guru? Dirty mouth, but funny as." She laughed loosely, then added almost to herself, "Wish I had that kind of self-belief."

Carrick liked her, self-doubt was a stranger to the other judges he'd met.

"Did you talk to him?"

"Wish I had."

Benny returned with half a dozen beers jammed into an ice bucket. He must have caught the last part of the conversation, "You wanted a bloody job from him in New York, that's why you wanted to talk to him."

She punched him in the arm but almost toppled herself.

"Keep it down, you dork, someone'll hear you and get me fired when I get back to Sy'ney."

"I don't blame you, McGain & Rainer's rubbish anyway, you should get out of Oz."

"You think every agency's rubbish 'cept whoever you're interviewing this week."

"It's a living," said Benny, taking a swig, "Did you tell Andy about seeing the head-hunter yet?"

"They're called Human Resources Advisors," she corrected, then hiccupped at last, "Did I hiccup out loud then?"

"No," said Benny, "Tell him what the head-hunter said."

Bec Woods looked around to see if anyone was listening. They weren't, the whole world was talking at once.

She wiped her fringe back from her forehead, focused and said to Carrick in a low voice, "Between us, OK? I was talking to someone about a possible career move, to the next level. Logical, right? Now I'm an international judge and all? Anyway, she told me in passing about some rather scallywaggish behaviour happening around the Qi pitch."

At last someone had something on the Qi business. Carrick leaned into her beery breath.

"These are just stories, you unnerstand? May not be totally true, but Benny said you might be innerested. You mustn't sell a soul ... tell a soul ... someone might get in real trouble."

"Sure."

"Well, seems he went to China and set up a fake agency, for the day, just one day — for some initial meetings with the top Qi client executives. A complete fake agency in some empty office space! Tricky, eh?"

"A complete agency? I thought the pitch was still in its early phase?"

"'Xactly," she slurred, "But it wasn't a real agency, everyone in the building was a fake! All of them face jobs."

"Face jobs?"

"'Xactly," she said again, nodding.

"What's a face job?" Carrick's mind whirring in various directions.

"It's what the Chinese call it when you rent *gweilos* to populate your office. You know?"

"Rent *gweilos*?"

Chapter 8.

"Fake caucasian office workers, it makes you look rool successful. The Chinese clients think your company's doing rool well if you can afford to employ lots of *gweilos*, lots of white people running round in dark business suits, all pretending to be working on the brand already."

Fake advertising people? Why not? They already had fake ads, thought Carrick. The *Prince of the Scammers*.

"When did Jonas do this?"

"Jonas?"

"Shackleton. You said he went over to China to set up a fake agency?"

"No, no, it wasn't Jonas," interrupted BS, "It was the CEO, Tony Maine."

Bec Woods nodded again, "'S'right. If it gets out they'd probably be thrown off the pitch quick smart."

She drained her beer.

"There's more. Go on with the story, Bec," urged BS.

"Give a girl a chance, jeez. Gimme a coldie, will you? Anyway, what I heard was that apparently some local agency in Beijing — not anyone involved in the pitch, just a local shop — anyway, their CEO somehow got wind about Tony Maine's fake show."

"So you think they'll be thrown off the pitch?"

"Well, no, maybe not. Apparently, this guy rang Tony Maine, told him that he knew about the face jobs, fooling the client and all that. I reckon the bloke figured it might be worth squeezing Maine a little or something like that. Asking for a payoff maybe."

Putting the squeeze on Tony Maine? Carrick was intrigued.

"What did Maine say?"

"Said he'd ring the guy back in two hours with a proposal," Bec paused for effect and a sip.

BS chipped in, "Here's the best bit."

"You're not going to write any of this, BS, you promised," she pointed a chewed fingernail at his face.

"Don't worry, I wouldn't dare," he held up his hands in surrender, "More than my life's worth."

"Go on," prompted Carrick.

"Anyway, two hours later Maine calls him back, like he said he would. He tells the local agency CEO bloke to stand up. What? says the guy. Stand up, says Maine, stand up and walk around to your reception area. Why? says the guy. Maine says, put the phone down, stand up, walk around to your reception area, then come back and tell me what you saw. The CEO thinks he's crazy, but says OK. He goes down the hall and peers cautiously around the corner, I don't know, expecting to see a coupla heavies or something. But instead there's like a dozen people there, not client type people, y'know, more like people off the street. Just standing there or sitting on the reception chairs or on the floor looking crook, blowing their noses, coughing, just hanging around. He goes to the receptionist and asks who they all are? She doesn't know, says they all arrived together like some bus tour or something and told her they must wait. The CEO goes back to the phone and tells Maine that there's a bunch of people in reception. So what?

"Maine says, yes, and they're not leaving until you courier a personal cheque for five hunnerd thousand US to my bank in Shanghai. The CEO says why the fuck would I do that? Tony Maine says, it's my insurance. If I ever hear a word about the face jobs, from anyone, I'll cash that cheque. You following?" said Bec Woods.

"Think so."

"You can imagine, right? The guy's amazed. He was supposed to be squeezing Tony Maine and now Tony Maine wants a half mil from him? A personal cheque? Five hunnerd thousand? He laughs out loud down the phone at Maine. You're crazy, why would I do anything like that, he says? I don't care how long they stand in my goddamn reception area."

"You should, Tony Maine said to him, you should get them out of your offices and away from your staff as fast as possible."

"Why's that? he says.

"Because they all have the H5N1 virus..."

"...Bird flu," said BS.

CHAPTER 9.

Less than ten minutes to get to the roof bar to meet Sammi Walton, he didn't want to be a no show for the second time that day.

Bec Woods' story about Tony Maine rattled around in his mind, more advertising smoke and mirrors. Ironic the only story he'd got about Qi so far was about Tony Maine and not Jonas Shackleton. If it could be believed, that is, who could tell in this town, could be just bar room gossip?

At the top of the Hotel White Palms the elevator doors parted like curtains at the cinema and he saw her straight away, fiery auburn mane backlit from the spots at the edge of the terrace. Sammi looked like one of those strong-boned heroine's from a forties movie. All feisty glamour. There was a resemblance to someone that he couldn't quite place.

But she wasn't dressed like one of those elegant silk and satin stars, she wore a tight T-shirt with designer claw marks torn revealingly across the chest, her long legs poured into jeans and high-heeled leather boots, across her shoulder a black S&M inspired studs-and-spikes bag that looked more like a medieval weapon.

"Champagne, m'lady?"

She smiled at him, a thousand watts for a moment, "Campari and soda."

"Shall we sit at the bar?"

"Let's live dangerously."

"Got your sea legs back after your day on the briny?"

"Don't worry about me,' she said, "I'm well balanced."

The stools at the bar were close together and they sat knee to knee. The barman slid a half-empty bowl of nuts in front of them. Carrick still hadn't eaten anything and he eyed them hungrily.

"So what happened to you this morning, Mr. No-Show, what was it that saved you from my evil clutches?"

"I had an interview of sorts with the local constabulary."

"The cops?" She looked genuinely concerned.

"I was picked up at the quay while I was waiting for you. Didn't have much of a choice in the matter; for a while there I didn't think they were going to let me go."

"Wow," she said, "that's some excuse. You are trouble on a stick Andy Carrick. Cheers."

"*Á votre santé!*"

They clinked glasses.

"What happened next?"

"They asked me lots of questions."

"You give them any answers?"

"Not as many as they would have liked, I suspect."

"But you do have some answers?" she looked directly at him, he liked the way she was so earthy, unafraid.

"I might have something," he'd meant it to sound vague, but it came out like a tease.

She sipped her drink, "Well, you *are* a fast worker. You didn't seem to have a clue the other day."

Carrick shifted on his stool, his bruised leg stiffening in the cramped position,

"I was wondering about you and Jamie Tan?"

Her eyes snapped back to him, "Why on earth would you wonder about Jamie?"

"You're just good friends?"

"What? Me and Jamie? Oh, no, not like that. He's gay," she laughed, "Bailey and Liang carry on about how great his job is, painting naked girls, but a straight guy wouldn't be able to do it."

That laugh, there was something familiar about it somehow.

"You kept in touch when you left Bangkok?"

"Sure. We were mates, that's all. Jamie's a gentle soul. He was so really talented."

"Was?"

"Still is. But wasting himself painting stupid girls in a greasy club."

She was nettled again, Sammi had such instant, raw reactions, it made her exciting to be around.

"Why did Shackleton have Jamie Tan's portfolio of work here in Cannes?"

"Did he?"

"In his suite in the Carlton," he watched to see how this information went down.

"Well," she said slowly, "Jamie was probably hoping to get back into advertising. Do something worthwhile with his life ..." she lowered her eyes briefly, "He probably thought Shackleton was going to help him."

"How?"

"Oh, show his folio to other creative directors here, I suppose. Why should I know?"

"I just thought you would ..." Carrick swirled his drink, pausing for effect the way Lacont might, "... after all, Jamie's folio was air expressed to Shackleton on your company's account ..."

Her eyes opened wider, a micro expression passed across her face, "How do you know that?"

"I saw the delivery docket. Backroom Boys Productions paid... You."

She smiled a brief salesman's smile, no warmth in it.

"Well, OK, I was the Good Samaritan who paid on my company's account to ship Jamie's folio to Cannes. True. So what? No biggie. I encouraged Jamie to put his folio together. He wanted to send it to Jonas. That wasn't my idea, far from it. But then he changed his mind, lost the energy, wasn't going to do anything at all. He lost interest in everything when he was using heavily. I told him I'd pay to ship it, anything just to get him motivated. He asked Jonas and apparently he said, sure, send it over."

"You didn't mention he was in a coma after an overdose when I asked about him the other day."

"When?"

"When we were here last time, after Bailey and Liang left."

"Really? What did I say?"

"You said Jamie couldn't have killed Shackleton because he wasn't here in Cannes."

"So?"

"It's just funny you didn't say, 'Jamie couldn't have killed Shackleton because he's in a life-threatening coma.' That's a watertight alibi."

"You're a really intense guy, Mr. Carrick. Not sure if I remember saying any of that. You got witnesses? Anyway, I've had a lot on my mind this week, sorry if I missed that it was so pertinent to you a friend of mine is ill."

Maybe she was right. But it was hard working out what might or might not be important in this case, Carrick was treating everything as significant.

Then she sat upright suddenly, all bright-eyed enthusiasm, "Look, let's have a real drink," she called the barman over again, "Tequila?"

"Guess I'm game," he said, unenthusiastically.

This time they got a fresh bowl of peanuts.

"Disgusting things," Sammi said, pushing them out of reach, "So tell me, where exactly are you with this investigation?"

"Collecting dots, hoping to join them up."

"Such as?"

"When you worked with Shackleton in Bangkok did he ever wear a large amulet around his neck?"

"An amulet?"

"A largish pendant on a gold chain?"

"What about it?"

"Shackleton was wearing it when he went up to his room; and he wasn't when he was found by the police. I think the murderer has it."

She took all this in, shook her head, "Can't help you there."

They threw back the shots.

Funny thing about tequila, after the open-handed whack of the first one you're more prepared the second time round.

Then the third's nothing.

Soon they were all laughing insanely. Andy, Sammi and the six tequilas.

"Look. Only suckers pay for drinks in Cannes. The Brazilian delegates have set up a samba bar around the pool at the Majestic for the rest of the week," she said, "Open bar. Come on, it's five minutes away, we can dance. Dancing tells me a lot about a man."

How straight is she being, he wondered as they lurched down La Croisette in the moonlight? She was holding something back about Jamie. Was she even as drunk as she was making out?

"Sammi, it was only yesterday someone near the market ruined my dancing career with a speeding car."

There was a sign over the entrance —*The Samba/r* — it quoted Brazilian poet, Vinicius de Moraes: *Whisky is a man's best friend, a dog in a bottle.*

Everything was themed in yellow, green, white and blue, including a pair of impossibly leggy dancers in feathers and tassels who were shaking in front of giant tropical fruit sculptures. A DJ was keeping the Latin beat pulsing.

They grabbed a table beside the dance floor while Carrick wondered what he was doing on a Cannes pub crawl? He didn't know whether Sammi was trying to get him drunk to avoid questioning or if she was trying to take advantage of him. The fact that he saw the latter as a possibility was evidence, he decided, that he'd already had far too much to drink.

They finished a round of caipirinhas and Sammi ordered another while Carrick contemplated the Brazilian girls on the gaudy stage, "Love Rio," said Sammi, "Did a shoot there for GBY&B last year. Even Sao Paulo's OK, so long as you travel everywhere by helicopter, the streets are the pits."

"Never been," he admitted, "And I don't get around in helicopters much any more either. Apart from the other day. Saw some nice yachts in the bay, maybe even yours."

"How come you were in a helicopter?"

"I was with Tony Maine," Carrick bit his tongue, he hadn't really meant to mention him to Sammi. Last drink, he promised himself. Then he saw movement in the crowd, "Here comes Francesco Ferreira."

Hand outstretched and smiling a host's smile, Ferreira walked across the dance floor, the leggy dancers parting ways for him.

"The sleekest lizard in the lounge," Sammi said.

"Mr. Carrick ... Sammi Walton ... what a delightful couple you make. Welcome to our samba bar. A temporary piece of contemporary Brazil."

Carrick stood, shook hands, Ferreira kissed Sammi on both cheeks, "You're looking well, my dear."

Did her colour rise slightly?

"We were just on our way out," Sammi reached for her handbag.

Francesco ignored her and sat down.

"How's everything, Mr. Carrick? Is Sammi assisting you with your enquiries?"

Sammi sat back down like a delinquent pupil. A waiter had followed Francesco to the table.

"Have you tried our Caipiroska Negra — Black Russian vodka instead of *cachaça*? *Tres, graças*," he ordered without waiting for an answer, "You'll like it. So, are you here tonight for business or pleasure?"

"It's all business with Andy Carrick," said Sammi.

"Where do you two know each other from?" Carrick asked.

"Oh, we go back a long way," Francesco smiled privately at Sammi, reached over and squeezed her knee, grinning at her unease, "Don't we? Since you were just a little girl." He turned to Carrick, "Through her father. When we first met young Samantha was just learning to ride horses, weren't you?"

"Let's not go there, Francesco."

He smiled indulgently. She was oddly stiff.

"As you mention business, Francesco, could I ask you this? Do you recall an amulet Jonas Shackleton wore around his neck?"

"Amulet? What is that? *Amuleto*? Like an *encanter*? A charm?"

Carrick nodded. "He was showing it to Eugene Choi just before he went upstairs and got murdered."

The Brazilian's mouth turned downwards, he shook a perfectly groomed head, "I don't notice these things on men," he smiled as the three drinks arrived, "*Vivar*".

Carrick drank before remembering that he wasn't going to have any more, his stomach was signalling an intention of going its own way unless he called it a night soon.

He tried another question, throwing dots into the air and seeing if they came down in a connecting line, "Do you know Jamie Tan, Francesco?"

Another shake of the silver head, "Is he a suspect or something?"

Sammi sighed loudly, "Why would he know Jamie for god-sakes? Jamie's nobody, a real nobody. Francesco only deals in rock stars, Andy, you've got to be a total rock-star art director or copywriter to be on Francesco's radar. Unless you're the rock-star of restaurants he won't eat with you, you've got to be a rock-star architect to build his house, a rock-star bartender to mix his drink, a rock-star dentist to drill his perfect teeth. Jamie's just another hopeless hopeful with the wrong personality for success. People like Francesco wipe people like Jamie off the soles of their designer sneakers. Don't you darling?" She put an arm around Francesco's neck, he looked unperturbed by her outburst, mildly amused if anything, "That's life in the jungle, right? Bad guys make the girls wet and nice guys finish in a coma."

Both men looked at her in silence, Francesco perhaps pondering what he'd said to cause her to flare, Carrick noting again the rawness of her feelings regarding Jamie.

"I might just explode," she jumped up and loomed over them, laughing loudly, grabbing Francesco's hand, "Unless you dance with me like a rock-star."

He allowed himself to be led to the dance floor and took her in his arms. Francesco was a natural fluid dancer, Sammi was enthusiastic, she rolled her hips to the samba with relish.

Carrick watched as they spoke together, their faces close.

The waiter came back and he ordered a large mineral water.

Then he saw a new arrival, BS, surveying the crowd before coming in. He registered Carrick and loped over.

"What are you doing here? Drinking alone? Not a good sign. Thought you were meeting someone?"

"I'm with Francesco and Sammi," he indicated in their general direction, "They're dancing. At least, I think they are, everything's swimming around a little in my brain at the moment. Thanks again for introducing me to Bec Woods, by the way."

"God, those Aussies can drink beer," said BS with admiration, "'specially the sheilas." Benny sat down in Sammi's chair, "I should get back to my hotel, unless I'm in bed by two my liver can't get through the next day. Just thought I'd drop in here to see who was around."

"I admire how you keep up the pace, years of disciplined training, I suppose. Anyway, you better move before Sammi wants her chair back, you know how she gets."

He grunted, "Don't know what you see in her." He stayed put, crowd watching. "I've been thinking. Have you considered it was an inside job?"

"Meaning?"

"Instead of someone trying to nobble InterGroup, maybe someone inside InterGroup?"

"Such as who? Ray Doyle, do you mean? He doesn't seem the type, frankly."

"Maybe," said BS, "Or Tony Maine?"

"Why would Tony Maine want his own network's creative director killed?"

"Wrong man in the job, maybe?"

Carrick grunted this time, "Is he the type?"

"You heard Bec's story. He's a tough guy."

"Sounds a little far fetched."

"Richard Blake told me a chilling story about him once, you'd know Blakey, the photographer? Always at the Groucho Club?"

"I've heard his name."

"Blakey's no bullshitter, he's been around too long. He's dead straight. Anyway, he told me last year he was doing a job for Maine's agency, big campaign launch. Anyway, the client wants to meet the famous photographer he was paying for — you know, the way they do — and the client's office is in Birmingham, so Maine says to Blakey that he'll drive them both up in his brand new Bentley. Give it a run. Chauffeur, fully stocked drinks cabinet, lunch first. Blakey's says why not.

"Comes the day, they're late, lunch went too long or something. So Maine says to his driver push the pedal, move it along a bit up the motorway. Anyway, the driver cuts in on this lorry on the M1 while changing lanes, right? No-one thinks about it until a few minutes after when there's a hold up near the exit. The lorry catches up doesn't he, and you can imagine this with some of the crazies on our roads, the lorry guy pulls right across the road and starts edging the Bentley towards the service lane, bit by bit, into the shoulder of the bloody motorway towards the safety rails. The chauffeur's got to stop or the Bentley's going to get scratched and the truck parks right in front, blocking the way.

"Then, get this, a bloody great feller jumps down from the truck. Huge bloke, Blakey said, checkered shirt, big gut and beard, the lot. And ... he's got a gooseneck jemmy in his hand. He lumbers over and looks down at the Bentley. Blakey thinks they're all going to be dog meat in a minute or at the very least the guy will smash the windows and kick in the side of the car.

"'Bugger, bugger, bugger,' says Tony, 'we're already late.'

"The guy leans down and stares into the back window, he can't see much 'cos the windows are tinted. He raps the glass hard with his big fist. Bang, bang. 'Open up, yer tosser.' No-one does anything for a moment.

"Then Tony Maine presses the automatic window button and the tinted glass slides down with a little hum — vrrrrrr. The lorry guy puts his great head down to the window and sees Tony Maine in his suit and dark glasses in the backseat, all total calm. He opens his mouth to say something but Maine stops him with his finger, beckoning him closer.

"The big bloke leans forwards and Tony Maine, real slow, in a half-whisper, says just one simple sentence, 'Move the lorry, son, or I'll have you killed.'

"You know what Maine's like, that voice, he can coat you in honey or cover you in acid. Then Maine closes the automatic window on him — vrrrrrr.

"Blakey said there was so much menace in Maine's voice that he almost shat himself. So did the lorry guy apparently, he stood up straight with his jaw open down to here. He doesn't know what to think, poor bloke, right? He takes two steps back, then decides to scarper. He turns and, Blakey reckons, he literally ran back to the cabin of his truck, jumped in and pulled away, tyres spinning on the lorry up the emergency lane.

"'Fuck me, Tony, that was amazing,' says Blakey.

"'I wasn't kidding,' said Maine, cold as buggery.

"I'm telling you, Tony Maine is a tough guy."

❧

"To the Aphrodite," Sammi laughed loudly, one arm held aloft, finger pointing the way; then she was waving goodbye to Carrick over her shoulder as Francesco escorted her towards the hotel taxi rank, "Catch ya'll later."

BS came back from the bar with a fresh drink, the waiter service had dropped off since Francesco left the table, "She going?"

"Looks that way, back to her floating pleasure palace I guess."

Carrick watched her go with a strong sense of unfinished business, but he was out to it, exhausted by the day and her resistance. He'd learnt nothing from her other than that she didn't want to talk about Jamie Tan and could outmanoeuvre him with a few drinks.

"What pleasure palace?"

"Some yacht her company hired for their big party."

"What party? The Backroom Boys had a party? First I've heard of it, I thought they were all in Morocco shooting an Apple spot, apart from her." BS pulled a disgusted face.

"You can't be everywhere, Benny. Though you're making a good effort tonight."

"Is Francesco coming back or is he tucking her into her bunk?"

"Don't know. Francesco seems to be an old friend of the family."

"Think she's got a thing for older men, you better watch out," he laughed, "Tell you what, though, women throw themselves at that Francesco. He's like a TV celeb back in Brazil, the gossip magazine do profiles on him, people recognize him in the street."

"Lucky Francesco."

"He's a talented feller. You know a US telco client once hired him to write a campaign for them, gave him an unlimited budget to make a commercial ... know what he did?"

"What?"

"He exceeded it."

BS laughed at his own anecdote as if he'd never heard it before, Carrick peered at him through scratchy eyelids.

"You should have seen those girls in tight black dresses at the Palais looking at him backstage this morning when they were doing run-throughs for the speeches."

"Speeches?" Carrick said without interest.

"Francesco's making the Chairman of Judges report and handing out the gongs on the award night," BS explained, "I heard him rehearsing a bit of his speech and he's really going to give it to them."

"Who?"

"Everyone. The big agencies at Cannes, the UK, the Europeans in general, the Americans too. He's basically telling us that all our advertising should be much better, he says most agencies have let their clients' middle management run the show. He's probably right. That's why I'm offering a download of the *Best of Brazil* this year for our lucky *InCreative* subscribers."

"Great," Carrick wasn't listening and wondered why he was even pretending to.

"Mind you, I think he's pouring a bucket over everyone else's advertising because South America didn't win the Grand Prix this year."

"Who won?" Carrick asked without thinking or caring, he was too drunk to get out of his seat.

BS was still bright as a button. "Couldn't say for sure. All rumours at this stage, that's half the fun of Cannes, guessing what's true and what's not."

That's all I've been doing, guessing what's true and what's not, thought Carrick. For a start he was guessing the Chinese Qi Project was not the reason behind Shackleton's death. Tony Maine was wrong, he was clearly obsessed with Qi. Nor was Shackleton's Bangkok girlie bar the reason for his murder, Ray Doyle's instinct was wrong too. Carrick was also guessing that Shackleton wasn't the victim of a lover's tiff with Pornthip, Lacont was wrong. Carrick was convinced it was something to do with the missing amulet and some sort of fakery. Shackleton was *Prince of the Scammers*. He loved fakery.

Just then Francesco came back looking fresh as a chewing gum advertisement. Carrick was ragged, he'd half made up his mind to leave but as most of him was still sitting in the chair he decided to stay.

Stay and push things with Francesco.

"You're still here, Andy? Hello there, Francesco Ferreira," he shook Benny's hand in introduction.

"We've met before. I'm Benny Sewell from *InCreative*. Off duty now, though, after midnight."

"Want another Caipiroska Negra, Andy?"

"No, please, I'm on Perrier or I'll be on a stretcher."

"They're going to close up here shortly, I'm taking some friends to a club that's opening soon, it sounds interesting, not too far from here. You're welcome to join us?"

Did Carrick detect a small change in Francesco's demeanour, his green eyes watching more closely? What had Sammi been whispering to him on the dance floor?

"No, thanks. But before you go I wonder can I ask about something that's been bothering me, Francesco?"

"Surely," he perched on the edge of chair sensing a change in the temperature of Carrick's conversation.

"You said before you didn't remember Shackleton showing off his amulet to Choi during the lunch, yet I'm told you were seated right next to him? I don't get that. To show it to Choi, who was sitting across the luncheon table, Shackleton would have had to half stand ... half bend across the table ... like this," he mimicked the action and leant forward a little unsteadily until he was less than twelve inches from the Brazilian's face and getting closer, "Come on, Francesco, Shackleton was a pretty big guy, stretching himself across a formal dining table, talking enthusiastically, probably loudly ... With due respect, you were sitting next to him, you can't have not noticed!"

BS was agape at Carrick's sudden aggression, but Francesco waved his hand lightly, "Vaguely, I suppose, I saw something of the sort," a sad, sympathetic expression grew across his face, "You see, I didn't want to look." He sat back in his chair, recreating a more respectable distance between them, "My impression was that Jonas was trying to talk Choi into something, it didn't do him credit."

"What was he trying to talk Choi into?" said BS.

"I believe he may have wanted him to take something back to China after the Lions are finished, I'm not sure what, art, *pinturas* or some *antigos* like his *amuleto*. The whole thing sounded to me like, how do you say it in England, *brincadeira* ... a wind-up? You understand? A joke, he was entertaining himself, I imagine. That was what Jonas was like. As for Choi, he probably just admired the design and was being polite, it was all nothing."

"Did you see the design?"

"I took no notice, I kept my back turned. It was a trinket, *bugigangas.*"

"I think it's more than that," Carrick said.

"You think it's special, don't you? Worth a lot?" said BS, antennae extended.

"I think it must have been worth killing for."

Next morning Carrick cancelled all the meetings he'd arranged with the bigwig suits during Shackleton's wake, convinced the murder had nothing to do with the Qi project and a lot to do with art forgery and Jamie Tan's special skills. He needed the time to prepare his presentation to Lacont.

There was a dog-eared English-Speaking Yellow Pages in a drawer of his hotel room, he found a digital photo print shop to get the best enhancement of the photo of Glanum's Hammer God around Shackleton's neck.

There aren't many surviving, Gabriel said.

Then how was it Shackleton wore one?

With two and a half hours left before he was due to meet Lacont, Carrick went to the library.

The Cannes Municipal library is not a typical suburban library. Originally built by Baron de Rothschild as his home in Cannes' first millionaires precinct in the 1880s, the young Andy and Robyn had marvelled at it as tourists.

"The Baron wanted to show off his good taste, as much of it as possible," Robyn explained, "So he used all the best styles; a touch of Classical, dash of Palladian, a little Renaissance, with a pinch of Baroque stirred in."

This time Carrick's research took in only the Art and Antiquities wing. He made some printouts, a couple of photocopies, gathered everything together with the digital enlargement of Shackleton's pendant and put them all in a natty red folder he'd bought at the print shop.

Chapter 9.

Presentation aids under his arm, Carrick was ready to sell his big idea to Lacont.

He arrived fifteen minutes early at the Carlton and looked for the double-crossing Duty Manager, Perott, but was disappointed he was not on duty; he would have enjoyed the schadenfreude of being seen in conference with the chief Inspecteur.

Going in he'd overheard an English tourist comment that the Carlton's famous Victorian four square façade reminded her of something that would be right at home in Brighton if only it was a little more run down. Chuckling to himself, he browsed the magazine stand in the lobby. It had been commandeered by a comprehensive selection of advertising and marketing titles in half a dozen different languages, Jonas Shackleton's face leering from the front cover of most.

Benny's magazine, *InCreative*, had the most arresting shot, Shackleton blowing a jet of cigar smoke from under his big moustache right into the face of the camera.

He was pleased with himself choosing the Carlton to meet Lacont, it was at the centre of things in Cannes and right now he felt centre-stage in Cannes' biggest mystery. This meeting would turn the investigation.

The Bar de Célébrités was only half-full as he settled into a pale peach chair and ordered a glass of white wine. The mention of Shackleton's name a couple of tables away caught his ear. Carrick shifted in his seat so he could look in the wall mirror for the voice: a young man with lank hair, acne scars and a NY Mets baseball cap, his friend in Hawaiian shirt and beanie. A copy of *InCreative* sitting on the table between them.

An American accent, "... knowing Shackleton, dude, it's probably totally true."

"So what happened? He thought she was a hooker or somethin'?"

"Yeah! Late last Thursday night, Shackleton's cruising Rue d'Antibes. It gets a bit quiet and dark in the middle of the night, OK? So Shackleton's cruising and sees this woman in a tight top and a short dress, standing in the shadows. He winds down his window and waves to her, she comes over straight away but he doesn't recognise her... even though they'd had a meeting together when she was quoting on his commercial that very afternoon! She's all glammed up, on her way to a party at some late-night club. She comes over to say 'Hi'. Anyway, he doesn't recognise her at all... "

"Oh no... "

"He's like totally trashed, right? He winds down his window and says, 'How much, luv?' At first she thinks he's kidding but then she's, like, mortified. She realises that he's really mistaken her for a hooker and she's totally humiliated. You know? She'd spent an hour taking him through the director's treatment boards and the reel and everything, the figures, the lot. She leans down into the car, looks him in the eye and says, 'Still a million two, you dick.'"

The Hawaiian shirt shakes with laughter, "Classic, man."

Last Thursday, thought Carrick. Shackleton had used his judge's suite at the Carlton for meetings the day before he died. Carrick willed one or other of them to mention the name of the producer woman in the story.

"Great story. A fitting memorial to the randy old goat."

They drank.

"You ever meet him?"

"No. You?"

"Nah. But a friend gave me one of the corporate T-shirts he did when he went to New York to join InterGroup-Publicity."

"Yeah? Any good?"

"It's funny. A plain white T-shirt, says, *I work for InterGroup-Publicity and I'm proud of it.*"

"What's funny?"

"The type is really, really small..."

"So?"

"... and it's printed on the inside label at the back of the neck where it can't be seen."

"Hah. Nice."

"He did some cool ads too, ya gotta hand it to him."

"Yeah, easier to do that in Asia, though. The clients don't know so much."

"One's thing's sure, he wasn't researched to death, ha ha ha."

Carrick's Sancerre arrived at the same moment the laughing Americans stood up to leave. He turned around in his chair, waved and grinned up at them, "Hi guys. Hey, sorry, but I overheard you mention old Shackleton. Didn't mean to eavesdrop, you know, but it's a great story. It was Jenny Arlington, wasn't it? From BBG? The producer you mentioned?"

He made up the name, hoped there was no such person and that these two didn't themselves come from the BBG agency.

The guy in the baseball cap said, "Hi, my name's Dean. This is Josh."

"Andy. Nice to meet you. Look, sorry to intrude, just asking?"

"No, no. It was Liza Lieberman. Don't know a Jenny at BBG. Do you Dean? Anyway, it was definitely Liza, she told me the story herself."

"I must have got it totally wrong," Carrick said, "Where does Liza Lieberman work?"

"You've never heard of Liza? She's Head Producer at Bingo! Films."

"Of course. I think I saw her the other night. She's staying here at the hotel?"

"Who knows? Where you from?" said Dean.

"Maine Hyland & Blix."

"Yeah? What do you do?"

Carrick hesitated, "I'm a suit."

"Great. OK."

The two looked at each other. "Anyway, we gotta go."

"Yeah, we got to catch that workshop session at the Palais."

Carrick pulled out his cell phone and rang Melodie, the last time he'd spoken to her she accused him of upsetting her judges and making Eugene Choi leave town early, he would have to put on his smooth-as-Francesco voice, "Melodie, it's Andy Carrick, I need your help."

"I am still angry wiz you."

"Are you pouting? I bet you look like a brunette Bardot."

"I am busy, Andy. I don't 'ave time for words, we've got rehearsals for awards night."

"I'm having a tough week too, someone tried to run me down and the police are talking about locking me up, otherwise I would have called earlier. I would have sent you flowers too."

"Are you serious?"

"Yes, pink and white ones."

"No, I mean are you serious about ze police? And being run down? Are you 'urt?"

"No permanent damage, but I think I'm onto something with the investigation. I need to find someone who saw Shackleton last week, the day before he was killed. Her name is Liza Lieberman, a producer at a company called Bingo! Films. She's in Cannes but I don't know which hotel. Know her?"

"You want me to find a girl for you!"

"I need to interview her. She was one of the last people to meet with Shackleton before the judges' lunch at Colombe d'Or."

"I just look after ze judges and help with ze awards presentation, I don't know any delegates, zere are zousands and zousands of zem."

"There must be a list?"

"If she's an official Cannes delegate 'er 'otel and local contact number will be in our networking book."

"Can you look her up for me, Melodie? I'll buy you dinner?"

"You were going to ask me anyway."

"Yes, but I'll make it a more expensive dinner."

"What sort of girl..."

"Please, Melodie, Liza Lieberman?"

"OK, I'll text you if she's in ze networking book. But now I must go." She paused, "Andy, take mush care."

Five minutes later Inspecteur de Détective Lacont came through the lobby's revolving door, Carrick stood to shake his hand, the policeman sat down ignoring the outstretched palm.

Chapter 9.

"Give me one reason why I should not arrest you immediately, Monsieur Carrique."

"I have an honest face."

"Why did you elude Inspecteur Adjoint Rolande yesterday?"

"No offence to Rolande, but I had no idea who it was tailing me, it could have been gangsters. Made me nervous, I've already been run down by one car this week. Besides, Inspecteur, I need space to work."

"It may have been that I assigned him for your own protection."

"It may have been, but more likely you were trying to find out who or what I was onto, even though I'd promised to fill you in today. It doesn't show much trust."

"Why should I trust you? Everything you've told me is a lie. Stupid lies. Why? I made a mistake letting you leave yesterday. Shackleton's throat was cut commando style one could say, you're an ex-special forces man intimidating witnesses under a false identity, suspicious, erratic... "

"But you wondered what I've turned up? The missing amulet was a clue you'd missed. So was the Avis car. Look, I've done my part, I've got you the photo I promised."

"Show me."

As he opened the red folder, Carrick saw Lacont take a quick look passed him, over his shoulder. He threw the enlarged image of the amulet onto the table between them; stapled to it a printout of Benny's original photo so that he could see it was worn by Shackleton at Nice airport.

Lacont picked it up as a waiter came over to ask his order, "*Rien, partir,*" he snapped and the waiter bounced away like a pinball.

Carrick looked around towards the grand staircase. To one side, near the Brasserie entrance, he spotted the hovering Rolande. The meeting hadn't started as well as he'd hoped.

"You were supposed to come alone," he said tersely.

Lacont looked up, holding the enlarged photo of the amulet, "What am I to make of this?"

"That was around Shackleton's neck just before he went upstairs and got himself killed. It wasn't when the police arrived. I assume the killer took it."

"Is it valuable?"

"Depends."

"On what?"

Carrick passed over the catalogue showing the amulet on the antique statue in St-Rémy, "Depends if it's real or fake. It could be a pre-Roman antiquity, in which case it's priceless. Or it could be a fake advertising prop."

"Where did you get this photo?"

"It was taken the day Shackleton arrived by one of the advertising press. Shackleton was showing the pendant off to Eugene Choi moments before he went upstairs to his room."

"You're saying the motive for the murder was robbery and the killer takes this pendant and nothing else?"

"And ... if the killer was Pornthip Sinn, why would she take the pendant and none of her luggage?"

"Maybe it was a gift from her to him in better times," he said, "Sentimental value."

"But she didn't even take her own jewellery from the room. If you stopped thinking of Pornthip as a possible perpetrator you might think of her as a possible victim. Have you turned up anything on the rental car yet?"

"I will decide who is a suspect, Carrique."

He didn't like the way Lacont had begun dropping the Monsieur. Didn't like D.I. Rolande lurking in the background either. Who else did Lacont have outside? He could feel invisible walls closing in.

"I'm trying to help here. I think I've found some interesting links that might help us, take a look at ..."

"Us?"

"You, me, my employer."

Lacont sighed, "And who is your employer today?"

"I told you: Tony Maine, InterGroup-Publicity, the network who employed Shackleton. Tony Maine's worried the killing of Shackleton has to do with an attempted nobbling of a mega-million new business pitch in China. But I'm not so sure it doesn't have much more to do with art and antiquity forgery..."

"Tony Maine says you are not working for him."

Lacont delivered it like a pistol shot.

"What?" Carrick's mind careered around, "I ..."

Lacont stared silently and Carrick trailed off. He had a bad premonition, "You've spoken to him? What did he...?"

"He says he met you a couple of years ago but has not seen you again, that is, until you accosted him in Cannes the other day..."

"Accosted?"

"... to extort money from him."

"No, he's paying me fifteen thousand to do this job."

"Fifteen thousand? He alleges you threatened him and his business interests and demanded one hundred and fifty thousand or 'what happened to Shackleton could happen to you or another one of your people'."

"That's ridiculous. I told you, he rang me last week from a mutual friend's house. It's true I hadn't seen him in a couple of years, but fifteen thousand is what he's paying me for the investigation."

"This mutual friend?"

"Emma Browning for god-sakes, I told you that too. Emma Browning-Luc is her full name. Look, Lacont, I don't know what you're playing at here, I gave you all this yesterday. And I know you checked, at least with Emma, because I saw your gendarmes at her shop in St Rémy."

"You went to see her?"

"I was in the area."

"To threaten her?"

"No, she's a friend of mine."

"She says she hasn't seen you for quite some time. Months."

"Well, no, not until last Friday night..."

"She says not then either, Carrique."

He didn't know what to say.

Lacont added, "Her husband corroborates, he also has not seen you."

"Didier wasn't there on the Friday night, I told you, just Tony Maine and Emma and me."

Carrick could hear desperation in his voice, though he tried to disguise it as exasperation. What was going on? Maine, Emma, Didier? Denied three time. *Christ.*

He saw Lacont flick his eyes at Rolande again, that meant that Rolande would begin closing in from behind. Carrick felt his options narrowing. The ceiling was crumbling towards him, the Carlton's tall columns leaning in like a cage, his beams and rafters were splitting, his palms moistened.

"You're making a mistake, Lacont."

"It's been suggested to me you might have a history of some, shall we say, mental instability?"

"What the...?"

"You have been spending your time very much alone here in France, socially isolated, yes?"

"What are you getting at?"

"You were treated by psychiatrists before you left the military?"

How would he know that?

"Now hang about, Lacont... that's normal procedure after hostile capture... "

"Were you questioned by police some time ago about the murder of a fellow military man?" he opened his notes, "one David Oliver Fergusen?"

Dave 'bloody' Fergusen.

"Where did you get this stuff?" Carrick said, "Look, I was questioned simply because I knew him. I was cleared of any involvement."

"Fergusen's neck was sliced, I understand, is that not so Carrique?"

This was not going in a good direction. Carrick was running out of time, Rolande was approaching.

"I think I need to put you where I can keep an eye you," Lacont was saying like a weary schoolteacher, "Then, we can have time to talk about your highly creative theories."

Carrick answered rapid fire, "I don't know what you're up to

Lacont, but Shackleton's murder wasn't my doing, it's part of an artwork scam, paintings and antiquities. Listen, someone here in Cannes knows more about it than I do. Sammi Walton. I told you about her already, she's staying on a yacht in the bay called Aphrodite. She knows the artist who I think has been making art fakes in Bangkok, supplying them to Shackleton. Look at the folio in his room here at the Carlton. I've checked the originals in art books, three of them are part of the collection at La Colombe d'Or. Look at this folder. I've done the research. Give me some space. Call your dogs off Lacont."

The room was intolerably smaller, the air was thinning, the Inspecteur glared steadily at him, "Yes, you told me about her yesterday. We checked it, Carrique," he stood up, "Both the port authorities and the coast guard have informed me there is no yacht called Aphrodite currently logged anywhere in the vicinity."

Rolande arrived, gripped Carrick's shoulder hard from behind at the same moment. He was too close. That was a blunder.

Lacont said, "This time, you can't talk yourself out of the holding cells, Carrique."

Carrick gave him a look of regret.

"You've given me no choice, Lacont. Please apologise to Rolande, but it's your fault."

"What do you mean...?"

Carrick grabbed Rolande's fingers and yanked them away from his shoulder, twisting the wrist around ninety degrees. As he cried out Carrick pulled down hard and turned the arm out of its socket. It's not a nice sound, but it's a much worse pain. Carrick used the limp arm as leverage to pull himself up from the chair and in the same motion swung Rolande's body weight around and into Lacont who was coming forwards from the other side of the low table. Their heads collided, loud as a couple of bone billiard balls, and Carrick made for the Brasserie.

Two bow-tied stewards sidestepped like a pair of weighted skittles as he bolted toward the glassed-in dining area that faced La Croisette and then through to the outdoor terrace.

Chapter 9.

"Arreter, Police!" Lacont was yelling from two rooms back, Carrick hoped he wouldn't think about drawing a gun in such a place.

The doors to the terrace were folded open and there was a full lunchtime crowd in mid-mouthful, Carrick ran an obstacle course of wicker chairs and round tables down the stone steps to the street. Shouts came from two sides now, someone had been stationed near the portico entrance.

Fleeing from the Carlton for the second time in two days, Carrick hoped he'd be able to look back on it and laugh sometime, but right now the only escape route was across the four lanes of La Croisette into the crowds along the promenade. He jumped over the yellow lines in front of a slow-moving delivery van in the first lane and rolled over the bonnet of a white stretch limo, launching himself into the median centre-strip between two palm trees. A woman screamed, there was more shouting from behind.

The westbound traffic was moving steadily but not fast, a blue convertible coming up the outside lane and behind it a motorcycle.

He stepped into the turning lane and made to jump into the convertible as it passed. The driver saw him and veered violently away directly into the path of the motorcycle in the inside lane. Its rider came off, skidding across the road in precisely the way you wouldn't want to. Fast and face first.

The unlucky bloke came to rest in the gutter and the bike slithered on its side onto the pedestrian pavement.

People rushed to the rider as he started to sit up and Carrick ran to his bike and heaved it upright. It started first kick, he gunned it down the pedestrian pavement towards the Palm Beach casino scattering wide-eyed delegates like pigeons for a couple of hundred yards.

After about two blocks he pulled back onto the vehicular part of La Croisette in an attempt to attract slightly less attention.

The name Boulevard de la Croisette translates into English as the Little Cross Drive. Carrick was more than a little bloody cross. He didn't have time in the moment to muse on why Tony Maine and Emma and Didier had each denied him, or how Lacont had dug up old skeletons, but he was furious with himself for going headlong into something that he clearly did not understand. Situation normal, all fucked up.

He wheeled left through the red light into the S-shaped Rue du Dr Zamenhof, a police siren wailing two blocks back.

Lacont would already be alerting every goddamned gendarme on the Côte d'Azur to look for a sandy-haired man in white shirt and black jeans riding a red and white Ducati without a helmet. All that had to change fast.

Priority one was to alter his visual profile dramatically.

Carrick reached the other side of the railway, took a left, a right and then left again to the roundabout, slowing enough to blend with the traffic and then he hooked onto Boulevard d'Alsace. This took him back in a semi-circle towards the Gare de Cannes. The sirens were receding in the other direction, his pursuers naturally assuming he was heading out of town.

He left the Ducati among a dozen other bikes at the railway station and walked into Cannes' central shopping district.

Trying not to hurry. Just another window shopper. He slipped casually into a boutique where he bought a purple shirt and a yellow pair of those over-length multi-pocketed shorts so beloved of Americans on holiday. He topped off the ensemble with a baseball cap and a new pair of sunglasses, depositing the plastic bag with his own clothes in a charity bin.

Then he crossed the street and took a chair at l'Esterel Coiffeur, asked for a colour job. Bright red, very close-cropped. He figured a hairdressing salon was the last place Lacont would be looking right now.

While the stylist chatted inanely, pausing occasionally to admire his work and groove to the Ibiza inspired chill music, Carrick caught glimpses of himself in the mirror cogitating, ruminating one moment then being overwhelmed by rushes of red banner emotions the next, thoughts racing across his mind like a screeching tabloid.

Betrayed!

Confused!

Chapter 9.

A Wanted Man!

Lacont alleged extortion, did that really come from Tony Maine or was the Inspecteur playing him? And then there was Emma and Didier! Denying he was even in their house on Friday.

No wonder they hadn't returned his calls.

He clenched and unclenched knotty fingers until the stylist noticed and asked if he'd had too much caffeine.

CHAPTER 10.

The mission had changed. It wasn't about Shackleton's cut throat any more, it was about saving his own neck.

Hung out to dry, played like a patsy, perhaps even fitted up for a murder. A 'commando style' murder, Lacont called it. The Inspecteur was building a circumstantial case and all Carrick's alibis had collapsed somehow.

How was that possible?

Calm, boy, the Major's instructing voice, *Adrenaline blocks thinking.*

Tony Maine, thought Carrick.

It was unavoidable. All roads led to Tony Maine.

He got me involved in the first place, sold me on the idea, briefed me right down to the tone of voice to use with the judges.

Tony and Emma both. Tony and Emma? Were they together in this? And more? Why? What's in it for them? What about Didier? Didier seemed completely surprised about the meeting at his own house. He'd sounded genuine. Hadn't he?

Carrick couldn't tell anymore.

The betrayed have trust stolen from them.

Until this point he'd been trying to navigate the arcane politics of advertising, searching blindly for a link between Shackleton's murder and the Qi pitch as per Maine's brief, drawing a blank with everyone he spoke to. The only substantial clue suggested a different scenario, the murderer had killed Shackleton then taken his pendant.

Find one maybe he would find the other?

Sitting in the salon waiting for the lurid red hair-dye to take, Carrick wondered about Sammi Walton. Lacont said that the Aphrodite yacht was a lie. Well at least BS would be relieved, he thought grimly, it explained why Benny hadn't been invited to the Backroom Boys' party. If there was no yacht, there had been no party.

What was that about? And why on earth had Sammi invented a yacht at all? To impress? Why try to impress him?

She'd first mentioned it when talking to Nick Bailey and Liang Weh on Monday, Carrick tried to remember the context ... He asked if she'd seen Shackleton in Cannes? She said no, just arrived. On the Aphrodite. Said they'd picked it up in Nice and only just sailed it into port.

A convenient alibi? It placed her safely away from questions about Shackleton, both in time and space.

How did she expect to get away with it? It meant she'd invited him out for a party on a non-existent boat yesterday? More disinformation. The idea was mad. The only reason Carrick didn't notice that Aphrodite was invisible was that the gendarmes jumped him soon as he arrived at the port. It made no sense. Nothing did.

Carrick needed her to come clean about exactly what Jamie Tan was up to with Shackleton, even if she didn't know who killed him, he was damn sure that she knew why.

He stepped out of l'Esterel Coiffeur a brand new man, physically different enough from the description police would have. But inside he was just as bewildered.

There was a cash machine across the road, he checked his bank account. It was a strange feeling to see the balance bulging. Exactly as Lacont said. One hundred and fifty thousand pounds higher. A sight that would normally bring a sigh of pleasure gave him a sick knot in the stomach.

Chapter 10.

You've lost control of the beast, he said to himself, events are galloping away. Was this how insanity starts?

His cell phone beeped and he went rigid momentarily, but it was a message from Melodie with the hotel phone number for Liza Lieberman, the producer who Shackleton had apparently mistaken for a prostitute. For a moment it grounded him. There was no choice but to crash through the chaos and find something solid.

He was about to call Lieberman when he realised that using his cell might be another mistake. Lacont had his number. Theoretically they could trace it by triangulating the signal from the nearest transmission towers. Carrick had no idea how long it would take to put that process in place.

He decided paranoia was a reasonable reaction given his situation, so he found a bar and used the pay phone.

A good break at last: Liza Lieberman answered straight away. He trotted out the insurance investigator story one more time and arranged to meet in half an hour at her hotel, the Noga. It meant going back to La Croisette's hotel strip but the risk was necessary.

It wasn't far to the beachfront but he used all the available time, choosing the most crowded streets, stopping frequently at corner shops to survey the next short leg of the route ahead. In a strange way it relaxed him, he was more at ease in action than in deliberation, an operational calm began to take over.

As they sat in a corner of the hotel's brightly lit coffee lounge, Liza Lieberman said in a raspy Brooklyn accent, "You sure don't look much like an insurance investigator, Mr. Carrick."

He glanced down. The new purple shirt had a winking sheen and the bright yellow shorts made him wince. "Oh, sorry about the clothes, I was on holiday when they called me about this."

He took off the goofy baseball cap revealing his freshly dyed hair. She raised an eyebrow.

Liza Lieberman was in her early forties, a generously-sized woman with intelligent eyes, a hard, tanned face above an expensive and tight-fitting outfit. Her arms and neck were all bangles and beads. Carrick gave her his card and got straight down to business,

"You had a meeting with Jonas Shackleton at the Carlton Hotel the day before he was killed?"

"That's right," she jangled her bling, hands and bangles moving constantly, "Bingo! Films is quoting on a commercial he's doing. Was doing, I guess. We really should have had the meeting in New York, but Jonas couldn't fit us in before coming to Cannes. We really wanted the job, so I came over here early."

"One point two million dollars worth, I hear."

"We're offering value, there's a lot of post-production to allow for. How do you know the amount anyway?"

"I heard a story that you met him on the street again Thursday night."

"Met him? He propositioned me in the street that night. Didn't even register that he knew me. Who told you?"

He decided to be honest, "A couple of guys in the Carlton bar."

"Oh, that's just great, I tell the story at just one Beach Club lunch and a random insurance guy hears it in some bar..."

"Can I ask how you found Shackleton during your meeting? Happy? Worried...?"

"Distracted."

"By what, do you think?"

"I don't have to think, I know. He had someone waiting for him in the other room."

"An Asian girl?" Carrick thinking of Pornthip.

"Well, I can tell you it was a female, I could smell Issey Miyake, I'd know it anywhere," she laughed, "And let me tell you, that's not the perfume of a hooker, if that's what you mean by 'Asian girl'. Apart from that I couldn't say."

"Did he talk to you about the amulet he wore around his neck?"

"No. Why would he?"

"Just wondered. Did he mention anything that struck you as odd? Did you notice anything unusual?"

"Not really. Well, there was this folio he'd been looking at when I came in, it was open on top of the coffee table."

"Did you see what was in the folio?"

"I made sure I did, but it was OK."

"How do you mean 'OK'?"

"I mean it had nothing to do with my job, the script I was quoting. My first thought was that it might belong to the person in the other room, that maybe my appointment had interrupted them. When Jonas went to the john I had a look in case it was a storyboard for someone else's treatment of the script, but it was just illustrations and paintings. He saw me looking at it when he came back and asked whether I'd ever seen the art at a restaurant called Columbus Door, or something? But I haven't."

"La Colombe d'Or?"

"Could be that. He went on and on about it, all the famous artists, like he'd forgotten why I was there. Like I wanted to talk about somewhere he goes for lunch? We're at the Cannes Lions, for god-sakes, the whole place is one long lunch, my God, we were meant to be having a meeting."

"What did he say about it?"

"About what?"

"The art?"

"The art? You too? That's what you want to talk about? Well, he named them all, you know, Picasso, yadda yadda, Matisse or Magritte, whoever, I can't remember which one of those is which. The whole history of the place he knew, the restaurant ... The Column...?"

"La Colombe d'Or."

"Yeah. He even knew who used to hang out there in the old black and white days, Hemingway and the rest, French film stars who got married there, I began to wonder if he had money in the place. To be frank, I wasn't really paying attention, I mean, who cares? I was trying to pull him back to my quote for our production, I really wanted him to look at it after making the trip out here early and everything. He was hardly listening to me."

"Why do you think he was so interested?"

"No idea. Probably just a way of talking down to me, I suppose. Using what we call their Creative License. Most of them have a superiority complex that places them beyond normal social expectations."

"Them?"

"Creative Directors. They love an audience. "

"I've noticed." .

"They're always selling a story in some way, it becomes a habit.
Sell a story. To consumers, to clients. It's a talent. I suppose they need
the charisma or the chutzpah to sell the marketing departments on
running with their ideas, and that ain't easy, a lotta big clients are just
dumb schmucks when it comes to communication, really uptight."
She laughed, "You know what Shackleton called clients? He said it in
a speech a coupla years ago right here in Cannes ... *Pigs with cheque
books.*"

"Did people in the industry like him?"

"As Oscar Wilde said, *He has no enemies, but is intensely disliked by
his friends.* Sums up Jonas, or any of them, really. Success is their only
friend and that's a one-night stand," she sipped her chai latte and
licked the froth from her top lip, "It's the worst job in advertising."

"From what I've seen it looks like the best."

"That's what people think, oh sure it has its perks, but there's a
big burnout factor, so much pressure. Agencies demand high
creativity but don't you dare make any mistakes. Creative Directors
move jobs more than anyone else. There's so much politics. The suits
make a big deal about the importance of creativity but it's just a
commodity to them, creatives are expendable, they don't really
respect them."

Carrick nodded, thought back to Tony's attitude, the way he'd
talked about the judges, the casual belittling of *Dear old Ray.*

"Truth is, Creative Directors are high-wire acrobats performing
amazing feats of skill without a safety net; the better they are the
more effortless it looks. Only other acrobats truly appreciate how
difficult it is. That's why they have awards like Cannes. Of course, it
helps if they have talented back up around them."

"Like the production companies they hire, you mean?"

"Well, yes, great directors can take a script and make it work,
sometimes even take a sow's ear and make it into a silk purse beautiful enough to slip an award into."

"Like your company, Bingo! Films?"

"Sure. We've got our share of talented directors on the books."

"What about the Backroom Boys?"

That made her bang her beads together as her hands fretted and she tensed the muscles in her neck, "What about them? Why do you mention them?"

"I heard they're one of the top production houses at the moment? An example of the type of companies you're talking about?"

"Perhaps," she said cautiously, "They've done some nice work, I suppose," she sighed, started again, "Ah, what am I saying? Shackleton's script is probably dead now ... pardon the pun ... so it doesn't matter anyway. Yes, of course they're good. Won a couple of Clios in the States this year."

"What doesn't matter?"

"Oh, I'm just a bit defensive. After I left Shackleton suite, once our so-called meeting was done, I saw one of the Backroom Boys' producers come out of the elevator. I didn't even know they were coming to Cannes, thought they were all tied up on a big job in Morocco this month."

Carrick leant forwards, "Tell me more?"

"Well, I had a stiff drink in the Carlton's lounge after seeing Jonas, to calm myself down a little, I was so frustrated with him. Then I saw her come out of the lift about twenty minutes later and I wondered, sheer paranoia, of course, whether it was her waiting in the other room during my meeting with Jonas? You know, making a pitch for the job for the Backroom Boys? I thought he was two-timing me. Sometimes they just use you as a check-quote. That's probably why I reacted the way I did when Jonas propositioned me on the street later that night. He thought I was a hooker, as you've heard. Anyway, that's why I spat out our figure at him."

"It was Sammi Walton who came out of the elevator?"

"Yes. You know her?" The painted fingers intertwined.

"I've questioned her. She said she hadn't seen Shackleton in Cannes."

"Really? Then I was being paranoid." Then she said, almost as an aside, "I thought maybe they'd got back together again."

"Back together? How do you mean...?"

Now it was Carrick's fingers tightening their grip on each other.

"Yeah. They were an item for a while in New York, maybe even before that in Bangkok for all I know. Oh my God, look at me, now I'm gossiping. Is this really any help to your investigation?"

He thanked her and assured her it had been. It had given him a lot to think about.

As she left she looked him up and down again, the hair, the short pants,"I hope you can get back to your holiday real soon, Mr. Carrick."

"I've got myself into another spot of bother, would you believe?" Carrick was using the Noga's lobby phone.

Sammi had answered her cell immediately, "Uh-huh. Nothing too fatal by the sound of it."

"Now, now. Be nice."

"I don't do nice, Andy."

"I need to speak to you."

"What about?"

"Forged artworks, antique rarities. About Shackleton and Jamie Tan, Shackleton and you. Why I shouldn't go to the police with what I've got about you all?"

It was bluff, but it was worth the try.

"I've told you already, I wasn't involved in any scheme they had going."

"You also told me you hadn't seen Shackleton here in Cannes."

A small hesitation, "So?"

"Let's meet and have a heart to heart, Sammi."

"I have to be at the Palm Beach Casino tonight for an important meeting and right now I'm about to have my hair done."

"You too?"

"What?"

"Nothing. Later, after the casino is fine. 11pm? I'll pick you up outside. It's important."

With the police looking for him he preferred his chances after dark.

Just before hanging up she said, "Andy, you better be there. All this stuff is freaking me out."

This admission of weakness surprised him, softened him a little. Am I being too harsh, he asked himself? Probably not. Why believe her? *They were an item for a while in New York*, Liza Lieberman said.

It was then he saw one of the Lions' delegates staring at a mute TV mounted behind the coffee shop counter.

Carrick followed his sight line.

The TV screen showed Pornthip Sinn's passport photo, the picture caption at the bottom read: *Cannes Lions VIP Murder —
Suspect's body found by fishermen.*

Then it cut to a commercial break.

On the bay water skiers chased frothing speed boats between billionaires' yachts. Burnt bodies iridescent with oil lay in row upon row like a military formation along the length of the beach, an invading force armed with ice cream cones. Carrick among them, sweating, a towel over his head, at the club across the boulevard from the Noga.

The beer was cold, the crowded area anonymous, safe as anywhere for a man on the run, a man without allies or local back up. He could stay the rest of the afternoon and turn over a few things. Like where to spend the night?

Not his hotel, Lacont knew where that was. Not his rented cottage, Lacont knew that too.

Lacont knew a surprising amount.

You were treated by psychiatrists before you left the military. How the hell did Lacont get that?

The PTSD diagnosis after Gorma was something Carrick did not advertise. Even people who knew him well didn't mention it, not in his hearing anyway. Not since he'd broken the nose of that trooper in a Richmond pub, his fingers still pinned and wired, after the boy made the mistake of having a laugh.

Then there was Dave 'bloody' Fergusen.

You were questioned by police about the murder of a fellow military man? One David Oliver Fergusen?

Dave 'bloody' Fergusen.

Even dead he was a pain.

Fergusen's neck was sliced, I understand, is that not so Carrique?

They'd served together, shared barracks, completed Special Duties in the same team. Before the debacle on the Noorullah mission they'd been comrades. Buddies.

Dave 'bloody' Fergusen had been in the forces two years longer than Carrick, born Boston, Mass., but an English citizen since age twelve. English mum, American dad.

He still had traces of the Bostonian's *wicked pissa* accent that, Carrick noted, the girls all loved. Robyn laughed like a drain when she first heard him describe his army crew cut as a *whiffle*. Unobtrusively handsome, straight American teeth, on the surface easy-going but cunning as a box of monkeys — attributes Carrick mostly lacked. Yet the orphan boy and the smooth cowboy found enough common ground until Fergusen added a notch to his belt called Robyn.

Too self-serving to be trusted, the Major once commented and, as usual, he turned out to be right.

Guess who I scooped on last night? Fergusen said to Jacko and a room full of squaddies after bedding Robyn.

As well as women, Fergusen's weaknesses were a love of guns and drugs. He could strip an M4 in under thirty seconds. Strip a Glock one-handed. He boasted he could strip slampigs even faster. That was his word for cheap Bristol girls.

But it was the drugs that Carrick always thought was going to be trouble, whenever he was on leave Fergusen had an appetite that was relentless and a wild west attitude that fed it. When Carrick heard Fergusen had been found dead in his bungalow he'd suspected it was a deal gone bad. He'd heard rumours Fergusen was supplying steroids and who knows what else to interested parties at the Credenhill Barracks. Fergusen played fast with unsavoury people, crowed about it, thought himself invincible, but the SF strut can be dangerous if you rub the wrong people the wrong way.

When he was killed the investigating police interviewed a number of guys from the regiment and came down from Hereford to speak with Carrick in London. Nothing unusual in that, they were trying to piece together background they said.

Carrick told them very little, certainly not the circumstances of their falling out. As for the drugs, in Carrick's view it was a matter of loyalty to the regiment to say nothing, Fergusen was still serving so it was the military's issue after all.

Yes, I knew him. Yes, pretty well, we served together. Yes, in the desert. He was a good soldier. No, not everyone liked him, but many did. No, I don't know of anyone who disliked him enough to kill him. No, I don't know anything about drugs found on his premises. No, I couldn't tell you much about his private life. No, I haven't had any contact with him for a couple of years, we drifted apart once I decided to leave.

As was his habit, Carrick asked a few questions of his questioners.

He'd heard a story that Fergusen was killed with a regimental sword but the police told him no, there'd been some kind of struggle and it was a broken bottle that caused the fatal wound. Strange choice of weapon considering the room was a virtual armoury, they said, a whole array of pistols, rifles, knives, even some restricted poisons.

Dave 'bloody' Fergusen. How did he get his moniker?

Live boldly, die bloody, Carrick told them, it was his motto.

Got his wish said one of the investigating coppers as they departed.

Where did Lacont hear of Fergusen? The English police? Tony Maine perhaps? But how could *he* know anything of Fergusen? And surely Maine couldn't know about the psychiatric sessions that continued for weeks after Carrick left hospital.

But Lacont knew. So maybe Maine did know.

Tony Maine.

Why hire him to investigate Shackleton's death then deny it, accuse him of extortion and plant suspicion in Lacont's mind that Carrick was the murderer? The obvious answer was Maine must have killed Shackleton, not personally, but he could certainly arrange it. Why?

The £2 million insurance pay out? That would be a pittance in Tony's world.

To get Shackleton off the Qi pitch? BS suggested that Maine might have considered he was the wrong man for the project, but why not just get someone else? He's the boss after all, must happen all the time. *Creative directors move jobs more than anyone*, said Liza.

Killing Shackleton *must* be about something else. If it was the amulet around his neck, what did that have to do with Maine?

Then there was the red car that tried to run him down; Maine's people? It wasn't a very professional effort. Why get him involved and then run him down? Everything was circular, each question begged the next until he got back to the first.

Carrick was giddy on the outside of the circle, spinning around the rim of a world he couldn't grasp, tumbling through events at the edge without understanding anything, caught in the gravitational pull but so very far from the centre. Too many unknowns to form a battle strategy, yet meantime he was taking fire from every angle.

The only time his intuition had been right was poor Pornthip. She must have run because she knew she was in danger. She knew something that was worth killing twice for. Something to do with the Hammer God amulet? Something to do with the fake paintings in Jamie Tan's folio? That was a notion Carrick couldn't shake off.

Prince of the Scammers.

Carrick's cell phone was beeping.

A voice mail from Didier Luc.

He didn't retrieve it, worried that using his phone might easily give away his GPS location.

A few minutes later it beeped again, this time a text.

Chapter 10.

Ur not answering my calls & I know I let you down. Can we meet? I need to talk. & apologise. Didi.

A set up? What else are friends for?

Before he could decide what to do a second text came.

Please. I want to fix things. I know about Tony and Emma. Call me. D.

Carrick pulled a face, picked up a handful of sand and let it filter out from his half closed fist. Then he decided to roll the dice.

It turned out to be a very bad decision, another one, but he wasn't to learn that for many hours.

A decision he would regret the rest of his life.

Carrick ambled over to the cabana and asked to use the Beach Club phone.

Even if Lacont *had* set up an automatic number identification on Didier's phone it would only give them the billing address of the caller, which for an international hotel chain could be anywhere. He dialled the number.

What other options were there? Running would solve nothing, where to, how long? Lacont would eventually win that game. *You can't go back*, the Major always said, *A soldier should never look back.*

"What's the story Didi?"

"Andy? Are you OK?"

"Thanks for asking," Carrick's terseness hung in the air a moment. On the assumption that the French police were listening at Didier's end, he added, "I asked for your help getting a local lawyer when Lacont started to suggest, wrongly, that I might be involved in Shackleton's demise, and you didn't help. Then you failed to corroborate my story about meeting Emma and Tony Maine at your place on Friday night. You lied to the police. Emma lied to the police. Maine lied to the police. Mate, all things considered you're doing a good job of making sure I'm not OK."

"Look, I'm so sorry, Andy, I made a mistake. I know. I need to explain things. Where are you?"

Wrong question.

"Explain things to me now."

"Look, I know you're angry, you've got every right. But they let you go yesterday, right? The police?"

"And then tried to arrest me today."

"Oh Jesus, Andy. I didn't know. What happened?"

"I managed to slip away quietly. But it's a little hotter right now than the South of France ought to be thanks to you and your wife and Tony Maine."

"Look, I know I let you down, I'm sorry, I'm sorry. I'll give you Etienne Balford's number, he's a lawyer I sometimes play tennis with, I've got it right here," it sounded like he was choking up, he made a glottal noise in his throat, "… You really did come to our house, didn't you, on Friday night, like you said?"

"Of course I bloody did, why would I make it up?"

"Yes, I wondered that too, but Emma said … she said … she told me point blank it wasn't true."

"Why did she lie?"

"I think she's been lying about a couple of things recently."

Carrick frowned. This wasn't the way the conversation would go if Didier had the police listening at his shoulder.

"What did she say?"

"Said you were crazy, that you'd lost it, that we should stay out of whatever it is you're mixed up in. Told me to not admit to the police that I'd spoken to you at all, not to get involved." There was a long pause, his voice was thick, "Andy, the problem is, oh God, look, I think she's having an affair with him."

There was pain in his voice that Carrick recognized, a cuckold's cry. *The guy's a bloody good actor if he's trying set me up.*

"Is it true, Andy? What do you think? Her and Tony? You were there, you saw them together, you'd be able to tell," he laughed wretchedly, a gallows chuckle, "Don't want to kill myself and find out later she's innocent."

Great, someone tries to run me down, I'm wanted by the French police,

Chapter 10.

and now an old mate is either setting me up brilliantly or about to commit suicide.

Carrick's eyes rolled round the afternoon beach scene, the line of palms, the blue Med crisscrossed with coloured sails, glistening tourists sipping bright cocktails spiked with miniature umbrellas.

But he was back in the sandbox.

How do you tell an innocent from an insurgent, friend from foe? They look the same, maybe are the same, until the day they betray you.

But you have to decide in an instant.

"Didier, have you got a car?"

The late afternoon was heavy with humidity, half the sky painted a polluted orange, flaccid flags hung at the entrance of the Palais des Festivals where posters announced tonight's big event, the New Directors' Showcase. Carrick stood at the top of the red-carpet stairway to Festival heaven, twenty-two steps to fame and fortune, advertising's best and brightest swarming around him. The crowd was good cover and he had a wide-angle view over the forecourt where the Promenade de la Pantiero meets La Croisette.

Agreeing to meet Didier in the centre of Cannes was dangerous enough, but he wasn't going to sucker himself by taking more of a chance than absolutely necessary. If Didier had informed the police, or perhaps the homicidal driver of a red Renault, Carrick wanted a little forewarning, wanted to see them coming.

He tried to shrug off maudlin thoughts. He felt an exhausting sadness that his messy life had brought him to this. One friend, one single ally would stiffen him against the flood.

Then he spotted Didier and moved down a couple of steps through the molasses crowd and gave the kid a nod. A Moroccan kid, saucer-eyed, whip smart. He'd given the boy a 20-euro note and told him to pass on a message; it was better money than the kid's usual shoeshine pitch and he agreed in an instant. Carrick watched him rush towards Didier, zigzag-ging through the crowd, grab his shirt, hiss in his ear to cross the road and wait outside the Le Porto building next to the gelato seller's pushcart.

Then he darted back into the crowd like a lizard under a woodpile.

Didier did as he was told. Carrick watched for a change of direc-tion from anyone in the throng, an alteration to the pattern, a ripple from a predator. No-one followed the kid. Or Didi. Some minutes passed.

Then at Carrick's signal the gelato seller leaned across and directed Didier to the plane-tree-covered park alongside La Pantiero, told him to keep walking until he reached the Hotel Splendide.

From his vantage point on the Palais steps Carrick saw no tail.

No one on foot, no dawdling car.

He moved in.

Reaching for Didier from behind he caught his arm just above the elbow at the *kyushu* pressure point, a good control spot but not too conspicuous. Didi didn't resist.

"Andy?" he did a double take, "Ouah, I hardly recognised you," then the familiar grin, "Great hair."

"Walk."

"Are the police still after you?" he said, looking around jerkily.

"Don't look. Walk and keep quiet."

They pushed through the motley tourists around the water feature at the Le Grande Café, crossed Rue Félix Faure and slipped passed the queue into the air-conditioned cool of the Arcade Cinema. Carrick pulled two tickets from the pocket of his yellow shorts and gave them to the usher at the doors of Cinéma Trois.

Now they were in the darkness, a couple minutes into a dubbed teen movie about crazy American college kids, Carrick chose two seats in an empty row near the corner exit.

"Speak to me, Didier."

He let go his arm.

Didier gathered himself, then started slowly and deliberately as if he were talking to a counsellor.

"Remember when you were training for Special Forces and you used to tell me, *When you're going through hell, keep going*? Well, I kept going and now I'm just in deeper."

Emma, he said baldly, lost their baby fourteen months ago. They'd been trying to get pregnant since they married. The miscarriage came while he was away in Frankfurt working.

For the next forty-five minutes Didier didn't stop, mesmerised by the telling of his own tragedy, pouring out his heart in a mixture of whispers and whimpers while the reflections from the movie screen played over his face in a surreal wash of light and colour, changing the shadows in his features in eerie ways, ghoulish sometimes, at other times clownish.

"I'm always away somewhere. One morning, Em rang me in hysterics. 'Just a bloody mess in the bathroom.' She kept repeating those words over and at first I didn't get what she meant.

"'What are you talking about?' I said, 'I've got a meeting to go to.' 'Just a bloody mess in the bathroom — our son,' she said, 'Our son is just a bloody mess in the bathroom.'

"Of course I flew home straight away, nothing to be done though. It went bad for her the next few months. A crazy sense of guilt, I think, a sort of *défailance*, a sense of failure. She sort of closed up into herself. I was mourning too. I did not handle things well, I think, Andy."

He stared into some unfocussed middle-distance, purple, red and white flashes from the screen painting him into a sad, carney face.

"She told me she didn't feel like she was a real woman."

Carrick said nothing, averted his eyes. This wasn't the way he'd anticipated the dialogue would go.

"Losing a baby is not the sort of thing people talk much about in France, women from the town told her to not worry, to pray, maybe she could one day have another to replace it. That wasn't what either of us wanted to hear, you can't replace someone you've already begun to love. He was our son, he already had a name. Giles. He was already a person. Our person.

"Em went back to the UK for a while, stayed with her mother, but her stuffy English relatives seemed more embarrassed about it than anything else," he looked down at his hands, "The doctors said she has some kind of a cervical incompetency. Fuck, what a word to use; anyway, it means it's unlikely she could ever to go full term."

The trembling light cut across his face in snatches and shapes, "Something broke inside her, Andy, I don't mean physically, in her heart, in her deep self somewhere; something I couldn't reach, even as her husband.

"Maybe something changed inside me too," he shook his head slowly, "I remember looking at her and thinking her belly would never swell with my love. What a selfish bastard to think like that."

Guffaws erupted from the audience in response to some gross sight gag involving the college kids and a gerbil.

"She said to me one night in bed, 'I will never be loved as a mother is loved, never be loved by you for mothering your child, never be loved by my child. I will never be a real woman.' What could I say, Andy? How do you make up for that? '*I will never be loved as a mother is loved*'".

Carrick thanked God for the background babble of the movie, the silences between Didier's sentences were distended with so much pain it was more excruciating than his utterances.

"I should have been strong for her at that moment, but I couldn't. I cried, Andy, I fell apart, I was weak, went out, got drunk, turned away. She told me I couldn't help her. She was right in a way. She was slipping away from me."

He blew out a long, sad breath from somewhere so deep it seemed to eviscerate him.

"She was so low for so long. Months later I thought I heard the dog whimpering in the middle of the night, I got up and found it was Em in the kitchen weeping, 'I have missed so much of the love a woman should have,' she said.

Carrick looked away, focussed on the wall to one side of Didier's head.

He thought about himself. Andy and Robyn. He would never be father to Andy and Robyn's son. Never be the father that he himself never had. Would never be loved by Andy and Robyn's son, the boy who'd be able to do all Carrick could, but better, who'd achieve something with his talents. A wise son. He would never gaze into that new face, part him, part Robyn, part his own father and father's father. His family tree, whatever it was, would stop anonymously at Carrick and fall away into rootless space. He would leave nothing behind. No family line, just a full stop.

He had lost his shot at the family he always craved through his own failures, his own kind of inherent incompetence. He put a brotherly arm on Didier's. Both men mourning lost sons as the cinema full of teenagers gawked and gurgled at the screen.

Didier didn't notice, he was saying, "Eventually, I thought Emma was getting over it, making an effort; she'd started to throw herself into work in St-Rémy, you know, her art shop, going to trade fairs, conventions, she started dressing better again, looking after herself. But thinking about it now, I can see a pattern, something else. A pattern and a name."

One day, while Emma was in the pool, Didier answered her cell phone. It was Tony Maine. He was going to be in Avignon doing a deal with Robbie Williams, the English singer, for some advertising campaign; there was going to be a concert in the Palace of the Popes Square. Maine had tickets, front and centre. But Didier was busy, an early flight next morning, so Emma went with Tony alone.

"Then she started going on buying trips, Paris, Bruges, she bought special papers for the shop, antique writing cases, exotic inks. Soon she was away as often as me," he laughed sourly, "I didn't think anything of it at first, after all there was nothing to keep her at home, we'd turned the nursery into a storage room.

"Tony's name was mentioned occasionally, she bumped into him at the Hotel Costas last month. Now this," Didier was morose, "I find he's been in my own home. I don't think it's the first time." Then he burst out like a true Frenchman, "Andy, she even smells different."

Carrick considered this for a moment.

"Issey Miyake?"

"No, I don't mean perfume, Andy."

Chapter 10.

Didier had always been the most straightforward of men when they were mates in the London days. With his cherubic looks and French accent he could have had any of the girls, but his love for Emma was total and true. They'd met at an ad agency Christmas bash and he never looked at another woman after he'd been with her a week.

Carrick hurt for him now, he felt worse for putting him through the meeting-in-a-park process and then subjecting him to the indignity of telling his intimate secrets in a cinema full of howling adolescents.

"What do you think?" Didier asked, "When you saw them at my house, could you see them together in that way? Was there *frisson*?"

Carrick remembered she looked radiant that night, her blonde hair loose, her shining eyes, the recalcitrant strap that kept baring one shoulder, he said, "I'm not sure, Didi, for most of the night they were briefing me about advertising politics and plotting out this damn investigation Tony convinced me to do. It wasn't a very romantic setting, more like a business strategy meeting."

A strategy meeting with four or five bottles of red, though now he realised the free-flowing wine was designed to soften him up, "I was being press-ganged."

"And when you left, Tony stayed?" said Didier, his voice tight with strain.

"I passed out in your spare room. In the morning Tony was gone."
Cold comfort.

They fell silent.

Carrick shifted the subject back to his own problems, ironically, it now seemed less emotionally fraught, "What happened yesterday after I rang you from the police station?"

"I didn't have Etienne's phone direct number with me in Portofino — he's the lawyer I was going to call for you, works for Morel & Balford in Nice — so I rang Emma to get it out of our teledex. That's when I told her all about you ringing me from the police station. She surprised me. Said you were flipped out, I'm sorry, anyway, her opinion was that you were losing it, she told me you hadn't been at our place at all. Neither had Tony. Said you were lying, I shouldn't trust you. She was adamant, she said ... she said, well, that she'd heard you'd been drinking a lot recently. Don't know why I believed that," he chuckled like the old days.

Carrick didn't find it funny, Lacont had asked about mental instability. He was being profiled. Ex-soldier. Loner. Drinker. Killer?

"She said that you must be up to something if the police were questioning you. She told me to ignore the whole thing, after all, I didn't want any scandal while I was doing this celebrity job in Portofino, did I? It's going to be a real showpiece. Anyway, Em told me I should forget you called, that it would blow over. Just turn off my phone, simple as that. I'm sorry, Andy, I'm not much of a friend am I?"

The slurries of colour and play of light from the movie turned his handsome face into a sorrowful mosaic, a stained-glass portrait of a sad faced martyr.

Inspecteur Lacont's dinner wasn't sitting well.

Neither were the facts.

One line of investigation at a time was the procedural rule he liked to follow, but this case was making that discipline difficult.

His head still ached after its collision with Rolande's skull during Carrick's escape, he was embarrassed and annoyed in equal measure, and now his digestion made clear thinking difficult. He didn't like Carrick. He was arrogant as the advertising judges in his own way, the same cockiness, yet Lacont had not expected the violence in the Carlton, the reckless escape. Carrick's motives perplexed him.

During the long-distance phone call to China yesterday afternoon, Tony Maine said that Carrick contacted him on Friday claiming to be investigating the murder for Lloyd's, he said he knew him slightly and it seemed plausible, so he'd arranged for him to meet with the judges. Then on Saturday Carrick came to Maine in person and demanded protection money, suggesting that otherwise "the same thing might happen" to Ray Doyle or even himself while he was in Cannes as had happened to Shackleton.

"What was your reaction monsieur?" Lacont asked the echoing telephone.

"I told him it would take 24 hours. What else could I do? I knew he was potentially dangerous. When I heard that Carrick had threatened all the judges I thought he might be setting up other agencies for the same treatment.

"The man needs help," Maine added glibly.

But if Carrick *had* killed Shackleton, as Tony Maine was suggesting (and how did he manage that without being seen entering or leaving the scene?), why would he make himself so conspicuous straight afterwards? Why offer an alibi so easily disproven? The fake identity of an insurance investigator with a theory about a Chinese advertising account was a farce. And then why concoct yet another theory about art fakes and missing amulets?

Perhaps he was as unbalanced as Tony Maine suggested?

When Lacont told his wife, Margot, over dinner of the bungled arrest at the Carlton, her rejoinder pulled him up short, "A very arid response to his predicament, *mon cher*," said Madame Lacont.

"Do you think so?"

"Well, if he is telling you the truth his actions were perfectly understandable. Maybe he is the dupe of his employer, this British businessman, maybe there is an art forgery syndicate? Open mind, open mind, Gerrard; stranger things have happened on the Côte d'Azur."

"You should have seen what he did to Rolande's shoulder," Lacont felt obliged to say, "He'll be in a sling for weeks."

But it was true, Tony Maine worried him. He seemed a hybrid creature, carefree in damning Carrick yet he considered himself guiltless in paying extortion money without contacting the police. Lacont keenly wanted to interview him in person. He was a charismatic and successful business leader with powerful friends, men like him were a constant factor in police work on the Côte, but that didn't make him honest. It did mean, however, that Lacont had to be careful.

"Unfortunately, I have no plans to return to France at the moment, Inspecteur, I'll have my lawyers supply you with statements and anything else you need."

"Monsieur, I will need proof of the extortion."

"I won't press charges at this stage," Maine said.

"If a crime has been committed," Lacont pointed out, "you don't have to; I shall charge him."

Maine sent him a copy of the bank transfer and provided a list of people who might corroborate his story:

Rémy Barré told Rolande that he witnessed Maine get an unexpected phone call backstage at the Palais after the Legends debate. "I remember it clearly. Tony was surprised and angry, he said something like, *Andy Carrick? Are you following me?* He then arranged to meet him at the helipad. Then I heard him say, *How can I believe you, Carrick, you're just after my money.*"

The helicopter pilot, too, remembered a brief exchange before they took off. "Mr. Maine said, *The money's in your account now.* Mr. Maine seemed very preoccupied. Worried, maybe."

One of the flight attendants at the private jet facility in Nice was also interviewed. "Yes, I remember Mr. Maine yelling at a man across the lounge, he said, *I'll talk to the police and tell them about you.* It made me wonder if something was wrong. Then, when we were crossing the tarmac to his jet he said, almost to himself, but loud enough for me to hear, *You murderous bastard.*"

Yet ... Lacont's instincts twitched.

The first thing was to bring Carrick in. But taking him might be difficult, he had melted into the festival melange and finding him was not going to be simple.

"*Is* it possible there is an art forgery racket?" Margot persisted as she put a plate of cheese in front of Lacont, "It would be so much more interesting."

"*Que sais-je?* What do I know? I'm checking with La Colombe d'Or the pieces in the Shackleton art folio. We will learn more tomorrow. Don't worry my dear one, my mind is open, it is just crowded and hurting."

Chapter 10.

He pushed the d'Affinois to one side and rubbed his head.

The American teen movie had wrung all it could from the themes of bodily functions and the humiliation of oversexed college kids. The next session started immediately, this time a comedy about a geeky city boy and a provincial girl.

Didier sat gravely quiet and then increasingly wide-eyed as Carrick backgrounded him on events in Cannes since the murder of Shackleton — Tony Maine's story of a link to the Chinese Qi project, the hit and run attempt on Carrick's life, the police suspicions once his cover was blown, Pornthip turning up dead in the sea, and finally his theory based on the amulet: an art scam involving Shackleton, Jamie Tan in Bangkok and unknown others, maybe Tony Maine, maybe the Chinese judge, Choi.

"My hunch is that Pornthip discovered the plan and paid a high price. I have to get more out of Sammi Walton, she knew Shackleton and Jamie Tan and she arranged for the folio to be sent to Cannes; she might be involved or she might be a stooge. If she's innocent of the scam she might be in as much danger as Pornthip Sinn was."

"Do you think Emma's in danger?" asked Didier.

"No. Anything Emma knows she got from Tony Maine. Though I can't actually link Maine and the scam yet, apart from Shackleton of course."

Now Carrick was thinking about Lacont. How had he got his potted history for the profiling?

"Didier, what exactly did you tell the police about me?"

"Only that I hadn't seen you, or spoken."

"It's just that you're the only one of these jokers who knows I saw the military psych after Afghanistan, PTSD is not something I mention to everyone. And Lacont knows about Dave 'bloody' Fergusen's death too..."

"I didn't say anything about any of that to the police," he

Chapter 10.

answered quickly, "Why would I?" then, "Ah, but I guess, um, Emma ... I probably told her, you know, at the time about..."

"Didier, we were mates, that kind of stuff's not for public consumption." Carrick protested pathetically.

"Just pillow talk, Andy, I didn't mean ... ah, Jesus, I'm such a failure."

So that's how Tony Maine knew.

And that's how Lacont knew.

"I'm sorry, Andy, I just never thought..."

Carrick cut him off with a dismissive hand, "Did you tell Emma you were meeting me?"

"Absolutely not."

"Did you tell her you were coming to Cannes?"

"She thinks I'm still in Portofino."

I hope you're right, thought Carrick.

By the time they left the cinema and made their way to Didier's car it was dark. Carrick was due to meet Sammi at the Casino Palm Beach in 40 minutes.

Didier's green Maserati Quattroporte cruised passed with Carrick in the passenger seat checking the parked cars, the people, the sight lines. No police presence or obvious *voitures banalisée*. There weren't any stray Lions festival-goers either, the Palm Beach gaming centre being at the opposite and less fashionable end of the Croisette from the Palais.

They doubled back to the outdoor car park near the health club entrance and Carrick got out.

The casino was a low-slung, somewhat dated building with an extended covered walkway leading from the entrance almost all the way to the zebra crossing on the Place Franklin Roosevelt. Not the most glamorous of playhouses for Sammi to choose, he wondered. The complex sat on a protruding tip of the peninsula where the main road does a sharp U-bend to follow the coast. Splitting the U, a narrow residential street running inland due north, Avenue de Lérins, which turned the shape of the junction into a kind of pitchfork.

Chapter 10.

Three ways out for Carrick if the police showed up and every-thing went to hell.

If Sammi knew the cops were after his scalp then Carrick had little doubt she'd consider fingering him, so he took the precaution of waiting out the time in La Cabane, a chintzy sidewalk café with a blue canvas awning and clear plastic walls to protect patrons from the sea breeze that funnelled along the apartment lined street.

Didier was around the corner, double parked outside the small yacht club, ready to pick her up when he got the call from Carrick; that way, if there *was* a police trap, if Sammi tipped had them off, they'd spring it on the wrong man. They'd jump Didier. And Didier was innocent of everything except being a cuckold.

Carrick asked for a "generous" pastis from the manager, an affable character with highlights in his hair, he wore bright blue shoes that matched the blue awning and table-cloths: his idea of corporate branding. Carrick gave him a €20 note saying he would soon need to use his phone for two local calls.

"*Vous êtes dans le pastis?*" said Blue Shoes, a polite French way of asking 'Are you in trouble?'

"I'll know after the phone calls."

Carrick sat in the corner with a direct view of the casino entrance about a hundred and thirty yards away. Between him and it the ghostly reflection of himself distorted in the uneven plastic wall, red crew cut glowing like a matchstick in the café light. He was glad to have Didi onboard, grateful to have an ally, it helped his clarity having someone to explain things to.

"You sure about this art scam thing?" Didier asked in the cinema.

Carrick shook his head, "I may not have much of an eye for art but some of the pieces I saw in Jamie Tan's folio look perfect copies of what's on the wall at La Colombe d'Or. I found a book in the library detailing the whole collection."

Not much to go on, but a drowning man has to clutch at something.

Sammi appeared at 10.58pm, striding in her mannish fashion along the length of the covered walkway to the street. She scanned both directions impatiently, waving away a hovering taxi cab. Carrick went to the café counter and Blue Shoes handed him the phone before discreetly retreating to the kitchen.

Carrick saw Sammi puzzle over the number before deciding to answer.

"Who's this?"

"It's your date."

He told her to get into the green Maserati that was about to pull up and say the words: 'Hi Didier.'

"Who the hell's Didier?" she demanded.

"Sammi, just do it."

Then he rang Didier's cell.

"Now."

"On my way, suh," said Didi in a mock military voice.

Watching for trouble from a hundred yards away up the Avenue de Lérins meant that Carrick was too far away to do anything when trouble came.

He saw Sammi at the road's edge, thin sleeveless top rippling in the sea breeze, bare arms toned, long legs shiny in black leather, at her hips the buckles on her long-strapped shoulder bag were highlighted in a brief flash of headlights.

The green Quattroporte pulled into Carrick's frame of vision on cue. As Didier leaned across and opened the passenger door for her, she bent down, looked into the car and saw him, stood up again, put her hands on hips and said something. Suddenly she looked up sharply towards the sound of a roaring engine, she shook her head and recoiled half a step, moving a hand to her mouth.

Carrick stood up too quickly and knocked his chair off its feet as he saw a black van speed onto the scene from the west, it stopped in an abbreviated screech, blocking his view of Didier's car, for a moment he had no vision of what was happening on the other side of the vehicle until two sharp flashes. Two lightening strikes from a black cloud.

Unmistakable.

Two muzzle flashes.

Chapter 10.

His stomach dropped to his bowels.

This couldn't be the police.

Carrick bolted from the café and sprinted towards them in slow motion like a bad dream. He heard a door slam, the passenger side of the van closing, and the thing sped off like a wailing banshee. There was still eighty yards between Carrick and the motionless Maserati.

He knew he was too late. It had all happened in thirty seconds from the moment he'd seen her exit the Casino.

"Sammi!" he yelled.

Now he saw her, hand to the side of her head, bewildered, still on the far side of the Maserati she stood frozen in place, unsure where the voice came from.

"Sammi!"

The few witnesses on the street were converging tentatively on Didier's Quattroporte and Carrick was now forty yards away running towards them like a crazed fiend. A woman screamed.

What he saw when he got there was as bad as his worst fear. Didier, head askew on the headrest, a bullet entry in his cheek, another where his right eye used to be.

Carrick looked at Sammi. She stared back, horror contorting her face, but untouched.

A man was running into the casino entrance yelling, "Ambulance, *immédiatement*. Police!"

All Carrick could think was this was the worst place in the world for someone already in a bad way with the police.

"Get in the back seat," he yelled.

The Maserati's motor was still running, he shoved Didier's dead weight across to the passenger side and jumped into the driver seat, "Sammi. Get in the back. Now!"

He crunched the car into gear as he heard her slam the back door, gunned it in a fury of smoke and rubber in the direction the van had gone.

"Who the hell was that?" he yelled.

"How the fuck do I know? Who the hell is this?" she yelled back.

She meant Didier.

Chapter 10.

A short way along Boulevard Eugéne Gazagnaire towards the D6007 self-preservation reasserted itself and he gave up trying to locate the black van, too much of a start, there were a dozen side road options it could have taken. He had to slow down and stop drawing attention to himself, get off the main roads.

Carrick looked up, Sammi blank eyed and pale in the rear vision mirror. He turned off the Avenue du Maréchal Juin and north to Boulevard Metropole, heading inland, driving in dumb silence. The winding road tightened into hairpins and the traffic thinned as they started climbing the tree-capped hill passed the villa-studded peaks of La Californie and Super Cannes. Didier's grisly head swayed across from the passenger side and onto his shoulder.

"Aw, yuck," said Sammi.

Carrick pushed Didier gently back, as if not to wake him. But the same thing happened on the next sharp bend, his shoulder was getting damp with dark blood and stuff that doesn't bear too much thought.

"Where are you taking me?" demanded Sammi.

"Somewhere safe."

He hoped.

But his first job was to get rid of Didier's car and poor Didier himself, he took a turn and they were on unmade road, white as a ghost trail in the headlights, he smashed through a yellow work barrier to a track that led to a wooded area atop one of the peaks. Some kind of quarry. No good worrying about Didier's precious Quattroporte now.

"Where are you going, you maniac?" Sammi shrieked.

The forested hill had a bald crown like a monk. He stopped the car at the edge of the clearing near the trees, switched off the lights and listened for pursuers.

All was silence.

He got out, opened the rear door for her, "Come on. We've got some walking to do."

She was on him with the knife before he knew it.

CHAPTER 11.

Carrick dropped his right shoulder and turned to dodge the thrusting blade but it sliced through his purple shirt and slashed across his belly. She lashed out again, he threw his weight sideways, lifting his knee to jam her wrist against the rear panel of the car. Her head came forwards involuntarily and he twisted, using the torque to jab her hard as he could in the forehead with the point of his elbow.

Once was enough.

She let go the knife and her eyes rolled back, she folded to the ground, right arm still pinned to the car like a doll pegged to a clothesline.

He stepped back, pulled up his satin shirt and surveyed the damage. The wound above his naval was four inches long but not deep, she'd only caught him with the tip of the blade but he was leaking like a pierced barrel. He picked up the weapon and examined it in the moonlight. A 4 1/2-inch dive knife, drop point tip, smooth side sliding down to a line cutter and a serrated edge on the back, finger scoops on the hand grip like a survival knife. Looked brand new apart from his blood on it.

Sammi groaned.

He pulled her up roughly, put his left fist against her throat and pushed her hard against the edge of the car door.

"Time we had a talk."

"Kill me, I don't care. But I won't make it easy."

"I'm not going to kill you. I'm trying to save you."

This was a ridiculous conversation. He eased the pressure and slipped the knife down the back of his shorts.

She snapped away from him suddenly and tried to knee him in the groin. He slapped her hard and increased the force on her throat again until her colour heightened to fire engine. Then he gradually released it and took her by the shoulders.

"Chill out, can't you? Stop attacking me and I'll stop having to defend myself."

She put her hand to her forehead and rubbed the lump that was already a golf ball, "Bastard. You're all the same."

"Hey, you came at me with the knife. Why are you carrying something like that?"

It was a damn good knife. Titanium. Well balanced. Expensive.

"Cannes is a dangerous place. Or haven't you noticed?"

He tilted her head into the moonlight to look at the damage, "You'll live."

She pulled away and leaned back against the car, taking deep breaths. Carrick took off his shirt, now paisley with his blood and bits of Didier, tore it into strips as a makeshift field dressing and wrapped his wound, neat and firm.

"Quite the boy scout," she said, watching him sullenly, "Except for the tattoos."

Carrick pulled the key from the ignition and opened the trunk, inside he found Didier's suitcase with the clothes he'd taken to Portofino. He grabbed a shirt. Didier was a couple of sizes smaller but Carrick wasn't going to be fussy, at least the flaps were long enough to cover the blood stains at the waist of his yellow shorts and conceal the knife nestled against his spine. He wasn't going to try struggling into Didier's trousers right now, he put the case under his arm, threw the keys into the trunk and slammed it.

He grabbed her shoulder bag from the back seat and opened it, "Any more surprises in here?"

Sammi turned her face away defiantly. Carrick found no more weapons but pulled out three small plastic bags of white powder and held them up to her.

"Awards night is Friday," she said simply, "You don't think I went to that lousy casino just to score on the slot machines?"

Carrick threw the cocaine into the bushes then, without taking his eyes from her, moved to the front seat to get Didier's cell phone. He stroked Didier's dead hand, then shut the car door.

"OK, let's go."

"Where?"

"Walk now," Carrick shoved her towards the road, "Talk later."

This bit Carrick had worked out while he was still at the Noga hotel beach club. At Shackleton's wake BS had said that Bobby Best's place was virtually the only vacant villa in the whole area during Lions week; property rentals are Saturday to Saturday so Carrick was betting the crackerbox palace would still be empty.

It wasn't far as the crow flies but it was hilly and frustratingly circuitous walking. They marched in silence, both brooding.

Didier's pointless death weighed leaden in Carrick's guts, over and over he replayed the events that he'd watched so helplessly. It was a professional style hit, no doubt, but how did they know the time and place? Sammi would have to answer to that. In the end he parcelled Didier carefully away in his mind, gently as a brother, and put him in a quiet place he knew he'd have to revisit. Right now he had to worry about the living.

"You're treating me like your prisoner," Sammi said at one point.

"Good. The interrogation later won't surprise you."

The moon rose high and their shadows trudged reluctantly behind them up the affluent hills. They were on quiet residential streets, the wealthy denizens dreaming peacefully in fortressed luxury.

"What's with the hair? Those awful shorts?"

Maybe she wasn't aware he was on the run? He said nothing.

Chapter 11.

With the app on Didier's phone Carrick found the right road and as they neared the high walls of the chateau Sammi noticed him slow down, scoping for any sign of life. She realised where they were now.

"Hey, this is … You're not thinking…?"

During Shackleton's wake Carrick had eyeballed the security, purely out of professional interest; one CCTV camera pointed at the driveway gates and another covered the length of the high fence.

The angle was poorly vectored on the second camera, maybe it had been knocked or more likely installed by someone who didn't care much about exactitude. He was confident its field of vision wouldn't reach the far corner where Bobby Best's ten-foot wall joined his neighbour's ten-foot wall. The spot was a pool of black shadow from the overhanging canopy of a broad-leafed tree so the neighbour's cameras were blinded too.

Carrick threw Didier's suitcase over and climbed up after it. Sammi was tall and strong enough to hoist herself up without assistance, they dropped onto Bobby Best's lawn together.

He guided her along the tree line in the shadows beside the white pebbled drive and around the side of the house to the door that led to the kitchen. Carrick figured they would likely set off an alarm so he used her knife to cut the phone landline; now it wouldn't be able to alert its call centre. Some systems use a back-up VoIP routing the alarm call via the internet, so he cut the chateau's power too, just in case. They wouldn't be needing electric light tonight.

Inside he anticipated motion-detecting sensors, probably the passive infrared type that pick up body heat. Most have a short delay allowing time for owners to enter their security codes and disarm it, as long as he could pop the batteries out of the control box within a reasonable time no-one should be unduly alarmed.

"You've done this before by the look?"

"I run a security business."

She nodded, "Well, it's obvious to anyone you're not an insurance guy."

By 02.10 they'd made their way in the darkness to one of the chateau's upper-floor bedrooms overlooking sparkling Cannes and the pricks of light that were luxury yachts anchored in the bay. As if it wasn't dark enough without electricity, the décor of all the bedrooms was black. Everything from the carpet, the walls, the bed linen.

"Let's talk about you for a while, Sammi."

"Look, all that shooting was nothing to do with me."

"They were after me," Carrick said, "that's obvious enough. But how did they know where I was meeting you?"

"You seem to attract antipathy."

He moved toward to her.

"You going to hit me again, big man?" she tossed her head defiantly.

"I think the score is pretty even," he indicated the dressing around his belly. "Did you tell anyone you were meeting me?"

"Like who?"

"Were you followed?"

"How would I know? How would I know if my phone was bugged? How would I know if your phone was bugged? You're the security expert." She looked into the darkness of the hallway, "Think they got anything to drink in this dump?"

"Tell me about Shackleton, Sammi."

"Look, I'm exhausted, I'm thirsty, I'm dirty, confused."

Outside, the sea breeze stiffened to an onshore wind, susurrant trees filled the silence in the empty villa, white noise pressing into the dark rooms.

"Sammi...?" he persisted, "Shackleton?"

"Tell you what in particular?" she spat it out, "That he was a misogynist bastard who humiliated women for pleasure and talented people for business?"

"You had an affair with him?"

"Who told you that?"

"Doesn't matter. It's true?"

"It ended. It ended after he raped me, sodomised me, made me the lowest goddamn grub in the universe, until I was snivelling like a beggar, pleading like a child. That he enjoyed."

Her voice splintered with the rawness of the memory, the wind rose up and rattled shutters in one of the rooms down the corridor. In the moonlight a large tear glistened on her cheek, it looked out of place on the proud face, like a statue weeping.

Carrick said quietly, "OK. Let's find that drink."

By the light of Didier's cell phone they fumbled their way to the wine cabinet in the dining room downstairs, but it was empty. They tried the kitchen, only the dregs of the cooking sherry in the pantry. Just before things got that desperate Carrick noticed a small arched door down the corridor. A cellar door. Padlocked.

"That looks promising," she perked up, "Where would the key be?"

Carrick rifled through the lowest kitchen drawers and brought back a screwdriver and a meat mallet, he placed the blade between the lock and the loop and hit the screwdriver sharply one blow with the mallet. The lock popped open. Cool air brushed against their faces, a musty smell rose up.

They edged down a dozen stone steps and at the bottom found Bobby Best's wine stocks, hardly overflowing but quite enough for the duration.

She seized two bottles without looking at them, "Grab a couple more."

"You're kidding."

"For choice. And don't forget a corkscrew."

Back in the upstairs bedroom she sat on the floor and necked a bottle of red in unladylike gulps, eschewing the glasses Carrick brought from the kitchen. After quaffing in silence for a few minutes she started talking about Shackleton, her voice sharp in the blackness and the quiet room.

"I'd kept clear of his grasp when I worked in the Bangkok office. He always had hot and cold running local girls on tap there, they love the leverage of being with one of the bosses, silly yellow sluts. We used to laugh at him, tell him he'd forgotten what a white woman looks like.

"Then I moved to New York to join the Backroom Boys, they were just becoming a really hot production company. Anyway, about a year ago Jonas and I hooked up at the One Show awards, he was spending time in New York for the InterGroup network.

"Somehow we ended up having a quickie in the Men's room after doing a couple of lines before the gongs were given out," she said matter-of-factly, "I didn't see him again until a few months ago. We got something going then."

"Something serious?"

"With Jonas nothing was serious, that's what people found attractive about him, he just didn't care. People love reckless certainty. We hooked up when we could and played. We went to Mexico one weekend. Another time we went to an orgy at a swingers club in some old bathhouse on the east side of Canal Street. We were quite wild. Catching up, he said, for not getting together in Bangkok."

She took another deep draught of red wine, wiped her mouth on her arm.

"It was an on and off kind of thing, couldn't be too regular, I was busy, he travelled a lot. That's one of the benefits of being a creative director: you can write commercials set in locations that you'd like to travel to."

She laughed to herself, "He brought back some yarchagumba one time from a shoot he did in Tibet, that was cool. Jonas always wanted to try it so he somehow talked this poor client into the idea that he simply must set his washing machine commercial on the Tibetan plateau."

"What's yucho gumbo?"

"Yarchagumba, it's an aphrodisiac, you sophisticate. It was so Jonas, costs like twenty thousand bucks a kilogram. It's really wild stuff, better for sex than coke or ekkies.

"They're like a skinny mushroom, but what he loved was that it only grows through the head of some kind of caterpillar at ten thousand feet altitude. Can you imagine anything so unlikely? The fungus invades the insect's body somehow, I can't remember, fills its entire body cavity and kills it, then it grows out of the caterpillar's forehead. Jonas loved extreme things, he used to call himself an 'extremophile'," she drank again, "That's why he liked Asia."

"Where does Jamie Tan fit in?"

"Jamie was always a misfit. Didn't fit in anywhere," she laughed sourly, belched, "He was my friend."

Again 'was' when talking about Jamie.

"Did he know about you and Jonas?"

"I told him all. Talking to a gay guy about your sex life is easy, they understand, they love the quirky details. We spent hours on the phone. Thank God for Skype."

"Then?"

"Then? Well, then I was furious with Jonas for getting rid of Jamie from the agency and rehiring him to work in his stupid strip club in Patpong. I was more furious with Jamie for letting him do it, to be honest. Such a waste. But Jamie said it was fine, in fact, he said, he was painting and working on other interesting stuff as well; so I thought, OK, wait and see."

"What kind of painting and other stuff?"

"Does it really matter now?"

"I think it might, Sammi. I think it's... "

"Can I go to the bathroom, please?"

"Of course."

After all, she could hardly climb out the bathroom window, Carrick already checked and it wasn't big enough.

She picked up her handbag and went into the large en suite with its jet black floor tiles, walls, ceiling, basin, shower, even the raised spa in the corner with a view of the unlit grounds was black. Wall-to-wall, surface-to-surface, black as pitch.

After a minute, Carrick heard the shower running.

"Hey, what are you doing, Sammi?" he called at the door.

"There's no hot water," she squealed.

"The power's off."

"That's right. Bugger, bugger, bugger."

A few moments after the noise of the shower stopped she unlocked the bathroom door and stepped naked into a shaft of moon glow, a pale shapely sculpture, shiny lines of water trailing over soft curves. Aphrodite, thought Carrick.

"There aren't any towels."

He found the linen closet and threw her a towel, it was black, "Direct from Bobby Best's colourful bathroom collection."

She raised her arms without modesty and towelled the back of her head. "I feel better. That was bracing."

She patted herself down slowly. Rested one foot on the bed, dried a long leg, then the other. The variety of ways Sammi had of diverting his inquiries were multiplying, this the most distracting yet.

"Are you trying to make it hard for me to question you?"

"How hard can it be?" Sliding a tease into her tone she moved to him, dropped the towel, a charge filled the space between them. She reached for his hand, placed it on her cool flank. His tan fingers spread on her whiteness. Fingertips gritty. Dried blood under his nails. Didier.

He stopped her in her tracks.

"Jamie started creating art forgeries for Shackleton, didn't he?"

The moment was gone. She turned from him and picked up her clothes from the bathroom floor, her silhouette framed by the window, breasts swaying slightly as the soft light from Cannes touched them.

"How should I know?"

"Because among the advertising illustrations there were at least three fake canvases in the folio Jamie sent to Shackleton at the Carlton. The folio your company paid to have couriered to Cannes."

She put her hands on her hips, squared up to him, "Doesn't prove I knew what was in the folio, that was between Jamie and Jonas, I already told you."

He watched her for a long moment, in appreciation as much as lust. Her distractions were working. He chided himself and looked away.

Then he heard a couple of short sprays of perfume. Without turning, he asked, "Issey Miyake?"

"A man who knows his scents, I like that. There's more to you than meets the eye."

"You saw Jonas in the Carlton..."

"I told you before, no."

"It wasn't a question, Sammi, you were seen."

"By?"

"A reliable witness."

He heard her pulling on her leather pants, the press-studs snapping into place, and looked back towards her, she still had no top on. She picked up the bottle and took another swig, one breast rising with her arm, "So what if I did see him there?" she thrust her chin out, insolent as a fashion model, "I was trying to help Jamie, I wanted to know if Jonas was really going to show his stuff to other Cannes judges and recommend him."

"Was he?"

"No," she said more quietly, "I don't think so. Honeyed lies." She drained the bottle, leaned her bare back against the wall.

"Strange you went to see him. You said he raped you in New York?"

She gathered herself, took a moment to answer. "He did."

She put on her T-shirt and sat on the edge of the mattress, "We got too out of it one night, I guess, too far gone. We'd argued earlier but drank ourselves through it. When we got back to his apartment he was wild. He was in full moon rut, had me on the staircase, we were trying to make it upstairs to his bedroom but kept getting distracted, you know? It sounds ridiculous, well, anyway, at some point I stuck my head through the balusters at the top of the stairs on the landing, playing daddy's little girl, pretending ... who knows why we do the things we do when we're fucking, right? Anyway, and don't laugh Andy or I'll kill you, in the heat of the moment I got stuck between the bars. It was terrible, my head was trapped and I was on my knees and everything. He wouldn't help, that was bad enough, he wouldn't even stop. I had a bit of a panic attack but he kept on going, loved it, laughed the more I panicked.

"Then he ... he left me there and went away to get things, giggling dementedly, he ... all kinds of..." she took a deep breath, "he sodomised me with humiliating objects, did things I couldn't even say. When he was done he left me there, God, I couldn't forgive that, he just went to sleep on top of his bed and snored like a grandpa. It was only then, once he stopped pushing and jolting, that I could free myself. I should've murdered him while he slept, instead I left, like a cowed dog whining to be put down."

Carrick swallowed drily, "You didn't tell the police?"

"In New York City? Come on."

Outside, the trees shook, the yowling wind filled the stillness inside the room. Carrick changed the subject back to the issues at hand.

"Was Pornthip Sinn there when you saw Shackleton at the Carlton?"

"She was shopping."

"How do you know?"

"He said so."

"Did you see Pornthip at all here in Cannes?"

"Why? Someone see me with her, too?"

"Why don't you just tell me of your own volition? I know when you're lying," he lied.

She sighed out the words like a spoilt teen, "Yes, all right, she came back from shopping while I was there. Happy?"

"You were jealous of her?"

"Don't make me laugh. Look, she was just a piece of fluff, a dime a dozen in the fun park of Jonas World."

"Sounds jealous."

"She meant nothing to me. Neither did he. You don't carry a torch for someone who shamed and belittled you like that. Anyway, I was polite and charming to Pornthip, I even invited her out on the boat when Jonas was busy with the judges lunch."

"The Aphrodite?" he scoffed.

"Yes."

"You're consistent, if nothing else," Carrick shook his head, "but you're lying, Sammi. Aphrodite is a myth."

"What are you...?"

"I know it's a lie. The Coast Guard checked."

She closed her mouth and glowered in the dark. Carrick stood up to release some energy. It was then he saw her silver cell phone on the soap stand in the shower cubicle, the only thing in the jet-coloured bathroom that was reflecting light. He froze.

"What the...?"

Had she used her phone when showering? When he was on the other side of the door, the sound of water drowning it out? Who would she ring? As if to answer his question, the screen flashed into life just as he reached into the glass cubicle.

A mute text, the cryptic words in blue, *They're coming.*

He turned to confront her.

Not quickly enough.

The descending blow caught him hard above the right ear, a full bottle of red wine, and the floor became his friend.

The black floor.

His hands and feet were tied. Curtain cords. His eyes searched around the dark room. Sammi sitting on the edge of the bed spreading neat lines of coke on the bedside table with a black Am Ex card, using the illumination from her cell phone.

Carrick's head hurt even more than usual after hitting the red wine, it took a moment before he remembered the last thing he'd seen.

The words, *They're coming.*

Who?

"What's the story, Sammi?"

His voice sounded foggy, it seemed to come from far away. He sat up slowly as best he could, summoning the most dignity possible, which was not much with hands and feet bound tight.

"Wish you hadn't thrown away the other three grams, Andy. Lucky I had this one in my pocket or I would've been very cross."

Chapter 11.

She rolled up a bank note and snorted two lines. "I'd offer you one but you don't seem the type."

"What's the plan? Going into the art business? You and Jamie? Forgeries'R'Us?"

"You've never had a clue, have you, Andy?" She stood over him like a triumphant Amazon.

It was true, she had him there.

"I'm new at this, I'll get better with experience."

"Any opportunities for further experience will be short-lived, I'm afraid. Your beginner's luck has run out, Mr. Insurance Investigator."

"Who are they that are coming?"

She laughed, "How should I know? Rough boys. Look in the Yellow Pages under *Armed Killers for Hire*. Only seen them the once, earlier on tonight, remember? My dear, um, father protector had them sent over from Marseille, I think. Wasn't my idea, I could've taken care of you eventually. I told him that. Anyway, as usual he wants to be in charge. I've told them you're a red head now so there won't be any more confusion. They got the wrong guy earlier, your friend, but I think they'll do better this time."

Carrick replayed the moment the murderous van pulled up outside the casino, Sammi shaking her head, he'd thought in confusion but she'd actually been trying to tell them no, it wasn't him behind the wheel. That it was Didier.

She picked up her shoulder bag and started for the door, "They certainly won't be needing me."

"Who sent them?"

"I told you, the eternally vigilant one. What is it with you older men, you can't let a girl have her fun?"

"Is he the one who killed Shackleton?"

"You are so stupid."

OK, different tack then. Carrick had to keep her there, keep her talking. "Tell me, Sammi, all that rape stuff about Shackleton, was that real or just part of your Aphrodite fantasy?"

She turned on her heels and kicked at his head, he swivelled,

241

taking it on the shoulder. She looked down as if she was going to grind him into the floor like a cockroach.

"It happened just like I said, you dumb troll, it's why I killed him," she screeched, "That real enough for you?"

The words bounced down the empty hall of the chateau and out into the night.

"*You* murdered Shackleton?"

"When I lived in Asia I learnt all about *diulien* and *sia naa*, you know, loss of face. And what it takes to get it back. It takes revenge, Andy. Revenge the echoing laughter. Don't frown at me, revenge is natural."

She bent down and shouted into his face, "He was a destroyer. He killed other people's chances, he drove Jamie to smack, stole his talent. He ... he did what he did to me. Now Jamie's in a coma, goddamn it! He was a destroyer of souls, a black hole. When I found out Jamie had overdosed, I knew what I was going to do."

"What about the forgeries?" Carrick asked, sitting up again, bracing against the wall.

"When Jamie told me he was doing forgeries, I knew Jonas didn't care about Jamie's folio, getting him a great job. It was only for Jonas's amusement, so Jonas could swap a piece or two on the wall of his favourite hotel and gloat over it. Get another one up on the world. If he got away with it maybe he'd give them to someone important in China, he said, or just put them in a drawer and laugh. If he got caught he'd tell them it was only a wind up, a practical joke, a comment on the commercialisation of culture.

"He had no respect for modern art, said it was just graphic design with a back story. The faking was the thing, the ego hit of replacing a Chagall or Braque or a ... Léger, however you say it, literally stealing their talent too."

"How did he expect to get away with it?"

"How did he get away with anything? Force of character. You know, he even had the gall to complain to the management at La Colombe d'Or that they'd moved one of his favourite pieces? They rotate their collection, he was really disappointed the Braque wasn't on the wall because he'd got Jamie to do that one. The management brought it out of storage and put it back up just for him. He was going to repay them by replacing it with the work of a depressed gay drug addict from a strip club. Some joke, eh?"

"Last Thursday you went to the Carlton to see him. To kill him?"

"I told you before, I wanted to know if Jonas was really going to show Jamie's stuff to the other Cannes judges," she paused, back in control of herself, adopting an almost coquettish face, "Though I did take my new dive knife with me."

"You couldn't kill him at the Carlton because Liza Lieberman had a meeting scheduled with him?"

"You have been snooping around, haven't you? Yes, that leathery old bag turned up and I had to sit it out in the bedroom for the best part of an hour. God, she practically begged him to use her second-rate production company — when she finally left poor little Pornthip came back from shopping."

"Inconvenient."

"Oh, I thought about doing the both of them then and there, then I realised it would be smarter to separate her off. Take her out and let her carry the weight for Jonas's death."

Separate her off. Just like that, a death warrant for an innocent girl.

"So you made a time to meet her nine am Friday?"

"Yes. How did you...?"

"Pornthip wrote the time down on a hotel notepad."

"Really? They underestimated you."

Bound hand and feet and completely helpless Carrick didn't really agree, he'd been way off the scent from the start, but now his job was to keep her talking long enough to think of a way out.

"You killed her and dumped her at sea somehow?"

"She said she was dying to go out on a yacht, so I invited her out on one... "

"There is no bloody yacht," he said crossly, despite being at her feet.

"Sure, but she didn't know that. She accepted the invitation and I met her at the Quai Saint-Pierre, I pointed to the yacht anchored

243

furthest around the point and we set out in a little 12-foot outboard I rented for the morning," she added with a tone that Carrick took as self-righteousness, "which by the way was called, Aphrodite."

"And you killed her and dumped her overboard?"

"Once we were far enough out."

"Why? What had she done?"

"She's no loss. I told her Jonas was scum, even told her that he was faking art, using poor Jamie, destroying him. Jonas's whole life was one giant fake. She didn't want to know, silly cow, she thought everything was just ... so exciting. She said, 'Nothing is real, Sammi.' For god-sakes, something she'd heard in a song. I tell you, she asked for it, she was a pain in the backside: 'Which yacht is it, Sammi? How much further, Sammi? Where are we going, Sammi?' All in her cutesy little sing-song-ting-tong voice. So I stuck a knife in her. It was a pleasure putting a diving weight belt around her long scrawny neck. Such a peaceful return trip, I can't tell you."

Carrick looked hard at her, the muscles of his jaw working. In the dark she didn't notice. She probably wouldn't have noticed in daylight, she was in a bubble of her own.

"I took her hotel key and put on her pink hoodie and went to La Colombe d'Or, walked right into Jonas's room and waited. I knew he'd be up soon enough."

"Pornthip had nothing to do with you and Shackleton," Carrick complained, but he was pleading for a life already taken.

"Don't sound sorry for her! Anyway, she was useful, everyone in Cannes would assume it was her who did it, at least they would for a while ... people jump to the obvious conclusion, specially cops," she half-suppressed a titter, "and advertising people. Poor little Pornthip was a born patsy. Like you."

"So that was going to be my fate too, when you invited me out on the Aphrodite, a one-way trip in an outboard?"

"Seemed a good idea. Though I did have to go back to the damn dive shop for more weights."

"Shame I couldn't keep the appointment."

"See what you've put us both through?" she smiled.

She was enjoying herself, she slipped two fingers into a tiny pocket at the front of her leather pants and out came the packet of coke again, she tapped some more onto her left fist and took a snort. Threw her head back and shook her auburn mane.

"What about the amulet around his neck, the ancient Hammer God symbol? Another Jamie fake?"

"You know about that too? Wow. In a way that's what started the whole thing off. Jamie made it as an experiment, he saw it reproduced in some antiquities book, made one and gave it to me before I came to Cannes that year. So sweet. It's the symbol of an ancient healing cult. But Jonas saw it and Jonas wanted it, the Hammer God — you can imagine — he loved the idea of being the Hammer God. Bang, bang, bang. Sexual healing, he said. Well, lust is blind, I suppose, I gave it to him. Then, last week, I took it back."

"And cut his throat."

Doesn't sound much like women's work, Carrick remembered saying when Tony Maine first told him about the murder. Depends on the woman.

She knelt next to him on one knee, her head close, and whispered, "I asked nicely first," she ran a finger around the curved edge of Carrick's ear lobe, "Said I'd do something verrry special if I got my Hammer God back. I went around behind, rubbing myself against him like the pet dog he wanted me to be. I undid the chain around his neck ever so gently ... 'Come on, give your bitch back her chain,' I said, 'and get something very special that you'll remember as long as you live...' Jonas couldn't wait, he made it easier by putting his hands behind his back to feel me up, he lifted his chin in pleasure as his fingers fiddled. Then I pulled out his own cut-throat razor and put it against his throat, like this ..."

Suddenly she had the blade of her diving knife against Carrick's skin, his Adam's apple wobbled involuntarily.

"Then he laughed that big guffaw I used to love. I don't know why he laughed. Why did he laugh, Andy? Why do you think he'd laugh? Because he didn't think I'd do it? Or because he did?"

The blade was burning a bar across his throat, he felt hot blood starting to seep down the side of his neck.

"I pulled the razor hard as I could across his throat, he fell straight to the stone floor with a satisfying slap, twitched awhile, and was dead." She chuckled, took the knife away from Carrick's neck and stood up again, victorious as a warrior princess reliving the kill, "You know, Andy, while he gurgled on the floor for a minute or two I was awash with dopamine. I do believe I climaxed I'm ashamed to say."

Shame sat strangely with her, he thought.

"Vengeance was done," he said.

"Justice was done," she corrected.

"I think the law would disagree."

"Justice and vengeance are the same."

"No, Sammi..."

"I was in New York City when they got Bin Laden and I saw the faces of those college kids in the street. That's the feeling I wanted and that's what I got. Satisfaction."

Revenge is hardwired into humans, every soldier recognises that. The satisfaction from a summary execution is strong, Carrick had seen it. For all he knew it might even be necessary sometimes, he thought back to Mullah Noorullah, but it wasn't the same as justice.

He changed the subject.

"How did you get out of the hotel?" remembering Lacont had told him the CCTV showed no one leaving.

"Out was easy, I've been to the Colombe d'Or lots of times. I left Jonas's door wide open so someone would find him on the floor, I knew it wouldn't take long, went down the staff stairs at the back, waited in the changing area near the pool until the screaming started and people began running around inside the building. Then over the back garden wall and onto the roof of my rental car parked at the rear. It was still a bit of a jump down, put a dent in the roof when I landed. You remember my rental car, don't you? It would soon enough collect some fender damage too."

It dawned on him, "The red Renault?"

She giggled, "I admit it was foolish to try and run you over. My father said I was a troublesome child. But when Bailey told me he and Liang were meeting with this so-called insurance investigator, I couldn't help but poke my nose in. It would be a scream. That's why I swanned into the White Palms that lunchtime. But I took a dislike to your questions from the beginning, Andy my lad. You started asking about Jamie straight away, it was OK when you thought it was about the Qi pitch, but you'd already made the creative leap to Jamie. You were supposed to be rubbish at this.

"Anyway, I couldn't believe my luck when I saw you mooching around the streets next day so I followed you. When you went into that bar near the market for a morning snifter I saw an opportunity. It was a long shot, but my car was nearby so I gave it a red hot go. If only you hadn't moved so fast," she scolded, "I realised I'd only winged you so I parked around the corner and came back to see. Later, I phoned the rental company and told them their car had been stolen."

"Very efficient."

"You forget, Andy, I'm a commercials producer, we organise the impossible on a daily basis. That's our motto. 'Nothing's impossible.'"

All these damned people lived inside catchy phrases. Carrick had one for himself, *Gullible idiot: works all hours.*

"Look, nothing personal, OK?" she put the dive knife back in her bag, "but I've been told to go before those nasty boys turn up again. And I don't want to see what happened to your driver happen to you. I mean, it is going to happen, I just don't want to see it."

"Didier wasn't my driver. He was my friend."

"Sorry, poor old Didier," she made for the door, "Poor old Andy, too."

She pouted like a little girl deciding it was time to throw a toy soldier into the fire.

"Sammi, wait, where are you going?"

"Need my beauty sleep; I've got a fancy award night on Friday to get dolled up for," she continued with mock enthusiasm, "Can't wait to see which of those grand agencies gets the Grand Prix."

She pronounced it grand pricks.

"Stop, Sammi —"

"I can find my way, I've caught the bus from here before, remember?"

"Sammi, who sent them...?"

She gave him the New York salute as she had the day of Shackleton's wake. He heard her footsteps click down the stairs and fade down the hall into the distance, then the kitchen door opened and closed. She was gone.

Leaning against the wall for leverage, Carrick pushed himself up to a standing position and jumped in little hops to the bedroom door. He had to find a way to cut the cords from his hands and feet.

Like an escaped jack-in-the-box he bounced into the corridor passed the other bedrooms to the top of the staircase. It was darker in the hall without the ambient light from the windows but his eyes were as accustomed to the dim as they would be. One by one, without too much haste, he jumped down the steps; he didn't want to take a tumble as there was no way to protect himself in a fall. This was no time to break his neck, he wouldn't give them the satisfaction.

The thumping didn't help his headache and worse it meant he couldn't hear much else. He stopped midway on the landing to listen. The wind was still whipping around the villa's fairytale towers and the trees in the garden sounded like the sea was crashing at the front door.

They could be in the lounge for all he could hear.

He hopped a little faster.

At the bottom he stopped and listened again for anything unusual. Had he heard car doors slam? Surely the street was too far away for that? There are times when a good imagination is a bad thing, like when you're tied up and trapped in the pitch black in the early hours of the morning waiting for an uncertain number of killers to come and shoot you.

He kept hopping.

Passed the lounge and its sunken play area, the knight's suit of armour glinting softly in the gloom, passed the formal dining room on one side and then the drawing room on the other. Now he was in the kitchen where he'd seen chef's knives on a magnetic rack. He levered himself onto the work bench to reach them and set to work cutting the cords.

After a minute he stopped sawing and listened, holding his breath.

This time he definitely heard noises outside. The front door of the villa was being tried. They were so confident that they were prepared to come in the front door to shoot him!

They.

How many?

All he'd seen when they shot Didier was the black-tinted windows of their van. So, a driver and a shooter at least.

If they came around the side of the villa the next entrance they'd find would be the unlocked kitchen door. Carrick hopped back to the hallway, eyes wide as any rabbit on the run. He needed more time to slice through the ropes. He saw the cellar door, hopped through it.

For the next few seconds the loudest noise was his heartbeat.

He heard the kitchen door being opened.

Under the thick timber door of the cellar came a thin white line. Torchlight.

His noisy heart skipped into his mouth, surely they wouldn't start a search in the cellar?

The light passed and faded in the direction of the staircase, but it would only be a short time before they checked every upstairs bedroom and then started a more determined search throughout the villa. Not knowing the number of enemy, their exact location or their fire power led him to the only rational decision. Give peace a chance and run, despite the anger he felt about Didier he wasn't after revenge.

Carrick took responsibility for Didier's death, he should never have got him involved. The thought of telling Emma was gut wrenching — she might have lied to the police and she may even be having an affair with Tony Maine, but Carrick had punished her many times over by getting her husband killed. She would never have their baby boy now. He shoved it all back down into the vault, the battlefield's no place for guilt. More pressing was making it out to the darkness of the garden while they were still upstairs.

At last the cords around his hands gave way with a tiny snap and he moved quickly to free his feet. He stepped into the hall, the kitchen was just five paces away but he was completely exposed, his white shirt bright in the dark.

Seeing movement at the bottom of the stairs he froze, the silhouette of a big man in dark clothes, the back of his bald head glowing like a bulb in the weak light. At the same moment there was an alarmed call from upstairs.

"Giles! *Personne!*"

They'd found no-one upstairs.

The bald goon took a step or two up the staircase. The voice barked at him to search the ground floor.

Meanwhile Carrick had made the kitchen.

Footsteps hurried down the corridor in his direction, he crouched low behind the marble-topped island bench in the centre of the room, kitchen knife in hand. There'd be no outrunning a bullet if he fled outside now.

Baldy's steps slowed as he reached the kitchen entrance.

Carrick held his breath again, trying to perceive Baldy's movements, it seemed he'd paused in the hallway near the kitchen door then moved on. There was a foot scuff on the tiles at the cellar door. He must have noticed it ajar.

Wardrobes and doors were being opened and slammed in the upstairs bedrooms, there were two distinct voices. So, at least three of them including Baldy.

Carrick had a simple choice, break for it or wait for it.

A clatter of feet coming down the staircase made up his mind, the other two were on their way. The footsteps split in two different directions when they reached the bottom of the stairs, one receding, the others advancing towards the kitchen. Torchlight ballooned into the hallway.

Chapter 11.

Carrick made for the outside door, silent and low.

"Giles?" called the Torchbearer.

Baldy answered that the cellar door had been open. "*Donnez-moi la torche*," he shouted.

The second man ran passed the kitchen towards the cellar.

Carrick opened the door and slipped outside. Just as quickly the wind rushed in, racketing and whining into the vacuum he'd created, as obvious as any house alarm.

He sprinted along the side of the chateau in the direction of the pool.

Two gun shots punched through the glass of the galleria into the darkness of the garden.

The Shooter must be the third goon, the one who had gone in the opposite direction to the Torchbearer and was now in the front section of the house. Carrick ducked below the window line and kept running.

As he reached the corner of the building he saw the other two come out the kitchen door behind him and give chase, the baldy called Giles and the Torchbearer.

Decision time.

If he sprinted for the tall trees lining the driveway it would mean no cover, the Shooter inside would have an unimpeded view of his back for the first twenty paces at least. There was nothing for it but to hug the villa wall and stay below his line of fire.

The only defence was attack.

Ducking under the windows Carrick doubled back to the corner he'd just come around and sank to his knees, ready.

The shaking torch was a headlight signalling the approach of the two goons, Carrick slashed hard with the carving knife at the first pair of running feet to come around the corner. The man made a girly shriek of surprise before sprawling full-length on the ground, grabbing at his cut ankle.

The bigger man, Baldy, was a few steps behind but unable to stop himself in time. Using the knife in both hands as a bayonet, Carrick

Chapter 11.

launched from a squat, Baldy's own momentum forcing the blade through his belly and up under the ribcage.

He would have been dead before he hit the ground except he didn't hit the ground; the dead weight fell on Carrick, knocking the wind from him.

Meantime the Torchbearer had lost the torch, its light now illuminating the swimming pool's low white diving board. He was groping on the ground for something else in the night murk. His gun.

Getting Baldy's weight from on top of him was like trying to run in a dream, Carrick flailed like an upturned tortoise, bucked like an epileptic, finally squeezed out after an age and dived at the Torchbearer's outstretched hand. They grappled on the gravel, Carrick pulled back the man's fingers until bones snapped.

Every moment Carrick expected a couple of rounds from the Shooter inside the villa to rip through his back, the angle would have been easy and the distance from the galleria was nothing. The fact that he hadn't squeezed off any shots probably meant he'd abandoned the position and was on his way outside.

There was no time for niceties. Carrick thrust the fingers of his right hand deep into the Torchbearer's nostrils and ripped the nose up his face until it came away. The man screamed and arched his back, put both hands to his face, blood and gristle oozing between his fingers.

Carrick got to his knees for more leverage. With both hands bunched together he hit him hard and sharp just below his jaw, the scratchy breath stopped and the Torchbearer lay still.

Leaping for the gun Carrick rolled over and aimed back towards the building, sweeping the house and windows with his aching finger tight on the trigger.

No-one.

The Shooter hadn't come round the corner.

Even in the dark Carrick could tell the gun was a Glock, fourth-generation .22. A fine piece. Should have seventeen rounds if it was fresh.

He got to his feet, sprinted low toward the twin cigarette pines outside the villa's entrance doors. It was cover in the dark but hardly protection. Where the hell was the Shooter? The moon tucked itself into a dark blanket of cloud. The wind was throwing the big trees in the garden around and the noise made it impossible to hear footsteps on grass.

Then a voice called, "Giles?"

Sounded like he was just around the corner of the villa. He would have seen Baldy's body from there but Giles wouldn't be answering, the kitchen knife still in his heart.

"Serge?"

That must be the Torchbearer's name. Serge had been put out too, it's virtually impossible to breathe with your nose ripped off and the blow to that point of the neck is usually conclusive.

But the Shooter wouldn't see anything until he rounded around the corner.

Carrick encouraged him to do just that.

He called back with a guttural groan, *"Arrghh ... Ici."*

It may not have been a great impersonation of Serge but Carrick hoped the turbulent night noises might forgive the performance and disguise the exact direction his voice was coming from.

"Ou sont vous?" the Shooter called without coming around the corner.

This time Carrick didn't answer.

He aimed the automatic at the corner of the chateau at head height and squeezed some tension into the trigger.

Waiting.

"Serge?"

Curiosity is a weakness in battle. The Shooter would eventually take a look.

"Serge?"

Peak around the damn corner...

But the Shooter didn't look, instead he came out firing.

Carrick would've had a clean head shot if he hadn't been aiming too high. Way too high. The Shooter was a goddamn midget and he'd come out spraying a half-dozen rounds in an arc. Carrick ducked instinctively, the Shooter saw the movement and narrowed the target area. Carrick hit the ground as more bullets ripped through the greenery above him and Bobby Best's gravel sprayed in his face.

He let fly a return volley from the Glock but with the muzzle rise the rounds only took some chunks off the wall. The gun's aim recovery was fast though, Carrick adjusted and the last few bullets hit close enough to have the guy thinking.

Both men stopped firing.

Carrick's problem was nowhere to run and the place he was hiding gave no protection apart from darkness. The little Shooter had an approximate fix on his position now, Carrick had to move. He crawled backwards on knees and elbows keeping the slim tree that flanked the entrance between the midget and himself. He squeezed off three more shots at the midget's corner and scrambled further backwards. Now he was in the double doorway of the main entrance to the villa, it was slightly recessed but not deep enough to provide real sanctuary.

Standing up slowly, his back against the big doors, right arm extended for a High Noon moment if the midget charged, he was surprised to hear his name come to him on the wind.

"Carrick? Can you hear me?" Thickly accented English, "We have no fight, you and I. The other two are dead, I see. Let's quit it. We'll both live. Go while you can. I'll tell him that I lost you."

I'll tell him that I lost you.

Tell who?

He had not expected a negotiated truce. He didn't answer, it would tell the little Shooter too much about his position.

"Carrick? You hear me?"

If he was to convince Lacont what was really going on, finding out who these goons were working for was mandatory. Despite everything Sammi admitted it had only been a kind of bar room bragging, there was no proof of anything she'd said.

Carrick turned the Glock towards the villa's entrance and shot the lock out, then he hit the double doors hard with his shoulder and stumbled inside. It was a tactical advantage to be back in the chateau because he knew the layout, he was gambling that the midget would follow. Carrick climbed down into the deep carpet of the sunken lounge area and waited.

Nothing happened, he saw nothing, heard nothing, only the wind filling the night and the roaring trees outside.

Maybe the midget had decided to call the whole thing off? If he'd skirted around the far side of the garden he could've made it to the boundary wall on the street side without ever being in Carrick's line of fire.

Carrrick listened for the engine of the van being started.

Still nothing.

No, he's here. These guys are in it for the money and a job that isn't finished doesn't pay well. Carrick didn't move.

At that exact moment there was the smallest of sounds behind him, the slightest brush of material against the wall of the corridor.

Smart little man. The midget had circled back and come in through the kitchen door again. Carrick could feel him moving more than hear him, he dared not risk the rustle of his own clothes by changing position to look.

Lying in his well of shadow, Carrick knew the Shooter had edged forward enough to be just inches above his head.

Then he saw him shaped against the white wall, the barrel of his gun leading the way. As he advanced he fanned the weapon slowly, left and right. In his other hand the torch he'd retrieved from outside, unlit but at the ready.

Carrick was below his sight line and could have taken him out right there, he had a strong urge to do just that, he was sure it was him who killed Didier. Then came a knight in shining armour. Literally. The moon emerged and the silver light caught an angle on the fake suit of armour against the wall on the far side of the lounge area.

The midget mistook it for movement and seeing a man-sized figure fired a group of three.

He was fast and accurate, the tin knight clanged thrice, spun around and toppled loudly to the floor in an explosion of metal.

Disconcerted, he turned on the torch to see what had happened.

At the same second Carrick leapt at him from below, the midget swore in shock as much as pain as his short legs went from beneath him. Carrick hit him on the cheek with his gun handle. It didn't slow him, he was strong and he was pumped. He brought the torch up hard and struck Carrick across the bridge of the nose.

Carrick pulled the trigger.

It was instinct more than intent because Carrick wanted him alive, he was relieved when the little man cursed again. He hadn't killed him.

The midget was crumpled in pain on the corridor floor, Carrick jammed his foot down on the wrist of his gun hand, and poked the barrel of his Glock into his eye.

"Don't move," he hissed at his face.

The midget stopped struggling. "*Salaud,*" he spat, "Bastard."

Carrick snatched the gun from his grasp and pushed it away across the floor, grabbed the torch and shone it over the small body. There was an entrance wound just above his right hip, "Who are you working for, little man?"

The midget didn't answer. Carrick pushed his fist into the hole and the little man screamed like a giant. Under his back a dark shadow of blood was growing across the carpet, his face was getting paler at the same rate.

"Don't die yet," Carrick shook him hard, "Who called you?"

"London, London."

"Who in London?"

His eyes glazed and rolled.

"No you don't," Carrick slapped his face, "No passing out. Who in London? Who called you in? Who?"

"Savage."

Carrick wasn't sure he understood.

Does he mean me?

"What?"

"Savage. Savage."

He was only semi-conscious, losing too much blood, going into shock.

Chapter 11.

Carrick picked up his gun and the torch, dashed down the corridor to look for towels in the bathroom and wondered how to get him to a hospital. A body count wasn't going to help his case with Lacont, but a live witness might.

When he got back only the slough of blood was left, it was like a nightmare, he'd only been away half a minute.

Swearing silently Carrick killed the torchlight and pulled the Glock from his belt.

He dropped to a crouch. The midget was ruining his chances of being taken alive.

It was some minutes before Carrick ventured outside, the eastern sky was already breaking light. He followed the blood trail across the white stones and found the little Shooter halfway down the driveway leaning against a plane tree like a sleeping picnicker.

Cold as the morning.

CHAPTER 12.

Carrick stared at the rising sky for a long moment wondering if it was the last he'd see as a free man. The night's rushing wind had called a truce and calmed to a soft stirring in the morning's first light and he breathed the new dawn down deep into his chest.

When you're going through Hell, keep going.

The Major's voice.

Reboot, boy, momentum is the soldier's friend; crack on.

He frisked the dead shooter and immediately found a piece of luck, a cell phone. Not locked, why would he bother? he was a gangster.

He thumbed a few keys. Recent Caller ID showed two incoming calls from the same number in the UK. London, the Shooter said, was where his orders came from.

London.

Savage.

Carrick pondered the timing of the calls and tried to fit them to the scenario. The older call came in forty-five minutes after he'd spoken with Sammi that afternoon and made the arrangement to meet her at the Palm Beach Casino. The second call was thirty minutes or so before the gang's arrival at the chateau, which matched the time Sammi could have alerted the gang from the shower cubicle.

Had Sammi told someone named Savage about the meeting? Had this Savage then called the midget Shooter to arrange a hit at the Casino? Was this Savage the protector she'd mentioned?

Was Savage a real name? A nickname? A person, a company, an organization?

Whichever, on gut instinct Carrick decided he would send them a message.

Taking the cellphone, he left the dead shooter and ran back inside the chateau to the pool of blood in the lounge where he'd shot him. Smearing a handful of the midget's blood onto the side of his own face and temple he lay down with the back of his head in the middle of the tacky puddle, the rusty iron smell rushing down his throat.

He placed his driver's license on his forehead, rolled his eyes back, opened his mouth, stretched his arm up and took the selfie.

Proof of death.

It just needed a headline caption before texting it to the UK number ... to Savage?

Supprimé.

French for deleted.

Was that how the midget would tell his client about the kill? In French? In English? Who knew? But if they believed he was dead, he reasoned, it might stop them sending anyone else to kill him.

Carrick hit *Send*.

Next he showered and changed into clothes from Didier's suitcase. The t-shirt was tight but acceptable, the jeans were more of a struggle. He couldn't button them and eventually threaded one of the cut curtain cords through the belt buckle and tied it into a knot at the front. It felt no more ridiculous than the baseball cap, purple shirt and yellow shorts he'd worn yesterday.

As he left the chateau, Didier's suitcase in hand, the events of the last hours seemed as unreal as the chipboard walls that held the chimerical building in place. He didn't look back.

A sleepy dawn cab picked him up about a mile from the chateau gates, his eyes opened when Carrick gave him the address.

"Oppéde? *Le village? Etes-vous certain?*"

The cabbie was even more surprised when Carrick told him the tip he'd get if they arrived before eight am. No-one is happier than a Frenchman being paid to drive recklessly.

Emma Browning-Luc stiffened when she recognised the face under the bright red haircut and the darker red gash on his nose where the midget hit him.

Before she said anything or had time to shut the door Carrick pushed passed her and into the villa. "Emma, I have some bad news. Sit down. You're not going to like this."

"I know you've had some trouble with the pol..."

This woman betrayed him and she'd betrayed Didier. He gave it to her between the eyes. "Didier is dead. He was killed in Cannes last night."

"What? What are you talking about? Didier's in Portofino. He's..."

"He's dead, Emma, in Cannes. I saw it happen."

"Look, Andy, I don't know what you're doing here, but... is that Didier's suitcase?"

She looked him up and down, seemed to register the clothes he was wearing.

"Emma, Didier has been shot. Murdered in his car."

"You're crazy, if you don't get out of here I'm calling the police."

"He was trying to help me. He was killed by three men sent to kill me."

It began to sink in, boring into her skull like a .45 calibre sound bite.

"But who would...?"

"The goons thought Didier was me. Listen, Didier came to Cannes to help me. These goons showed up and they shot him before I knew it. Before he knew it."

Chapter 12.

"You're lying!"

"Seems to me it's you and Tony Maine who have been doing all the imaginative work, Emma. Starting last Friday night right here in this kitchen. But Didier didn't buy it, he wanted to help a friend, not set me up as some stooge."

She shook her head dumbly and made little fists, "I don't understand. It wasn't meant to be anything like this," she said more to herself than Carrick.

"What was it meant to be like?"

"He really is...?"

Her face crumpled like paper in the flames of a fire, pained animal noises pitched from her throat. She staggered, sat down. He didn't go to her, he stayed hard. Her hair fell over her face and her shoulders started to shake.

"Where is he? Where's Didier...?"

"I had to leave him in his car."

It sounded outrageous, beyond callous.

He explained quickly, "I've got the police looking for me, thanks to Tony and you, and the killers were still out there at the time. I had to leave him. He didn't suffer, Emma."

It sounded so weak.

Her eyes welled up with hatred. Who for? Him? The killers? Tony Maine? The whole treacherous world? We all deserve it, he thought. What have I become?

After a silence as long as the winter, "What happened?"

The room was still. Emma motionless now. The quiet of the morning all around.

"After shooting Didier they came back to try for me again. Now they're dead."

"You ... killed them?"

"You're going to have to come clean with me Emma. It's gone too far. There are six people dead now including Didi."

She stared, vacant, unmoving. White and fragile as porcelain.

"All I got out of them was two words: 'London' and 'Savage.' That mean anything to you?"

Nothing.

She had frozen.

"Emma? 'London' and 'Savage'?"

"I... no. I don't know. Savage? You mean Sidney Savage?"

"You know him?"

"'*Sid Savage before lunch ... Sid Vicious after*'. You mean him?"

"I don't know, who is he?"

"Sidney Savage works for Maine Hyland & Blix, he's the production department's fixer."

"At Tony's agency?"

So it was true.

Carrick hung his head. From the beginning cast as the fall guy, not the action hero. Blinded with a crazy fee, set up with a false story. Little wonder they say no one makes friends in advertising.

"Savage is the go-to guy if Tony's agency has any trouble, Mr-Fix-It. He knows the wide boys down in Soho. But why would Tony take it that far? Oh, Andy..." She lurched out of the chair and into his arms, sobbing onto his shoulder, "What have I done?"

He stood with arms at his side. Maybe he wanted to see the same amount of hurt in her as he'd seen on Didier's face in the cinema, the same hurt he'd felt about Robyn and Dave 'bloody' Fergusen? — equality of suffering, an equal sharing of hell.

He eased her back into the chair, "Let's start at the beginning: you're having an affair with Tony."

She looked up slowly, years older, "Did Didier know? I didn't want..."

"How long has it been going on?"

She blew her nose on a tea towel that had been lying on the table.

"It's been going on and off for years, more 'on' in recent times I suppose. It started a long time ago, when I still worked at Tony's agency. After the stress and strain of a new business pitch. Gladiator sex we called it, letting off steam after the battle when everyone was gone home," she spoke in a monotone, all spunk gone. "When Didier and I married and moved here, I stopped it, but I guess I needed something after ... after ... after a while. Being a shopkeeper doesn't get the adrenaline going quite like Adland."

She wiped her face with the back of a hand, "Get me a glass of water, will you? I don't think I can stand up."

Something about this broke through and Carrick felt wretched as he walked across the kitchen to the sink, this was not the way Didier would want me to treat his wife he told himself.

He remembered Didi's sad tale in the cinema: *"She was so low for so long. Months later I thought I heard the dog whimpering in the middle of the night, I got up and found it was Em in the kitchen weeping, 'I have missed so much of the love a woman should have,' she said."*

Carrick rebuked himself. I had more responsibility for his death than she did, I put Didier in harm's way. I made her a widow.

He gave her the water and put a hand on her shoulder. "Didier wasn't bitter. He loved you, Emma."

She collapsed into uncontrolled tears and Carrick held her as her whole body was wracked.

Later Carrick made tea and between tearful fits Emma explained how Tony Maine arranged to see her on his way to Cannes, knowing Didier was away on business.

"But he rang en route saying he had a problem, also that he had a plan. Disruption, as usual. He asked if that bloke, Carrick, was still in our rental cottage just down the road?"

Yes, he was.

Tony was pleased, he wanted her to help him convince Carrick to mount an investigation around the death of Jonas Shackleton. The Qi Project was the red herring. Any conspiracy theory has currency if you throw in the Chinese, he said.

"I didn't see any great harm in it, in the circumstances," Emma didn't look at Carrick when she said that, "He was going to pay you handsomely."

A hundred and fifty thousand pounds..."

"Fifteen thousand," she corrected.

"He transferred a hundred and fifty thousand so he could tell the police I extorted the money from him."

"Oh my God," Emma shaking her head, "I had no idea."

"Part of a larger plan to make the police suspicious that I might have murdered Shackleton?"

"No, he was just trying to sew confusion. The plan was that you'd be a distraction, that's all, draw everyone's attention. I didn't think you'd get into any actual trouble."

"Even when the police came to question you about me?"

"Tony said that might happen. Told me to deny any knowledge. I thought it meant the plan was working."

"Oh, it was." Carrick was thinking of Maine after the helicopter, before he boarded his plane in Nice, *I thought you'd be talking to the police at some stage.*

"Where did the police get my military history so that they could start profiling me? You?"

"What history?"

"The military psych, the divorced loner, the murder investigation about Dave 'bloody' Fergusen."

"Tony told the police that? I'm so sorry, I didn't think he'd use it against you, I was just gossiping ... I don't know, we were brainstorming, making it up as we went along. He said that glass half-empty people were easier to manipulate and I told him you were pretty low these days ..."

"Glass half-empty people?"

"Sorry. His words, Andy, not mine. He has a bloodhound's nose for people's weaknesses. The point is that it was all just a smoke screen, a disruption. He said you wouldn't get into any real problems, you'd just look a bit foolish, that's all."

That's all.

Carrick swallowed drily but let it go.

"Why did Tony want a smoke screen? What was Shackleton's murder to him if it was nothing to do with Qi? Was it the art scam?"

"What art scam?"

"Shackleton's"

"I don't know what you're talking about, Tony never mentioned anything about art."

"Shackleton was planning to replace some of the art on the walls at La Colombe d'Or with fakes he had done in Bangkok."

"Really? I don't think Tony knew anything about that."

Carrick was more lost than ever. *So much for all my detective work.*

"Then I don't understand why he's done all this, what's it all for?"

"For Sammi, of course."

How did this intersect with Sammi? Her motives were purely personal, 'pure' perhaps the wrong word when applied to Sammi Walton, but it was clearly a domestic violence murder. Shackleton abused her and she'd been vengeful with extreme prejudice.

"I don't understand? Tony knows Sammi...?"

"Tony knew it was Sammi killed Shackleton as soon as he heard about it, he knew straightaway somehow. He had to protect her. Create a diversion."

"Why?"

"Why?" she looked as if it were the most obvious thing in the world, "Loyalty. He loves her."

"Loves her?"

"She's his daughter."

"His daughter? Sammi Walton?"

"Walton's her mother's maiden name, Dame Elizabeth Walton. Tony's ex-wife."

Carrick remembered Sammi's words as she told him the gangsters would be coming to the chateau.

My dear father protector had them sent over from Marseille.

"Why didn't you say 'Tony Maine' when I asked who you were working for?" lectured BS, "I could've set you straight. I could have told you Sammi Walton was his daughter if you'd just asked."

Carrick closed his eyes for a long while. Life turns on the inconsequential, things so negligible we don't see the fatal drift. Things could have been so different with that small piece of information at the beginning.

Chapter 12.

It was two hours since he'd left Emma desolated in the sunless kitchen. They hadn't parted as friends exactly, more as comrades-in-arms, she'd promised to be there for him if he could get Tony Maine back to Cannes. Something he was determined to do.

Getting Benny Sewell on side was pivotal to this plan, Carrick needed his network of contacts and support. The irony of crawling to the gutter press for help didn't escape him.

"There's this thing called client confidentiality," Carrick answered eventually.

BS laughed, "So?"

"You're the press, Benny."

"Yeah. But I'm hardly Rupert Murdoch, I've got scruples, you know."

"Well, I've given you the whole story now. You're up to date. And you'll be up to your neck in it if you help me. Understand the risks."

"Thing is, old cobbler, I could have told you a thing or two about Tony Maine if you'd just put me in the frame earlier."

Benny sniffed and contorted his face in the particular way he had of soaking up attention, it meant he had something more to say. He scanned around for non-existent eavesdroppers (how could there be? the two of them were sitting in Benny's hotel room), then looked back at Carrick from the corner of his crow's feet, "Remember when Tony Maine went through that purple patch, his agency I mean, this great phase of winning all the new business pitches? Amazing run, millions and millions of pounds worth. You remember, a few years back?"

"No, but what about it?"

"It was unbelievable, ten or twelve new business wins in a row."

"So?"

"So, I was just laughing to myself when you say 'client confidentiality'. You see, he'd always have the prospective clients brought to the agency pitch in a chauffeur-driven limo, make them feel special ... then the team would do the campaign presentation ... afterwards they give the clients a drink and a piece of cake, shake their hands and wave goodbye at the lift … and then the chauffeur would drive them back to their offices. It was a nice little touch, yeah?

"The thing is, though, clients always discuss the agency's presentation on the way back, good or bad, what they liked or hated, who they thought was a git and who made sense in the meeting, all that. The chauffeur couldn't hear a thing, that was important — he was behind glass, right?"

Carrick recognised his cue, BS expected to be coaxed, "But...?"

"But Tony Maine heard everything, didn't he? The elevator they took to the car park was wired. The limo was wired. By the time the clients were back at their offices, Tony's people were already beavering away on refinements to the campaign they'd just presented, filling in the holes and revising the misjudgments, little things that Maine could ring the client about the next day and suggest as 'improvements' to their proposal. It worked a treat."

"You wrote about this at the time?"

"'Course not," he snorted, "Not as such, I'd never work in the industry again if I let out all the trade secrets. Anyway, word did start to get around somehow and clients stopped accepting his limo ride. Tell you one thing though, even now his employees don't talk about him when they're in the elevator."

Carrick smiled, but said seriously, "Do you think you'll be able to work in the industry again if you help me with this?"

"After this little caper I won't need to."

Earlier that morning, at the chateau, Carrick had experienced a certain clarity. He remembered a big poster he'd seen somewhere along the Croisette with the headline, *The most direct way to predict the future is to create it yourself.*

He started being creative.

Sammi had told him she was staying in Cannes long enough to go to the Lion Award presentation night and that had given him the germ of an idea.

Could he somehow get Tony Maine back to Cannes too?

Looking down from Bobby Best's chateau at Cannes' croissant

shaped beach turning into a golden smile in the morning sun Carrick realised the solution was right in front of him.

The Lions.

Defining a problem properly usually suggests the solution, says the tactics manual. Cannes itself was the answer, the magnetism of the festival. Tony Maine's ego would surely bring the rest of him along if his agency was going to pick up the Cannes Lions Grand Prix. All Carrick had to do was fix it so that his agency won the festival's biggest prize ... how hard could that be?

Ludicrously hard, of course. Nevertheless, the thought persisted and began not to seem such a crazy idea after a while.

Cannes thrives on rumour, BS had said. *Nothing is impossible*, Sammi had said. *Create the future*, thought Carrick.

Maybe it simply needed a believable rumour to bring Maine back? And where better to start than the gutter press?

Rather than being shocked by the things Carrick was outlining, BS was in turns intrigued, fascinated and finally enthused. He even started jotting down notes.

"What a great idea."

Then Carrick realised Benny was constructing chapters for some lurid treatment even as they spoke.

"This is big," Benny gushed, "This is my way out. I can do a book about old Jonas, and if you actually nail Tony Maine I'll sell twice as many. It's a real story and it's an exclusive. I'm going mainstream!"

"A book?"

"Yeah, I've even got the title, *Cannes of Worms*."

Three hours earlier Inspecteur Lacont received one of the most memorable phone calls of his career.

He was leafing through the reports of a crime committed overnight. Forest workers had discovered a green Maserati Quattroporte soon after dawn, parked near the walking track at a reserve not far from Le

Cannet. A dead man inside with two gunshot wounds to the head, either of which would have been instantly fatal. The police attending the scene said it had all the hallmarks of a professional hit, robbery did not seem to be at play, the man's wallet was still in his pocket.

It was a different modus operandi from the killings of Shackleton and Pornthip Sinn so Lacont hadn't drawn any connections. Until he learnt the name of the victim.

"Sir, the deceased appears to be one Didier Francois Luc. Husband of Emma Browning-Luc, the woman Carrick tried to use as an alibi for his movements last Friday," Inspecteur Adjoint Rolande informed him gravely, "Strange coincidence, no?"

"I don't believe in coincidences," Lacont said.

Then his phone rang.

It was Andy Carrick.

"I'd like to report a murder, Inspecteur. I was a witness. We need to talk."

"Carrique?" Lacont signalled to Rolande to pick up the extension, "Where are you?"

"Never mind that now. My friend was shot last night, Didier Luc."

"We have already found the body and the car. Carrique, I want you to go to the nearest Commissariat and hand yourself in."

"Didier was murdered by a hit squad outside the Casino Palm Beach at precisely 11pm, a gang of three men in a black van. Professionals from Marseille."

"We received reports of an incident at the casino, but found nothing," Lacont said evenly while writing a note to Rolande to try and arrange a trace on the call.

"They were sent to kill me. You'll find my fingerprints in Didier's car, I used it in a futile attempt to pursue them."

"You know these people?"

"No, but I know who sent them. A man called Savage. Sidney Savage. He works for a man called Tony Maine."

"You accuse Tony Maine? Why would he do such a thing?"

"Because I know who killed Jonas Shackleton."

"You think this gang murdered Shackleton?"

"No. That was a crime of passion."

"*Le críme passionnel*?" Lacont was back on familiar ground, "The girl, Sinn?"

"No, not Pornthip, sadly she was already with the fishes by then. It was another of Shackleton's women. Sammi Walton. She also murdered Pornthip."

"Monsieur, why don't you come in and talk to me about all your ideas."

"These aren't ideas, they're facts. After killing Pornthip she walked into La Colombe d'Or wearing Pornthip's pink hoodie over her head and waited in Shackleton's room for him. Find the hoodie and do a DNA test, I'm sure there'll be traces."

"How do you know all this, Monsieur Carrique?"

"Sammi Walton admitted most of it. The Tony Maine connection I learned from the gangsters."

"Ah, the gangsters you pursued but who got away."

"There's a small chintzy chateau in Le Cannet, they found me there a couple of hours after they shot Didier. They didn't get away the second time."

Carrick gave him the address where to find the bodies.

"Bodies? All dead?" gasped Lacont, "Are you serious? You killed them all?"

"Them or me, Inspecteur."

Roland appeared at the office door. With his good arm he gave the thumbs up, he had a location from the phone trace. Lacont read the note. *La Croisette — entre les rues François Einesy et Frédéric Amouretti.*

Carrick was at the beach front.

Lacont cursed to himself, there would be hundreds in that small area at this time of day, not easy to find one man who could be either on the street or the beach. Lacont nodded the go ahead to Rolande, silently mouthing the words, *Envoyer tout le monde.* Send everyone you can get.

Meanwhile he played for time.

"I am confused, monsieur, what has this got to do with the art fakes you told me about when we last met?"

"Ah, you've looked at my folder. Did you find the forgeries in Shackleton's black folio?"

"The paintings? *Oui*."

"Shackleton was going to swap one or more of the fakes from the portfolio for the originals in La Colombe d'Or some time this week."

Lacont thought about the CCTV footage in the dining room, Shackleton examining the frame of one of the paintings on the wall. "And this Sammi Walton is involved with the art?"

"Much as it pains me to tell you, Inspecteur, the art scam was incidental, a folly of Shackleton's alone. I was completely wrong, art had nothing to do with the murder of Shackleton or Pornthip. It was pure, mad hate. I'm a lousy detective."

"What about the pendant stolen from the body? The amulet?"

"It belonged to Sammi originally. I think it's what inspired the whole fake art idea in Shackleton's mind. He took it from her ... and now she's taken it back."

"And where is this Sammi Walton now?"

"Wish I knew."

"She is alive then?"

"Very much so. Look, I don't expect you to believe a word of what I'm claiming..."

"*Ça c'est bon*," Lacont said drily.

"...But I'm telling you the truth. It's a technique of persuasion foreign to everyone I've met in Cannes so far, I know, but I thought I'd try it. Please interview Emma Browning-Luc again, she'll tell you. She's waiting for your call. Be gentle, she's just lost her husband because of Tony Maine. She'll explain how all this began."

"How did it begin?"

"I was duped, used as a disruption to take everyone's eye off the real murderer. It's all been a conjuror's trick, distract the audience with misdirection while using a sleight of hand. Tony Maine framed me as an extortionist and then he tried to take me out when I got too close to the truth."

"Give yourself up, we can protect you."

"Not necessary. Savage and Maine think I'm dead. I sent them a message via the gangster's phone. It gives me an opportunity."

"An opportunity to do what?"

Carrick took a deep breath as he saw the first of the police cars arrive.

"There's one last thing I'd like you to think about, Inspecteur."

"What is that?"

"I'm hardly likely to have been Shackleton's killer and yet be ringing you now with all the details of the case, including the bodies at the chateau, am I?"

"You might be crazy enough to do anything from what I've seen. Carrique, I advise you to hand yourself in to the nearest policeman and attend the Commissariat. We will talk more and also you will be safe."

"Arrest me now and we lose the chance to catch the real culprits. I need space. Talk to Emma"

He hung up.

As the police swarmed in all directions, a hundred metres offshore from the beach club a red headed man in swimming trunks put the dead shooter's cell phone down on the floating pontoon and dived into the sea, backstroking his way to the far end of the beach.

"Publishing an utterly false rumour about the winner of this year's Grand Prix is a breach of journalistic ethics, of course," pronounced BS.

Stevie J. Rockett, the leprechaun-like commercials director and host for the awards night looked at him curiously, "And you care?"

"It's no biggie, but to tip such a lame ad? I'll look a right dick in certain creative circles."

"Will anyone notice the difference?"

Rockett was an arrogant little man and happily admitted as much, the world's *Directeur du jour* he called himself when BS introduced him to Carrick.

"I'm an arrogant little feller, that's why I chose this particular room," he grinned as he showed them around.

They were in an expansive suite at the Carlton, brainstorming. The suite was named after a famous fifties movie star and had its own private lift, an unexpected bonus as far as Carrick was concerned, he didn't want to chance being seen by anyone who might recognize him.

"I don't need all the extra bedrooms, but this is where Jean-Paul Goude shot the original Égoiste commercial yonks ago. I'm going to do the latest one, you see, and I'm going to blow him away. If I do say so myself."

"Égoiste?" asked Carrick.

"A Chanel scent for men," explained BS, "The original TV spot won the Grand Prix at Cannes in the late eighties. Bound to I guess, being set in the hotel where the judges stay. It's a classic."

Carrick shook his head at the deep-seated inbreeding of the award system. Stevie parted the french doors to the terrace and opened a bottle of Dom Perignon over the edge, the cork flying high into the view of the Meditteranean before crashing down on the palm trees below.

"Here you go, lads, some fizz courtesy of René Barré and the Cannes Committee to thank me in advance for my brilliant presentation speech tomorrow night." He filled their glasses to overflowing before jumping onto the middle of the white couch and sitting cross-legged like a skinny Buddha, "Now, tell me this adventure story that BS says is so hush-hush."

"Andy knows who killed Jonas Shackleton and his girlfriend. They tried to kill Andy too," BS made the second statement an afterthought. "We need your help to nail them."

"If you're willing," said Carrick.

"I'm willing to listen. Old Jonas was a character. It was shocking what happened to him."

"Did you know him well?"

"Not really. He was supportive when I had a little crisis last year."

"What happened?" said BS with an air of one who should have been told already.

"Oh, it was nothin'. Silly little thing. I'd bought a Quinn blood sculpture, you know the ones? It's a sculpture of the artist's head made from his own blood that's been frozen in a cast."

"Oh yeah," BS nodded.

"Left it in a freezer in my place in Dublin while I was working on location, didn't I? Me builders turned off the power while they were doing some renovations and you can imagine the rest."

"It melted? That's funny," hooted BS like a schoolboy.

"£50,000 worth," said Rockett, "Anyway, I was on location in the Himalayas doing a washing machine commercial for Jonas when the housekeeper rang and told me what happened. Jonas gave me a Bloody Mary to drink every half hour to ease the pain. You gotta laugh, he said."

BS cackled, "Bloody Marys! That's Shackleton all over."

"He said it served me right for dabbling in modern art. It's all a con, he said."

"That's a good segue for my story," said Carrick, and so told Rockett the whole saga.

Rockett fidgeted and twitched, asked for the occasional clarification, but mostly listened in silence.

"I'm an Irishman," Rockett said, when Carrick finished and asked what he thought? "I love stories, convoluted ones especially. Forlorn ones best of all."

"I've had my forlorn moments the last few days, I can tell you that. Will you help me?"

"Sure. Be proud to. But where do the police stand with all this?"

"Sitting on their hands," answered BS before Carrick had a chance to open his mouth. It seemed a reasonable summation, so he didn't add to it.

But it wasn't entirely accurate.

Inspecteur Lacont was at that moment fully occupied contemplating Andy Carrick's dilemma.

A message taped to a cell phone had been found on a floating pontoon, *Urgent. Give to Inspecteur Lacont — Cannes Police.* An American tourist handed the cell to one of the gendarmes that Rolande had hastily dispatched to La Croisette. The Call History revealed it was recently used to ring the Inspecteur himself.

"Carrick," Lacont muttered to his deputy.

Apart from the Inspecteur's number, the last Sent text was also noteworthy.

It featured an attached photo of a bloodied Andy Carrick, dead eyes staring, and the single word message, *Supprimé.* Deleted. It was sent to a UK number. The same number had called the cell twice the day before.

Rolande's urgent check showed the number belonged to one Sidney Savage in London.

This is what Carrick meant when he said Savage and Maine thought he was dead, Lacont realised, he had faked a proof of death photo and used the gangster's phone to send it.

By now the police had confirmation of the bodies strewn around the Le Cannet address that Carrick had given him. One suffocated, one stabbed, one shot. Among them was the Corsican, Jean Levy, also known as Little Big Man, a notoriously violent gangster associated with the organized crime Milieu in Marseille.

Carrick certainly had powerful enemies, but achieving such carnage working alone was formidable. "I worry what this man is capable of," he said to Rolande.

Rolande rubbed his dislocated shoulder.

An hour later Lacont had Emma Browning-Luc brought to him.

Her admissions, delivered in monotone, that she had indeed schemed with Tony Maine to use Carrick to draw attention away from Sammi Walton shocked Lacont.

She was naive. She kept saying how 'out of hand it's all got'. English understatement.

She confirmed that Carrick's plan was to entice Tony Maine back to Cannes and confront him and Sammi Walton at the same time. Clearly he was going to set some ambush, but how? And how severe was his revenge going to be? A betrayed man is dangerous as a wounded animal.

Emma Browning-Luc was a troubled woman but she was compliant, she would cooperate with the police now, he felt sure of that much.

"She seemed hollowed out," Rolande commented, "Like someone who just lost their belief in God."

"She seems like a woman who just lost the husband she loved by the hand of a lover she doesn't," replied Lacont.

The cold detachment of Maine's strategy also struck him as perfidiously English, and momentarily he wondered if that notion was mildly racist or merely insightful. Nevertheless, if he could prove Maine and his employee Savage hired Little Big Man and his cohorts to take Carrick out then it would be a blow for civilised society. He didn't care much for Carrick but he finally understood him. Margot, his dear wife, had been right.

"What's he going to do?" Lacont mused out loud.

Rolande, his right-shoulder aching constantly and hanging heavily in its sling answered, "Carrick? I know what I'm going to do when we find him."

From Carrick's point of view it wasn't about revenge. He was a soldier, it was about winning. It was about clearing himself from suspicion, absolving himself by solving the problem before him.

He didn't despise Tony Maine, characteristically he blamed himself for the weakness that attracted Maine to him. *Glass half-empty.*

He'd come to France for a new start and this felt like the tail end of his old life wrapping him up in a Gordian knot. All his past mistakes brought him to this moment, the bad decisions had become septic, the infection spread and damn near killed him, first with depression in the cottage and then violently in Cannes.

But this was the turning point.

Chapter 12.

Thinking back on it in the weeks and months that followed, Carrick wasn't sure why Stevie J. Rockett helped him so readily.

Was it the gravity of Carrick's need or because Rockett enjoyed the sheer theatricality of the ploy he devised to deliver Maine and Sammi to justice?

Like so many of the creative people Carrick had met it seemed more about the adventure than the substance of the matter for the hyperactive director. Which is not to say Rockett didn't take the idea of flushing out the perpetrators seriously — on cue he deplored puppet-meisters like Tony Maine, manipulative businessmen without a soul, he said, conniving suits riding on the coat tails of creative people the world over.

Maybe.

Carrick suspected the opportunity for a killer performance outpointed principle every time with people like Stevie J. Rockett.

"I think we can have some fun with this," the diminutive director said, pouring more champagne.

"What have you got in mind?" BS leaning in, the arch co-conspirator.

"Mine is a collaborative art and this is the South of France..." a sly grin to telegraph the humour, "... Where better to collaborate?"

Rockett said he'd already planned Friday night's presentation around a salute to Jonas Shackleton and an extravagant celebration of creativity, his death was too big an event to ignore so it had to be embraced.

"The first thing is to work with the punters early, stir things up, the audience have to be part of this. We'll need them to help raise the emotional temperature. I'll have to make some revisions to be sure, but they won't be major in terms of what the production people have to do. I love anarchy meself, but the technical crew won't, not at final rehearsal stage."

"How will you get the crowd on side?"

"Us, Andy me lad, you'll be up there too."

"Is that wise?"

"We're going to have to get rid of that lipstick-red hair of yours.

Then we're going to tell the delegates that things in Adland aren't what they used to be, that usually gets the blood going. That's how we'll use the Shackleton thing, a metaphor for what's gone wrong with creativity."

"Creativity?"

"Advertising creativity."

A metaphor for what's gone wrong with advertising creativity? Carrick wasn't sure how that would help nail Tony Maine and Sammi.

"Don't worry your pretty head," said Rockett, "We can do that and more. Get Walton and Maine to the awards and I'll make them sweat."

"How do you mean?"

"Confucius say, 'What is expected is as much as people will believe'. The audience will see the presentation they expect, but I think we can make our murderers see another presentation altogether. With me?"

"Um, in principle."

"With luck we can get your Sammi and Tony to play their parts in our little bit of theatre. We're going to play with their nasty little minds."

"Sounds good," said Carrick, none the wiser.

Rockett jumped to his feet and ordered room service.

When he put the phone down he clapped his hands together and turned to BS, "That's the important stuff taken care of, now let's get down to business. What's wrong with advertising today, Benny?"

"Well, the creative standard is mostly rubbish. Except for what we see here in Cannes, of course."

"Yeah, but why is it mostly rubbish? Including most of what we see here in Cannes. Write me a list."

He threw a pad of notepaper across the table to BS. He snatched a pen from the desk and threw that too.

"What?" said Benny.

"Why is advertising creativity so much shite? Scribe me a list, you're meant to be a journo."

Benny put down his champagne reluctantly and looked at the

blank pad, "Well, any agency guy will tell you that the clients' competence is usually below the demands of the job, there's so much piddling about at middle management level. You know, bozos who've done a marketing unit at business college and think they know it all."

"OK. Write down *'Middle Management'*."

"That's pretty dull, isn't it?" said BS, as doubtful as Carrick about where Rockett was headed.

"Not when I'm done with it," said Rockett, "What else?"

He sat down on the edge of the couch for a moment, then jumped up and went to the mini-bar. He moved constantly as a bird. Pulling out a bottle of Grey Goose he poured a shot, added some Dom Perignon to it.

"Champagne Slammer," he grinned at Carrick, "Want one?"

"No, thanks. I think I'm going on the wagon a while."

"Researchers?" said Benny, "They bugger up more ads than anyone, convincing cowardly clients that a focus group is scientifically ..."

"Great," interrupted Rockett, "Write down *'Concept Research'*, I don't need a sermon. What else? What about shrinking production budgets?"

"Everyone complains about how much you charge, Stevie. You may not want to go there."

"Righto, forget that one then. What about crowdsourcing?"

"Yeah," BS nodded, "Social media's dumbed-down advertising, it's back to the days of direct mail and snake oil caravans. Click bait is ..."

"That's the way. Write down *'Social Media'*. Next?"

"Suits that can't sell edgy ideas to the clients?"

"Jaysuz. Agency creatives blame everything on suits. Do they ever give them credit for selling the occasional good idea not to mention running the business profitably?"

"Nah."

"OK. Write down *'Empty Suits'*."

And on it went until they had a list of a dozen or so key words. Carrick was reminded of Tony and Emma's excited briefing a week earlier. A week ago? Felt like a year.

He was deeply tired, nervous and excited, mixed with a dull worry that things were slipping into a different realm where the loonies were running amok. Suddenly he knew how a client exec must feel with agency types taking over something his livelihood depended on, putting his life into the hands of someone else's eccentricities.

The room service trolley arrived. It was from behind a piece of lobster that Rockett revealed he was going to use a psychedelic coffin "as the central image" of the show.

"You don't mind squeezing into a tight spot do you?" he said to Carrick.

"A coffin?" Carrick lost his appetite.

BS spent the next hour writing blogs. The first one tipped an obscure Maine Hyland & Blix ad would win the Grand Prix, *Long Shot Ad to Scoop the Big One?*

"Publishing an utterly false rumour about the winner of this year's Grand Prix is a breach of journalistic ethics, of course," pronounced BS.

"And you care?"

Almost immediately it attracted sceptical comments on Twitter.

"Once the conversation's started it can't be stopped," said Rockett.

A second post, scheduled to go up on the *InCreative* website at midnight, planted the bones of the other story they wanted circulated, the headline read, *Shock Brit Connection in Shackleton Murder.*

In vague but punchy language Benny recapped the killing of Shackleton at an official judges' function and the discovery of his companion's body in the bay by a fisherman weighing anchor. The last paragraph mentioned rumours of a former British soldier posing as an insurance investigator who had been involved in a shootout at a nearby chateau.

Carrick thought it read like a cheap novel.

He wandered around the enormous hotel suite while Rockett and BS worked, feeling like a fifth wheel and trying to keep out of their way. He found the same Lions Welcome Kit he'd seen in Shackleton's room a few days earlier, the same invitations to parties, events, presentations and the whole palaver.

There was a pile of unread complimentary magazines too. He flicked through the glossy pages of the hotel's inhouse magazine. Grace Kelly's face stared back at him from a PR pic for the old movie, *To Catch a Thief*, shot at the hotel in the mid 1950s. The article was mostly nostalgia about the off-set romance between Kelly and the real star of the region, Monaco's Prince Rainier, a fairytale come true.

It didn't mention the movie's scenes of the future Princess Grace driving the hairpins of the Corniche too fast and Cary Grant begging her to ease up.

Melodie was right, *To know Cannes is to see its ironies.*

Carrick realised he was trying a similar idea to Hitchcock's. Set a trickster to catch a trickster. Using Stevie J. Rockett to catch Tony Maine.

He tossed the magazine aside and opened the latest copy of Time at random. The page had an inset box that caught his attention, a picture of a psychologist called Catherine Widom, who'd run an advertisement to attract subjects for a landmark study: *Wanted — Charming, aggressive, care-free people who are impulsively irresponsible but good at handling people and looking out for number one.*

Flipping back a page to the beginning of the article, it was entitled, *Is Your Boss a Psychopath?*

Carrick scanned the first few paras and settled on a sentence or two ... *Psychopathy is hard to define but it involves personality traits that fall along a continuum, with those at the extreme end characterised by superficial charm, callousness and a lack of empathy ...*

Tony Maine came straight to mind.

Researchers use a brief personality measure that assesses three socially undesirable traits: Psychopathy, Narcissism and Machiavellianism - the Dark Triad ... yet the individual can operate smoothly and with great success, as one author puts it, behind a "mask of sanity" ...

Carrick mouthed the words to himself, a mask of sanity.

Tony Maine to a T.

... a personality disorder characterised by superficial charm conjoined

with a profound dishonesty, callousness, guiltlessness and poor impulse control ... Carrick felt he was watching Tony Maine squirming in a Petri dish. Every word pinned him down precisely, the man was a psychopath.

Being able to define him, explain him, somehow helped Carrick. He didn't know why. Maybe it made him feel it was he who was the better man after all.

... Not surprisingly, psychopathic individuals are more likely than other people to commit crimes ... He must show this to Lacont ... *They almost always know when their actions are morally wrong, it just doesn't bother them ...* Carrick smiled with real pleasure.

He felt sane, wholly sane in the face of Tony Maine's disease, superior against Maine's success and the charming certainty that masked his insanity.

... The world's premier psychopathy expert, Canadian Robert Hare, once quipped, "If I weren't studying psychopaths in prison, I'd do it at the stock exchange..."

Lacont would see the pattern when he explained some of the stories BS had told him about Tony Maine.

... If you combine the traits of a psychopath with a high IQ and good communication skills you get more or less the definition of Leadership ...

Carrick felt vindicated, or at least less of a sap. It wasn't until he read the article's last paragraph that his euphoria evaporated and he threw the magazine violently across the room against the window and the view of the blue sky beyond.

... Studies show that people with pronounced psychopathic traits may be found in disproportionately large numbers in certain niches, notably politics, business, law enforcement and special operations military services.

Once more Lacont was reviewing the CCTV footage from the day of Shackleton's murder.

Carrick had claimed that Sammi Walton murdered Pornthip Sinn Friday morning and then wore her pink hoodie to go to La Colombe d'Or. The camera at the hotel entrance showed a girl identified as Pornthip Sinn leaving the hotel at 8.17am. The same camera showed her, or at least someone wearing a similar outfit, returning some six hours later, at 2.35pm, an hour before Shackleton's murder. The fur lined hood is pulled up and obscures the face.

Lacont went back and forth to study the walk. In the morning her gait was bouncy, short steps, a young person's spring. In the afternoon it was a stride, purposeful, confident. A difference in mood? Was she the same height in both? Tall, angular in the first, he decided. Statuesque, imposing in the second. Was he quibbling or did they *feel* different? The semantics of body language, nothing determinative he decided, certainly nothing that would stand up in court.

He told Rolande to order a DNA analysis of the hoodie as Carrick had suggested.

By this time, just a few blocks away, BS was arranging what he called 'the final ninety-five per cent' of the scheme devised in Stevie J. Rockett's hotel suite, and for once in his life that probably wasn't an exaggeration.

Hours earlier Carrick tried to find which hotel Sammi Walton was staying at by calling Melodie and asking her to check in the directory of delegates again ("Why is it always women zat you are trying to find?"), but Sammi wasn't a delegate so there was no listing. This was bad news, what if she had already flown out of Cannes? When she'd left him at the chateau Sammi told Carrick that she would be at the award night, but Sammi and Truth kept a wide berth.

It was Benny who suggested using Nick Bailey and Liang Weh to make sure she turned up. Carrick had mentioned all three were desperate to meet Rockett the day they saw him with Annie Leibovitz.

"That's the answer then," said BS picking up his cell phone and arranging to meet the creative team poolside at the Martinez in half an hour. "Don't worry," he said to Carrick as he left, "I won't tell them the real reason, those two wouldn't be able to keep a secret to the end of the hallway."

"Got a bit of graft for you if you'll do me a favour," BS announced after buying them each a beer.

"Do you a favour?" sneered Bailey.

"I've got three Backstage Passes for the award night from Stevie J. Rockett, I was thinking you guys might like to meet him?"

"Wow," said Liang, "Thanks, Benny, you're great."

"Access all areas."

"How'd you land them?" said Bailey.

"Persistence is genius. Look, there's just one thing. Stevie J. told me one of the passes had to go to a good-looking producer; I think he's actually wanting a new producer in America. Keep it quiet."

"Wow," said Liang.

"I was thinking Sammi Walton. Don't suppose you know where she's staying?"

"Sammi? Wow. I'll call her. Don't know where she's staying."

"Bring her along. If Stevie likes her he'll have you guys to thank."

The inside track was a Benny speciality, very 'Cannes'.

"Whatever," said Bailey, but he was already looking for her number in his cell phone Contacts.

Next, Benny worked on luring Tony Maine.

That meant working on Ray Doyle.

The sun was going down poolside as he was waylaid by a young Scandinavian creative duo who were fancied to pick up a couple category awards, "What about the interview you promised you'd do with us, Benny?"

"Yeah, yeah, why not now?"

Benny put his digital camera on the plastic table, resting it on an ashtray and angling it up at their faces.

"OK, guys, over to you," Benny grinned as he backed away, "Just ask each other some questions and take turns to answer them. It'll be cool. I'll edit it and put it up on the site tomorrow."

The pair looked at him, piqued, "What? You are not going to do it with us?" said one.

"It'll seem less staged if you do it, more creative," Benny was already on his way inside the hotel, "Just don't let anyone nick my camera, I'll be back in ten. It's already rolling. Action!"

Inside the bar Ray Doyle was at a corner table, drinking green tea, looking like a sad owl.

"Thanks for coming," BS sat down and ordered another beer. This was thirsty work but he was loving it.

Of course, he was setting Doyle up to lose some skin, but if Maine ended up being arrested then poor old Ray could be a bit of a hero with a little media spin. Benny would see to it.

Doyle nodded sullenly to him. He'd had a bad week. Nearly everyone in Cannes assumed that he would either be replacing Shackleton in the worldwide position out of New York or at least be running the creative side of the Qi pitch. To Doyle's way of thinking that tainted him, it looked like he was the one benefiting most from Shackleton's death. Now, to make matters worse, BS had asked him to lie to his boss.

"Look, I've been thinking, is this really the best way to play it?"

Benny cut him off, "It's how Rémy Barré wants it. Who are we to argue with the President of the Cannes Lions?"

"Barré never mentioned anything to us at the judging about Tony getting a Lifetime Achievement Award."

"'Course not. Wouldn't be a secret if anyone else knew, would it?"

"Why didn't Barré organise something when Tony was here for the Legends speech?"

"Yeah, I asked him that. Said he assumed Tony was staying the whole week. Most of the leading CEOs do."

"You can't assume anything with Tony. He's always got an agenda no one expects. Look, there must be another way to get Tony back to Cannes without lying to him?"

"Like what?"

"I don't know. I think I'm having a mid-life crisis."

"How old are you?" said Benny.

"Forty-eight."

"More like an end-of-life crisis then, isn't it?"

"He's going to be furious if I tell him we've won the Grand Prix and we haven't."

"He won't care, not when he receives the Inaugural Cannes Lions Lifetime Achievement Award. He'll probably give you a raise."

"You don't know Tony."

"Oh, I know enough about him, don't worry. Look, I've prepared the ground for you, I've hinted at it online in my latest blog. I've started the rumour mill, all you've got to do is ring him and tell him to come down 'cos the agency's won the Grand Prix. Call now while I'm here."

Ray did nothing for a full minute. Benny gave him an encouraging shoulder massage, "Come on, champ, you can do it."

"Alright, I'll do what I can," he said with a sigh and dialled the number. "Tony? Ray. Great news. I think the agency's won the Grand Prix award for Best of Show."

"You're bloody kidding."

"Looks like we've pulled it off."

"And you're telling me today? Now? You're one of the bloody judges, why didn't you tell me earlier?"

"The vote for the big one was close, Tony. Tied, in fact, without Shackleton's vote it was a hung jury. The chairman got the casting vote so we other judges were in the dark for the sake of secrecy. But I think we managed to jag it."

"I saw the gutter press rumours, but I'm not flying down on the off-chance. You know I don't attend award shows unless we win," he growled, "Why sit with rows of losers?"

"I wouldn't call unless I was sure you won't leave empty handed. I thought you should collect the award, Tony. For the sake of appearances," he paused, "It doesn't look good if I go up to get it, being on the jury and all."

"It's a bloody inconvenience, Ray. Look, here's an idea: why don't you get the creative team who wrote the ad to go? I'll send them down on the next flight. They'll be... "

"Can't do that, they resigned two months ago, remember? They're the team moved to HypKno, wanted to work with Malcolm White for some reason."

"Them? Bugger, bugger, bugger. I've got luncheon with Lord Mayfield on Friday. Oh, I suppose I could cut him short, boring old fart. Oh Ray, you are a nuisance."

"That would be great, Tony. Shall I tell them what time you're coming?" but Maine had already hung up.

"Good job," BS told him.

Doyle sighed deeply, "Yes. It was."

CHAPTER 13.

Breathe, breathe.

Crunch time and Carrick didn't even know if Sammi Walton had turned up or if Tony Maine would be in the house.

He was sick in his stomach at the thought of appearing in front of so many people with so much at stake and so little control. Wishing he had never got involved with creative people. It was a bad dream. Any sane person would think twice, Fate is mocked when a living man willingly climbs into a coffin.

You don't mind squeezing into a tight spot do you? Rockett had said the day before.

Breathe, breathe.

"Everyone's asking if you're dead," BS said brightly that morning over room service croissants and faintly burnt French coffee.

"I must admit I'm not feeling that bright."

"It's all good, the blogs are getting traction. Maine's got contacts everywhere, he'll hear. Look. Here's a text from another journo asking if it's true. And the police are refusing to comment about the chateau apparently, which is handy," he preened, proud as a peacock, "Benny's patented Three Big 'I's are working their magic."

"Big eyes?"

"Insinuation. Innuendo. Invention. All the big 'I's. My stock in trade."

"Oh good."

"What do you think I was doing all night? You're going viral, mate."

Carrick had bivouacked on Benny's hotel room couch overnight but hadn't got much rest. Benny was up and down endlessly, texting, checking emails, updating his blog, rattling the mini-bar. Carrick realised that this was his normal life, no wonder he looked like a scarecrow. Carrick was tired after no sleep the night before, but too keyed up to manage more than a couple of hours kip.

Friday had been a blur of preparations and now, too soon, curtain time had come, the award night had begun and Carrick was being packed into the awful crate for his part in the performance.

It was ten minutes since Rémy Barré had made his entrance to open the world's biggest award show, welcoming the delegates to "This glittering night at the pinnacle of global creativity…"

That was the cue for Carrick and Rockett, concealed behind the curtain, to climb into opposite sides of a specially-fitted coffin, painted gaudily as a magician's box to disguise its oversize proportions, suspended on a pulley high in the rigging far above the stage.

Bird-boned Stevie J. Rockett fitted snugly one side of the thin dividing wall, back to back with Carrick on the other, jammed into an equal half of the box and already sweating profusely.

"You've made your bed and now you're lying in it," BS winked, "Whatever you do, don't fuck it up."

Should be my motto, thought Carrick.

Melodie whispered, *Toi, toi, toi,* as they closed the lid. Break a leg.

The hard-edged shadow of the coffin lid wiped across his freshly shaved skull and filled the casket with darkness. The lift lines tautened. Suddenly, powerful spotlights from the rafters were shining white-hot through the joins. Inside the glitter-coated coffin Carrick was immediately cramped, hot and gulping for air.

Military training says the body has no memory of pain, but Carrick's imagination disagreed. No, this had not been a good idea. It

Chapter 13.

was small as the steel oven that the mujahideen stuffed him into when they baked him in the desert sun. This was too familiar. Images of Robyn suddenly returned, his old embedded survival program kicked in even though the application was way out of date.

Stevie J. Rockett hadn't told Carrick exactly what he planned to say on stage, just smiled whenever he tried to pin him down during the afternoon.

"Just listen for your cues, boyo, and then do your bit."

Suddenly they were on.

The opening bars of *Also Spake Zarathustra* boomed around the theatre, rumblings from deep in an orchestra, a martial kettledrum punctuating the air with thirteen ominous blows like the boots of an approaching army. Mighty trumpets sounded three long, clear notes and crescendoed to a pair of clashing chords that hung like infinite possibilities in some huge space.

The wildly painted magic coffin was lowering slowly from the ceiling on invisible wires through a giant plume of smoke, a surreal space ship landing on the right-hand half of the stage in massive, music-video-style pomp.

It touched down end up and stood there, a strange vertical sentinel. A psychedelic monolith.

Carrick couldn't see, but he knew that three leggy assistants in high-heels, blue sequins, top hats and little else but big smiles would now be standing beside it, stroking it adoringly. With a flash of light and a theatrical puff of smoke the coffin rocked as Stevie J. Rockett's side burst open at the music's climax and he sprang out onto the stage in full magician's outfit, black topper, tuxedo, cummerbund, red-lined cape and shiny boots — as Carrick had seen him photographed by Annie Leibovitz.

The spotlight followed him across the stage and the coffin lid was closed again by one of the sequinned girls, then the box began to slowly spin like a mirror ball at a cheap disco, Carrick inside gripping the supports with his fingertips, denying his anxiety, clenching his teeth, swearing to any of the gods willing to listen.

Stevie J's amplified brogue cut through the night, echoing and strident, "Welcome my friends to the show of shows ... bristling with all-new brilliance ... a night some of you will never forget ... ladies and gentlemen, I give you ... the once in a lifetime, super sized, superlative-filled, best of the best ... this 60th Cannes Lions Festival ..."

Generous applause.

"I, the Stevie J. Rockett of your dreams, will be your humble MC, but the Lions are king in this town tonight ...

"After my little bit of theatre, the Chairman of Judges, the legendary Mr. Francesco Ferreira, will pass the juries' judgment on your entries, category by category ... the gongs will go to the victors ... the brilliant among us will shine and the losers will pine ... Once the presentations are done, we shall move onto the after party with music supplied by Mr. Roger Daltry and his band, a veritable who's who ...

"But first, tonight we pay homage," he stretched out the word in an Irish-cum-French accent that sounded like he was being ill, "... omm-ahh-gg ... to those who've done the work that makes us all proud ... the conjurors, magicians, illusionists and storytellers who observe our complex and baffling world ... adroitly boiling all of life's emotions down to powerful pith and promise...

"All in all it's going to be a jolly bit of fun, so let's have a laugh while we're loving ourselves up..." he pulled a rabbit out of his top hat and handed it to one of his beautiful assistants, "... Some of you lucky little bunnies will get the Rockett ride of your life tonight, I guarantee it."

In a puff of smoke, the rabbit disappeared again.

The audience was lubricated, comfortable, happy to clap the old illusion. Carrick could see nothing from inside the slowly spinning box, just a narrow sliver of light, but Rockett told him later it was at this moment he saw Tony Maine slip into his seat in the front row, glancing around at which other agencies were in the special guest seating, nodding greetings at one or two.

" ... Like any great magic act, I shall require a volunteer from the audience to join me here on stage, please."

The lighting operator had been briefed to scan the audience with swirling spotlights on the cue.

"Hey, now, who do I spy up front in the expensive seats? Who better?" he proclaimed in mock reverence, "Who better to help us create magic, than the wonderful ... Mister ... Tony ... Maine...?"

The audience applauded as all the spotlights found him in perfect sync.

"Britain's Maine man ... the master prestidigitator ... the wiz of ads ... the harlot of Charlotte Street ...," laughter from the audience, "Come on, who thinks Tony Maine is the ideal man to come up and assist me with my trickstering?"

Cheers, chants, more applause.

Reluctantly but indulgently, Tony Maine stood, turned and bowed to the rows behind him, then climbed up to the stage on the arm of a sequinned assistant.

"Now, most of the night will be about the voodoo that you do ..." Stevie indicated the audience with a sweep of his hand, "The gongs are just around the corner ... but first, ladies and gentlemen, please indulge me, we must do justice to the magic mountain that was the late Jonas Shackleton. A fallen hero to many," he paused theatrically, "a bit of a naughty boy to others."

The crowd 'ooohhed', still willing to go along with the camped up vaudevillian delivery.

"I come not to bury Jonas, but to raise his spirits ... his creative spirit that is. Delegates, do you think we could cast a spell here ... tonight ... right now ... fellow magicians, wizards, witches and whorelocks ... do you...? Do we dare conjure up the creative spirit of Jonas Shackleton's dark magic...?

"What do *you* think, Mr. Maine? Speak up."

Maine gestured that his hands were empty, he had no microphone.

"Oh, sorry, what an oversight," said Rockett and gestured to one of his assistants.

The crowd tittered. A blue-sequinned girl picked up the spare hand mic and walked across the stage to give it to Maine.

He said something into it but it didn't work.

"Tap it a couple of times," Rockett prompted.

Maine tapped the mic and jumped as it magically turned into a bunch of flowers. The crowd guffawed.

"Oops. Oh well," said Rockett, "The show must go on."

The leggy assistant took the bunch of flowers from Maine and curtsied.

It turned back into a microphone as she walked away. The crowd clapped.

The stage lights began to lower as Rockett signalled for the audience to quieten down, a couple of nervous giggles erupted. Tony Maine stood awkwardly on the stage not knowing what to do as Rockett opened the lid of the coffin and paused, about to climb back inside but drawing out the moment to wave regally, one foot in and one foot out, the gleam in his eye bright enough to shine into the back row. A thunderous drum roll began.

From his spot high up in the fly gallery, BS thought he noticed Tony Maine's focus shift momentarily passed Rockett to the stage wings. Had he seen Sammi Walton standing there with her backstage pass? Even in darkness a father knows his daughter. It was probably his first intimation of potential trouble.

On the opposite side of the stage, Francesco Ferreira was waiting for his cue to enter and make his speech. To anyone who knew him, Ferreira's usually equivocal expression was strangely uneasy.

"He was dancing from one foot to the other like he wanted to pee," Benny told Carrick later, "I'm sure he suspected something was up."

If Maine saw him too as he glanced to each side of the wings, he must have wondered what kind of upcoming stage trick could cause such behaviour in the unflappable Brazilian, was Rockett going to do something outrageous? Or dangerous even? There'd been some flamboyantly regrettable moments in award presentations past.

Also there were two loitering figures in uniform behind Ferreira, were they holding Francho SPAS semi-automatic shotguns? Was Maine wondering if they were part of the show? Real? Performers in costume with props?

Whatever he was thinking, Maine began to look apprehensive, squinting deeper into the dark wings, a little lost on stage without being able to speak or control the action.

A spotlight beamed onto the coffin, "Watch me closely as I con...coct ... a ... spell," Rockett looked over his shoulder at Maine and then back to the audience, "Let the faint of heart beware, I'm about to summon a presence from another world ..."

Maine's attention snapped back to the show as Rockett proclaimed in a flourishing cry, amplified to ear piercing levels, "Zim zella bim ... it's time to brrriing ... baaack ... himmm!"

Suddenly Stevie J. Rockett disappeared into the star-spangled coffin and slammed the lid in an explosion of smoke. A strobing light show began to flash on the beat as dramatic rock music filled the auditorium, the effect was sudden and disorienting. The sparkling coffin revolved several times on the spot under the dazzling light-show; inside, Carrick tried not to throw up.

"We need a magic wand ... a magic man ..." came Rockett's disembodied voice from inside the box.

One of the magician's assistants handed Tony Maine a large sword, she mimed that he should plunge it into the coffin in the style of the old sword and box trick. Maine was mortified — a suit stabbing at a creative guy in a box just a week after the death of Jonas Shackleton? Not a golden PR image, but what could he do? As the upright coffin came to rest, the sequinned girl, carefully briefed, lifted Maine's arm up in a hammy way, laughing at the absurdity of it too; then she deceived him by quickly pushing his elbow, forcing the sword into the coffin with him holding the handle.

Off stage, watching from the wings, Sammi Walton was agape.

So were many in the audience, like swirling seaweed whole rows shifted uneasily in their seats wondering, as Maine himself did, exactly what the stabbing of the coffin was symbolizing? The old 'Suits versus Creatives' or something more sinister?

In the judges' reserved seats Ray Doyle squirmed and saw his career flash in front of his eyes.

The second sequinned girl gave Maine another sword and indicated that he should add it to the first, the famous ad man looked at a loss. Some of the crowd started slow clapping. They'd lost their sympathy for the over the top performance, many were mumbling something about bad taste to their neighbours.

Maine was shaking his head in resignation, he shrugged an 'on with the show' gesture and reluctantly slid the second sword into the casket.

Then a third sword and a fourth.

Cymbals crashed and new music started.

Again, a big puff of smoke and ... bang!

The coffin lid burst open and it wasn't Stevie J. Rockett who exploded onto the stage.

It was ... it couldn't be ... it was Jonas Shackleton.

The crowd gasped.

Carrick exploded from the sub-compartment of the coffin like a boxed devil, his head shiny, shaved bald of its red fluff, and a great black moustache in the manner of Jonas Shackleton pasted to his upper lip. The face of a murdered man.

Stevie J. Rockett's spectral voice rang out through the speakers like Jehovah, "Ladies and Gentlemen, the immortally immoral Jonas Shackleton ... a man possessed ... though still he lies ... a spirit like Jonas will never lie quiet..."

The bald Carrick moved across to centre stage arms outstretched.

Tony Maine stood aghast. Like he'd seen ghost. He was rooted to the spot in frozen alarm, Carrick saw it pass across his visage. Maine recognized Carrick under the Shackleton guise, what he saw on stage with all the lights, fog and sound was something twice killed, twice bewildering. Carrick's phantom manifest as Shackleton's. There was a time when men pronounced dead did not argue. The audience could see Maine was strangely moved at the bald and moustachioed figure and some misread it as respect for the dead advertising guru.

The wailing music grew louder, an orchestra of Aztec Death

Whistles, Rockett's voice seemed to grow in power and depth, "We can't let them kill the creative spirit..."

Carrick turned to the wings on the far side and saw Sammi Walton.

The crowd was puzzled, politely applauding this strange celebration of Shackleton when Rockett went up another gear. "This man is not Jonas Shackleton, of course, ladies and gentlemen," as a red spotlight pinpointed Carrick, "He is a spectre, isn't he Mr. Maine? A presence from another world summoned to help us find out who it is dares murder creativity. Isn't that right...?"

Carrick nodded gravely for big effect and bowed slightly.

The loud music stopped abruptly and the lights suddenly calmed.

The crowd hushed.

Then Rockett's voice blasted the silence away, "Let's hear it for Tony Maine, ladies and gentlemen — he is paying to bring Jonas Shackleton's killer to justice! Let us thank him for his magnificent generosity."

The crowd applauded, non-plussed but respectful. Tony Maine looked pained, powerless without a microphone.

Over the clapping, Rockett's voice boomed, "Can you tell us, mischievous apparition, tell us, what kind of evil thing is it that dares murder creativity? Who tramples our creative spirit? Who is to blame? Who killed the guru in *us all*? Hmm? Who ... killed ... the gu ... ru? Who? ... Who?"

Rockett's voice became digitally altered into a techno gurgle as he chanted rhythmically to an insistent drum beat so loud that it echoed in the chest of everyone in the theatre.

"Who ... killed ... the guru? ... Who ... Who?

"Who ... killed ... the guru? ... Who ... Who?"

Now big white words were being projected onto the stage in massive capital letters, the typeface distressed and scratchy, folding in waves over the back curtain in an effect that made the material look alive. It was the list Rockett and BS had come up with in his suite at the Carlton.

As each appeared, Rockett chanted, "Who ... killed ... the guru? You? You?"

MUDDLE MANAGEMENT ...?

Each word flashed on cue with Rockett's chant.

"Who ... killed ... the guru? You? You?"

BLAND MANAGERS ...?

"Who ... killed ... the guru? You? You?"

RESEARCH AND DESTROY ...?

"Who ... killed ... the guru? You? You?"

EMPTY SUITS ...?

"Who ... killed ... the guru? You? You?"

FATAL DEADLINES ...?

"Who ... killed ... the guru? You? You?"

Every copywriter, designer, art director and director in the audience whose artistic sensitivities had been bruised in the hurly burly of commercial life felt their hackles rise, they got the point now, creativity was suffocated on a daily basis by these things.

Carrick turned to look stage left and paused for an instant.

Tony Maine, standing limply, followed his eye-line to where the audience could not see. Standing in the stage wings where Ferreira had been was Emma Browning and Inspecteur Lacont, flanked by two uniform police. Emma stared at him with undisguised malice.

The energy seemed to visibly drain from Tony Maine.

"Who ... killed ... the guru?" LOWEST DENOMINATOR CHOICES ...? "You? You?" COMMITTEE INDECISIONS ...? "You? You?" CREATIVITY BY NUMBERS ...? "You? You?"

The projected words screamed out the failings of the industrialized creative development process, everyone in the crowd recognised his or her own particular nemesis in them, they struck at the emotional core of each of the ten thousand frustrated people in the Palais. Every working day, they faced such barriers to making their ideas the pure unadulterated diamonds they could have been. Should have been.

CLICK BAIT STRATEGIES ...? "You? You?" ME TOO-ISM ...? "You? You?" DEATH BY A THOUSAND CHANGES ...? "You? You?"

Chapter 13.

The delegates saw what Rockett was saying: How could the average creative person compete against such odds? How could originality and inspiration rise above the culture of mediocrity these words embodied? If nothing else they knew Shackleton was a maverick struck down. They understood that was the metaphor. Slowly at first, but then strongly and in heartfelt force the audience picked up the throbbing chant, row after row joined in and railed against the natural enemies of their delicate genius, minute by minute becoming incensed as a wronged football crowd.

But from the darkness of the wings Sammi couldn't see the projections of the words that everyone was focused on, she could only hear the chant repeating, *You ... You.*

You ... You.

It was tribal, stupefying.

Then a news cameraman jumped up on stage, camera on his shoulder, eye to the viewfinder, baseball cap backwards on his head, weatherproof jacket emblazoned with the *France 24* satellite network logo. Real or part of the act? He advanced on Tony Maine to get a quick shot. Then he wheeled around and turned the camera to the side of the stage. Sammi realised he was focusing on her, she stared transfixed as a deer in the headlights at the red 'live' light flashing beside the lens. The cameraman was coming closer and closer.

Carrick too was staring her down from the stage, Tony was looking at her strangely, trying to process it all, she felt eyes on her everywhere even though the audience could not see into the stage wings. As Stevie J. Rockett predicted, in Sammi's mind like most sociopaths, it was all about her.

"Who killed the guru?" someone in the audience stood and yelled between the beat in a call and response, "Who killed the guru?" called another as the crowd's zeal became infectious, soon it was being chanted from every tier of the auditorium, roaring through the Palais like the din from a Roman coliseum, "You ... You."

"Who killed the guru? You ... You. Who killed the guru?"

The big words from the projector flicked on and off, repeating, faster and faster, insistent and hypnotic. Taken up by the whole theatre now, thousands of feet stamping in rough rhythm, the chant became a demand, a primal baying, "Who-killed-the-guru?-You?-You?-Who-killed-the-guru?-You?-You?-Who-the-killed- guru?"

The two gendarmes from the wings near Emma walked purposefully onto the stage, straight to Tony Maine. The crowd swivelled as one to watch. Caught off guard, Maine took an unsteady half-step back towards the apron of the stage. Some in the crowd howled with laughter at the slapstick.

Stevie J. Rockett's voice boomed out of the speakers again: "Can you tell us who killed the guru...?"

The gendarmes surprised Tony Maine by veering off and instead taking flanking positions either side of Carrick, like nearly everyone else in the auditorium he thought they were coming for him.

Carrick gestured for the gendarmes to follow and they headed stage right towards Sammi in the wings.

The chant reached a crescendo of jeers, "Who ... killed ... the guru? You! You!" THE BIG 4 NETWORKS ...? "You! You!""

Sammi Walton saw Carrick striding towards her from upstage, pointing the way with the two gendarmes behind him. She dropped her champagne glass on the floor, the smash heard as a dramatic offstage sound effect by the first few rows. It was high melodrama.

Then it was farce.

As the gendarmes turned, Tony Maine and the audience realised as one that the pair of cops had the backside of their uniform cut away and were as bare-assed as policemen in a gay bar show. The crowd guffawed and rocked in their seats, this was absurdist comedy par excellence and their own laughter made them roar again.

Hearing everyone laugh as Carrick and the fake gendarmes advanced, Sammi panicked. The spotlight that was following him into the wings blazed into her face and he was a great, bald silhouette advancing toward her. Tension cascaded through her in sickly confusion, it was like a bad trip.

A group of performers wearing sandwich-board signs inscribed with the words *Who killed the guru?* were performing a circuit of the stage, marching faster and faster in rhythm to the chant.

Chapter 13.

They formed a tight little group and faced Sammi too. She stared in horror. The human billboards had cardboard masks strapped to their heads, a nightmare chill rippled through her as she saw they were printed with the great moustachioed face of the Hammer God.

Did *everyone* know?

The penny dropped for her. A trick. Rockett didn't want to meet her, there was no job offer, it was a fraud, it wasn't real. *Nothing is real, Sammi*, fucking Pornthip said.

Hate sprang up in a sudden rush of animal heat. She looked at her father on stage, powerless, unsure, a pathetic figure. She despised his weakness. She always had. Emotions peeled across Sammi's pale features in a succession of jerky micro-expressions.

The manual says create confusion in the enemy. Carrick didn't have overwhelming force, air back-up or even covering fire, what he had was Stevie J. Rockett, his smoke and mirrors, his sound and fury, his sonic weaponry, his burlesque.

"You bastard!" Sammi screamed, pulling the dive knife from her shoulder bag.

She rushed out towards Carrick ready to stab from shoulder height. Was it him or the image of Shackleton she was trying to kill, Carrick wondered?

Stranded on centre stage Maine cried out in dread, "No! No!"

At the same instant, in the gloom of the wings, a man with his arm in a sling stepped straight into Sammi's path to block her attack on Carrick. It was Deputy Inspecteur Rolande. She halted long enough to knee him in the groin, he doubled up and concertinaed to the floor, but three real gendarmes broke from the darkness at the edge of the curtain and were on her a fraction later.

Maine, stranded, helpless and alone in the centre of the stage saw it all, understood the ruse; he looked back to Carrick.

Carrick was mouthing something to him over his shoulder as he exited stage right, unheard in the cacophony, saying it slowly enough so Maine could lip-read.

"Whatever it takes."

EPILOGUE

Two months later ...

8.15PM. A shirtless Carrick lying on his back, flat out keeping the brand new couch company, the late August heat boiling him in his own juices.

He sipped at the mineral water balanced on his chest.

The farmhouse restorations he'd started were progressing steadily, repointing the chimney was keeping body occupied and mind numb with fatigue by the end of each day. He was obsessed with the idea of completing it all before the trials began.

Across the far side of the room the phone started ringing.

He jumped up and answered in his best French, "Allo."

"Hello you."

Robyn's quiet voice.

An electric shock went through his body.

He opened his mouth but no words came.

She said nervously, "Some of the things I've heard... I thought I should call. See how you are?"

It was two months since Carrick's torrid week in Cannes, his hair had grown back almost an inch and the scar on his belly where Sammi slashed it with the dive knife had healed to a red seam. But the battle had barely started.

Tony Maine had a top defence team, a distinguished French *advocat* and deep pockets.

Subpoenaed phone records showed an incriminating trail from Sammi to Maine to Syd Savage and the hit men from Marseille. But the Prosecutor's Office said that was circumstantial. Getting evidence from Sid Savage in the UK was going to be a challenge. The Prosecutor's best chance lay with Emma's evidence about the conspiracy. At Carrick's insistence, she'd formally requested witness protection and it was still being considered in the methodical way that the French bureaucracy grinds. So he'd decided to stay close to look after her, in the Bonnieux cottage, *just down the road*. Meanwhile doing a bit of restoration work to help out.

As for nailing Sammi Walton, things were more promising. Lacont's men found the dive shop where Sammi bought the weight belts that she'd attached to Pornthip Sinn, the *vendeur* remembered a tall American-accented girl buying a knife and weights.

She'd come in a second time to buy another set of belts a few days later. In preparation to use on Carrick.

Lacont also found the runabout named Aphrodite and her handwriting (under a false name) on the hire contract.

No matter how many enhancements Lacont tried with the CCTV footage showing a tall girl dressed in a pink hoodie arriving at La Colombe d'Or an hour before the murder, it wasn't possible to see a face. But forensics found a red hair inside the hood and eventually the good news came through that it matched Sammi's DNA.

Police also found Shackleton's Hammer God amulet in Sammi's luggage.

"It already seems a lifetime ago, back in the pre-Cambrian era," Carrick said to Robyn on the phone.

There was much to say but little he wanted to talk about.

They'd spoken only a couple of times since their divorce. At the Major's funeral, after catching each other's eyes across the open grave. As they walked away he'd almost broken down when she touched his arm in consolation, her lips twisting with uncertainty.

"You've had so many lifetimes," she said now, "Like a cat."

"I'm going to need all nine at this rate."

Robyn said nothing for a moment, trying to gauge his mood.

"Did you know the Stone Age was only five hundred and seventy lifetimes ago?"

When she was nervous her conversations were often tangental, unpredictable new directions set off by word associations. He used to find it endearing. Except during the final days of their marriage (when she was still trying to be companionable and he wasn't). Then he'd found it annoying, thinking she was hedging away from facing the real topic.

This evening, in the still, clear twilight, he understood it was her way of not pushing too hard.

"Puts things in perspective."

Another silence, each giving the other careful space.

"Let's hope we can trust the court to see things in perspective," she said tentatively, like a small animal lifting its nose to sniff the air or a deer in a shaft of sunlight turning its ears this way and that.

"Trust?" he grunted. Trust. The word pulled at old wounds, "Who was it said, *Trust no one, not even yourself*?"

"Um. Wasn't that Stalin?"

"Oh," he grunted again.

"Who was it said, *You live in torment if you don't trust enough*?"

"Haven't heard that one."

Another awkward silence.

Or was all the awkwardness at his end of the line, he wondered?

She said, "How's Emma?"

Was that the real reason she'd rung? She was always trying to save the baby bird fallen from the nest. She was a good person.

"OK. Not great." He sighed, in truth he worried she was suicidal, "It's hit her hard. I try to keep an eye on her, but I don't know what to say. After everything."

"It's good of you to stay there for her."

"Not really. I feel duty bound. Didier ... his ... you know ... it was my fault." He wasn't wallowing in self-pity, just explaining things.

Robyn stayed quiet, processing it. She knew not to press him about circumstances, details.

She said the only thing anyone can say about the dead. "I'm sorry he's gone."

"Despite what she did to me I owe her, I would've been lost unless she'd sacrificed Tony. They were having an affair. Unless she'd come forward and told the police everything, I don't know how things would have turned out."

He had small confidence that justice would ever be done, though he was pleased when he learned that Tony's parent company, Inter-Group-Publicity, failed to win the Qi pitch in China. The business went to Unicom. BS was keeping him informed, told him Tony's agency lost all its government business in the UK too. Schadenfreude didn't amount to much, but it didn't hurt either.

"There's been a kind of PR campaign in the UK supporting Tony Maine," Robyn said, "in the Sunday supplements."

"Image is everything."

BS had also told him that Malcolm White replaced Ray Doyle as Executive Creative Director at Maine Hyland & Blix. Just that morning he'd heard Doyle was still looking for a job.

"I'm sick of thinking about it all to tell you the truth."

"You think too much, Andy. The world has always been too much with you."

There was truth in that. He'd relived every moment of the investigation over and over, seen his mistakes. Shouldn't have been so needy with Maine, shouldn't have been so trusting. Shouldn't have lied to Lacont at their first meeting, shouldn't have heavied the judges like a pillock. Shouldn't have ... shouldn't have ... shouldn't have. Shouldn't have been suckered into becoming an amateur shamus full stop. He'd been as big a fake as Shackleton. There were dozens of shouldn't haves that added up to one fatal mistake. Poor Didier. Didi shouldn't have trusted him.

There were a few winners out of it all, however.

BS would be a winner once his book about Jonas Shackleton hit the stands — *Cannes of Worms: The Death of a Guru* — to be published by a Murdoch subsidiary; he'd been given a healthy upfront fee and apparently advance orders were strong both sides of the Atlantic. Carrick was glad for him.

Nick Bailey and Liang Weh were winners too. They'd won the actual Cannes Grand Prix. Even BS hadn't picked that. It was a free-lance campaign they'd written for a client of Vince Delahunty's office in Bangkok for the client, *Aussie Cossie.*

Bailey said they'd knocked it out sitting in the downstairs bar at *Inn the Pink* one afternoon. Liang said the Gold Lion must've been a parting gift from Shackleton's ghost.

Later Carrick heard Nick Bailey began an affair with Melodie the night of the awards at the after party, but he tried not to think too hard about that.

Stevie J. Rockett was a winner. The day after the awards when everyone read the news that French police were holding Tony Maine and his daughter over Shackleton's murder, the true nature of Rock-ett's theatrics sunk in and instantly became legend to those who saw it. The delegates were really impressed with themselves at being there, at the centre of the interesting universe.

An Arresting Night at the Cannes Lions ran the headline in Benny's blog. It was picked up by the international press. Another by-line.

Carrick, too, had been awestruck by Rockett's performance and told him so, the idea had sounded banal when Stevie first explained it but in execution worked a treat.

"Banal? Never underestimate the power of creativity," Stevie scalded, "A play to catch the conscience of a king."

Carrick smiled contritely, realised his opinions had been shaped by Maine who'd derided creative people as coddled flakes, but now he saw that the big ego stuff gave them the push to be bold; after all, no one achieves much being unassuming. Maybe those "haughty bastards" he'd despised that night at the wine tasting deserved to be coddled. If only they spent their talent on something better than attracting pigeons onto casino roofs for the benefit of the shotgun wielding rich, he mused.

Spooking Sammi and Maine into a flap had given Lacont substantial leverage when questioning, holding and finally charging them.

Sammi exploded at the police station. Why had Tony messed with a perfectly simple idea, she screamed? "… The beast was slaughtered and dear Pornthip was going to wear the blame, you idiot, why overwork it like a second-rate suit by adding complications?"

It had taken several gendarmes to subdue her at one stage.

Benny interviewed Stevie J. Rockett for an *InCreative* video blog and he held forth like a true auteur, "If you create a visceral emotional response, then action will surely follow," he said, "As for the show, what can I say? Reality leaves a lot to the imagination, you never need worry too much about the logic."

As he pulled the cork from a bottle of Dom Perignon and held the foaming neck close to Benny's lens, it fizzed up and a tiny galaxy of bubbles folded over the rim, "Our nervous system feeds impulses directly to the brain — they bubble up from both the conscious and the subconscious, you see? — so in reality, poor emotional creatures as we are, we're quite unable to discern the difference between the real and, let's say, the vividly imagined. Know what I mean?"

Carrick didn't. He only ever understood half of what Rockett said. But now he trusted the persuasiveness of his creativity. The Irishman flew to L.A. the next day to start pre-production on his first Hollywood film.

Looking at the photos of Maine and Sammi side by side in Benny's piece, Carrick realised for the first time why she'd looked familiar to him when they first met, the red hair, the dimpled chin, the family resemblance was obvious once you'd seen it. She even used the phrase, 'bugger, bugger, bugger', the way Tony Maine did, he remembered one morning while shaving.

Inspecteur de Détective Lacont was a winner too. While the antics of the award night were deeply unwelcome, he was quietly pleased by the result. The three bodies at the chateau were career criminals from Marseille with violent histories and organised crime associations, it was on the strength of this as well as Emma's evidence that he'd agreed to post his men backstage. Though, of course, he'd anticipated their presence would mean less drama, not be part of the show.

If Lacont couldn't decide about Carrick, neither had he ever been quite sure about Tony Maine.

Such an important man should be taken at his word but, "At a certain level of society's power strata there's a point where morality flips," he said in an exclusive interview for Benny, "A point where a man comes to believe the rules that apply to others no longer apply to oneself. In fact, they're reversed. The Côte d'Azur has taught me this many times."

Even Remy Barré, at first outraged by Rockett's show, came out of it looking good and was photographed the day after the arrests with the two local Mayors congratulating him on the terrace at La Colombe d'Or.

It was followed by a long lunch.

The same day the chairman of the judges, Francesco Ferreira, told Carrick that Tony Maine had rung him three times to check if the rumour that his agency's ad won the jury's Grande Prix was true, leaving messages asking if he should fly down for the awards show?

"But you didn't call him back? Why?"

"I've known Tony since my first D&AD awards dinner in London, twelve years ago. We sat at the same table."

The following weekend, he explained, Tony invited him over to Stockholm to see a Rolling Stones concert with sixty of his closest friends.

"That's where I met Tony's teenage daughter, Samantha; she would have been fifteen year old then. During *Sympathy for the Devil* she'd told me, quite nonchalantly, she had recently killed a neighbour's horse. She fed it poison hemlock, she said, after it threw her 'on purpose' the month before. She thought it a marvellous thing. Tony was forced to sort it out with the wretched people next door, she said. At the time, I assumed that she was stoned or fantasising, I didn't believe her. Then she boasted, 'I *made* him fix it up for me.'"

"How?" Francesco asked.

"'I said to him: *I'm all you've got Daddy, I'm your blood. Mummy doesn't love you anymore and all the rest of your family is dead.*'"

Francesco told Carrick that the night he'd danced with Sammi in the Samba/r at the Majestic he'd sensed something.

"Your presence provoked it," he said, "I've known her a long time, she was very skittish. Then I half-remembered something about an affair between her and Shackleton and it all clicked in my mind. Perhaps she'd been thrown from another horse? Perhaps Tony was having to fix something else for her?"

He flashed that patented suave smile, "They are a flamboyant family."

Carrick wanted to know something. Something about the nature of betrayal.

"Tell me, when Maine rang to ask whether he should come to Cannes for the awards night, you knew he wouldn't win... you knew it must be a trap?"

"It was not an easy decision," Francesco smoothed his hair, "In the end, I said to myself, what would Tony do if our positions were reversed?"

So, a pre-emptive betrayal, Carrick reflected, do unto others before they do unto you.

Betrayal seemed the pivot of the modern world. Slick promises betray consumers' trust on a daily basis. Small betrayals, big ones too. Corporate lies about washing powder, government lies about war, all the same seamless deceit. Why wouldn't people betray each other just as heedlessly? Francesco betrayed Maine. Emma betrayed Didier. Shackleton betrayed Sammi. Maine betrayed Carrick.

The Afghan terp betrayed the Gorma mission.

And who had he betrayed, he asked himself? His wife through neglect? The Major's legacy? Himself in his dissolution? The son he'd never have?

We're all double agents, all green on blue traitors, empathising and building relationships and being accepted and even loved and then we betray. It's the hard-wired animal deep inside us. Carrick saw it clearly. All of us populate a universe of one. Betrayal is as human as love or violence, twisted snake-like into our DNA, natural as breathing. It's the way the world turns.

Yet he was still trying to ruffle Francesco, "So you stabbed him in the back," he'd said, "Metaphorically?"

"I thought it might give our holding company a better chance in the Qi pitch," the smile without a trace of awkwardness, "Correctly, as it turns out."

And with that Francesco walked away a winner too.

Characteristically Carrick counted himself a loser in the scheme of things. Lacont had accepted the three killings at the chateau were self defence, but he'd still been charged with resisting arrest and assaulting a policeman at the Carlton, as well as the theft of a motor bike. He hoped that with a good word from Lacont he may get away with a slap on the wrist, but who knew? Carrick paid Rolande's physiotherapist bills as a gesture of goodwill.

He'd hired Etienne Balford, the solicitor Didier recommended, whose first instruction was to put Tony's money (less the expenses incurred to date) into a trust fund until the court case was run. Etienne saw no irony in recommending a trust fund.

"Take no risks," Etienne said, "while the facts are in dispute."

Too late, Carrick thought grimly, I've spent my life doing the opposite.

Freezing the money wasn't good timing; business at the security firm in London was drying up. Ad agencies and production companies were wary after seeing a figure as big as Tony Maine go down with Carrick driving the case. The dog has bitten his master, Jacko said.

It didn't help that the UK tabloids characterised the three deaths at the chateau as 'frenzied'. Carrick suspected Tony Maine had some influence in spinning the story, he expected there'd be smears worse than mere adjectives to come.

"They'll probably dredge up Dave 'bloody' Fergusen's death at some stage too and try to link me with it, like Maine did with Lacont," Carrick was saying to Robyn, "The tabloids will love it."

"Oh no," she said tensely, "Oh God, I see that."

There was a particularly long silence on the line this time. He hadn't really wanted to bring up the Ferguson thing, so much darkness and harm clung to that whole time, but he felt he needed to be utterly honest.

Finally he said, "I didn't kill him, you know. Dave Ferguson."

He felt certain she knew that, but it was good to say it out loud. He didn't want any misunderstanding, this conversation was too fragile a thing.

But there was a change in atmosphere at her end of the line, almost too quickly she said, "Yes, I know."

He heard her swallow, her mouth close to the phone, "I ... I should have made it clear to you before now..."

"I don't want to talk about all that," Carrick pulled the phone away from his ear in a moment of irritation.

Fuck him. Dave 'bloody' Ferguson was getting in the way again.

"... but I thought you might have worked it out," he heard her say, her voice small in the receiver.

"Worked it out? What?" pressing the phone back to his ear.

"Worked out who it was killed Dave..." There was something in her voice that caught him, a certain cadence, a hesitancy before something of moment.

"Killed Ferguson...? What do you mean who...?"

"... It was me."

Carrick stopped breathing.

~

"IT'S NOT a story I really wanted to tell you over the phone ... tell you at all really."

"You can't just drop that on me, Rob? Are you serious?"

Her voice became tight, hoarse with agitation. She said quickly, "It was an accident, in a kind of way. Self defence. It just happened."

"But he was stabbed in the neck?"

"It was a weird time, horrible. You'd gone, moved out and already down in London, but I was stuck in Herefordshire and still saw everyone we used to know. They all wanted to take sides about us splitting up, yours, mine, it didn't make any difference. It was awful. Some of your so called mates dropped around to give me comfort. What they called comfort."

"From the regiment?"

"Bastards," she said bitterly, "Sniffing around like, like ..."

"You never told me."

"We were getting a divorce, what would you have done about it?"

He said nothing. He didn't want the temperature to rise. Nevertheless he wanted names. He waited.

"Anyway, someone told me ... I heard ... that Dave had been boasting that he'd ... that we'd ... had a little romp or whatever when you were in Afghanistan. Guess the others were game to see if I was up for it after it was official that you and I were over ... they all think they're God's gift."

It was true the men in the regiment expected girls to want them, they attract an easy female following. He could imagine things playing out that way. But Carrick had no idea any of this had happened to Robyn, it didn't make him proud of his former mates.

"Look, I..."

"Don't defend the ..."

"No, I wasn't. Go on."

"Sorry, it's just so hard to tell you this, that's all, I've never told ..."

"No, I'm sorry. Don't apologise. Take your time."

"I went to Dave's place down at the river to confront him, but he was really drunk, totally out of it. I hadn't seen him at all for so long. It was a mistake. God, all you guys used to drink so much. Are you still like that?"

"No, not now."

It was true. He'd been sober since the Lions' award night.

"Well, Dave was bouncing off the ceiling, he had bottles and pills everywhere. We argued, but it turned into him pacing around making a speech at me, waving his arms. He was practically incoherent, but he said a couple of things ... I got really upset ..."

"How do you mean?"

"He said ... Andy, he let slip that when he'd come round that weekend ... and I know you never believed me but I didn't invite him, he just turned up. Anyway, when he and I ... at our place ... when you were on operations and we ended up, you know, well, he knew that you'd been captured. He said he didn't think you were coming back, thought you'd be killed for sure. Oh Andy, I was furious. Beyond furious. He knew and said nothing. No one had told me anything at that stage. It's really so twisted. How could he do that to me? To you? How could he be screwing me in our bed knowing you were being tortured or killed somewhere in Afghanistan at that very moment?"

Carrick could hear her breathing hard down the phone. His fingers tightened painfully around the receiver.

"He said you should have stayed buried."

"What did ..."

"So I punched him in the face."

Carrick laughed despite himself, "You..."

"Then he slapped me three times really fast and hard and pushed me against the wall. I thought he was going to choke me he was so wild."

Fergusen's side business included selling Dianobol, the anabolic steroid the lads in the regiment call the breakfast of champions. Sounded like he'd begun overusing them himself. They can make people very aggro.

Rob's voice came thinly over the line, "He called me a silly slut and I got really scared, he was shouting, swearing and cursing, his veins popping purple, he ... loved that I was scared," she paused to take a slow breath and said steadily, "Anyway, he still had hold of me but I grabbed a bottle of vodka and smashed it on the wall behind me and held the jagged piece up to his neck like you showed me."

Carrick could feel his own blood rising as he visualised the scene. When Robyn first started working at the jody bar Carrick taught her some emergency street fighting self-defence, showed her the carotid artery just under the ear.

"I tried to scream at him to let me go, but couldn't. Dave punched me in the stomach and kept crushing my windpipe and yelling and I

... I ... I guess I just shoved the bottle into the side of his neck. It was very, very quick. Just instinct. I don't even really remember deciding to do it or anything."

Carrick swallowed drily.

Depends on the woman.

"Why didn't you go to the police?"

"Oh, I don't ... everything would have ... I was in shock. I didn't know whether anyone would believe me or... and you'd've been dragged back into it. You'd gone through enough already, in the desert, in hospital," she said quietly, "I'd done enough to you already; I could hear you saying that."

Would he have said that? He didn't know. He didn't deny it, didn't want to rake over the coals of how he'd been in those days.

She calmed herself. He heard another deep breath, "Anyway, if Tony Maine is going to dig up Dave's death to discredit you, I just thought you'd better know the real story, the whole story."

Carrick was blown away, lost in unanchored thought.

"...Andy?"

"Sorry. I was thinking."

"Me too. Andy," a new note to her voice, "I was wondering about ... about coming to visit, if you don't mind, I mean? I thought I might visit Emma. I'm going down to Genoa for work, I'm working with a film location search company now, you probably didn't know that?" she went on tentatively, "Anyway, I was thinking I could take a day or two next weekend and come over and see Emma ... and... ?"

He was still trying to take in everything. He paused even longer than Lacont could have.

"... Andy?"

There was something he wanted to ask.

"Rob, you didn't ... when you killed him, I mean ... it wasn't because of ... I mean, it wasn't for... for... because of ...?"

He couldn't say the word 'me'.

When you killed him, it wasn't because of me? It wasn't for me?

He didn't know how to ask, didn't know if he really wanted to ask. Didn't know what answer he wanted.

But she knew.

"Of course not," she cut in, "I did it to save my life."

"Of course, I... yes ..."

In his mind's eye he saw her putting a finger to his lips, the way she used to when they were Andy and Robyn, Robyn and Andy, when he got too intense about something. The image calmed him now.

"You won't mind if I come... it won't ... crowd you ...?"

All noisy thoughts slipped away.

He missed the comfort of her touch more than anything in the world. His stubble scratching her chin when they kissed, sudden smiles washing away self doubts, her instinctive goodness, her shining bliss when she spoke about the "purity of moments".

Whatever you do, don't fuck it up. His new motto, the slogan BS gave him before the award night performance.

"... I hear it's a slice of Eden around there?"

"Yes, it is. I mean, I'm... I'd like... " then quietly, "Yes. Please, come."

Suddenly she laughed the way people do when they're comfortable with each other. When a shadow or a cloud has passed. And with that Carrick felt a tensile thing inside him relax, some emotional muscle unknot itself, there was a feeling of space, some cage that he'd constructed was opening, a feeling more like a beginning than an end.

He gave her the address and basic directions to Bonnieux. They set a date. He didn't know what to say next.

"I must tell you about a snake I found in the kitchen," he blathered, "It's a very funny story."

She gave a puckish laugh, "No Eden without snakes, Andy."

fin

NOTES

• Catherine Widom is a real psychologist who did a landmark study of psychopathology; Robert Hare is also a distinguished expert in the field. However, the article in *Time* magazine is imaginary, a pastiche of other writings.

• *T'Aint What You Do* is a song written by Melvin "Sy" Oliver and James "Trummy" Young, Copyright Ⓒ1939 Songs Of Universal Incorporated/Universal Music, Universal/MCA Music Ltd.

• The story of the Monte Carlo pigeons was told in John le Carré's memoirs, *Pigeon Tunnel*, 2016.

• Carrick's pack in Afghanistan pays homage to Andy McNab's account of the *Bravo Two Zero* mission, Bantam, 1993.

ABOUT THE AUTHOR

Michael Newman has published two non-fiction books and has been translated into Chinese, Korean, Hungarian, Russian, Turkish, Kazakh, French, Italian, Portuguese and Spanish.

He's written for magazines in the UK, France, Turkey, Singapore, Indonesia, Malaysia and Australia.

His creative work has won major awards in Europe, UK, US, Asia and Australia.

He lives on the east coast, in a forest, near a lake.

DON'T DIE WONDERING is his first novel.

info@dontdiewondering.info

www.ingramcontent.com/pod-product-compliance
Lightning Source LLC
Chambersburg PA
CBHW071204020726
47502CB00002B/539